The Fortescue Diamond
Monique Ellis

ZEBRA BOOKS
KENSINGTON PUBLISHING CORP.

ZEBRA BOOKS are published by

Kensington Publishing Corp.
850 Third Avenue
New York, NY 10022

First Printing: September, 1994

Printed in the United States of America

ZEBRA REGENCIES
ARE
THE TALK OF THE TON!

A REFORMED RAKE (4499, $3.99)
by Jeanne Savery

After governess Harriet Cole helped her young charge flee to France—and the designs of a despicable suitor, more trouble soon arrived in the person of a London rake. Sir Frederick Carrington insisted on providing safe escort back to England. Harriet deemed Carrington more dangerous than any band of brigands, but secretly relished matching wits with him. But after being taken in his arms for a tender kiss, she found herself wondering—*could* a lady find love with an irresistible rogue?

A SCANDALOUS PROPOSAL (4504, $4.99)
by Teresa DesJardien

After only two weeks into the London season, Lady Pamela Premington has already received her first offer of marriage. If only it hadn't come from the *ton's* most notorious rake, Lord Marchmont. Pamela had already set her sights on the distinguished Lieutenant Penford, who had the heroism and honor that made him the ideal match. Now she had to keep from falling under the spell of the seductive Lord so she could pursue the man more worthy of her love. Or was he?

A LADY'S CHAMPION (4535, $3.99)
by Janice Bennett

Miss Daphne, art mistress of the Selwood Academy for Young Ladies, greeted the notion of ghosts haunting the academy with skepticism. However, to avoid rumors frightening off students, she found herself turning to Mr. Adrian Carstairs, sent by her uncle to be her "protector" against the "ghosts." Although, Daphne would accept no interference in her life, she *would* accept aid in exposing any spectral spirits. What she never expected was for Adrian to expose the secret wishes of her hidden heart . . .

CHARITY'S GAMBIT (4537, $3.99)
by Marcy Stewart

Charity Abercrombie reluctantly embarks on a London season in hopes of making a suitable match. However she cannot forget the mysterious Dominic Castille—and the kiss they shared—when he fell from a tree as she strolled through the woods. Charity does not know that the dark and dashing captain harbors a dangerous secret that will ensnare them both in its web—leaving Charity to risk certain ruin and losing the man she so passionately loves . . .

Available wherever paperbacks are sold, or order direct from the Publisher. Send cover price plus 50¢ per copy for mailing and handling to Penguin USA, P.O. Box 999, c/o Dept. 17109, Bergenfield, NJ 07621. Residents of New York and Tennessee must include sales tax. DO NOT SEND CASH.

A MOST AWKWARD MEETING

There was a sudden lurch, and the elegant chaise gave up the struggle, settling drunkenly on its side with a crash.

Louisa attempted to right herself, blushing at the sight of her legs sticking straight up in the air. "Blast," she muttered, squirming desperately, but it was no good. As a head rose over the side, she shut her eyes, dangled her hand artistically and moaned.

There was puffing, the tinkle of broken glass, then a slight lurch as a body landed beside her. Through slitted eyes, she glimpsed a pair of gleaming black Hessians, and an expanse of soft buff leather ending in—She snapped her eyes shut, hoping her face with its telltale blush was indistinguishable in the murky confusion.

"Turned fairly top over tail, aren't you," a deep voice said. "Yes, I know—you can't hear a word I'm saying, as you're in a dead faint! A Mrs. Siddons"—there was a sudden tugging at the robes tangled around her waist—"you definitely"—a grunt, and the tangle came free—"are not!"

Powerful hands grasped her forearms and brought her to her feet. She wavered, not entirely acting, and was supported firmly against a hard male body.

"Better?" the voice asked.

For Kate, with all my love:

The most wonderful daughter, best friend, severest critic, and most patient and encouraging fan any mother ever had.

"Le coeur a ses raisons, que la raison ne connaît point."
"The heart has its own logic which no logician will ever comprehend."
—*Blaise Pascal*

One

"So, you see . . ." Lord Henry Beckenham, sixth viscount Marleybourne and late of Wellington's Peninsular Army by way of an unfortunate incident at Salamanca, lifted his clear blue eyes with a certain trepidation from the papers he had been rearranging on his father's desk, placing a folded sheet of heavy cream-colored stock atop the stack. ". . . there it is," he concluded, flushing under his sister's unwinking gaze. "Gwendolyn allows me a year."

The late winter sun streamed through the library windows of the massive stone Court, burnishing his fair hair to a golden helmet and creating shining epaulets in the heavy tweed of his old shooting jacket. Backlit so, his empty sleeve was almost unnoticeable. Only the break in the smooth planes of his handsome face betrayed the fading scar which ran like an irregular boundary from hairline to mouth corner, but the lingering pallor under his weather-beaten skin revealed the twenty-eight-year-old erstwhile major for what he was—a man who had suffered so much that he deserved, if possible, to be spared further misery.

It was on this basis that Louisa, seated in a low chair by the dancing fire, answered, "Most generous," after a slight pause, her voice neutral, her finely sculpted features an unaccustomed blank. "Most exceptionally generous."

"Gwendolyn's an angel!" her brother agreed fervently, eyes glowing. "She says even my arm and face don't matter—that they're badges of honor! What, in all my worthless life, I've done to earn such good fortune . . . Gwendolyn is the purest, the sweetest, the kindest, the most beautiful girl any man ever dreamt of during three years of—Well, there's more than castles in Spain, love."

Louisa's sea-green gaze flicked to his empty sleeve, back to his eyes, missing the scar she still found so hard to accept. "I know, my dear," she said softly.

Around them the old library rose, ancient oak paneling polished to glowing amber, the leather-bound volumes glinting gold and garnet and lapis and dusky emerald. It had always been their favorite room—at once refuge and place of adventure, where journeys to other times and places lay near at hand. Here Harry had chosen to give her his great news, pulling strength and confidence from shared memories.

"You're accepting this with amazing calm," he beamed as he leaned back in his chair, hand now lying gracefully across the cream paper. "Three years ago I'd've expected a fusillade to rival poor Edward Whinyate's rockets—at the very least!"

"That was then. This is now." Louisa frowned, thinking furiously. "Let me see if I have it correctly. The requirements *are* the slightest bit unusual, you know. I am to be married before your betrothal can be announced?"

"Wedded *and* bedded," he nodded, coloring.

"And, should I not be wed by the end of one year—*and* bedded—your Gwendolyn will cry off from the private understanding which has existed between you since just before your departure for the Peninsula?"

"Since the night before," he specified. "Lord Fortescue was most reluctant to grant even that provisional approval. It required every fact I had at my command—my prospects for promotion, my position as Father's heir, the nature of the entail and the possibilities of its being broken, a recital of my personal finances, and of Father's as well in so far as I knew them, and a will in Gwendolyn's favor should anything happen to me in the interim—to convince him to grant even conditional approval!" He smiled ruefully. "I learned to count myself cheap indeed that night! A salutary lesson, I suppose, but one I was close to resenting in spite of understanding my darling deserved every possible protection a fond parent could devise.

"It came to this: If Gwendolyn formed no other attachment during my absence, I could present myself to her as an approved suitor on my return, but with the proviso that there be no clandestine correspondence in the interim. I left for Spain with little hope of a successful conclusion," he sighed. "Such a pearl, and so young, so beautiful and innocent, to still be free whenever I might return, no matter how great the interval? It was hardly worth dreaming of! But, I dreamt . . ."

Louisa's eyes glinted. The room was silent except for the crackle of the fire, seeming closed in on itself, near stifled, in spite of the thin sunshine streaming through soaring arched and mullioned windows from which heavy bronze velvet draperies had been looped back. Far beyond the sky rose in winter's sharp blue, the tops of trees shifting in a wayward wind.

"And no one to be told," Harry continued, jaw clenching at the memory, "not even you or our father, or all would be at an end. That, perhaps, was the hardest to endure."

There was a chill to the air despite the fire, an odor of time and dust which not all the cleaning and polishing of generations of servants could banish. Louisa shivered in her burgundy merino gown with its worn lace collar and cuffs, drew her heavy wool shawl closer around her shoulders. Not even her brother's tweeds, she suspected, were proof against a cold which seeped from the very walls at this time of year.

"Understandable, of course," she stated after taking time to consider. "Had anyone known—even if only our father and myself—she would have been bound in honor to listen to no other proposals until your return, whether a formal announcement had been made or not. Only—" Louisa took a deep breath. "Only, the stipulation of a will in her favor should anything . . . *happen* . . . seems, perhaps, a trifle odd. There was no formally sanctioned understanding between you."

"A pledge of the degree of seriousness with which I viewed the commitment," Harry explained quickly. "As Lord Fortescue stated, I was only assuring Gwendolyn's future should the worst happen. You certainly had no need of my personal fortune; and, should Gwendolyn have accepted another offer, I could easily change my will."

"The will remains in effect?"

"Of course. That portion of my fortune which is at my own disposal is hers unless she should wed another. You *do* understand their reasons?"

"Oh, yes—quite clearly. The most prudent of parents."

"They are that . . . I barely had time to arrange everything before I left, but Fortescue's solicitor was most efficient. Never could have muddled through without him."

"Lord Fortescue's—? You didn't go to old Pennington?"

" 'Course not!" Harry sputtered. "He'd've contacted Father immediately. No—going to Fortescue's man was the only way to maintain secrecy. You must see that."

"*Most* prudent parents! Oh, Harry," she sighed, not for the first time wishing their father had survived until his son's return. Wisdom, on this chill February morning of 1813, was hard to find. "It was all merely sensible, I suppose," she said finally, "at least in their eyes. Your return uncertain as to time——"

"Even as to the event itself," he interrupted hardily, "do not forget that, and they have kept their word despite my arm."

"Fortunes of war," Louisa responded with an insousiance she was far from feeling. "Naturally they kept their word! You're no longer a love-struck young lieutenant departing to an uncertain future, but a viscount in possession of considerable property, and one of Wellington's heroes as well."

"There's nothing particularly heroic about getting your arm blown off, love—it's merely damned uncomfortable. A nuisance, too," he added wryly, "though I manage most things fairly well now—even riding, since I've copied the cavalry trick of tucking the reins beneath my knee at the gates." A lurking smile, at once humorous and self-deprecating, lit his eyes. "You do forgive me for being so anxious to get to London as soon as I had my strength back? Though London wasn't really my goal."

Louisa smiled into the fire as it flared suddenly, a log dissolving in a shower of sparks. "So it was not just a visit to Scott's," she said teasingly. "I did wonder at the time, for you seemed more truly anxious to leave than you had been delighted to arrive, and you've never aspired to the dandy."

"Lord, no! My excuse was lame as a parson's nag," he chuckled. "Didn't even get *near* London, but I *couldn't* tell you then—not and retain my honor. Still can't bruit it about beyond the family, but at least there'll be no more secrets between us now."

Louisa smiled, held her peace.

"And, there's some duke or marquess lurking in the background. Got hints of that from Norval. Won't tell me which one, dammit, or I'd—sorry . . ."

Louisa's smile broadened as she tilted her head, firelight dancing in her golden hair. "That's all right, Harry," she said gently. "No one could expect you to break *every* Peninsular habit so soon." Her hand curled around the arm of her chair, white-knuckled. "My merely removing from the Court would not suffice? Establishing myself—with a proper chaperon or companion, naturally—in, say, Bath?"

"Louisa! That would give the appearance of your being chased from your home, which is far from the case, of course."

"Of course," she responded dryly.

"Imagine the stories that would run through the neighborhood!"

"Your lady's own sweet nature—"

"My love—you're so well established here, so respected and admired, that at the first hint of such a thing poor Gwendolyn would be cut right and left. Do stop being selfish and consider her position. Consider mine!" His voice rose at her willful obtuseness, hand clenching on the heavy cream-colored paper. Then he shook his head, assuming a look of omniscient male reasonableness. "Were Father still alive, there would be no question of this, but he died while I was in Spain, and now you can properly make your home only with me, or with your husband had you one."

"I'm more than seven, Harry!"

"You're a green girl, love, a sweet peagoose with not even one season in London, no proper come-out, and your life spent for most part between the bounds of the park. What a spitfire you were, to be sure! 'I will not be paraded like a prize filly at Almack's! Let us at least do the thing honestly and place me on the block at Tattersall's,' " he mimicked.

She bit her lip, fighting back words which begged to be spoken. Louisa had not seen the sparkle of humor and joy now lighting Harry's eyes since before he left for Spain. To cause it to vanish would be unbearable.

"I've been mistress of Marleybourne since Mother died," she finally protested gently. "That's ten years, Harry, and I've run the estate since Father's death. I am neither a green girl nor a peagoose, and I'll thank you not to call me such names!"

"No—you're an old, wise woman of twenty-five with gray hair and a cat to keep you company on cold nights," he teased. Then, as he studied her face more carefully, sun-struck by a bright band from the window and side-lit by the fire, the laughter drained from his face to be replaced by a look of tender concern. "My love, you've been mistress here in the same manner, and with the same grace, that you would have been of your own establishment had you wed out of the schoolroom. You've not even had a chaperon since old Tibby retired! *That* is the issue, Louisa. Ten years, as you say, or pretty near. My God, girl—some *marriages* don't endure that long, at least not in a meaningful manner!"

"I know."

"Gwendolyn is thinking of *your* comfort and security, *your* happiness and peace of mind—not her own. And mine as well—she made that very clear," he insisted. "It would be damnably uncomfortable for you here, seeing another in your place. What would happen when it came time to ring for a guest's carriage?"

"I suppose I would reach for the rope without thinking," she admitted with a sigh, "and then be forced to hang myself from it in mortification."

"Exactly."

"Yes—I begin to see. My presence would be most . . . disturbing."

"A house cannot have two mistresses, Louisa," Harry said almost regretfully, "and I'm afraid precedence will have to be granted my wife. Just consider—always forced to cede your formerly rightful place to another. Having your desires given last consideration, if they were considered at all. You would hate that."

"Indeed I should," she said, eyes large at the vision his words created. "Very much indeed!"

"You have been of first consequence at Marleybourne since you were fifteen," he pressed. "Suddenly you would be last. It's *you*, and *your* comfort and peace Gwendolyn is considering. For her own part, she would be delighted to have you make your home with us, but I am forced to admit that what she and Lady Fortescue require is neither shocking nor lacking in proper feeling. It is, rather, natural and wholesome for all."

"Yes, I do believe you are right," Louisa agreed hesitantly, barely noting the unaccustomed pomposity of his words, busy with her own thoughts. "I don't think it would do at all—to have me and your Gwendolyn under the same roof. Poor Bedloe! He would be so afraid of giving offense to me or insulting your wife that he wouldn't know where to turn." A smile flitted across her face like a cloud before the sun, darkening rather than brightening her features. "Has your lady been so good as to select a husband for me?"

"Heavens, no! The choice must be yours."

"She is all consideration."

"And delicacy," Harry prompted.

"And delicacy," Louisa acquiesced.

But, it amounted to much the same thing, she learned after Harry scowled a moment, his expression that of a schoolboy attempting to recall a difficult lesson hardly learned, and on the proper recitation of which depended being spared a painful birching.

"There's Bentick, of course," he began, "and her Cousin Norval—Norval Quarmayne, that is. Old name, that one—back to the Conqueror, Gwendolyn says. Domesday Book, and all the rest. No title, but *very* historic.

Excellent connections, both of 'em, and quite plump in the pocket. Your pin money would be generous. Then there're Hastings, Scrivendale, and Portmandle."

"Mercy—they sound like a firm of solicitors!"

"Do be serious. I know there's another one . . . Gossmar—that's it! Ephraim Gossmar. Vicar, holds the living attached to Fortescue Lodge."

"A *vicar?*" Louisa quavered. "Truly? You're certain he's not a curate?"

"No, goose! A widower with three grown sons. As I collect, one's taken orders, the second has a secretarial post, and the youngest's a tutor in some nabob's household."

"Goodness! How old is the vicar?" Louisa choked.

"Fine-looking man—fine-looking! Bruising rider to hounds, Norval tells me, and very impressive in the pulpit, too. Seen that more than once for myself. Voice like a cathedral organ. Reads from Fordyce's *Sermons* every Sunday. Says his own wouldn't be half so elevating, which shows you what a fine mind he has," Harry enthused, "and the vicarage is more along the lines of a small manor with its own attached farm. Eminently suitable establishment. Oh—Gossmar keeps a good cellar."

"I am certain he does."

To scream or laugh would have been equally fatal. It was better, Louisa decided, to view this as a charade for the entertainment of an unseen audience, or better yet, the farce which followed a wrenching drama. It could not be real—except it was.

"I'm glad the vicar interests you," Harry continued with satisfaction. "Certainly he's Lady Fortescue's first choice, and would make any woman a fine, steady husband. Best of all, he's most anxious for a wife—widower almost a year now."

"No, Harry—I think not."

"That's where you're out, love—he *is* anxious. Told

me so himself. Wants a steady, biddable, refined girl. His first wife was a bit flighty according to Lady Fortescue, and not properly conscious of her place. Wore *silk*, if you can credit it! A *parson's wife!* And gave herself airs . . . Too, she was a perfect shatterbrain when it came to managing, and *that* even a well-fixed parson's wife must do, for these things are relative."

He was quoting someone, Louisa told herself. She wouldn't believe any of this was truly *Harry*. It *couldn't* be . . . She cocked her head, waiting.

"If you had seen how his eyes lit up when Gwendolyn described you—" Harry concluded on a note of triumph, certain this evidence of predisposition would do the trick.

"How *could* she!" Louisa spat, staring first at her brother, and then beyond him to the windows. The divisions of the panes loomed like prison bars, the walls closing around her in an implacable trap. Then the lids sank over her eyes, raised slowly. "Describe me, I mean," she said more evenly. "We have never met."

"Well, you see—you do run the Court, and even—"

"I do see." She smiled. "Open: Position as housekeeper to aging cleric who treasures his tipple. Did your Gwendolyn also happen to mention my inheritance from our mother, and the provisions for me in our father's will?"

"It *is* a matter of common knowledge, more or less," he protested uncomfortably.

"Among those with whom I am in no way acquainted? Amazing!"

"They are acquainted with *me*," he blustered.

"Indeed they are."

"See here—I had to tell them, back before I went to Spain. All part of the agreement."

"I fail to see how your sister's fortune—Or lack of it!—could affect your impending nuptials."

"Wanted to be sure you wouldn't be forever hanging

on my sleeve," Harry mumbled. "Could prove very inconvenient, that."

"I see. Of course. How silly of me!" Louisa's voice had the sweetness of honey on velvet. "Then Miss Fortescue *did* bring forth the matter when discussing me with the amorous cleric?"

"Something along those lines may have been mentioned in passing by *Lady* Fortescue, among various other advantages to the match."

"An elderly cleric fond of his tipple who desires not only an unpaid housekeeper, but that she bring him a fortune as well? What images of marital bliss *that* engenders. Your lady and her mother are all heart! No—I think we'll dispense with the vicar."

"He *is* a Fortescue connection on the distaff side—some sort of second or third cousin at several removes—and he puts off blacks for his wife in a fortnight. Plenty of time to arrange a wedding—a quiet ceremony, naturally, out of respect to his former wife—no fallals or special clothes. The dress you're wearing now would serve admirably. Then Gwendolyn and I could be married in the fall," Harry said with a lingering trace of hope.

"I have had this gown going on four years, Harry," Louisa returned tartly. "I generally wear it when I am doing the accounts, and it is covered with ink stains."

"Well, I suppose you *could* have something new if you deem it essential, but Lady Fortescue believes it would be extremely wise in you to accept the vicar's offer without further—Ah, well, so are the others all connections of one sort or another, and you can't afford to be too nice, love. You're solidly on the shelf, and must be grateful if any respectable man offers for you."

"Must I, indeed? I'd not realized I'd become such an ape-leader, buried here at Marleybourne. Thank you for telling me." She did sound truly grateful for the information. "But, tell me, Harry—how can I at once be at my last prayers, and a green girl? They would appear incompatible states."

"Not at all! That you cannot see it for yourself merely proves the point."

"Ah . . . You say all these other gentlemen are also connections of Lord and Lady Fortescue?"

"Some *are* rather distant."

"Even so, they must think *extremely* highly of you to desire such a doubled connection! Let us at least decline the vicar, if you don't mind?"

"No—no. Not at all, if you insist on it. He whuffles, if you must know. I didn't mention that, did I?"

"Whuffles?"

"When he speaks, except when he's in the pulpit. Needs something to read from, you see, or he's never quite certain what to say. Magnificent on horseback, though. Sweetest seat and gentlest hands I've ever seen on a man his size, but he's forever pursing his lips and blowing them apart while he determines the most appropriate comment—sort of a 'whuffle' sound. Rather annoying, after a while."

"It must be," Louisa agreed with a genuine laugh. "No—I must definitely cede the whuffling vicar and his excellent cellar to some other 'biddable girl.' The honor he would do me in offering would be far beyond my merits."

" 'You would adorn any position you condescended to grace with perfection of manner,' " Harry said with a smile. "Those are Gwendolyn's very words."

"How generous!" Louisa inclined her head graciously. "Charitable, even, as she can know me only from your reports."

"I thought so. Very prettily expressed, it was." He leaned back in the chair, completely relaxed now the first fence had been cleared and it was only a question of devising the means to meet the terms he had been set.

"Well, Gossmar's not the only fish in the sea. There's Norval, of course: Slightly weak chin, and his mind isn't quite as first-rate as the vicar's, but he's got a nice little place in Kent. Very pleasant fellow, dresses bang-up-to-the-nines, always in Town for the season. You'd like that, Gwendolyn said, but Bentick's the best of the lot for my money. A *baronet*, Louisa, and he's looking to set up his nursery. Even given up his high—well, never mind that, but he's seriously hanging out for a wife."

"To be sure, he is," she twinkled, "if he has given up his *high*-whatevers! Husbanding his strength, no doubt."

"Yes, well, ah . . ." Harry took a deep breath. Louisa's combination of tartness and humor did not overly concern him. Certainly it was better than the tempest he had expected, for she had never been one to consider matters calmly or acknowledge any point of view but her own. As for seeing the consequences of an action, or the ability to judge what she ought best to do—never had there been such a pudding-head! "Bentick's not much of a gamester, either. White's, Wattier's, that sort of thing, but never to excess, that's Bentick. No Cocoa-Tree, or—Well, never *anything* to excess. Solid, good family—title's a couple generations deep. Something to do with Charles II and a female ancest—well, never mind *that*, either! Thing is, a dependable man. Very plump in the pocket, generous to a fault, but the estate *is* entailed, which might prove a drawback eventually, I suppose, if you failed to produce an heir."

"No . . . I don't think so."

"Yes, it is, I tell you! Believe me, Louisa—I'm protecting your interests as best I can. Had it from Bentick himself when we were, ah—"

"Did you discuss my 'circumstances' with him as well, Harry?"

"As much as was necessary." Harry flushed, eyes roving the bookcases as if searching for a favorite title. "Very pleased Mother had a son right off," he muttered. "Liked that even better than your dot."

Silence stretched between them, unspoken words dancing in the air like dust motes. Harry dreamed longingly of a dressing-down by Wellington—far less disturbing than this interview with his sister. And Louisa? Louisa envisaged daggers, poison, and pistols at dawn, and regretted her family name was not Borgia, that this was modern England where certain things were not done.

"Is it you who has been so busy on my behalf, Harry?" she asked when the silence had built so thickly that another moment and it would have become an impenetrable barrier, "or, is it your fair Gwendolyn?"

"Both of us, I suppose," he admitted sheepishly after clearing his throat. "She *has* waited three years, Louisa. Why, she's almost twenty-one! People are beginning to whisper. To have to wait another entire year—You *do* understand, don't you? Gwendolyn's only trying to help, bless her, for she understands your predicament far better than you do. There's not a chance you'd find someone suitable yourself with no mother to guide you."

"And so I am to accept the guidance of a—Never mind that! But, Bentick and Cousin Norval and the whuffling vicar and the rest? I think not."

"I don't understand. What *possible* objection can you—"

"They won't do, Harry," she said gently, "not any of them. We shouldn't suit."

"You can't reject them out of hand!" he protested in exasperation. "Why, you haven't met a one of them! Even Gossmar has his good points."

"I'm certain he does—on a point-to-point."

"And Lady Fortescue is planning a house party at the Lodge in three weeks' time so you may meet them all and make your selection. Not every woman is given such an opportunity, or granted such latitude of decision!"

"How exceptionally kind of her."

"Isn't it? A great condescension, as generally she detests vapid gatherings of that sort, but in *this* case—"

"Her graciousness humbles me, Harry, but I am afraid I shan't be free to attend."

"Not free?" Whatever do you mean?"

"Just that, Harry."

Louisa stood, staring down at the old carpet with its dusky brown and gold pattern of Greek keys. As children they had transformed it into classical battlefields via crumpled cloth mountains and silver paper seas across which had stormed cardboard armies fashioned by their father and delicately painted by their mother. Eccentric, they had been called. It did not seem possible this could be the same room, the same carpet, with the same thin winter sunlight streaming through the same tall windows.

A sad smile twisted her lips as she thought of Hannibal and his elephants, of Caesar and his cohorts. More inexorable than the march of Roman legionnaires had been the march of time, and no greater than the crumbling of Rome before the invading barbarians was the threatened destruction of her home. Slowly her head lifted and her shoulders straightened.

"You will make my excuses, won't you?" she asked, interrupting the flood of protest that washed over her like those phantom silver seas, neither touching nor moving her. "And say everything that is proper?"

"I shall not!"

"What a pity, as Lady Fortescue will then think me lacking in proper manners, and that will only reflect on you."

"But—but—it's been decided! You *cannot* do this! How shall *I* look? What will *you* appear? The invitations have been sent. Look here—I brought yours with me!" He seized the heavily embossed piece of cold-pressed paper lying in front of him, thrust it at her. "Here, take it!"

"I was not consulted, nor were my sentiments or convenience considered," she said, hands gripped behind her back.

"Louisa!" he roared.

"If I must marry—and it appears I must, or cost you your Gwendolyn—it will be in my own time and in my own way, and the gentleman will be one of *my* choosing, not the selection of your bride or your future mama-in-law. Let that be very clear at the inception."

"But—what will you do?" he spluttered. To lose Gwendolyn now—and to Louisa's childish, egoistic stupidity and stubbornness—would be more than he could bear! "How will you go on if you refuse their assistance and guidance? You'll make a perfect mull of everything! You turned down every eligible candidate in the district before you were eighteen. They're all leg-shackled now, and we've no new neighbors, dammit!"

Louisa smiled slightly. "Perhaps," she said, "it's time I considered that London Season Aunt Daphne's carped about for years."

Relief spread over her brother's face. "Famous! I never thought you'd agree, or I'd've made the suggestion myself. Town's thin of company just yet, but that will change as spring comes on, and naturally you'll stay at Fortescue House. They have entry everywhere." Enthusiasm and joy rang in his voice. "Why, under Lady Fortescue's aegis, you might even be granted vouchers for Almack's! She offered to come down if you proved diffi—if *only* I could convince you, but I thought you'd prefer the other thing."

"I'm glad you approve," Louisa laughed, "but there's no need for Lady Fortescue to alter her plans. I shall do quite well with Aunt Daphne."

"But it would be such a perfect opportunity for you to get to know my angel," he wheedled, "learn to love her like a sister. She *is* the dearest thing, Louisa! And always, *always* so gracious to everyone—"

"It would be far too particular, Harry—my staying there. How tongues would wag, with my own aunt in town and her entry at least as good as theirs! Besides, if it must come to it, I prefer to be sponsored by a member of my own family."

"Well, perhaps that would be best," he admitted grudgingly, "so long as Aunt Daffy can bring someone up to scratch in time."

His tone, so doubtful as to be an insult, Louisa ignored. Whether he considered the problem lay in her being unable to attract any man, or whether he was remembering their father's sister too clearly for comfort, there was no way to tell.

"Believe me, it would be best," she said, "and as for Aunt Daphne's bringing someone 'up to scratch,' I'm not at my last prayers yet, no matter what you and the Fortescue contingent think of my advanced age!" She came over to the desk, caught his hand in both of hers, held it against her cheek for a moment, smiling with love and compassion. "I promise to do everything in my power short of shackling myself to someone totally unsuitable, Harry. Don't scowl at me! Truly—I swear it. Come what may, I want to see you as happy as you deserve."

"Gwendolyn's not the only angel in my life, you know," he said fondly, kissing her hands. "No fellow ever had such a sister!"

"I pray you will say the same in a year's time." She hesitated an instant. Then her smile broadened. "I am truly anxious to meet your Gwendolyn. She must be exceptional!"

"She is," he beamed. "Wish me the happiest man in Christendom, Louisa, for if I gain her for my own that is exactly what I shall be!"

"I do, my dear, with all my heart. The happiest man in Christendom—not just this year, or the next, but for all the years of your life."

Two

"Damn him!" Louisa Beckenham stormed into her room, shut the door with a snap more pointed than the loudest slam, seized the first pillow she found and hurled it at the far wall. "Damn him! *Damn him! DAMN HIM!* The poor, blithering clodpole . . ."

She plunked down at her dressing table, stared furiously into the glass, chin on clenched fist. It was no gentle, serene face that met her eyes, but rather a thunderous, scowling mask which no more resembled her than—Well, in truth, it resembled her now, she admitted ruefully. Her sea-green eyes were almost black with anger, and sparks seemed to fly from her golden curls.

"Damn the vixen!" she muttered. "Harry would *never* have concocted such a preposterous scheme—never! To *force* me, willy-nilly, into parson's mousetrap . . . And with the first candidate to hand, however dull or disreputable or dandified? She's *despicable!*"

She should have anticipated something of the sort, and she had—eventually. In perhaps five years' time, when Harry had adjusted to his civilian status, his missing arm and uniform, his face. To being alive. When she could finally believe she had him back, whole or not, to love and cosset. She had dreamed of watching the courtship, fostering it like a good fairy, and then retiring quietly to Bath while they were on their honeymoon—in France, of course, because by then Boney would have been *rompéd*—after ensuring everything at the Court and in town was perfect for their reception.

And his bride? Sweet and gentle and shy and adoring, having to be brought out of herself, too sensible of the miracle of Harry's loving her to demand her rights. Fair as he was fair, with eyes like a summer sky and diminutively feminine to set off his great height and manly vigor—*that* was the girl she had picked for Harry, though she had yet to find her. She had thought there would be time enough . . . Instead, it was to be a cold-faced statue with a cloud of russet hair and steel-gray eyes no artist's skill could soften.

Beautiful? Yes—she would grant the harpy that. A diamond of the first water, both from the miniature Harry had proudly shown her and from Aunt Daphne's gossipy letters. Oh, yes—she had heard of the chit! Perfection in all things which ranked as perfection in the ton, that was Harry's Gwendolyn—graceful, well-bred, with never a thought or hair out of place, of excellent family and respectable fortune—and as hard as the gemstone to which she was so often likened. Nothing but a simpering, overbred, overbearing pattern card with a determined look about her chin . . . *DAMN!*

Harry had been in the habit of falling in and out of love with every fair face he glimpsed since the middle of his third year at Harrow, penning execrable schoolboy sonnets and sighing with the force of a blown horse at the miracle of his love's left earlobe. Well, this time she doubted he'd had time for sonnets—just for penning his will . . . Much more practical as an expression of undying devotion.

Slowly the scowl faded, the eyes regained their accustomed tint, the hair subsided. Louisa watched the blanking of her face with satisfaction. It was a mask she would have to wear until this damnable situation was rectified . . .

According to Harry, he had known the girl but a few weeks, seen her all of six times during the short period between his return from Corunna in January of '09, and his departure for Lisbon in April—and those at balls, where even a favored suitor might beg only two dances with the same fair damsel without setting tongues flapping, she'd accept only two if she were not to be considered fast—when he requested an interview with her father. And then? Then he had departed instanter for three years in Spain—endowing her with all his worldly goods should he fail to survive.

Louisa performed some rapid calculations. At half an hour to a set, and allowing Harry two sets on three of the occasions (which was generous reckoning, given Miss Fortescue's reputation for rigid propriety), he had asked for her hand on the basis of barely more than four hours' acquaintance! Perhaps even as little as three . . . However many the hours, they would have been highly fragmented, with conversation halting at best—"Is the room not hot, sir?" and "Indeed it is, Miss Fortescue!"—knowledge of the character and personality of his beloved restricted to her taste, perhaps, in books or flowers.

Then, night and day for three intolerable years he had dreamt of his paragon, longed for her, elevated her, created her much as Pygmalion had created his Galatea, out of the whole cloth of his desires and imagination. It was time the statue was set in motion, brought to life so Harry could truly become acquainted with her.

Marry for the convenience of Gwendolyn Fortescue? Not likely!

Naturally she would have to play the game, present every appearance of ladylike willingness to accept some sot's "most gratifying proposals." Fortunately, there were no hot-air balloons from whose high-swinging gondolas one could peer into hearts and souls as one could into the hidden parts of the countryside.

Of course, if Harry *truly* loved the chit, and she was both worthy of his regard and returned it in full measure, the situation would be altered. After all, she had *intended* to set up her own establishment whenever Harry married, even idly considered whom she might ask to join her as a companion to preserve the proprieties. It was its being *demanded* that rankled, and in the attendant stipulation that the only proper place for her was in some man's bed, filling his nursery and running his household and overlooking his faults, lay the greatest part of the insult. Well, if needs must . . .

Sighing, she rose from the dressing table, went to the windows overlooking the lawns and park of Marleybourne. She had never thought to leave in such a manner. To be *chased*, like an unsatisfactory scullery maid.

Before her the dearly loved landscape unfolded itself from near to far in tones of gray and brown and russet and amber. Winter-Marleybourne, the spare limbs of trees knotting black lace against the sky, the lake bordering the home wood a pewter mirror, ice-girdled and still under a sky now leaden with the approach of clouds from the far hills. Snow would fall before night, a clean white blanket. Let it be thick! she prayed. Let it be thick and silent and deep, clogging roads and granting a few extra days' leave-taking.

She closed her eyes, wearily leaning her forehead against an icy pane as tears spilled down her cheeks. At least it was not as bad as it could have been—Harry dead, Oliver Beckenham and his scrawny wife and sniveling brats come to take possession as next in line under the entail—but it was bad enough. And, she would have time for all the small domestic details which must be arranged with Mrs. Cruickshank to ensure Harry's comfort, for

seeing Potts about draining the west field, for conferring
with Abner Gossett about—

But, no—it was Harry who would give those orders
now. Perhaps it *was* better that she slip silent and unre-
gretted into Marleybourne's past, no matter what the
impetus. She hadn't realized until this moment how many
reins she had held effortlessly in her hands for so many
years, how automatically she had manipulated them.
Time now, with Harry home and their father gone, to
relinquish them with the best grace possible.

Time, then, to change the guard . . .

If Marleybourne had been at its most winter-glorious
when she left, sparkling under a *diamanté* blanket of snow,
London, when Louisa Beckenham arrived, was at its
worst.

The roads had been close to impassable for most of
what should have been a two-day journey, forcedly
lengthened into five and taken in easy stages in her
brother's new traveling chaise. That they had had no
upsets was due solely to Robert Coachman's imperturbable skill, his refusal to hurry the pace as adamant as
Louisa's refusal to turn back and wait for the weather to
regularize itself. The thought of being forced to leave the
Court a second time had been more than she could bear.

The countryside, under today's thaw and subsequent
rain, had been as bleak as her thoughts. Nature and
emotions in concert, she admitted wryly as Robert
Coachman maneuvered the chaise through the crowded
city streets in the late afternoon of a sodden day under a
sullen sky.

Louisa leaned against the deep maroon squabs, staring
blindly at the confusion just beyond the window, the hot
brick at her feet long since cooled to uselessness. On the
opposite seat Matty, a maid from the Court sent to play

propriety, pressed her red nose against the window, babbling of sights too exotic for belief—of tumblers and jugglers and a man with a dancing monkey, of Corinthians with short-cropped hair and Cyprians with painted faces, even an aborigine from the Colonies in full regalia of leathers and feathers and beads. Hawkers' cries swelled above the din, raucously touting silver sand, tarts, meat pies, oranges, apples, and pears.

Louisa's lids sank over her eyes, shutting out the world she wanted neither to see nor join, turning back instead to the leave-taking at the Court, much in the manner of one who probes a sore tooth with questing tongue to determine exactly how much pain will ensue. As with the tooth, the pain was there—sharp as she thought of old Abner Gossett handing her a posy from the hothouses, sharper yet as she remembered Bedloe personally overseeing the stowage of her portmanteaux rather than leaving the task to the footmen as he customarily did, dull at Harry's barely veiled exuberance, mind clearly not on her despair at the ending of one world, but on his own joy at the incipient beginning of another. And then, gingerly, she examined the moment when she had turned back for one last look at the dear old gray stone pile, smoke wreathing its tall chimneys, towers like soldiers on picket, and they had passed around the first bend in the drive and the house was lost to view. To never be able to return as one who *belonged*—only as a guest, tolerated for brief periods but intrinsically unimportant to the life of Marleybourne and its future . . . To have no right to hold an opinion, however well founded, let alone express it, or if she did—Heaven forbid!—to have it attended to . . .

There was a sudden lurch, a grinding that shook the chaise as horses squealed and voices hurled insults. Robert Coachman's gruff voice rose above the chaos in stern exhortation to the unfamiliar team of job cattle.

Louisa's eyes flew open as the chaise tilted alarmingly.

Matty screeched. A sporty red curricle was jammed tightly against the off side, wheel apparently locked between those of the chaise. Louisa braced herself, grabbed the girl's shoulder to push her back in her seat. The chaise seemed to hesitate, teetering. Matty's screams redoubled. There came the agonized groan of tearing wood. The curricle caught against the off door and wheels ripped forward, horses plunging. The elegant chaise gave up the struggle, settling drunkenly on its side with a crash—but sedately, like an ancient toper who knew just how far the world was skewed when he was in his cups, and navigated accordingly—so that she and Matty slid rather than flew down the seats to land in a jumble of muffs, shawls, petticoats, bandboxes, lap robes, straw, and cold bricks, legs in the air and dignity ruffled.

"It needed only this! Damn Gwendolyn Fortescue . . ." Louisa muttered, and then, "Hush, Matty," as the robust maid beat a violent tattoo with her heels, voice soaring. "We've only been rather gently overturned. Neither of us is in the least injured."

The voice of reason failed to stem the avalanche of sound. Louisa attempted to right herself and administer a sharp slap to the hysterical girl. It was hopeless, she realized, blushing at the sight of her legs sticking straight in the air like a pair of dead limbs torn from their parent tree by a high wind. The tangle of travel impedimenta held her as firmly pinioned as the strongest chains in the deepest jail.

"Blast!" she muttered, squirming desperately, but it was no good. She was well and truly trapped, probably exposed to the waist, though all she could see through the welter was her feet encased in half-boots of jean and a fair expanse of warm woolen stocking covering shapely calves. As a head rose over the side, she shut her eyes, dangled her hand artistically and moaned—though she doubted she would be heard through Matty's din. Would the girl *never* stop?

"There's two of 'em in here, Jasper," a deep male voice called. "At least, I *think* it's two. Lend me a hand here— the door's hopelessly jammed."

"We're going to die!" Matty moaned. "Dear Lord, forgive me, a sinner!"

A blast of cold air ran up Louisa's legs, twining itself into recesses she prayed were hidden, followed by drops of icy rain. There was puffing, the tinkle of broken glass, then a slight lurch as a heavy body landed beside her with a grunt. Through slitted eyes she glimpsed a pair of gleaming black Hessians somewhat the worse for their encounter with the elements, and an expanse of soft buff leathers ending in—She snapped her eyes shut, hoping her face with its telltale blush was indistinguishable in the murky confusion. There was the sound of a scuffle, a sharp crack, and Matty's screeches faded to despairing whimpers. That was a mercy, at least. A man of direct action, was Lord Leap-to-the-Rescue.

"Ooh, my lady," Matty snuffled, "what ever will Lord Harry say, an' this his spankin' new chaise!" The voice climbed toward its overtaxed shriek. "Leave me be! *I'm a'dying!* Ooh, my head . . . Jesus, Mary, an' Joseph! What're you after doin' to me?" Where did the girl get the wind!? "Mother of God—leave me be!" Another sharp crack, another squeal, more whimpering.

"Hi! Jasper! One coming up!" the deep voice called.

"If you're thinking I'll be leaving my mistress what's fainted dead away, poor lady, alone with the likes of you—"

"Be still, girl! You'll do as you're told, or I'll give you a set of fives and *then* you'll do as you're told—believe me!"

"Help! Call the Watch! Libertine! Rakehell! *Help!*"

screamed Matty, back in full possession of her lungs and intent on proving their power. *"He's attacking me!"*

"Of course I am—do it every day! Perfect place for a cozy bit of dalliance—an overturned chaise in the middle of London with every man and his uncle crowding about wondering if they'll have the good fortune to glimpse a corpse—preferably young, female, only partly clad, and distinctly bloody! Don't be ridiculous, girl. Up you go!"

Louisa cringed at the laughter in the stranger's blunt words. Certainly no gentleman!

"Catch her hands, Jasper, and haul away. Brace yourself! This one's no sylph, and I don't want you doing yourself an injury. She's not worth it."

Another scuffle, a muttered curse, a shriek, what sounded like a sigh of relief. Louisa counted ten, moaned.

"Turned fairly top over tail, aren't you," the deep voice said unsympathetically. "You might at least thank me for stopping that creature's caterwauling—and don't *you* start in! Yes, I know—you can't hear a word I'm saying, as you're in a dead faint, Madam Rosy-Cheeks! A Mrs. Siddons"—there was a sudden tugging at the robes tangled around her waist—"you definitely"—a grunt, and the tangle came free—"are not!"

Louisa rolled bonelessly into the footwell, fetching up against what she assumed were the Hessians, eyes grimly clenched, face suddenly fully exposed. The almost-silence was broken by a single breath deeply and harshly drawn, slowly expelled, almost as if it were a sigh. Something brushed her cheek, and then her wrist was seized, her glove pulled roughly back. Cool fingers searched for her pulse, found it. Then came a low chuckle as her eyelid was unceremoniously pulled back, dropped. Powerful hands grasped her forearms and brought her to her feet. She wavered, not entirely acting, and was supported firmly against a hard male body, her skirts jerked to their customary position, her bonnet straightened.

"Better?" the voice asked. "You've as neatly-turned an ankle as it's been my privilege to observe in a fair number of years given over to that pleasurable pastime, madam— nothing to be ashamed of, if it's any consolation to you. Lord Harry's a lucky man . . . Well, here you go. Eyes open now, or you'll regret it. Reach up as far as you can, and Jasper'll catch you."

The hands slid to her waist, fingers biting deeply. Her eyes flew open as she soared through the air, and then she was standing on the muddy cracked cobbles surrounded by a shifting crowd of urchins, sweeps, ragpickers, cits, beggars, peddlers, and every other imaginable and un-imaginable ragtag of humanity. She leaned shakily against the carriage, grasping the wheel which stretched above her like the ribs of a giant denuded parasol. Just beyond the roof marched posts dividing the carriage and pedestrian ways. Another foot, and one would have come crashing through the side of the chaise. Louisa blanched, wavered. Fingers plucked curiously at her skirts, snatched at her bonnet, her pelisse.

"You, there—leave the lady be!" a new voice barked. "Leave be, now, or I'll take my whip to you!"

She stared around her dazedly, head swimming. A wiry, ragged stranger stood at the team's head, broad hand soothing their quivering necks and withers.

"Robert Coachman?" she implored weakly.

"Right here, m'lady."

"You're all right?" she asked muzzily, turning toward the voice.

"A bump here, a knock there. Nothing to signify," the reassuringly familiar gruff tones came at her side. "An' yerself?"

"A bump here, a knock there. Nothing to signify," she responded with a half-chuckle, shaking her head to chase the last of the cobwebs and determinedly ignoring the line of iron posts. Dear God—so close . . . "You're all right then, Robert. And Sanders? And the horses? It's plain to see Lord Harry's chaise—"

"Now, don't you go aworritin'," the burly old coachman grinned down at her. "Horses'll be fine. Nothing but a scratch here and there, though they ain't much use at t'moment—pulled up lame as they can stare. Chaise can be put back together—I've seen worse!—but how I'm to be getting you—"

"Come a fair distance?" the deep lazy voice inquired as a figure landed lightly beside her, and began inspecting the mud-encrusted undercarriage of the chaise.

"Yes," Louisa replied curtly, turned her back, determined to depress pretension. "And Sanders, Robert?"

"Thrown clear. Head's ringing a bit, but no bones broken."

"Well, that's a mercy, anyhow! I presume we can procure a hackney, even in this benighted area. You can join us at Aunt Daphne's after Harry's chaise has been hauled off and the team seen to. We haven't much in the way of—"

"Your jewel case, madam."

She turned, face glacial, to meet a pair of laughing gray eyes set in features too sardonic by half to be considered handsome. The man towered over her, and she was no pocket-Venus . . . He held out her mother's old leather case, rather scuffed from its late ordeal, the clasps still firmly latched.

"Thank you," she said frostily.

"And two bandboxes, the contents of which I did *not* inspect, you will be relieved to know. Delighted to be of service, madam."

"I am certain you were," she muttered, inspecting him coldly from the dark silver-flecked curls of his head past the shabby but well-cut coat of thick dark wool to the toes of his muddied Hessians, then set the boxes at her feet, pointedly turned her back once more. "Robert—"

"Madam, this is not a neighborhood in which I would suggest leaving a jumble of rags, let alone a jewel case, unattended at your feet."

She clenched her teeth, shuddering with the effort to restrain a sharp retort. "My thanks for your well-meant and timely caution," she managed finally. "Robert, if you would be so good as to ask Sanders to take charge of our effects and have Matty—"

"Your footman, madam? He's still off-pin. My tiger's seeing to him and the screecher. Jasper! Keep an eye on these things, will you?"

"That will not be ne—" Louisa began.

"I apologize for contradicting you, madam, but it *will* be necessary—unless you intend to detail me as chief guard and constable *pro tempore?*"

"No, I thank you," she spat.

"Oh—you're most welcome! My pleasure entirely. And now, if I might suggest, things will be in something of a muddle here for quite some time. The young fool who collided with you got rather more than he bargained for when he tried to catch the squirrel. A bit above par, is my supposition."

Louisa glanced around her, only now registering the debacle's aftermath.

Not only Harry's chaise was on its side. The trim racing curricle had overturned as well. Its team stood with heads hanging low, foam-flecked sides heaving while a groom attempted to soothe them. Sprawled against the curricle's side was a ginger-haired youth in a torn puce coat and very high shirt points, a gash over his eyebrow dripping blood down his pasty features. Just beyond, a drayer's cart had spilled its baskets of turnips and cabbages onto the broken cobbles. The confusion was lit by smoking torches held by link boys. Wavering shadows flickered across the tangle, transforming it to a writhing nightmare.

"Good heavens!"

"Exactly so. I suggest you permit me to send you and your maid on to your destination in my carriage—especially as you haven't much luggage. Jasper can return for me later. In the interim I can lend your men and that foolish young chub a hand."

Insufferable, overbearing, encroaching, officious—"Thank you, kind sir," she said sweetly, "but we shall do very well without your further assistance."—mushroom!

"Now, you be seein' here," Robert Coachman broke in with the assurance of an old family retainer, "Lord Harry would be tellin' you hisself to—"

"*Extremely* well," she said, an edge to her voice there had been no mistaking since she first put up her hair and let down her skirts. "Fetch me a hackney, Robert!"

The grizzled coachman shook his head, turned away. In this part of London, in a mizzle, with night coming on and himself chilled to the bone, *besides* being wet and muddy and with a lump on the back of his head the size of a hen's egg—But, when Miss Louisa took one of her starts there was nothing for it but to do as she commanded, or at least make the attempt, no matter how nonsensical. She'd taken the gentleman in dislike, a reaction as automatic with her as breathing, and as little considered, just the way she'd been turning her nose up at all the young blades since she left the schoolroom.

An understanding look passed between coachman and rescuer, and Robert grunted. At least the gentleman *was* a gentleman. No matter how uppity Miss Louisa got, he'd see she came to no harm. And then there were Sanders, and that fool Matty. Between the lot she'd survive until he returned—but not as comfortably as she would have in the buck's carriage, the more fool she!

Close to an hour later, mortified, shivering in the dispiriting drizzle, Louisa admitted defeat and permitted herself to be handed into the still waiting town carriage, portmanteaux and bandboxes stowed around her, Matty

crowded into the far corner. Somehow Louisa managed
to avoid meeting the ever-laughing gray eyes and insufferable grin of her rescuer, barely containing herself as she
said her thank-you's with a chilly politeness that would
have cowed a true gentleman, but only seemed to tickle
this commoner's risibilities.

His parting shot—after handing her up and instructing
Matty to see to it her mistress had a glass of brandy, a hot
bath, and a warm bed in that order once she reached her
destination—murmured as he bent over her hand, made
her want to claw his face. " '*Much* too neatly turned for
those woolen sausage-casings, madam,' " *indeed!*

As for presenting his compliments to Lord Harry, she'd
flung his heavily embossed card in the mud where it
belonged, rapped on the carriage roof, and leaned back in
relief as they pulled away.

"What!?" Daphne Cheltenham, Dowager Countess of
Stoker, collapsed against the rosy chaise-lounge pillows
staring at her niece. "You *cannot* be serious!"

The incident of the overturned carriage and encroaching demi-beau had been dealt with in what Louisa considered unnecessary detail over a dinner taken on trays in
Lady Daphne's cozy parlor—once a stiff brandy and hot
bath had been administered. As soon as the trays were
removed, the servants banished, Louisa had launched
into those reasons for her sudden trip to London which
she had been reluctant to commit to paper when she
wrote to accept her aunt's oft-repeated invitation. Beside
Harry's stupendous news, the mysterious ne'er-do-well
with his laughing eyes and arrogance—"Who could he *be?*
Gray eyes, you say, and dark hair silvered at the temples,
and a manner such as *could not* be pleasing to any lady?"—
fortunately paled to insignificance.

"Quite, *quite* serious," Louisa said smiling.

"They insist you—They must be mad, *totally* mad, *all* of them," Lady Daphne fumed. "Perfectly *Gothic*, my dear! And, if you *don't* wed, I suppose they'll chain you in a dungeon and reduce you to bread and water! I've always suspected *some* sort of scandal lurked behind that formidable Fortescue facade, and *now* I know what it is! Pure, unadulterated *madness*, coupled with an arrogance which passes all—And *Harry*, just as heartless and Gothic as they are!"

"No—he's just a boy," Louisa said with a sad smile, "who's spotted something he thinks he can't live without in a shop window. There's no meanness or cruelty in him."

"Then he's every *bit* as mad as they are!"

"Don't the poets claim love is a form of insanity?"

"Perhaps, but they don't mean it *literally*. Wait until I tell Sally Jersey about *this* latest start!"

"Oh, no, Aunt—please! You can't!" Louisa leaned forward imploringly. Sally Jersey, one of the patronesses of the fabled Almack's, and nicknamed "Silence," was the ton's most skilled and dedicated, if not its most vicious, gossip. "If word were to be bandied about, Miss Fortescue would be sure to hear of it and cry off, and Harry would be both furious with me—which I couldn't bear—and desolated, which would be even worse."

"You don't mean to tell me you *favor* this match!"

"No—but I won't be the cause of a rupture if I can help it. Some other method will have to be found for disentangling Harry, though the dear Lord knows what it may be! Wait until you see him. If love *is* a disease, Harry has contracted the fatal form."

"The man *cannot* cry off," Lady Cheltenham said thoughtfully, "so . . ."

"Naturally, but *how?*"

"*We* must find a substitute, higher of rank and plumper of pocket. *Rank* poses no insurmountable difficulty, but the *pockets* may be something of a problem. Our dear father was rich as Golden Ball, and Rockford and Isabella did nothing to dissipate the fortune, living retired as they did. I shall consider . . ."

"I wish it were possible, but when you see Harry, you'll know you're whistling in the dark. He's been well and truly caught."

"Even the weakest fish can slip the hook, if it wants."

"But, he doesn't *want*," Louisa rejoined with a sigh. "You should hear how he speaks of her!"

"I shall—all too soon, I imagine—and it will probably sicken me into a decline."

"You? Never!" Louisa said with a sudden chuckle. "Into a towering rage, perhaps, but never a decline!"

Lady Cheltenham's eyes twinkled. "That's better, my girl," she said. "Faint heart and long face *never* solved anything. Of course, the *idea* of your marrying is not in itself a bad one . . ."

Around them Lady Daphne's rose-bower parlor glowed with warmth and understated luxury. Never one to follow fashion slavishly—she considered the recent Egyptomania foolish beyond permission, as being both uncomfortable and impractical—she created little havens wherever she turned. The town house's exterior might be in the coolly elegant style of Robert Adam, but the intimate parlor spoke of sunlit meadows and high summer in the midst of raw winter. Icy rain might slash the panes hidden behind deep rose velvet draperies, the wind howl unforgivingly around the eaves—as both most definitely were. Here flowers bloomed perpetually, tender flames licked wood over shimmering coals, and not a vestige of a draft was permitted to insinuate itself.

With a flutter of shawls and draperies, Lady Daphne subsided on her plump cushions, eyes flashing.

"But, to place a *time limit* on it, and *such* a time limit! Only a year . . . Of course, a matter of a single *season* is often considered adequate by mamas anxious to fire off the eldest before the next is ready to leave the school-room. As if *genuine* attachments could march to the same drum as overly-fecund females! *Idiotish . . . !*"

Louisa's eyes sparkled. "Not even a year, dearest Aunt," she chuckled. "Only nine months remain. What do you say to placing a notice in the *Morning Post:* 'WANTED: Husband. Must be neat in person, of tem-perate habits and reasonable lineage. Sound teeth and good wind required. Neither hair nor wit mandatory. Fortune of no consequence. Age: under senility. Appli-cants to present themselves the twelfth instant—' "

"My dear!"

"Well, that's what it will amount to," Louisa insisted with a touch of resentment, not quite meeting her aunt's clear blue eyes. "The moment I appear in public at your side, everyone will know my purpose in coming to Lon-don."

"They will know you are come to visit *me*—nothing more," Lady Daphne said firmly, tilting her silvered head as she studied the young woman across from her. "Not unless you *want* them to know. What they *suspect* won't harm you—unless those abominable Fortescues poke their fingers in our pie."

"Which they have already attempted! Do not forget the vicar and the house party."

"Ah, yes—the good whuffling vicar of the excellent cellar and sweet bottom . . . 'What sorrows the flesh is heir to,' " her aunt quoted not quite accurately, restraining an impulse to chuckle. Louisa's description of the interview with Harry had been devastatingly accurate, and quite hilarious in spite of the circumstances. *"Forget* the vicar! *I* intend to." Lady Daphne took a deep and steadying breath, bosom atremble with flutters of lace and sparkle of jewels. "Your dear brother must be all about in his head to even *dream* of placing you in such a bumblebroth, especially if he thinks that—"

"Oh, I've agreed to it, Aunt Daphne," Louisa interposed with a twinkle. "There wasn't much else I *could* do."

"What—to *all* of it?"

Louisa continued to smile, but her face hardened.

"I mislike that look, young lady!"

"As well you might," Louisa chuckled, struck by the germ of an idea. "You must understand—I have agreed to wed before the end of the sainted Gwendolyn's year, but I shall be—Well, I shall not permit them, or *anyone*, to select a husband for me, and perhaps they won't be best pleased with *my* choice."

"It won't fadge, my dear," the older woman sighed, "though I do admire your spirit. Marriage is a more or less permanent arrangement, and it wouldn't do to select a spouse purely on the basis of unsuitability. You'd come home by weeping cross that way. As well find your knight-errant of this afternoon and wed him tomorrow!"

"Never!" Louisa laughed. "That much I can promise you. Had you but seen him, or, worse yet, *heard* him!"

"He sounds *quite* well set-up, in spite of your scathing tongue. Dark gray eyes, you say, and a sardonic grin?"

" 'Lecherous' would be the better term. He looked a hardened rake, and his manner was everything that is insulting!"

"Still . . ." Lady Daphne's eyes narrowed thoughtfully. "Precisely what did he say or do which you found so objectionable?"

"I refuse to discuss it," Louisa said, reddening.

"Not turning *missish* on me, are you?"

"Hardly!"

"Because it won't do if you are, my dear. Won't do *at all! Nothing* is more off-putting in a young woman . . . And, no idea at all as to who he might be," her aunt grumbled.

"I suppose you didn't bother to look for a crest on the carriage?"

"No—my mind wasn't on the social niceties."

"*Think!* You noticed *nothing?*"

"There may have been—I don't know," Louisa responded in exasperation. "His manner was so insulting that I—No!"

"A message of thanks should be sent, at the very least," her aunt grumbled.

"To that insufferable coxcomb? No, no message of thanks. He *wasn't* a gentleman, and so no thanks would be required, even if I did know his direction."

"That is *precisely* when thanks are *most* essential, you little peagoose," her aunt protested. "You'll learn *that* soon enough. Nothing like a properly worded expression of gratitude to depress pretension, if he is what you claim." Lady Daphne studied her niece narrowly, the slightest of frowns contracting her features. "You have someone in mind to assist you in assuring Harry of his diamond?"

"A type—no more."

"And, that is—?"

"I shall seek out a gentleman who has no more interest in the married state than I have myself. Once the ceremony is performed he shall go his way, I mine, and so we shall rub along tolerably, I should think."

"Grim! Believe me, my dear, *grim!* How your parents' daughter could contemplate such a thing with equanimity—Not that it isn't done, and quite *commonly,* too. I could name you any *number* of—But, *you?* No—quite out of the question. Such 'marriages' are descents into hell for any female of the *slightest* sensibility. If you *truly* intend such a thing, contemplate the possibility of wedding your lecherous coxcomb out of hand! *That's* the type of whom you speak, whether you realize it or not. You wouldn't survive a week!"

Louisa's answering laugh was brittle. "I've survived worse," she said, a touch of acid to her voice. "You should attempt a conversation such as I had with Harry that morning!" Then she smiled with genuine warmth. "So, you see, you shan't have me on your hands much over half a year, if that, for I'm determined not to stand in Harry's way—at least not in that manner. He shall have all the freedom he could wish to court and wed his paragon. If he makes a cake of himself in the process, and some kind soul has sufficient bottom to point it out to him, I shan't complain . . ."

"You'll leave the difficult tasks to others? That *isn't* like you."

"My hands are tied. Harry would never listen to any woman on such a subject—least of all his sister. He'd claim spite and jealousy caused the caveats, and not concern for his happiness. Now—the first requirement is clothes. You'll have the vapors when you see the little I've brought. I suspect I should be less out of fashion were I to appear in that which the Lord, rather than Madame Céleste and her *confrères* provide as covering!"

Three

The first flowers arrived the next morning as Louisa and Lady Daphne were finishing a hearty meal in the breakfast parlor—fortification against a day to be divided between several silk warehouses and three exclusive modistes, and capped (if something suitable by way of evening dress could be contrived for Louisa from Lady Daphne's extensive and youthful wardrobe) by an appearance at the opera.

They were jonquils, golden-yellow and dew-touched, nestled among the most delicate of ferns. No card. No message. Only a single silk stocking, binding the flowers in lieu of ribbons.

Lady Daphne chuckled into her chocolate. Louisa blushed and instructed Hoskins, her aunt's antiquated and unflappable butler, to have the flowers thrown out—preferably where they would be in clear evidence should the monster have the temerity to appear on the doorstep inquiring how she did after the yesterday's misadventure.

That first day in London passed in avalanches of silks and satins, in torrents of muslins and laces and spangled gauzes, the persistent drizzle in no way deflecting Lady Daphne from her self-appointed rounds. Whisked home with a burgeoning headache, an unwilling Louisa was thrust into the capable hands of Holfers, her aunt's austerely superior dresser, to be washed, rinsed, coifed, perfumed, jeweled, and garbed. It had become *imperative,* Lady Daphne proclaimed in a tone which brooked no opposition, that they attend that evening, no matter *what* Louisa was forced to wear. Too many eyes had noted them at a distance. That actual *introductions* had been avoided mattered not a whit. Louisa had been spotted. Now she must be *seen.*

The results of Holfers' expertise, Lady Daphne admitted as she watched Louisa descend the stairs three hours later, were not entirely to be despised—so long as one did not peer overlong at the wan face or recognize the decorative banding as masking a lengthened skirt. Her niece was a confection of glossy golden ringlets, Lady Daphne's hastily altered gown of palest Nile-green silk swirling at her ankles. The deep-green velvet roses and darker satin leaves, the frothings of lace and flutterings of ribbon had vanished, replaced by garlands of delicate crystal flowers and silver arabesques at neckline, high waist, and sculptured hem. The dress, in its new guise, was unrecognizable.

She ignored the girl's halfhearted pleas of exhaustion and a desire for her bed, propelled her into the dining parlor for a dinner suited to depleted constitutions and overwrought nerves, and then once more into her elegant town carriage.

"I but want you *glimpsed,*" that lady stated as she settled herself comfortably against the squabs, rapped on the roof, "so you may as well come out of the dismals. We shall appear only after the overture and mysteriously disappear before the end of the first act. You have but to maintain an intriguingly remote expression for that short period, and I shall be *quite* satisfied."

Louisa Beckenham sighed as the carriage pulled away from the house. Keeping pace with her father's charming but formidable sister was no sinecure. She was beginning to suspect that actual resistance to Daphne Cheltenham's edicts would prove yet more difficult, should she be so foolish as to make the attempt.

"Yes, Aunt," she acquiesced wearily. "I am not to be interested?"

"I doubt you will be. It's Gluck tonight—*unbearably* dull, with all that caterwauling and not a *scrap* of comprehensible plot or spark of humor to enliven the proceedings. Only noise and posturing. And *deaths*—quite a few, and all very *bloody*."

"I don't see why anyone bothers," Louisa sighed.

"My dear! One doesn't go to the opera to be *entertained*," Lady Daphne riposted tartly. "One goes to be *seen!* Tomorrow we shall be positively deluged with callers, but you shall be indisposed—the excuse for our sudden departure, naturally." Lady Daphne gave a pleased little smile, only half-visible in the soft light of the carriage lanterns. "Otherwise, we should be inundated during the interval, and while at a distance, this *thing*"—she indicated the stunning gown which Holfers and two upstairs maids had labored most of the day to alter and disguise—"will do quite well, for your first *true* appearance we must await your new gowns. *Nothing* is more critical to a successful social career than the nod a proper wardrobe elicits."

"Clothes do not make the woman."

"I should hope not! What a silly thing to say. Or, the *man*, for that matter, but nothing is of greater importance when one is dressing for dinner. Your dear mother came to town *at least* twice a year to smarten herself. Rockford, dolt though he may have been in *other* respects, still liked to see Isabella well turned-out."

"Mama was very beautiful . . ." Louisa's voice fell on the words, longing for a time long-past shining through.

"As are you, my dear! Did I not launch *four* daughters successfully?" Lady Daphne demanded. "*And* five nieces, one of whom was a positive *antidote*, for all her excellent dowry and pleasant disposition; *and* two distant cousins who were as portionless as they were witless; *and* the youngest and *excessively* plain daughter of an old friend?"

"I suppose you must have, since you trouble to pose the question."

"Yes, I most *certainly* did," Lady Daphne chuckled. "The tally of those ventures was an earl, a marquess, *two* viscounts, *three* baronets, a baron, three gentlemen, and a nabob—not *one* of whom was possessed of an income of less than *twenty thousand!* And not one, mind you, a *younger* son! Of course, not one was a *duke,* which would have been most gratifying. His Grace of Rawdon *did* offer for Marianne, no matter what anyone may tell you, but the silly goose had already determined on the nabob. Still, they're disgustingly happy, so I mustn't repine . . . Only time Rawdon ever made an *honest* offer to a female, and that must have been all of fifteen years ago—not that he's been wearing the willow! Now, *there* would be a catch, but he'll run shy of any young woman *I* sponsor after the debacle with Marianne. That tribe is unfortunately cursed with excessively long and inconvenient memories, so you may as well put him out of your mind."

"Certainly," Louisa chuckled. "No great task, as I've never even heard of the man."

"*Rawdon?* My word—you *are* countrified! The caps that have been set at him! The lures that have been cast! But, to no purpose. Elusive as a cloud on the wind. Something of a Corinthian, something of a rake," her gesture indicated they were equivalent, "and an inveterate prankster with *far* too much in the way of looks, charm, and fortune for his own good!"

"And too great a paragon for comfort or ease. An amiable younger son of modest circumstances would suit me rather better, as I have fortune enough for both."

"Don't be ridiculous! A *younger* son? You'll do a deal better than *that* under my sponsorship, even if Rawdon and his circle *are* out of reach. I don't know, though—perhaps not *entirely* . . ." Lady Daphne gazed abstractedly out the small carriage window, hand gracefully grasping the strap. "He *is* highly connected with the military—friends at the Horse Guards, that sort of thing. Younger brother was killed in the Peninsula—the Corunna retreat, I believe—and they were particularly close. Rawdon has maintained the ties, speaks up for Arthur Wellesley and his Peninsular Army in the Lords every chance he gets. An introduction from me would be a dead loss, but perhaps *Harry*—"

"No!" Louisa laughed. "I've no desire for a duke, or anything approaching it. A quiet gentleman of steady habits and retiring character will do very nicely, if I am forced to it in the end."

"Just as well, I suppose. Truth to tell, Marianne *was* the purest fluke. Caught him in a weak moment, and he's been doubly wary ever since. No desire to make a fool of himself again, I imagine. Skittish . . . Besides which, according to Tabitha Brassthwaite, His Grace is rusticating at Rawdonmere. *Most* inconsiderate! To stand up with him would *almost* be the making of you. A *second* set, and—He owes me that much!"

"A man with *far* too much power," Louisa responded lightly. "If I ever encounter His Grace, I believe it must be my duty to refuse him the honor."

"Don't be ridiculous!" The laughter which had lit Lady Daphne's eyes died. "The essence, my dear, of a successful campaign is to never once repeat a recognizable strategy while grasping every opportunity offered. Trust me! I have been planning this particular campaign since you left of the schoolroom."

The next flowers were hyacinths. Then came violets, roses, daffodils, tulips, and snowdrops, each offering devoid of card or message, each bound with a single silk stocking.

Matty, her promised week in London at an end, returned to Marleybourne with Robert and Sanders, replete with a stock of tales to regale the servants' hall for months to come. Louisa parted from them with regret, the last tangible ties to the Court severed. For Lady Daphne it was a moment of quiet satisfaction. She had feared, until the wrench of parting was past, that Louisa might bolt, Harry's future and her own abandoned in a fit of bathetic *cafard*.

Louisa's new feathers deluged the house in a sudden flood of boxes stuffed with the finest tissue. Harry wrote that their mother's diamonds had been sent to Rundle and Bridge for cleaning and resetting. Louisa shrugged. She had had the pearls since her unofficial country come-out at fifteen, and never particularly cared for the harder gems.

It wasn't that she was recalcitrant or ungrateful. She submitted to lessons in deportment, conversation, dancing, and the finer points of light flirtation with a deference for Lady Daphne's opinions which would have been remarkable in a schoolroom miss determined to take the ton by storm, let alone a young woman of five-and-twenty accustomed to being the mistress of what amounted to her own establishment for the past ten years. Only animation and pleasure were lacking.

Finally, in desperation, Lady Daphne decided Louisa must make her first semiofficial appearances or the game would be lost before it was well begun. She initiated a round of mild socializations culminating in a mid-week dinner for twenty. Among the guests were an elderly scholar of great charm, a widow and her dandy son, a pair of spinster connections with their man-about-town nephew, a widower general and his granddaughter, and—duty-bound—the eldest son of an old friend sent down from Scotland to acquire a little town bronze for himself and a bride for the succession.

"Except for that slow-top of a Harald Donclennon—who will never be of any use to anyone, even himself, more's the pity, for his mother was a joy—they're all *talkers,*" Lady Daphne explained of the rather dull list, "and talkers are precisely what we want now. I've hidden them away amongst others who are quite unexceptionable, and may prove useful eventually. Never does to show one's hand—remember that. As for you"—Lady Daphne patted Louisa's cheek with every appearance of a satisfaction she was far from feeling—"you'll do, now most of the country edges have been chipped away. Back straight, remember! Voice soft and low. *Float* across the room, and *never* look at a chair before you sit. *Sink*—don't plump—and *always* assume a gentleman will be there to position one properly in time. The signal?"

"Languor. A faint inviting smile. An abstracted look," Louisa recited parrotlike. "Then a *delicate* gathering of skirts followed by a *half*-step to the rear."

"Excellent! With the *exact* position of the chair previously noted upon entering the room. Remember *that,* too! Avoids tedious embarrassments. Once you have 'em trained, then start sitting from a point farther and farther from the chair. Works *wonders!* All the gentleman must watch you *most* carefully for fear of an unpleasant incident, and so are forced to ignore every other female present. Haven't used that one since my own come-out. *My* record was twenty-four feet, and with an intervening clot of dowagers who made things rather difficult for poor Roger Mainwaring. Not that he didn't have the chair there in time, mind you! I hope you're honored."

"I most certainly am, dear Aunt," Louisa chuckled, imagining a scene replete with mile-high coiffures, powdered wigs, and panniers. A tumble in such surround-

ings would have been daunting indeed for all concerned . . .

This first formal evening party passed without incident,
the man-about-town nephew and the dandy son vying for
Louisa's attention like two wasps circling a single rose,
while the rotund Lord Harald hovered tongue-tied in the
background, spilling his tea, spotting his waistcoat, and
treading so heavily on Lady Daphne's foot that she later
declared she was crippled for life. General Maitland proclaimed Louisa a delightful puss. The spinsters thought
her most properly modest and retiringly ladylike, not putting herself forward unbecomingly despite her excellent
pedigree and bruited dot. The scholar, who had the good
fortune to corner her briefly during the flurry of arrivals,
proclaimed her to possess a first-rate mind—an en-
comium which puzzled the others not a little, and caused
Lady Daphne's brows to soar in consternation. *That*
would have to be scotched on the instant! The granddaughter called her elegant. The plump widow dreamed
of nuptials in which Louisa's dot figured prominently, and
breathily exclaimed how lovely the unspoiled young thing
and her handsome son looked together. The smitten Scots
laird was content merely to let his eyes drink their fill, and
if his words were few and disjointed, his looks were speaking.

And the two gentlemen of fashion?

Each wasp-waisted, buchram-wadded spark saw a
coldness toward the other in Louisa's quiet manner, encouragement for himself in her infrequent smiles, and
came away satisfied he had quite cut out his supposed
rival.

The ton had been permitted to *see*. Now, they would
hear . . .

* * *

And still the flowers came, morning after morning—always in the best of taste, often shockingly out-of-season—consistently bound with their single silk stockings. Lady Daphne, after acceding to Louisa's first fit of pique, insisted the persistent offerings be permitted to adorn at least the public rooms of the tall house. Bright splashes of color were everywhere, as if draperies and upholstery had replicated in three dimensions.

As the days passed, Louisa became inured to the anonymous floral tributes, even going so far as to allow an occasional posy in her own rooms if she were particularly partial to the flowers. Mysteriously, those suddenly became the flowers of preference—not to the exclusion of all others, but arriving with sufficient frequency that before one bouquet passed its prime another took its place—yet not of such overwhelming preference that Louisa felt forced to question the servants concerning the donor's uncanny perspicacity. The silk stockings she at first attempted to bestow on the maids, but their embarrassed titters and sly glances left her no alternative but to throw the things out or stuff them in the bottom of a chest in her dressing room.

Mist alternated with chill rain and drizzle as the weeks passed. London was by way of becoming an aquarium, the wags joked, and examined their coteries for nascent gills and incipient scales. Bets were laid at White's and Brook's as to how long the inclement weather would last, and Harriette Wilson was heard to proclaim that the greatest ladies in the land were now perforce her sisters, their petticoats damped by nature as revealing as hers damped by art.

Through it all Lady Cheltenham kept a weather eye on both sky and social calendar, reducing their public appearances to ensure Louisa would not be too much seen, and so fade to insignificance when that year's crop of predatory young debutantes gathered for the seasonal hunt and capture of the unwary eligible male.

Restricted almost exclusively to the pastimes and society of her aunt's aging intimates—the only relief a call paid by the two sprigs of fashion with the purpose of confirming that this newly unearthed Incomparable retained her beauty and grace in morning's cold light before touting her perfections in the clubs, and a stultifying promenade in the Park with a pink-faced and incoherent Lord Harald at the fashionable hour of five, Lady Daphne uncomplainingly in attendance—boredom descended on Louisa to such a degree that she would have welcomed any diversion. Shocked at her own inconsistency, she found herself anticipating the daily bouquets with something akin to pleasure, as relieving a tedium so endlessly gray as to be insupportable. She dreamed of Marleybourne and longed for her lost independence.

Then, on a trip to Madame de Métrise's for the fitting of yet another ball gown, Louisa found herself watching the crowds less than idly for a glimpse of the long lean figure, the broad shoulders, the laughing devilish eyes and curling black locks touched with silver of her erstwhile rescuer. That this traitorous exercise followed hard on three days of unremitting rain and three evenings of patience was no excuse. If truth were told, it was not the first time her eyes had roamed the hurrying figures with more than cursory interest.

Conscious or not, it was a futile exercise. Of Lord Leap-to-the-Rescue there was no sign. He had vanished as neatly as at the wave of a magician's wand, leaving only his flowers as evidence that he was more than the figment of an overwrought imagination.

They returned from the mantua maker's that day to find Harry ensconced in the back parlor, long legs encased in muddied Hessians stretched to a well-built fire, a decanter of claret and a glass at his elbow along with the remains of a substantial platter of sandwiches, coat of olive superfine damp, neckcloth and shirt points wilted.

"Hoskins said you had but a single errand!" he exclaimed, surging to his feet as they appeared on the sill. "You've been gone three hours, and more! I could have been to the Clarendon and back ten times over, instead of which you find me here in all my dirt—nothing but your own faults, though I do apologize for miring the carpet. Whatever have you been doing all this time?"

Louisa froze in the doorway, then rushed to him, dismay at his appearance (and the probable reason for his sudden unannounced arrival) warring with genuine delight at his unexpected presence, hands outstretched.

"Darling Harry! You're all wet and cold!"

"Nonsense—with this fire? I've survived far worse. Merely bored beyond endurance waiting for you. What *have* you been doing?" He backed off slightly, surveying his sister with unaccustomed care. "Very smart. In fact, complete to a shade, if Gwendolyn's customary style is anything to judge by. Why ever didn't you look like this at home?"

"There was no need," returned Louisa with a twinkle, "and less opportunity."

"And *that*, young man, is what we have been doing," Lady Daphne proclaimed with more than usual vigor as she swept forward. "Such a transformation is not accomplished on the instant, no matter what you may think. You *do* approve?"

"Approve?" Harry dropped Louisa's hand and turned to his aunt, grinning like a schoolboy. "How could I not? You've worked miracles—not that you hadn't good material to begin with, but this is more than I hoped for—far more!"

"Merely a simple afternoon gown covered by a most undistinguished pelisse and crowned by a hat which is only barely passable," Lady Daphne smiled offhandedly, but with immense inner satisfaction. "Something sturdy enough to survive the inclement weather. Wait until the first ball of the season! *Then* you'll see what I've wrought, and it *is* miraculous, my boy—*indeed* it is!"

Harry laughed, catching his aunt in a great one-armed bear hug and dropping a kiss on her soft scented cheek. "You always were an intrepid old dear, Aunt Daffy," he chuckled, "but how you've gotten Louisa to agree to all these—I don't know what you call 'ems, but the improvement is truly astonishing."

"Well! With the assignment you gave her"—the slightest touch of asperity colored Lady Daphne's voice—"nothing *less* was possible. It's best you don't inquire too deeply into the cost, my boy, or you may change your mind about the entire project, and the investment has only just begun."

"Whatever it takes," Harry said magnanimously, "I'll stand the nonsense gladly, if only to see Louisa take the shine out of every other girl in London. Of course she won't outshine Gwendolyn—we're speaking of possibilities, rather than reaching for the moon—but there's no need for her to do that to snare a husband."

"None at all," interjected Louisa cordially before Lady Daphne could do more than draw herself up and open her mouth. "I've never aspired to be acclaimed a diamond of the first water."

"That, nevertheless, is exactly what you *will* be called the moment you're launched! Gwendolyn Fortescue, outshine Louisa?" Lady Daphne almost spat the words. "Not likely!"

Harry chuckled at this evidence of family partiality. Lady Daphne, her say having been said, instructed Harry to stop blathering, fetch his traps, and return in time to change for dinner. The Clarendon was shockingly expensive, and there was no need—Harry demurred, but did accept the summons to dine. There were certain matters, he informed them, which required frank family discussion.

The presence of a man, young and strong and handsomely virile despite his missing arm and cicatriced visage, wrought a magical change in the hitherto staid household. The maids' eyes sparkled. Cook went into a flurry which sent the pot boy and scullery maid flying, and left her assistants gasping at the meal she proposed to conjure out of thin air, for as Maisie said to Bess, "The larder's set for the two of 'em ladies, with a bit o' veal an' some 'sparygrasses, but buttered lobster? *An'* goose? *An'* boiled mutton with caper sauce? *An'* a blank-manger? *An'* all them removes? 'Tween the cookin' an' the cleanin' up, we won't be a-seein' of our beds 'til dawn!" But, the words were uttered without complaint—indeed, with an almost prideful satisfaction.

Hoskins saw to the selection of wines with unusual care, even resurrecting a particularly fine port from the deepest recesses of the cellar, and lecturing the brace of footmen on the proper manner in which to address the young viscount—"Just as if we never 'ad no nobs 'ere!" Charles remarked to Matthew as they gave the heavy plate a final polish before setting the covers. "*I* knows I can't call 'im Master 'arry no more, even if I 'as knowed 'im since 'e were a nipper, an' so does you! As for me aitches, I'll watch 'em good an' proper once 'e gets 'ere. We allus does when there's nobs to 'ear us!"

Lady Daphne decided to sport her rubies rather than the garnet set which would have been her customary choice with her dinner gown of deepest wine-red velvet, and commanded Louisa to don one of her new evening dresses—a sea-green confection with an overlay of palest blue gauze shot with silver threads, its lines flowing in the Grecian style, flocks of delicate silver birds embroidered

at the low neckline and hem—and her mother's diamonds rather than the pearls to which she had been
restricted heretofore.

"You'll be a nymph, my dear, just springing from a
fountain—or do I mean a dryad touched with dew?
Doesn't matter. You'll be *delectable!*" And *then* they'd see
who Harry, if he had one scrap of sense left in his cockloft,
would think just might outshine whom . . .

Harry had already returned when Lady Daphne and
Louisa swept down the stairs, his reaction to his sister's
elegance everything Lady Daphne had hoped—except
for his quick aside concerning doubt as to the suitability
of silk (and of such a color!) for a debutante, and the
propriety of diamonds on an unbetrothed woman. Perhaps he had made a mistake in sending them? Gwendolyn, he knew, restricted herself to white, or the palest of
pastel muslins, and pearls in the evening. Wasn't that
more in keeping—? Lady Daphne snorted, told him not
to worry himself over things of which he had no knowledge.

Certainly there was delight in Harry's eyes, and a most
unusual ceremoniousness to the manner in which he
treated his sister, but beneath lurked not only an apprecia-
tion for the beauty Louisa had revealed herself to be.
There was unease as well in the veiled glances he threw
in her direction, combined with not a little confusion.
This splendid young woman was no longer the sad romp
of a chit who lived to climb trees and ride neck-or-nothing
across the countryside when her nose wasn't buried in
books unsuitable for a schoolroom miss—or any female,
if truth were told, no matter what her age. His playmate
had vanished, along with Marleybourne's assured but
rather dowdy chatelaine, and the bluestocking was well-
enough masked that only the most perceptive would spot
her—and then only when she fell into one of her mischievous moods.

He did not quite know what to make of this metamorphosed Louisa, and wished devoutly that she had agreed to the house party at Fortescue Lodge.

There was danger in her new looks—danger to *her,* he insisted to himself. Every rake and fortune hunter in town would be trailing after her. He foresaw an uncomfortable spring fighting them off. The whole point of the exercise was to get her suitably and quietly wed as rapidly as possible, and in this new guise that might well prove impossible. The staid type of gentleman Lady Fortescue recommended as best suited to Louisa's advanced years would be frightened off by a young goddess of expensive tastes, and he feared Louisa might find herself so well entertained by the bucks and their fulsome attentions that she might not accept the first respectable offer, head turned and sights set on some totally unsuitable rattle with pockets to let.

London, with its wider choice of potential suitors, had seemed ideal when he had been comfortably lounging before the fire at Marleybourne. Now he could see London mightn't do at all—not if this was the appearance she was determined to present. She looked downright . . . *inviting!*

What their aunt had done was reprehensible, but he'd have to take care, not get the old lady's back up. She came, after all, from a looser generation, and probably didn't understand the modern proprieties. She undoubtedly meant well enough, but one *didn't* advertise a lady's, well, *wares,* and Louisa's were on full display. The dress clung in a manner he would *never* have permitted had he been consulted, and as for its décolletage, and the gentle swell of bosom it revealed . . . !

And then there was the impropriety of the contrast Louisa would present to Gwendolyn—far above any station to which she could reasonably aspire.

A damnable muddle, and he wasn't certain how to go about rectifying it.

Conversation sparkled nevertheless, when it didn't lag due to sudden fits of abstraction on Harry's part. Finally, desperation overcoming common sense, he blurted—"I can see the changes, of course, Aunt Daffy—only a blind man wouldn't. But . . . what progress have you made?" as soon as Hoskins had deposited the ten o'clock tea tray and departed.

Lady Daphne's brows rose slowly. "My dear boy, you must not be so cryptic," she protested with deliberate obtuseness, chuckling to herself at the troubled looks she had seen Harry throw his sister's way. The boy was well and truly shaken. Good! He'd soon learn Louisa was not a cipher to be sacrificed to his convenience . . . "Progress? You can see it for yourself! Other than that, I cannot think what you might mean."

"Louisa," he said with a vague wave of his hand. "You know—*progress!*"

"No, Harry—I am certain I do not, except for bringing her up to snuff for the season." Lady Daphne selected a cup and saucer from the tray. "You must be more explicit. Communication in the form of abbreviated military dispatches is *not* what I am accustomed to. Do you take sugar? I have quite forgotten."

"No—no sugar, thank you. Got out of the habit in Spain. *Progress.* You know! Suitors. Beaux. Offers. That sort of thing. Why she's here, after all, isn't it—to nab a husband?" he blustered, determined to see it through.

"The Town continues *extremely* thin of company," Lady Daphne responded evenly. "You yourself only arrived today. The Season is exceedingly slow in opening because of the atrocious weather. Who wants a hundred-guinea gown mired on the first wearing?"

"Is *that* what Louisa's getup cost?" Harry exploded, momentarily diverted from his course.

"More or less—not *this*, of course, but—"

"It had damn well better be less rather than more!" he fumed. "Lady Fortescue would never approve such outlandish expense—or such a gown for a connection of hers!" he spat before he thought. "Bad ton! Gwendolyn's apparel is always of the utmost modesty."

"My dear boy, there is nothing in the least *immodest* about Louisa's—"

"*And* simplicity!" he added triumphantly.

"So is *this*, my boy—which is why it *costs*. Furbelows are relatively cheap. Perfection of line and impeccability of taste are not. You'd be surprised at how much Miss Fortescue's 'utmost simplicity' sets her father back."

"I would, indeed! Gwendolyn's mind is far above fripperies."

"Then she is unlike any other young woman I have encountered in quite a few London Seasons."

"Indeed she is, for which I thank the Lord if Louisa's rig-out is any gauge!"

"The expense of my wardrobe is my own, Harry," Louisa broke in with smooth sweetness, "not yours, so you needn't go into a pelter. As for the dress, I rather like it, and I trust Aunt Daphne's taste. Since I know nothing of Lady Fortescue's talents in that direction, and as she is no connection of mine, I shan't let her opinions prey on me."

"The gown is *quite* unexceptionable," Lady Daphne said, sending Louisa a quick frown. "You have been out of the country several years, my boy, and are not conversant with the current mode. Leave such matters to those who are."

"I've never seen Gwendolyn appear in such a—a—"

"No? But then, calling to mind her coloring and figure, I doubt it would suit her," Lady Daphne interposed. "Truly, Harry, I would hold my peace if I were you—unless you are *determined* to make a cake of yourself?"

Harry subsided, disgruntled, clenched fist resting on his

thigh. The damnable part of it was, there was little he could legitimately do or say. Louisa was of age and her own mistress, with nary a trustee or guardian to restrain her, no requirements in their father's will to guide her, and she *was* under their aunt's protection and sponsorship. Damn their father! No woman should ever have been given such autonomy, for look at the mull they made of things the moment they were permitted the least freedom! If Louisa went on as she had begun, he would spend half the season calling out a trail of unsuitable suitors, and the other half apologizing to the ton for her appearance and deportment. And just how much time would *that* permit him with Gwendolyn? Precisely none! And if Louisa chose to ignore his caveats there was nothing he could do short of cutting her—and a pretty dust-up that would cause, aside from assuring no respectable man would offer for her, and so he would lose Gwendolyn in any case. *That* he refused to allow, no matter what it took . . .

"Have you made *any* progress?" Harry asked with stubborn determination after a slight pause in which Lady Daphne turned her attention to the tea tray and Louisa stared abstractedly at the shifting patterns of light and dark in the fireplace. "Has Louisa not met *anyone?* Anyone at *all?*"

"Well, there *is* the silk-stocking gentleman," Lady Daphne admitted, eyes twinkling, after a moment's consideration as Louisa's head whipped around, "though I'm not *certain* we should count him."

"No! Most definitely not!" Louisa spluttered, torn between laughter and vexation.

"Silk stocking—? What is he—a tradesman with aspirations?"

"We don't know," his aunt replied, giving Louisa a quelling frown along with Harry's cup. "A stranger came to Louisa's assistance after your chaise overturned the day she arrived, and we suspect it is he who has been inundating her daily with flowers bound by silk stockings, but as to his identity we haven't a clue."

"Mushroom!" Harry chuckled, diverted.

"Turnip," Louisa corrected, "or worse!"

"A common vegetable? Not bad! Some mushrooms do have a touch of elegance to 'em. But, *flowers? Every* day? Bound with silk stockings? He may not be a gentleman, but certainly he isn't in dun territory."

"Unless he considers them an investment," Lady Daphne retorted tartly. "Louisa is not exactly poverty-stricken."

"How could he possibly know who she is?"

"Your chaise has a crest on it," Louisa responded reluctantly, "and he sent me on to Aunt Daphne's in his carriage. Yours was in no case to continue, and the weather was such that Robert couldn't procure a hackney."

"Of all the hen-witted—"

"What would you have had me do, Harry? Stand out there in the rain waiting for the ark to sail by and rescue me?"

"Well, certainly *something*—"

"Night was coming on," Louisa explained with exaggerated patience, close to grinding her teeth, "and I was wet and cold and shaken. Had you not been so intent on hot-footing it back to Fortescue Lodge, and instead been willing to accompany me to London as I requested, I would have had the benefit of your protection. As it was, I had to rely on myself, which in the event meant relying on the kindness and chivalry of a stranger. Certainly he seemed to have more concern for my comfort and welfare than you did, no matter what his station!"

"I sent you to town in my new chaise," Harry exploded, goaded beyond endurance, "and just look what a shambles you made of it!"

"I? I made a shambles of your chaise? Apparently Robert failed to inform you of the young sprig in his cups who—"

"No—Robert told me. I don't mean to imply you caused the accident personally. The fact remains that, if you'd had the least sense, you'd have come to Fortescue Lodge with me as you were bid, and none of this would have happened. Any undesirable acquaintance forced on you by your pigheadedness is your own responsibility."

"I had no desire to go to Fortescue Lodge," Louisa responded tightly, "or have you forgotten that minor fact?"

"Forget your insufferable rudeness to my betrothed's mother? Not likely!"

"Was it not rather," Lady Daphne interposed, irritated by the spat between brother and sister, "that Lady Fortescue showed a certain lack of consideration in assuming Louisa would be at her instant disposal? Such an assumption would not have been at all the thing in *my* day! Indeed, it would have been considered an insult of the *most* provocative type. As for the proposed company, it could *certainly* have offered little enticement, *nor* the intent of the gathering. No"—she put up her hand, forestalling both Louisa and Harry—*"none* of this is to the purpose, and is only engendering ill will between you. Should you *insist* on continuing your tiff, I shall have no choice but to send you up to the attics and let you pretend they are your old schoolroom. Come to cuffs *there* if you wish, but *not* in my parlor!" Her eyes flashed from one to the other, but the minatory gaze that she bent on Louisa was tempered by a quick wink invisible to Harry from where he sat. "I *believe,"* she said with asperity, "we were discussing a certain turnip before you so thoroughly derouted us, Harry."

"Yes, we were, weren't we," Harry agreed, stifling the retort which he longed to spew and forcing himself to lean back in the chair, relaxing his tensed muscles one by one. "No idea at all who this demi-beau might be?"

"No," Louisa snapped. "Does it matter?"

"It might. He must have been very taken with you, if indeed the flowers come from the same man."

"After almost a week of travel in sodden weather, tumbled in the bottom of an overturned chaise with bandboxes piled on top of me, and what could be seen of me tangled in fur rugs? In my old brown pelisse and a gown which was *démodé* when it was *new*, and my bonnet—such as it was—knocked over my ear?"

Harry laughed at the picture her words conjured, shook his head. "No, I suppose not," he said almost regretfully. "More hoyden than siren to you at that point. He's probably just a social-climbing cit with an eye to the main chance. You'll have to guard yourself when you ride in the Park, though. I wouldn't put it past one of that stamp to try to force himself on your notice. Still," he concluded with a wave of his hand, "the 'transformation' hadn't been worked yet, and I can't imagine you were particularly memorable turned top over tail like a discarded dustmop. Any idea why the silk stockings, if it is the same man?"

"I haven't the slightest clue," Louisa said frostily. "One never knows what notion the lower orders will take into their heads."

"Perhaps he was intrigued, and perhaps not," Lady Daphne interjected, misliking the fiery glint in Louisa's eyes, and handing the young woman a cup of tea to keep her occupied. "Still, we won't count him unless *you* insist, Harry. Beyond the silk stocking gentleman, Louisa has made several pleasant acquaintances among the ton, but it's early days yet. I have insisted she not encourage the attentions of one gentleman over another until she has considerably wider exposure. This period merely gives her the opportunity to learn how to go on, so that when the season does begin she will have that sense of ease and assurance which is indispensable to a lady." The hint of a smile quirked Lady Daphne's lips. "There is time in *plenty*, my dear boy."

And with that Harry had to be satisfied, however unsatisfactory he found it.

Before he left he informed them that the Fortescues had arrived from the country three days earlier, and would soon be paying a formal call. The news, however warmly the two ladies greeted it officially, caused their hearts to sink and their chins to rise in unison. Not so the news, tossed off by Harry as an afterthought, that several of his old comrades-in-arms were in Town on leave, and he planned to bring them 'round.

"I *refuse* to swoon over scarlet regimentals!" Louisa stormed once the door was firmly closed behind him. "Of all the insufferable, obvious ploys I have *ever*—"

Lady Daphne cut her off with a laugh. "No one asks you to *swoon*, my dear, but a handsome officer or two dancing attendance won't do your stock any harm." Then she frowned slightly. "You really *must* learn to handle men more skillfully," she scolded lightly. *"Bludgeoning* is a tactic totally lacking in finesse, though I must say, in Harry's case nothing less seems to have much effect."

Four

But, it was not until another week had passed that Lady Harriet Fortescue (a formidable matron in puce, feathers, and jet), Miss Gwendolyn Fortescue (a vision in palest primrose muslin whose fragile delicacy and fluttering manners demanded protection from an uncivilized world), and two simpering and spotty younger sisters (Misses Sophronia and Belinda, plump girls in training for their eventual come-outs), darkened the Cheltenham steps, escorted by a stripling bearing an uncanny resemblance to the dandified youth who caused Harry's chaise to overturn.

In the interim Louisa and her aunt had been treated to an almost constant stream of military visitors introduced to their notice by Harry, some tongue-tied by extremes of youth or bashfulness, others possessed of a grace and social ease that won Lady Daphne's instant approval and even Louisa's reluctant liking—though she preferred the task of bringing the younger ones out of themselves to fending off the accomplished blandishments of the elder. As Harry's friends, however, they must all be welcome. These scions of the best of the Upper Ten Thousand (and the few who were not, merely springing from respectable county families) quickly learned that forthright camaraderie served far better with Louisa than skilled flirtation and soulful looks. Firm, lighthearted friendships began to blossom amid amusing tales of Portugal and Spain, and the inventive shifts to which Wellington's men were often put in the face of extreme privation and hardship—hardship and privation given all the aspects of privilege hardly won, and danger scoffingly ignored, only that which was light and humorous granted weight.

In competition with these came lords and honorables of every age, girth, fortune (and lack of it), determined to lay siege to the dot encased in such a delightful package. Their conversation was of ancestral manors and daring-do, connections even to royalty (if only with a bend sinister across the escutcheon), of mothers prepared to retire to dower houses, and of their own prowess in curricle, with pistols, on horseback, at card table and in ballroom. The most prepossessing of the counter-military contingent were Lord Harald Donclennon, doggedly assiduous in his attentions since Lady Daphne's dinner party of weeks before, and Lord Peter Sackett—only slightly less pompous and self-important than the best of the rest, and only slightly more entertaining, though he believed himself totally charming and irresistible to the ladies. His pockets were plump, his teeth his own, his estates fecund, his hair thick, his profile aristocratic, and his intentions the most honorable—to acquire a brood mare and beget himself an heir. What more, truthfully, could any gel want? That he tippled a bit more—and exercised both mind and body a good deal less—than was strictly good for him were minor matters.

The first tentative events of the season had at last taken place—a single ball so poorly attended as to cause the hostess to retire to the country in mortification, and a rout which the wags termed a "disqueace." The ton, or most of it, might be in town, but they watched one another and the sodden skies warily, waiting for some unmistakable sign that the revelries might at last begin in earnest. Indoor public entertainments—the opera, the theater, Astley's—did well. Tradesmen, confectioners, caterers, musicians, hostesses, and debutantes prayed for sunshine.

As for the flowers, they continued to arrive steadily and without fanfare, each offering bound by its silk stocking. So accustomed had Louisa become to their presence that, had they failed to make their appearance one morning, she would have been seriously put out. That other posies had begun to join them made not a jot of difference.

Now, as the Fortescue contingent filed into the drawing room reserved for formal callers, Louisa studied the Honorable Giles as best she could without appearing rude. There was no way to be certain. The somewhat puppyish face wore the same look of juvenile discontent she had glimpsed in the uncertain torchlight following the accident. The hair, of a distinctive coppery-red, appeared the same. The build—whippet-thin—was similar, all angles and knees and elbows, with an uncoordinated manner which spoke of extreme youth and a body too rapidly grown to permit ease of control. That Giles Fortescue colored when he felt Louisa's eyes on him was certain, but whether from lack of poise or conscious guilt there was no way to tell. The red mark on his brow, imperfectly hidden by a romantically sweeping lock of ginger hair, could as easily be an unfortunate blemish as a fresh scar.

The ceremonious flurry of greetings and the punctilious presentation of Gwendolyn to Louisa (which sequence put Harry's beloved quite out of charity with her hostess) successfully negotiated, the company settled into chairs, arranged skirts and draperies, and regarded each other for a moment in silence, a measuring in each glance, a finding of fault in each expression.

"Interesting room you have here," Lady Fortescue finally proclaimed, her sharp black eyes assessing furnishings and bibelots with a money lender's acuity, "if a trifle *bright*. Such obvious colors! And not *at all* in the current mode, though perfectly charming, I am sure, in its own way, and most individual. *Exactly* what I would have expected of you, Lady Cheltenham, had anyone troubled to ask my opinion. I'll warrant such particularity of style, with materials so outré as to be virtually unobtainable, must have required not only genius, but a small fortune to execute."

"No more than was warranted," responded Lady Daphne coolly. "*Such* inclement weather we're having, is it not?"

"*Quite* uncustomary. The town is as insupportable as the country under these conditions. Poor dear Gwendolyn has been in a state of despair awaiting the season's diversions." Lady Fortescue looked pointedly at Louisa, as if the cold, the wet, the mud, the inconvenience of a delayed season were all to be laid in her basket. Her eyes swept the young woman from curly crown to dainty toe, missing nothing between, in an examination as minute as it was demeaning. "Passable," she concluded after a sufficient pause to lend her words weight. "Figure's well enough, though the hair's much too girlish, and someone with sense should have the dressing of her. Such extremes of fashion are not intended for one of her age and position. Still—those are details, easily rectified. A good thing I insisted on coming to town, no matter how great the discommodation. I shall put her in the hands of my modiste—a very superior sort of woman with no nonsense about her, and a clever understanding of what is suitable to an unwed female past her prime. With proper management, there is no reason your niece shouldn't do well enough for herself, and speedily at that. Good bones, sound teeth, broad hips. That's all it takes, when they reach a certain age—which she has already passed. Of course, the *dot* will help. Too bad the girl didn't have a proper come-out at the conventional time. Might have taken almost as well as dear Gwendolyn."

"Perhaps even better," Lady Daphne responded. "This is your daughter's fourth season, I believe. Or, is it her fifth?"

"Fifth," snapped Lady Fortescue, "but then, her circumstances have been quite extraordinary. Gwendolyn's faithfulness to one particular gentleman in the face of constant importunings by others not so favored has been highly exemplary—though Lord Fortescue and I often urged the dear child to reconsider, given the uncertainty of a happy issue. In the event, it has turned out for the best, however. Young Beckenham is not to be despised."

"No, I should think not." Lady Daphne threw a sparkling smile at the two young women. "Certainly neither my niece nor I could contemplate such with equanimity."

"Everything that is charming," agreed Lady Fortescue, "or almost."

"Title, fortune, lands, position—all are in his favor," Lady Daphne returned with mischievous complacency.

"Lord Beckenham's attractions and attributes are many. It is only unfortunate that he did not receive proper guidance as a boy, and so avoid the unpardonable error of military service. His darkened skin is as deplorable as his facial disfigurement and missing limb, and should be held up as a warning to any youth foolish enough to contemplate such a departure from acceptable behavior in a gentleman," Lady Fortescue proclaimed.

Her eyes bored into her son, spearing him where he stood. The Honorable Giles pretended not to have heard—a neat trick, as no one else was speaking—but his easy blush played him traitor.

"Still, despite these deficiencies," Lady Daphne responded, "there remain the title, the fortune, and so forth." Her tone was almost apologetic.

"They have weighed heavily in his favor. Without them, Lord Beckenham would have been beneath consideration, crippled and scarred as he is."

Louisa's hands buried themselves in her skirts, nails biting into soft palms.

"A young girl such as Gwendolyn," continued her mother, "acclaimed by all not only as a rare beauty—an Incomparable, a veritable Diamond—but possessed as she is of those maidenly attributes which render mere physical beauty pale by comparison, could have demanded perfection in a mate, instead of which she has condescended to honor a man not only unwhole, but unsound. He is properly aware of her magnanimity in making such a startling exception in his case." The woman's eyes had swiveled to Louisa, lashing her like whips, then to Lady Daphne. "In such circumstances," she stressed, "any stipulations or conditions to be met prior to an announcement of their betrothal are not only proper, but mandatory. A young girl of such rare value and unsullied virtue and innocence as Gwendolyn must not be permitted by her fond parents to stand unprotected, but rather must have her ease, security, and comfort given first consideration by *all* concerned. Do you not agree?"

"I agree that you—and Lord Fortescue—are most fond and caring parents," Lady Daphne responded after a moment's silence in which desire for clear self-expression plainly warred with social convention, convention winning the day. "As to the rest, it is certain that a lady of your refinement and intelligence will understand that as you view your daughter, so we view Lord Beckenham. Thus, total agreement on all points may not be possible, however similar the principles we espouse."

"He desires the connection," Lady Fortescue declared flatly. "We have agreed to it—reluctantly. He claims his whole happiness is centered in our dear daughter. Such being the case, it behooves any claiming to hold him in affection to give particular attention to her desires. Should they not, they will prove the exact degree of their supposed affection!"

A log crumbled on the hearth, sending up a shower of sparks. The younger Fortescue girls squirmed on the small sofa they had selected as an observation post, it being in equally easy listening distance of their mother and the position selected by their elder sister. One played with the ruffles at her pudgy wrist. The other twisted the ribbons catching her high thick waist below unripe breasts. It was all very exciting, if decidedly boring, as on the one hand they were not personally involved, and on the other Mama always carried her point. Miss Beckenham would marry Cousin Norval, or possibly Cousin Gossmar, just as Mama had declared she should. Still, it was amusing to watch Mama put the dowager countess and Lord Beckenham's sister in their places, and explain their duty to them. That was an art at which Mama excelled. Goodness knows, she did it to them, and to Papa and Giles and Gwendolyn, often enough that she had the trick of it down well.

The silence stretched. Louisa's and Lady Daphne's faces remained social masks from which emotion, intelligence, even thought had been purged. Lady Fortescue's back stiffened, her eyes snapping.

"How do you find London, Miss Beckenham?" Gwendolyn Fortescue inquired sweetly as her mother turned back to Lady Daphne with the ponderous majesty of a ship of the line.

"Rather as I expected it to be," Louisa replied, trying to ignore the conversation across the room, which was continuing in much the same vein as it had begun despite her aunt's efforts to turn the subject to the weather, recent theatrical offerings, even the latest of Lord Byron's scandalous poetry.

"Oh? And, how is that?"

"Overrated."

"Indeed? I have always found it most pleasant."

"You have not just endured nigh on three months of winter rains here, I collect."

"No, indeed." Gwendolyn smoothed her fragile muslin skirts with an air of self-satisfaction, raised fluttering lashes to reveal a look in her clear gray eyes which was almost an apology. "We always retire to Papa's seat for the winter," she admitted graciously, "and so I have no experience of London under such faults of climate and paucity of suitable companionship as you mention. All the best families do the same. To stay in Town past the little season implies the lack of an ability to do anything else, you see." Her eyes flicked to Lady Daphne, then away, a hint of contempt marring her perfect features. "And *that* implies even more disagreeable possibilities. You have found it tedious?"

"In the extreme."

"And, of course, so lamentably thin of company in such an unfashionable period."

"It has been that," Louisa agreed, "though I am beginning to learn that lack of company is not necessarily a deterrent to pleasant social intercourse. Indeed, where some are concerned, absence is a positive pleasure, rather than a penance."

"You cannot expect me to believe you include Lord Beckenham in that stricture, surely!"

"Harry?" A martial light glinted in Louisa's eyes. "Heavens, no! *Him* I am always delighted to see."

Rain slid greasily down the panes of the windows that rose behind the two young women. They eyed each other, faces wearing the conventional expressions which marked their ages and social standing. Across the room Lady Fortescue's voice rose stridently, culminating on the words "—prior to any announcement, make no mistake, Lady Cheltenham! In this our dear daughter is quite determined, and we support her most fully. She has been, indeed, more than generous in the few paltry requirements she has voiced." And then that lady's voice fell following a flick of the eyes to ascertain whether, in the silence, her words had been attended where they were truly directed.

"I have often wondered," Gwendolyn said archly of a sudden, "whether those who find themselves dull in London would not find themselves dull anywhere? A lack of inner resources and imagination, in all likelihood. Such a failing is to be sincerely lamented in one of our sex, as evidencing lack of proper education, guidance, and supervision when a child—do you not agree? Of course, there are those females of uncertain gentility who might employ such a pose in an effort—spurious, no doubt—to render themselves interesting to the gentlemen in any manner they can."

"A fascinating observation," Louisa returned between her teeth, "though certainly I have never found myself dull in the country, and so must put down my unease to lack of familiar employments and surroundings."

"Indeed? You might have done better to accept your brother's guidance, then," Miss Fortescue returned in dulcet tones, "and joined us at the Lodge for a time, if the country is more to your taste than the town. Mama had many special entertainments planned for you, and was most put out by the lack of consideration and proper feeling evidenced by your refusal."

"Yes—Harry informed me of the 'entertainments.' Certain connections of yours, I believe—all male."

"There would have been other ladies present," Miss Fortescue protested, coloring becomingly.

"Oh? Wouldn't they have presented an impediment to your schemes?"

"Hardly!" Gwendolyn Fortescue's silvery, well-bred laugh hung in the air, then faded. "They were as carefully selected as the gentlemen, and would have had the good breeding to understand they were purely a guard against such appearances of particularity as must have led to unwelcome speculations at this juncture, and not on their own accounts at all."

"What amazingly forbearing friends you must have!"

"Such complaisance is not uncommon toward those who have earned the respect, and, indeed, the gratitude of their acquaintance. Mama is always most correct in such dealings. Indeed, you would do well to be guided by her in the coming Season." Her eyes shifted briefly to the two older women, Lady Daphne resplendent in a youthful morning gown of softest dying rose lustring and a delectably alluring lace cap, Lady Harriet a contrasting vision of social rectitude in tightly laced heavy silk and jet. "Your dear brother is quite concerned about the unwholesome influences under which you currently reside," she said gently, leaning forward to place her hand over Louisa's. Louisa snatched her own away as if scalded. "I trust you are not offended by my mentioning the matter, but what concerns Lord Beckenham *must* concern me also."

"Do you also assist him in selecting his cattle?" Louisa bit out, not able to stop herself.

"Oh, my, no! I wouldn't presume. Such knowledge is not part of a lady's education, and any opinions I might venture on *that* subject would be highly suspect."

"But not in this," Louisa said.

"You are offended at my mentioning your dear brother's concern for you," Miss Fortescue pouted.

"No—not at all. I am always glad to hear my brother's opinions, though I am more generally accustomed to hearing them from his own lips."

"There are some matters of great delicacy on which a brother may not feel comfortable speaking to his sister," she said primly. "I am only a very poor messenger, I know."

"No—I think you are quite an excellent messenger."

"How delighted I am to hear you say so!"

"It is only that I cannot help but wonder if the message, as delivered, is as Harry gave it to you. Harry," Louisa said with a bluntness she knew to be far from *comme il faut*, "has always held our father's sister in highest respect and deepest affection."

"I am certain his sentiments in that regard remain unchanged, and indeed must do him credit, as a proper respect for his elders is the first mark of a well-bred gentleman," Miss Fortescue smiled tolerantly. "As an aunt, as a father's sister, I am certain Lady Cheltenham remains all that is charming and delightful. As the chaperon of his sister, however, and the one responsible for introducing her to the ton and guiding her steps so that not one goes astray—*there*, perhaps, he does not find in her the same perfections."

"My goodness!" Louisa took a deep breath. "I had no idea . . ." she said faintly.

"No—of course not. It would have been quite improper in Lord Beckenham to have mentioned such a delicate subject to you—hence my temerity. In this regard" —the young woman paused, appearing to collect her thoughts—"Mama has suggested to your dear brother, in an effort to assist both him and you, you understand— though perhaps you might not quite like it, seeing objections which have escaped our poor brains . . . ?"

"Your speech is somewhat disjointed. I might not like what?"

Miss Fortescue's head tilted to the side as a winsome smile decorated her already decorative features—*crème Chantilly* on a blancmange. "Sophronia will not be making her come-out until next year, and Mama and your dear brother did discuss presenting you at a ball from our home. There is certainly no ballroom in *this* house. It is such a tiny place, really—though *quite* elegant, I suppose, if one cares for such idiosyncrasies of style. Certainly the address is at least *acceptable*, though very *new*, but the house itself is totally unsuited to entertaining on any respectable scale, and truly——"

"I think not."

"Oh, but to be considered worthy of attention among the ton, Miss Beckenham, one *must* have one's own ball! Nothing less is acceptable—believe me. Naturally you, unaccustomed to the ton and Town ways as you are, may be in ignorance of this fact, but I should have thought your dear aunt would have pointed out the unforgivable solecism such a lack would entail. Why, you would receive no attention at all!"

Louisa took a deep breath. "If that is so, then my brother can have our home on Berkeley Square opened, with my aunt to act as hostess. *It* has quite a respectable ballroom. Larger than the one available at *your* home, I dare say."

"To go such such expense and effort merely on a *missish* whim, when Mama is prepared——"

"I am sorry, my dear Miss Fortescue, but it is impossible for me to accept your mother's gracious offer. It *is* her offer, and not *yours*, I collect?"

"Why, naturally! I would never presume——" Miss Fortescue expostulated in pretty confusion. "It was thought best that I be the one to—And, as your future sister—It is only that"—she took a deep, revivifying breath—"with my mother's sponsorship and guidance, and the cachet of residing under my father's roof, you understand, you would be assured the guests would be of only the very *highest* respectability, your position and reputation within the ton thus assured."

"Your mother kindly offers to lend me countenance while I am residing under the roof of my father's sister— who happens to exceed her in rank? How exceptionally kind," Louisa commented wryly.

"Mama is noted for her attention to those less fortunate," Miss Fortescue agreed, "and you are both uncomfortably and unfortunately situated here. That you do not appreciate the fact speaks well of your innocence, though it does demonstrate your lamentable country-breeding and lack of sophistication. Elevated rank does not always equate with respectability, you see," she explained kindly. "It would have been much simpler, naturally, had you been willing to attend the party which Mama planned in your honor at the Lodge, as well as causing far less needless expense and upset. *That* was not well done of you—a subject on which we have already touched—but penance is invariably inherent in any misdeed. Had you but joined us there, you would have avoided the dullness of London in the off-season, and passed your time both agreeably and profitably in the superior company of those who *truly* have your best interests at heart. Indeed, you might actually be already wed," she simpered. "Cousin Gossmar was *most* anxious to make your acquaintance, as his current unhappy solitary state bears heavily on him as not being consonant with the laws of God and Man; and, Cousin Norval has reached that age of reason when a man begins to long for the comforts of hearth and home, and the delights of children in his image prattling at his knee."

"Oh? A shame, perhaps, and I've no one to blame but myself if these last weeks have been dullish, but then they could never be a total waste when I am with my dear aunt."

"Indeed?"

"Most definitely," Louisa responded. "And then, of course, there was my wardrobe to see to—so dowdy and out-of-fashion that I would have put you to the blush had I joined you at the Lodge, seeing how you are garbed and remembering my own poor appearance."

"Oh, there was not the least need for such frivolous

expenditure!" Miss Fortescue caroled. "Indeed, such self-indulgence could not but be counterproductive to your goal, as being most off-putting to any gentleman who might consider you a suitable spouse. You are not, after all, a girl making her come-out. In no way should you judge yourself against the appearance which *I* am forced to present! Your age alone renders that unnecessary."

"In no way—appearance, or *any other*—would I presume to compete with you, Miss Fortescue," Louisa said, then smiled gently, the perfect picture of maidenly propriety, "for in all ways you shall ever put me to shame."

"How very kind in you, Louisa! But, I am not such a paragon, as you will swiftly discover—no matter what dear Lord Beckenham may say to the contrary," she simpered winningly. "Come, will you not call me by my given name, as we are so soon to be sisters, and so must perforce become the very closest of friends?"

"I think not. As the private understanding between you and my brother remains only that, such evidence of intimacy with a relative stranger could not but give rise to gossip of the sort which would be most unwelcome to you."

"But surely in the privacy of our own homes—"

Louisa shook her head with determination, cutting the younger woman off. "I would never unreasonably discommode you in any way, Miss Fortescue," she said with a certain asperity, "but in this I am determined, and in the event you might find such an appearance of particularity deleterious to your best interests."

"Had you *truly* my best interests at heart—*and* those of your dear brother—you would not only grant me this small favor, but would have joined us at the Lodge rather than making this foolish and unnecessary journey to London!"

"Ah, but then, I never go where I am neither known nor *truly* wanted," Louisa said succinctly, "nor is it invariably my policy to place the whims of others, if ill-considered, above my own inclinations."

Sophronia and Belinda, watching this encounter with widened eyes and perked ears, giggled behind chubby hands. Their sister flushed and threw them a speaking glance, causing them to subside amid titterings and side-long glances at first her, and then their mother. "By Jove!" the Honorable Giles muttered, waking from his air of fashionable boredom to stare at Louisa with something akin to respect.

"You place a very high value on yourself, Miss Beckenham," Gwendolyn Fortescue commented finally, tight-voiced.

"I have never been taught to hold myself cheap, Miss Fortescue, if that is your meaning," Louisa responded, rising.

"Indeed?" Gwendolyn captured the folds of Louisa's sky-blue gown in a determined, if definitely feminine, grip. "Then you will permit me another moment of your time, will you not, for it does appear that you are holding yourself cheap indeed!"

Louisa sank back in her chair, staring at the girl. "Whatever can you mean?" she inquired hesitantly, eyes flying guiltily to that morning's tribute of palest-pink roses.

Miss Fortescue sighed, releasing Louisa's skirts—sadly crumpled by her urgency—as she did. "Far be it for me to criticize your dear brother," she said softly, almost whispering, "but we understand there has been a steady stream of—not to put too fine a point on it—*military rattles* invading your aunt's house these past days. This is *not* wise, for such men can never lend consequence to a young lady of fashion, casual as they are in dress and manners, crude in speech and conversation, *and* of uncertain ante-cedents. The Corsican Monster's recent depredations have caused virtually *anybody* to be acceptable to the

Horse Guards. You *must* discourage their presence here. Indeed, if you are the loving sister you claim, you will assist Mama and me in separating your dear brother from these improper associations. *That* part of his life is over. The sooner he comes to realize the unsuitability of intimacy with these ramshackle parvenus, both as escorts for you and companions for himself, the better for his consequence *and* yours within the ton."

"I am amazed that your parents permitted even an unofficial understanding between you and my brother, if these are indeed their sentiments regarding the profession! *Or,* that you thought Harry worthy of a second glance!"

"It was most gracious and understanding of them," Gwendolyn explained *sotto voce,* "and a tribute to the depth of the attachment between us. But then, of your dear brother's worth I have never been in doubt, as my constancy proves. *Do* distance yourself from these unwholesome, and indeed *tawdry,* associations, Miss Beckenham, for your brother's sake as much as for your own! They cannot do you good, and may do you great harm."

"Do you then have a policy of cutting such men?" Louisa asked, half curious, half infuriated.

"Great heavens, no!" The silvery laugh rang out, shattered against the stronger rocks of her mother's voice. "In such a climate of general approbation as the military currently enjoys in even the *best* society, that would be impolitic. I am universally gracious, as you must be, and indeed pride myself on standing up with any such individual as may ask me to partner him. But, it must never go further than that. It is not that they are refused the door," she smiled, "but rather that intimacy is consistently and gently discouraged. Every intimation of particularity, such as you and your aunt have clearly shown, is improper to say the least, and actually deleterious to your good name."

"I see." Louisa rose, towering over the young woman who had captured her brother's heart. "I thank you for your kind advice. I shall know exactly how to act on it. And now, if you will excuse me, I have been remiss in my duties because of the fascination of our conversation, and must see to refreshments for you and your charming family."

She fled the room, shaking, to lean for a moment against the closed drawing room door. What she had imagined, when Harry informed her of his plans in the library at Marleybourne, had been bad enough. The reality, she concluded as she forced her trembling limbs to still, was far worse. Harry saw a beautiful face—and quite out of the ordinary that aristocratic face indeed was, with its perfect features and cloud of russet hair, the nose expertly modeled, the lips so delicately sculpted and tinted as to present an affront to every other young woman of breeding and aspirations—and a lithe, graceful form, and had created a personality to match the physical perfection. If there were any justice in the world, Louisa fumed, this cool and self-possessed young diamond would on the instant be transformed into a lump of coal!

"Hoskins," she said hollowly as he appeared in the hall, "bring tea, chocolate, biscuits, cakes, fruit—whatever Cook has to hand. And arsenic, if any is to be found!"

Five

"Farouche!" declared Lady Fortescue when apprised of the conversation between the two young women by her eldest daughter. "She may 'take,' of course, but that won't help matters—aside from the other disadvantages she presents. Separating her from her brother and la Cheltenham is of at least as much importance as weaning him from that military rabble he frequents. Norval must come down from the country immediately! We have a serious problem."

And, "Insufferable, *both* of them!" proclaimed Lady Daphne, when Louisa performed the same service for her. "Show Harry's friends the door? Sponsor *you?* Harry, a *cripple!? Something must be done . . .*"

But what, or how, neither lady could imagine at that moment. Harry saw only what he wanted to see, heard only that which fed his *amour propre*.

"I wonder if they'll dare attempt to 'guide' him away from his friends," Louisa asked thoughtfully, once both ladies had retreated to the back parlor and given vent to their considerable spleen.

"They'd catch cold," Lady Daphne returned flatly, "which is no doubt why that sweet young thing was instructed to approach *you* on the subject. Though *why*, with the military held in such high esteem, and Wellington the hero of this and every hour, they seem so desirous to sever Harry's military connections I *cannot* understand! Such friendships only *add* to his consequence."

"Perhaps they see Hugh Malfont and Colonel Winthrop and the rest as a divisive influence, coming between them and Harry," Louisa suggested tentatively.

"Of course—*that* goes without saying! The same is true of you—hence the great rush to marry you off, preferably to someone they control who will then whisk you off to his country house, and there immure you to molder for the rest of your natural life. Still, it won't wash. There's more to it . . . Harriet Fortescue was never anyone's fool, even if she *did* send her delightful daughter on a fool's errand today. A testing of the waters, I think that was. But, why should they attempt to separate Harry from his fellow officers *now*—and *you*, too—when once the marriage takes place, that will be the inevitable result! His friends will return to the Peninsula, and he and his bride will retire to Marleybourne, and that will be an end to it."

"There's nothing sinister," Louisa said with a bitter chuckle at the sight of her aunt's puzzled face. "It's jealousy, plain and simple, on the part of the Glorious Gwendolyn. She wants Harry to herself, with nary an influence around him beyond her own sweet self."

"Jealousy is *never* plain or simple," Lady Daphne retorted, "and I don't think the Fortescue chit has enough depth to *feel* jealousy in any case—certainly not as a sensation connected with the *warmer* passions. No, it's something else . . ."

But what it was, or if indeed anything more than social self-consequence and overweening pride were involved, Lady Daphne gave up on after a few moments. The day was too dreary to add to the gloom with such speculations, which were cut short in any case by the advent of Colonel George Winthrop, Captain Hugh Malfont, and Major Lord Percy Fenton, come to propose a theater party for the Friday next, and whatever the ladies might enjoy in the interim.

The remainder of the day passed quietly and pleasantly, the Fortescues and their demands, if not forgotten, at least dropped from active consideration under the good-humored influence of these three men who were among the closest of Harry's friends. He had served under Winthrop, whom he regarded with something very close to reverence, for some months prior to being struck down at Salamanca, and credited his continued existence to Fenton's quick actions when he was wounded. Malfont was the perfect foil for the livelier Fenton—the butt of his pranks and jokes—as well as the clear medium between the often-serious colonel and the more flamboyant young baron. The only impediment to perfect felicity came when Colonel Winthrop, during a slight pause in the conversation, asked where Harry was keeping himself. The three officers had called at the Clarendon, and found him gone—where, his man could not say. While they had not come to Lady Daphne's precisely to find him, they had rather thought, given the weather, that he might be bearing his aunt and sister company.

Louisa proffered the explanation of a possible appointment with his man of business, at which Lady Daphne snorted and said, given Harry's propensity since his return from the Peninsula to delay anything demanding more than superficial cerebration as long as possible—and sometimes rather longer than that!—he was far more likely to be dancing attendance on the Fortescue diamond, or some other young lady of equal social prominence. A quick look passed between the colonel and Hugh Malfont, but the only comment was offered by Lord Fenton, who noted that he had never known Harry to be much in the petticoat line before, and therefore the neophyte stood in grave danger of putting the diamond so out of countenance from lack of flowery compliments that she might be incapable of sparkling for at least a fortnight. At this involved sally the others chuckled, and the subject turned to the ubiquitous weather.

Harry remained notable by his absence, and at last the three officers made their departure, intending to stop by White's to see if perchance he were there, and then continue to Manton's to test a brace of pistols Percy Fenton had ordered.

Left to their own devices, Lady Daphne snoozed while Louisa determinedly forged her way through a highly sensational tale of intrigue, false identities, and abductions residing within the marbled covers of the latest Minerva Press offering. The rain persisted, not heavy enough to be considered a true storm, not light enough to be considered a mizzle suitable to be ignored, as the chilly gray day dragged down to an even chillier gray evening, and they climbed the stairs to change.

"Anything," as Lady Daphne declared with disgust, "to relieve the tedium—even primping for our own sakes—is *highly* preferable to a fit of the screaming dismals."

The rain continued unrelentingly into the evening, the skies beyond the rosy draperies of Lady Daphne's back parlor low and leaden, the streets mired. Those unfortunates forced by profession or social inclination into the inclement weather scurried to their appointments with grumbling voice and collar turned high, shivering at the sudden gusts of biting wind. It was a night suited only to hovering by one's own well-built fire, perhaps even seeking the additional cheering solace of a warming glass of claret or port. It was as if the elements, in a fit of pique, had decided that this year London should be placed on a steady diet of damp and misery to which the despairing young ladies of the ton come to make their bows added their own donation in the form of copious tears.

"She is indeed lovely," Louisa said carefully when Harry burst in on them unexpectedly just after they had retired to the back parlor following a quiet *dîner à deux*. "A diamond of the first water, just as you said. I would not presume to compete with her."

"Isn't she? Such sweetness and grace! Such purity of form and elegance of mind! And, such a complete angel! Of all men on this sorry earth I am the most blessedly fortunate," he beamed. "She thought you were delightful, you know, if not quite in the common style."

"How kind of her to say so."

"Wasn't it?"

"Indeed, yes," interjected Lady Daphne, settled comfortably by the fire with a screen to one side, a footstool beneath her feet, and a tambour frame with her latest piece of stitchery in front of her to lend a semblance of industry. "I can't think of a *finer* authority—three London seasons on which to base her expertise. Or, is it four? I never *can* remember, for she seems to have been forming part of the scenery at Almack's forever!"

"Five. And the visit went off well?" he inquired anxiously, pacing and whirling as if determined to wear a path through to the room below.

"Everything was exactly as could be expected given the circumstances, my boy," his aunt informed him placidly, sorting through her wools. "This may be your *sister's* first season, but it isn't mine! I know how to comport myself when a prospective bride and her family call."

"Aren't they charming, all of them?" Harry demanded, temporarily coming to rest on the other side of the Adam fireplace, eyes sparkling. "The younger sisters—so unaffected and natural. They're sure to take the ton by storm when their turns come! And Giles is quite a fellow when you get to know him, in spite of his silly foppish airs. Bruising rider, and handles a team in form."

"Amazing in one so young," Louisa murmured. "Just

recently down from Eton, I believe he said. He never comes a cropper?"

"Oh, the occasional mishap to be expected in a cub his age. More bottom than sense sometimes, but that only raises him in my estimation. Lads of his stamp were often all that stood between us and disaster in the Peninsula."

"So long as his horses don't come to grief," Louisa fished.

"Well, there has been a problem or two when he's shot the cat, but nothing to be overly concerned about. Once Gwendolyn and I are leg-shackled, I'll take the boy in hand, and that nonsense will stop," Harry said with determination, sounding rather more like the former officer he was, and less the besotted suitor. Then his face cleared. "And how did you find Lady Fortescue?" he asked, turning to his aunt.

"Much as ever. I have been acquainted with Lady Harriet these twenty-five years and more," Lady Daphne said sweetly as Harry resumed his pacing, "and I'm certain she has not changed by so much as a hair since she made her come-out."

"Remarkable woman, isn't she," he agreed. "Forthright to a fault—which is unusual in a female. Not an ounce of trickery to her. Handsome, in the first stare of elegance, and with a manner and address that would outshine most royalty. And of such high principles! And with such a deep and genuine concern not only for her own family, but for the welfare of others as well!"

"She is indeed quite remarkable. For pity's sake, Harry—sit down!" Lady Daphne protested as he began yet another rapid tour of the cozy room. "All your pacing will give me the headache. Have you eaten?"

Harry perched on a chair between them, leaned forward, arm resting on knee. "Yes—yes, of course. At Fortescue House."

"You were there all day?"

"Hardly! I didn't call until late this afternoon. Because of the delicacy of the situation"—he threw a black look at Louisa, who pretended indifference—"I am not to run tame there, you understand. Indeed, I am only to call upon invitation, and then only in the company of others."

"I see. And they fed you well?"

"Extremely well. Lady Fortescue sets an excellent table. Her French chef is superb, and the company is always of the best. They set thirty covers tonight."

"Just an intimate little family dinner . . ."

"Well, hardly that, but Gwendolyn must be protected from the least appearance of impropriety. The same strictures obtain as when I was in Spain, except that I may have an occasional word with her. When Gwendolyn mentioned their visit this morning, I *had* to make my excuses and come to see what you thought of them all—especially my own very bright and particular angel."

"Oh, Louisa has it right—your young lady is a diamond of the first water, and her character is *exactly* what I would have expected from my long acquaintance with her mother."

"I couldn't be more fortunate," Harry sighed, a beatific glow on his handsome features. "You can't know how difficult it is—pretending she is nothing to me, nor I to her, when we are in company. An exquisite torture—each smile she bestows on another, each word she speaks for other ears . . . But, such a joyous torture! At least I am in her presence. Do wish me happy, Aunt Daffy! You haven't as yet, you know."

"It's early days yet for that, my boy. There have been neither banns called nor announcements made."

"Not at *my* behest!"

He surged to his feet, resumed pacing the comfortable little room, its mirrorlike tables reflecting his formal black evening dress, the blinding white of his waistcoat, shirt, and neckcloth, his single heavy gold fob. Louisa smiled to see him so, hand pushing distractedly through his severe "Brutus" cut, disarranging the carefully positioned red-gold locks. If one forgot the lady involved, and concentrated on the gentleman instead—which was, of course, nigh on to impossible—his ardency presented a charming picture . . .

"I'd climb to the top of Saint George's-Hanover and shout it to all of London, if only they'd permit it," he groaned.

"Better not. You'd slip, and then Miss Fortescue would find herself a widow before she was a bride!" his aunt retorted. "Harry, if you *cannot* compose yourself, I shall *have* to insist you leave. All this restlessness is *quite* unsettling when one has just eaten."

"Sorry, Aunt Daffy." He glanced quickly from one woman to the other, neither of whom seemed to appreciate the damnable situation he was in, and forced himself to return to his seat. "Any—any progress?" he inquired without much hope.

"Pardon me, Harry, but I do not grasp your meaning," Lady Daphne said, generations of dowager countesses at her back. *"Such* a non sequitur!"

"Yes, you do, Aunt Daphne," Louisa responded wearily. "It's the same as last time. 'You know—*'progress!*' " she quoted with a wave of her hand. "Harry wants to know if I've anyone prepared to leap into parson's mousetrap."

"Inelegant, Louisa, and *quite* beneath you. If that *is* your meaning, Harry," Lady Daphne continued, turning to her nephew, "which I doubt, as you *were* raised a gentleman, and would therefore *never* pose such an indelicate question to a lady—the answer is 'No,' most unequivocally."

"I'm not a lady so far as Harry is concerned," Louisa threw in. "I'm only his rather annoying younger sister. He sees me as standing in the way of his happiness, and viewed from his perspective, I suppose I do. Under such circumstances, the question may be indelicate, but it is not inappropriate."

"You grant your brother more latitude than I am willing to permit." Lady Daphne's elegantly coifed head rose, eyes sliding in their sockets until they were boring straight into Harry's. Even gowned for an intimate family evening, she presented the appearance of royalty, the soft silk of her evening dress swirling around her slim ankles, the silvery gray of the slip brightened by the gossamer rose lace overdress giving the illusion of dawn as the sun tips the earth. A distinct flush appeared above the points of Harry's collar, fled upward. "This is *not* some barbarous country where a young woman can be *forced* into wedlock against her wishes on the whim of a self-consequential and insensitive male. *This* is *England!*" Lady Daphne proclaimed coldly. "And, *this* is the nineteenth century! While such travesties may occur even in *these* modern times, they *never* occur in the *best* families—only among those who hold *fortune* and *rank* to be of greater importance than *character and proper feeling*. Is that clear, Nephew?"

"Very," Harry mumbled, giving every appearance of strangling on his neckcloth.

"And the issue will *never* be raised again in this house. Is that *also* perfectly clear?"

He nodded, a schoolboy caught playing with his grandfather's dress sword.

"I beg your pardon, Henry. I did not hear your response."

"Very clear, Aunt Daphne."

"Good. I *will not* have Louisa badgered in this house! Now, let us pretend the past few moments, and the unfortunate comments they engendered, never existed. How long do you intend to waste your blunt at the Clarendon?"

"I—"

"You sound as if your throat were *parched* my dear boy, and it is *far* too early for the tea tray. Louisa, ring for Hoskins, and request some brandy for your brother. Or, perhaps you would prefer port, Harry? I always keep a few bottles at hand for friends."

"Brandy would be fine, thank you," he said stiffly.

"See to it, Louisa. *Now,* Harry—the dibs may be in tune, but it won't do to outrun the constable. The Clarendon is *shockingly* expensive. How long do you intend to remain there?"

His initial reaction—that he was a man grown and would remain at the Clarendon precisely as long as he damn well pleased—he did not voice, saying mildly instead that he intended taking rooms in the vicinity of Buckingham House within the week. As Louisa was comfortably established with her aunt, and as her come-out would be held under the aegis of Lady Fortescue, there was no need to open the huge barracks on Berkeley Square, and indeed every reason not to given the bother and expense that would entail, as both Louisa's season and wedding, and his own, would not come cheap. When the time arrived, he did not intend half measures for either of them.

Laudable, his aunt informed him graciously as Hoskins appeared with a decanter and three crystal glasses, as far as it went, but then no Beckenham had ever been known as a nip-farthing. It was far too soon, however, to be talking of bridals—his *or* Louisa's. Far more to the point were events which lay in the near future, rather than in some misty land of forever, or perhaps *never*.

Harry watched his aunt from under veiled eyes as Hoskins presented him with a liberal portion of brandy, setting the glass on the table by his side and throwing him a sympathetic look before silently departing. Voices, on this evening, had carried well beyond the elegant carved doors leading to the little parlor, and staff was well aware that things were going well neither for the young lord nor his sister. While their sympathies lay rather more with Louisa than Harry, Hoskins was a man, and he had faced Lady Daphne's temper more than once. The boy had his empathy, if not his approbation.

Harry understood his aunt, and her tactics all too clearly. Wellington would have approved. At first on the attack himself, he had been routed by a skilled counteroffensive, and was in a fair way to being forced into a precipitous and ill-planned retreat. A dressing-down by Arthur Wellesley might make one feel ten times a fool and twenty times an incompetent worm, but it left one feeling a man. With his aunt, the years were stripped away until only a grubby boy remained, knees bloody, shirt torn, face bramble-scratched and dirt-stained.

How he could safely press his case with either his sister or Lady Daphne he was uncertain. Given the fact that Louisa was of age and in full control of her fortune, there was little he could bring to bear in the way of financial pressure. Rather, it was a case of having to enlist their sympathy—a task he had thought already accomplished. Yet, even after spending a morning in the company of his Gwendolyn, they remained intransigent. Didn't they understand how incredible her selection of him over all other men in the world was? Why, she could have looked as high as she wanted—at least to a marquess or duke, if not to royalty itself—and instead had condescended to— It was a damnable situation when a man's future was controlled by a totty-headed old woman and a bacon-brained chit who, from the way she was behaving, belonged locked in a strong tower before she gave the entire ton the impression she was a light-skirt! Tonight's gown was even worse than the last—an amber thing which hinted at everything it did not blatantly reveal—immodest, unmaidenly, brazen—there weren't words enough! Lady Fortescue would be justified in showing him the door simply on the basis of his sister's wanton appearance . . .

He leaned back and waited, determined to force the next maneuver on his aunt. Assist her in her damnable ploys he would not!

Harry had not long to wait to discover which flank she would harry next as she, too, leaned back in her chair, giving every impression of ease and assurance. For several moments there was a measuring silence between them, even Louisa holding her peace at some signal from Lady Daphne which he had missed. He could tell that silence did not sit well with his sister—unspoken words trembled on her lips like berry juice.

Then Lady Daphne smiled, an almost-bored expression of complaisance until one noted her eyes, as she leaned forward with a suddenness which startled him into an involuntary flinch.

"So," she said, "you do *not* plan to open the Berkeley Square house for Louisa?"

"No," he retorted curtly, convinced the fewer words he used, the safer he was.

"When *do* you plan to set the old mausoleum to rights?"

"In my own time."

"To celebrate Louisa's nuptials, perhaps?"

"Hardly. She will be wed from Marleybourne."

"And what if she would prefer a Town wedding?"

Louisa's mouth sprang open, then snapped shut at a look from her aunt.

"I hardly think the fuss and feathers of a Town wedding would be in keeping with her age and position," Harry said mildly, "nor the circumstances of any potential groom of whom I have knowledge. That will be a quiet affair, though naturally in the best of taste."

"I take it this has already been a matter of some discussion between you," Lady Daphne said, eyes darting from brother to sister.

"No," Harry returned curtly, "not between Louisa and myself. There has been no need up to this moment, unfortunately. Were she to insist on a town wedding, I presume you would have no objections to her being married from this house. These things will sort themselves out when the happy occasion arises."

"Then, when *do* you plan to open the house? Upon your own betrothal?"

"I *am* betrothed."

"Upon the official announcement, then?"

"That is my intention."

"But *not* for your sister—only for yourself and your bride. How generous! What of Louisa's come-out?"

"That is already settled. Lady Fortescue has kindly offered to see to the matter, and I have accepted her gracious proposals on Louisa's behalf. Naturally, I will bear the expense of the thing."

Concerning the ball, and Harriet Fortescue's sponsorship, Louisa and Lady Daphne quickly disabused him, Louisa declaring that she had no desire for a formal come-out—rather the opposite. Lady Daphne stated firmly that if ball there was to be—and, unlike Lady Harriet, she did not view it as essential in the least—it would be held in Berkeley Square, with him as host and herself as hostess, or it would not be held at all. The Fortescue contingent might attend as guests, but in no other capacity would their services be required, and if *he* wasn't willing to sport his blunt for the affair, *she* was.

Harry attempted to remonstrate, protesting that such a refusal was tantamount to an insult to his betrothed and her family, and that furthermore both his aunt and his sister seemed determined to place every possible obstacle in his path to the altar. Lady Daphne corrected him on the matter, declaring that where there was no announcement there was no betrothal, and therefore no betrothed with whom to be concerned. She and Harriet Fortescue were little better than distant and uneasy acquaintances, and the woman was a total stranger to Louisa, no matter how *he* viewed the matter. That he might consider such an arrangement fitting was his affair. *She* had greater experience of the ton, and informed him that such a proceeding would be ramshackle at best.

"And exactly *what* sort of affair is it to be, Harry," she inquired tartly, overriding his continued protests and objections. "How many couples? Who would determine the list of guests? From Louisa's recounting of Miss Fortescue's proposals, it appears the invitations would be at the complete discretion of Lady Harriet, with neither of *us* consulted. And are we talking of a true ball, or only an evening party with *perhaps* some dancing, and the governess doing her poor best on an antiquated and out-of-tune pianoforte?"

Protest however he might, it devolved that Lady Daphne had the right of it, and the projected Fortescue guest list was more or less the same as had been planned for the house party at the Lodge, not excluding the whuffling vicar.

Louisa stared at her brother, then burst into hysterical laughter.

"*A come-out ball?* You have the temerity to characterize such an atrocity a *come-out ball?* This is not Lisbon!" Lady Daphne snapped. And then, "No vapors, Miss! This *ain't* the time for 'em."

Tears streamed from Louisa's eyes as she regarded her aunt helplessly, shoulders shaking. "B-but, don't you s-see?" she gasped. "Front door or b-back, it matters not a wh-whit to them!"

"I see at *least* as much as you do, miss, and a *deal* more than your brother," Lady Daphne responded tartly. "Don't concern yourself with that. And, *stop* that silly cackling. You sound like a witch! This 'ball,' " she continued forcefully, turning back to the irate Harry, "will *not* take place. If it does, we shall *not* be in attendance. Should Harriet Fortescue persist in her plans, and bruit it about that such an *abomination* is to be your sister's come-out, I shall know *exactly* with whom to speak to scotch the disgusting rumor, *and I shall do it!* Make no mistake, Henry Beckenham: You cannot force Louisa into anything which is either unseemly in itself, or repugnant to her personally. Her hand and her fortune are *both* hers to dispose of as she sees fit. You will *not* sell your sister for a mess of pottage. I won't permit it!"

"And what of *my* future?" Harry roared.

"Your only future, if you persist in this folly, is as the laughingstock of London." Lady Daphne's voice was so low, so gentle, after the fireworks of the last minutes that it sent shivers up Louisa's spine. "The come-out of the Viscount of Marleybourne's young and beautiful and charming and wealthy sister—an evening party over which she has not even control of the guest list, and at which those in principal attendance would consist of distant and undistinguished bachelor connections of the Fortescue beldame and her consort? I thought you had more intelligence!"

"Anything more elaborate would be out of keeping with Louisa's spinster status and circumstances!" Harry exploded. "They are attempting, with exemplary kindness, to ensure Louisa does not make a fool of herself, which is more than you are doing, Aunt! The point is to introduce her to the notice of suitable gentlemen—not to watch her spin around a ballroom like a dewy-eyed innocent in the arms of some hardened rake or gazetted fortune hunter, for God's sake!"

"I see—not even a superannuated governess at the keyboard. *Whist,* I suppose, and flannel waistcoats. Why call it a 'ball,' then? *Auction block* would be more in keeping with the purpose as you state it."

"That *is* the purpose!" Harry bellowed, not caring if the servants, or indeed all of London, heard him. "At least, it is *my* purpose! It has always *been* my purpose—to see Louisa suitably established, and *as rapidly as possible!*"

"That may be your purpose, my boy, but it is not mine."

"No—I can see *your* purpose in the damn dresses you permit her to expose herself in!"

"I doubt it," Lady Daphne responded, voice unremittingly gentle, but with a firmness to it that registered with Harry, infuriated though he was. "Five-and-twenty is not such an advanced age as some have led you to believe."

"Louisa is on the shelf," Harry protested hardily, forcing his voice to a more reasonable timbre. *"You* know it. *I* know it. *She* knows it. The entire *ton* knows it! The best she can hope for is a gentleman of modest birth and moderate means, with her fortune as inducement to overlook her shopworn status, along with an indisputable family characteristic of breeding sons often and well. In such case, her disporting herself among the ton as if she were a girl fresh from the schoolroom, with all the advantages of youth and innocence, would be ludicrous, and make her an object of ridicule, and myself as well. My God—it would give every decent man a disgust of her!"

"Have you examined the guest list?" Lady Daphne inquired.

"Yes," Harry admitted, shifting in his seat.

"Do your military friends figure on it?"

"No." He swallowed, took a deep and steadying breath. "I did at first protest their omission, but Lady Fortescue is quite right in this. Such men are not the sort with whom I would wish to have Louisa's name linked. Far better to restrict the guests to more sober and steady-minded gentlemen, and not muddy the waters with extraneous and unsuitable rattles of possible libertine propensities and uncouth behavior who are in no case to seek out a wife. *They* will be looking for youth and beauty in a bride when they do wed, though they may accept something rather less for more informal liaisons. None would have any *serious* interest in Louisa, and interest of any other sort would not only be insupportable to me personally, but go far toward ruining her chances with more respectable candidates. *A-suivi* flirtations are *not* the thing these days, no matter what the case may have been in your time!"

"Then why did you introduce them into my home?"

"An error, which I admit freely. I was not considering the situation properly. They must be refused the house. I shall instruct Hoskins before I leave."

"No, I think not," Lady Daphne disagreed. "Firstly, this is *my* house, Harry, and no one has given you permission to take charge of the running of it. Secondly, I find them all most gentlemanlike, and *perfectly* unobjectionable. Their attentions to Louisa have been only that which is proper. Harriet Fortescue's opinion on the subject concerns me not in the least, as I have never considered looking to *her* for guidance in matters of propriety."

"Then you should! Military friendships cut across lines of class distinction," Harry stated firmly. "You must bow to me in this, as my knowledge and experience of the world are perforce superior to yours. What may be suitable as a comrade in the field is not necessarily suitable as even a casual acquaintance following the cessation of hostilities. As I have stated previously, I made a grievous error in introducing these men to your notice. You will oblige me by dropping their acquaintance."

"This is not a battlefield, Harry," his aunt said even more gently, "and we are not troops subject to your orders. You must leave the habits of command behind, my boy, or you will constantly come a cropper."

They parted that evening—brother and sister, nephew

and aunt—in no very great charity with one another, Harry barely restraining both temper and impatience at what he viewed as their unreasonable obstructionism, Lady Daphne and Louisa presenting a brave and concerted front, but inwardly quaking at the thought of what direction Harry's infatuation with the Fortescue diamond would next take.

One issue, at least, was resolved. While Harry might protest as much as he liked, Lady Daphne informed him, his military friends would always be welcome in her home, and he had best resign himself to meeting them there and treating them with proper civility. Moreover, Louisa was free to ride with them, stand up with them, speak with them, flirt with them should she so desire. She was even, Lady Daphne stated firmly, free to marry one of them, should she choose. Harry would do well to accept such an outcome gracefully should it occur.

"After all," the old lady said tartly, "that's what you brought 'em around for in the first place, isn't it, informing us they were all the best of good fellows, loyal to a fault, gallant beyond what is common, and gentlemen born? You should not be permitting Harriet Fortescue or her daughter to dictate your friendships at this early date, Harry, or you will have people saying you already live under the cat's paw!"

Later, as they climbed the stairs to seek their beds and what sleep they might find there, Lady Daphne commented acidly that she would never have believed Harry could be so quickly turned against all he had been and known and loved—family, principles, friends, courtesy, even common decency—then muttered something incomprehensible about a little head leading the bigger one.

"It hasn't been quick at all," Louisa returned sadly. "It's been three years in Spain, and total separation from the girl he thinks he loves, combined with the loss of his arm and the scarring of his face and, yes, the passing of his youth, or what he sees as his youth. He's frightened, and he's desperate, and he's grasping at what seems to him to be happiness. He doesn't care whom he must trample to gain it. In a way, I don't blame him. I just wish she were a worthier object for his affections."

"The fact remains," Lady Daphne commented at the door to her room, "that he is being excessively perverse and tiresome. I hope, should you be so indelicate as to contract the same malady, that you will show better sense."

"If I do not," Louisa smiled wanly, "you will have every right to throw me on Lady Fortescue's tender mercies."

Six

They had not long to wait to learn the shifts to which Harry would next resort in his pursuit of the Fortescue diamond.

He arrived two mornings later, traveling unicorn with the *Morning Post* and a delicate nosegay of violets done up with the usual silk stocking, offering to take Louisa for an early ride in the Park as the weather had at last broken and the day was exceptionally fine.

"I've had Commendatore brought down from Marleybourne," he informed his sister with obvious pride in his foresight and kindness. "Old Ben's walking him out front this very minute. If you won't keep me cooling my heels for above half an hour—"

Louisa flew from the breakfast table to the window. Below were her handsome chestnut gelding and Harry's big bay, being paraded in front of the area way.

"Commendatore? You dear!" she gasped. "You darling!" She whirled on Harry, threw her arms around him. "You best of all brothers! Oh, Harry . . ."

"Thought you'd be pleased," he grinned. "Here, now—stop crushing my neckcloth! I'll be unfit for human eyes if you continue in this manner."

She backed off, tears shining in her eyes.

"I can't believe it," she sputtered. "How did you know?

I didn't *dare* suggest such a thing, for I know maintaining a stable in London is frightfully dear."

"Thought you deserved a little fun. You were used to ride him every day at home. I don't know how you've stood it this long."

"Neither do I! I've attempted a rented hack a time or two when it was unavoidable," she admitted, smiling through tears which were half tenderness at his matchless kindness, half guilt at how she was standing in the way of this best of all brothers' happiness, "but it wasn't the same. What is considered suitable for a lady in town *you* wouldn't suggest as a mount for a dim-witted two-year-old!"

"Dull?" Harry asked with an indulgent laugh.

"Ever try to ride a mechanical statue?" Louisa burbled. "If it moves, it jolts. If it doesn't jolt, it just *stands* there and chews grass, no matter what you do. Mouths like leather! And then, it—well, it does things best not mentioned in polite society!"

"Flatulence?" Harry asked with a twinkle.

"And *other* things! Loudly . . . And, odoriferously."

"Poor Louisa! Get on with you," he laughed. "Up the stairs, and into something a bit more suitable, or I'll leave without you—and then where'll you be?"

"Hurling things after you, and cursing as no lady should." Her lips trembled. This was the old, pre-diamond Harry, considering her pleasure and desires with an imaginative thoughtfulness that was unmatchable, no matter how many cares might be weighing on him. "Harry, you *are* an angel. A positive *angel!* I'll be down directly."

Harry laughed as she flew from the room, breakfast forgotten, and took his place at the table.

"I see the flowers continue," he commented, still chuckling.

"Yes—most attentive, whoever the man may be," Lady Daphne agreed.

"Too bad he doesn't show his face. Might not prove a bad sort, and he's certainly bold enough!"

"Persistent, at the least."

Lady Daphne instructed the waiting footman to place the flowers in the back parlor, then glanced through the morning mail he had just deposited on a tray in front of her. It was crammed with invitations. The Season appeared to be starting in earnest at last.

Hoskins whisked away the soiled covers, a look of approbation lighting his solemn eyes as he replaced them with fresh, and deposited coffee and generous portions of grilled kidneys, buttered eggs, bacon, muffins, and wigs in front of the young viscount. One breakfast had never been enough for the boy. He doubted it was for the man.

"Very kind in you, Harry—bringing Louisa's horse down from Marleybourne," Lady Daphne remarked dryly, not as easily satisfied Harry harbored no ulterior motives in this conciliatory gesture toward his sister. "Maintaining her mount must be quite an inconvenience and expense, when added to your own considerable stable. What is the current tally? Two or three for hacking, I presume, your matched bays for tooling about town, and I believe someone mentioned you picked up a team of chestnuts from Beaton's breakdowns. If *that's* the pair I'm thinking of, they must have set you back a pretty penny! Then, of course, there are the carriage teams, and whatever your groom rides. I presume you left your hunters at Marleybourne, along with any racing stock."

"No hunters yet, Aunt Daffy," he said around bites of kidney and egg. "Haven't had time to see to that since I got home. Otherwise, you've got it pretty close. Stabling Louisa's gelding is no inconvenience when one considers the rest, and she *does* deserve a treat now and then."

"I agree." Lady Daphne gave Hoskins a sharp nod.

That worthy silently glided from the room, leaving them to themselves. "Trying to sweeten her up?" she asked as the door closed. "The way she was carrying on, one would assume you had spent your last ha'penny to procure her pleasure. Silly chit! Still, it is kind in you to take Louisa riding when I am certain there are other companions you would prefer."

"Oh, it's a beautiful morning," he returned offhandedly. "She *is* my sister, and she had been having rather a dull time of it. I feel responsible for that to a certain degree, though if she'd had any sense she'd've come to Fortescue Lodge as we planned, so she'd no one to blame but herself if she's been subject to fits of the dismals. Still, it was a wrench for her, I suppose—leaving Marleybourne."

"A considerable wrench," Lady Daphne agreed tartly, "and she didn't *leave*. She was *chased!*"

"You, of all people, should understand the necessity for it, Aunt Daffy." Harry reached for another muffin, reconsidered, then fortified his plate from the platters of bacon, kidneys, and eggs held at the ready over warmers on the sideboard. "Can you imagine Gwendolyn and Louisa under the same roof? Not that I mean any disrespect to either, but they are so different in all ways."

"Indeed they are!" No, she could not imagine Louisa living in harmony with her prospective sister-in-law—nor indeed, that any *man* could after the first few days—but she held her counsel. "Where did you go after you left us yesterday?" she inquired chattily. "Colonel Winthrop stopped by with Fenton and Malfont, on the prowl to discover your whereabouts. Somehow I neglected to mention that last evening. Did they ever find you?"

Harry grinned. "I'd promised to take Giles to Cribb's Parlor, so I returned to Fortescue House to collect him. Then he and I were off for some 'depraved male activities,' in which George and the others joined us later."

"Isn't the lad a trifle *young* for such a place?" she protested, remembering the tales she'd heard of the former pugilist's drinking establishment. "Blue ruin is not exactly recommended for sprigs who can't hold their liquor!"

"It was that, or a cock fight. Far better company at Cribb's. Back parlor was taken, unfortunately, but it was all quite proper otherwise—or as proper as such evenings are meant to be."

"And Miss Fortescue approved?"

He laughed, polishing off the last of a second helping of kidneys. "Didn't know a thing about it! I'd more or less promised the boy—a bribe, I suppose. I *don't* want him taking his team out when he's above par. By the bye, he was the one caused Louisa's accident, but don't tell her. That's between him and me . . . Believe me—Giles will come to no grief in my company! Rather the opposite. I'd like to turn his thoughts in another direction, if I can," Harry said thoughtfully, as he handed a muffin to his aunt for slathering with preserves.

"And in what direction are they turned presently, pray tell?"

"Petticoat-line, and he's definitely too young for that! Determined to cut a dash, the lad is, no matter what the cost. No—Cribb's, Gentleman Jack's, Manton's—*much* safer."

"And where is his father while you are sponsoring this young spark about town?"

"Lord Fortescue?" Harry shrugged, refilled his cup, accepted the muffin. "At one of his clubs, most likely. Practically lives at 'em, from what I've observed. Plays rather deep more or less constantly—that, or tipples. Boy comes by his love of a glass honestly, more's the pity. Rather a nonentity, Fortescue. Hasn't much understanding of lads of Giles' stamp, either. What the boy really wants is employment, but that isn't under consideration. A pair of colors would be the perfect solution, and either

George Winthrop or Percy Fenton would take him in hand for my sake—even Gracechurch, though he's still in Spain, or Heath—but I know better than to propose it. The boy may be army-mad, but he isn't even being permitted Cambridge, or to learn the management of the estates which will one day be his," Harry grumbled. "All that's being required of him is to acquire a little town bronze and play the gentleman without making a complete fool of himself. Boy lives under the parental roof, you see, though he's been given an allowance—generous enough to permit his getting into trouble, but not sufficiently generous to permit his extricating himself. I've pulled him from the River Tick more than once since I returned . . . Where Giles is concerned, Lord and Lady Fortescue are foolish beyond permission! Even Gwendolyn agrees with their strictures, sweet innocent that she is, but Lord Fortescue, at the least, should know better."

"You have taken it on yourself to bear-lead this precious twig of the Fortescue oak?"

Harry smiled disarmingly. "Not much else I *can* do, Aunt Daffy. I'll soon be a member of the family, and their concerns are mine. If I can assist in preventing the unpleasantness which is certain to ensue if Giles is permitted to continue his present course unchecked—"

"Having been acquainted with Harriet Fortescue somewhat longer than you, Harry, and Dexter Fortescue considerably longer than that, I should caution that if your interference comes to their ears, they will not be best pleased—no matter how laudable your intentions. Indeed, they would consider your self-involvement officious, and I am afraid I would be forced to concur."

"To stand by and permit a lad that age to make a mull of his life for want of a little effort would be unpardonable!" Harry protested.

"Giles Fortescue is not your concern. This is not some young, nameless subaltern in Spain, family and friends so distant as to be nonexistent. This is a boy in the bosom of his family, the counsels of father and mother instantly available."

"If Gwendolyn understood the dangers the lad is running, I would have her complete support. Naturally, she does not—no one would desire such understanding in an innocent young girl. However, in serving Giles I am serving her, and care for nothing else."

Lady Daphne leaned back, surveying her nephew, caught between a frown and a smile. How Harry had come to be so often and so rapidly promoted would have been clear to any but a fool! Well, she had warned him. On his head be any problems that might arise. And, wouldn't it be delightful if some did . . .

At that moment Louisa returned, resplendent in a form-fitting sapphire-blue velvet riding habit of military cut with epaulets and frogging of silver, the stock edged with silver lace. A shako of deeper blue perched on her sunny curls, white ostrich plumes curling to touch her cheek in most unmilitary fashion.

Harry stared at her, brows rising. "Bit rakish, aren't we?" he asked, an edge to his voice.

"Nonsense!" Lady Daphne snapped. "I am *certain*, were I a subaltern in Wellington's army, *you* could tell me how to go on, Henry. When it comes to *la mode*, please leave the decisions on what is proper to me. I do not want to be forced to touch on this subject again. *Twice* is more than enough! Turn around, Louisa. How is the fit across the shoulders? Yes—excellent! They've eliminated that annoying crease quite satisfactorily. *Very* fetching!"

"Question is, what will it fetch?" Harry muttered.

"You spoke?" Lady Daphne's brows rose ever so slightly.

"No—nothing of import." Harry rose hastily from the table. "We'd best be going before it starts to cloud over again, Louisa. Besides, the horses have been waiting quite long enough. At home it wouldn't have taken you above five minutes to change!"

"Ah—but *this* is London," Lady Daphne threw after him, "and Louisa is no longer a brass-faced hoyden, but rather a lady of fashion. You had best take *that* into your future calculations!"

They rode through the streets, Louisa's mount taking exception to each carriage and curricle, each cart and pedestrian, each stray dog and cat. Fully occupied with restraining Commendatore's more ambitious flights of fancy, she had no time for her brother other than to comment that her horse had apparently been stable-bound for an excessive period.

Harry was more pleased than not with the lack of conversation. Louisa's appearance did not meet with his approval, and he was restraining himself with considerable difficulty from giving her a well-deserved tongue-lashing. That he had instructed her to find a husband—and as quickly as possible—was one thing. That she should be going about it garbed in the manner of a high-priced bit of muslin was another. Whatever Aunt Daffy might have claimed about the dresses, the habit—no question about it—was *fast*, highest kick of fashion or no. A hint from Gwendolyn that she was exposing herself in a most unladylike manner, combined with Gwendolyn's own demure perfection, might do the trick, but he doubted it. Louisa was becoming entirely too independent and flighty.

A damnable situation, no matter from which side he examined it, Harry decided as he watched his sister carefully, ready to wedge his reins under his saddle and seize the playful Commendatore's bridle should the need arise. It was a good thing he had trained Thunderer to the slightly unusual maneuver while still at Marleybourne. The horse was even fresher than he had realized . . .

It was as if, he mused, Louisa—while giving every overt evidence of falling in with Gwendolyn's requirements—were in some subtle female way doing her best to prevent not only her own nuptials, but the announcement of his betrothal as well.

Gwendolyn had promised to try to bring Louisa to a proper understanding of her position, and the advisability—indeed, *necessity*—of falling in with their plans. Her brother was, after all, the head of his family. A certain deferential respect was due him, his desires deserving of first consideration. But, Gwendolyn had cautioned him, Lady Cheltenham (charming though she might be) was known throughout the ton as a vain, expensive, flighty, and slightly disreputable woman—a fact of which he could not have been aware when he selected her as his sister's sponsor, having been so little on the Town. Her influence over Louisa could not help but be pernicious at best. Louisa's continuance under her roof would do her no good, and might do considerable harm.

And certainly, thought Harry grimly, if Louisa's new getups were anything to judge by, this assessment of his aunt was charitable in the extreme.

They came to the gates and entered the Park, quickening their pace to a staid trot. Harry glanced at his sister, misliking the determined set of her chin.

"Out of charity with me of a sudden?" he asked.

"Hardly!"

"Out of sorts, then?"

"How I long for a good gallop," Louisa said wistfully, "rather than being forced to poke along in this manner."

"Not here!" Harry protested, reaching for her bridle.

She pulled Commendatore's head away, laughing even as she sent him a narrowed look. "I am already aware that a gallop in the Park equates with no vouchers for Almack's," she said tartly. "Aunt Daphne cautioned me. Keep your hand to yourself—there is no need for you to attempt to control my mount as well as my life!"

Harry bit back the retort trembling on his lips. Nothing would be served by brangling with his sister at this juncture.

Above them the tree canopy spread sun-spangled fans of spring lace, the branches losing their crisp definition against a clear sky from which the last vestiges of damp had been wrung. The lawns had turned the bright fresh green of newly sprung grass during the last week, and flowers were bursting into riotous blossom. Nursemaids and their small charges strolled the gentle paths, the children's voices rising in the crystalline air to join the carol of birdsong that gave fresh testimony to the ending of a long and unpleasant winter.

"I wonder how things are at Marleybourne," Louisa said longingly. "The gardens must be just—"

"Look! Up ahead!" Harry exclaimed, a trace too much surprise in his delight. "Isn't that Gwendolyn?"

"You would be the authority. I have seen her but once."

"Surely you recognize her? That elegant form, that grace, that perfection of manner could only be hers!" He paused, looking down the alley, his frown more expressive of a desire to convince than of actual puzzlement or distress. "I wonder who her escort might be? Well set-up man!" The words hung in the soft spring air like bad lines from a bad play.

"Her brother, perhaps?"

"I think not. There's an air of worldliness and assurance to this man that wouldn't fit Giles." Harry shrugged. "No matter—let's catch them up. I've no desire to see myself cut out!" he declaimed, and set the big bay to a smooth canter.

Louisa hung back, a wry twist to her lips, watching as

she maintained her steady, decorous trot on Commendatore. The three figures merged far ahead, presenting a pleasant tableau she had no wish to disturb. The sun beat warmly on her shoulders, and the breeze on her cheek was what she imagined a lover's first caress might be, at once tentative and suggesting greater pleasures to come. She shook herself as a pair of riders swept past at a fast canter, military men from the cut of their coats, backs straight and heads high, mounted on what looked to be a pair of matched grays. She enjoyed the handsome picture they made, a slight smile softening her earlier look of uneasy self-absorbtion. They were so much of a type, these men, with Harry and his friends—one posture, one tailor, one correct angle at which to set a hat or sit a horse for them all.

The two riders passed Harry as more hoofbeats pounded behind her—the thunder of a heavy horse being allowed his head by a master in firm control. She glanced back in curiosity. A magnificent black was bearing down on her, the rider hunched over his neck, stirrups so shortened that his legs were bent almost double—the most uncouth, ungainly seat she had ever seen. They hurtled toward her, then past, the rider's face hidden by the horse's flying mane. Commendatore danced, snatching at the bit, clearly longing to race the fidgets from his legs in a mad dash after the powerful black stallion. Louisa struggled to restrain him, but was almost unseated as the normally well-mannered gelding tried first to free himself of her weight, then break down the alley. Branches whipped past her, one snatching at the flying plumes of her shako. Suddenly the black was snorting beside her, Commendatore's bridle seized in a firm grip.

"Good morning, Miss Rosy-Cheeks," a familiar voice laughed as her mount came to a trembling stand and she struggled to regain her seat. "My apologies! Had I any idea I would be seeing you, I would have omitted the violets and taken more care with my appearance—as well as El Moro's gait! In the future, don't select a mount whose strength is above your own."

Louisa stared at the man as she resettled her hat, lips compressed to a thin line. "And just who might *you* be, to be issuing me orders!" she seethed. "I've had enough of that recently for a lifetime!"

"Come, now—can't you take a little teasing?" The eyes were as laughter-filled as the voice. "No—that's right, you respond atrociously to being quizzed. That's something you'll learn to accept with proper tutelage." The bright glitter of the man's dark eyes softened. "You may even learn to enjoy it, and return what you receive in good measure."

"Good God!" she said before she could stop herself.

"Hardly! Only James—ah—Morrison, at your service," he said with a flourish, doffing his scuffed hat, his other hand still firmly gripping Commendatore's bridle, keeping the two horses shoulder to shoulder.

Her eyes swept him, his magnificent horse, his dusty garb, his disheveled appearance. The cut might be good, but his rumpled brown hacking jacket had seen better days, and no valet had been within many a league of his linen. Yet his air was unconscious of these solecisms, and his address—in spite of its rakish impropriety—was that of a gentleman. A gentleman, then, who had, like his coat, seen better times, magnificent black stallion or no. The only possible conclusion was that he was in some manner employed to train or exercise a wealthier man's cattle— hence the extremely luxurious carriage at his disposal the night she arrived, and this wonderful mount clearly so far beyond his purse as to be laughable.

"I am pleased at this opportunity to thank you for the assistance you rendered me at the time of my accident," she responded primly.

His head flew back, his laughter ringing over the twitterings of the birds, the high voices of children calling in the distance.

"Don't be ridiculous! Admit you'd have much preferred never to see my face again." And then he looked at her, grin almost conspiratorial. "Let us always have truth between us, Miss Rosy-Cheeks—a minor precondition I set with all my acquaintances."

"If you prefer."

"I much prefer!" And then his face turned serious, as if a cloud had of a sudden obscured the sun. "What kind of hoydenish behavior are you indulging in, riding unescorted? It's not done, you know. I wouldn't like to see you have trouble with the sticklers. You should have a groom with you, at the least."

"My brother is just ahead," she shot back, torn between vexation and embarrassment. "I was about to join him and his friends when you so unexpectedly appeared, bent on tearing to perdition."

"He left you back here by yourself? Of all the irresponsible—" Morrison scowled, glancing down the alley over his shoulder to where Harry and the fair Gwendolyn formed an intimate twosome. "You might easily have come to grief. The hour is so early that I customarily use it to banish the cobwebs after a late night. Usually I have the paths to myself—beyond a few hardened barracks-cases who know not what to do with themselves once dawn arrives."

"I am sure, had my brother been aware of your intentions, he would not have left me unattended, Mr. Morrison."

"I am certain he would not," Lord Leap-to-the-Rescue replied with a chuckle. "Harry Beckenham is not generally known as a fool—except in certain matters." He glanced back over his shoulder, then at Louisa, eyes searching hers. "Is that, perchance, the scintillating

Fortescue diamond to whom he is paying such determined court?"

"So he said."

"You would do well to separate him from *that* influence," James Morrison informed her, voice flat and un-
compromising. "Diamonds are known to be both sharp
and hard if they are genuine. If they are not, they are
merely glass, and so beneath notice. In either case, not
precisely what one would desire for a Peninsular hero."

"I cannot see that my brother's friendships are any
concern of yours!" Louisa spat.

"Come—don't eat me. What concerns you, concerns
me. That much should have been apparent at our first
meeting," he smiled. "I would have much preferred to
ignore your caterwauling *bonne,* but her shrieks were pat-
ently an affront to your ears, and so she had to receive first
assistance, no matter what my personal inclinations.
Surely you do not hold that inverted attention against
me?"

"Coming it *much* too strong, Mr. Morrison," Louisa
retorted acidly. "All you could have observed was a jumble of assorted rugs tangled with miscellaneous lumpish
forms."

"You think so? Have it your own way," he grinned, "if
that makes you more comfortable. However, if you truly
desire *that* connection"—he jerked his head, indicating
the group down the alley—"you are a far poorer judge of
character than I take you to be."

The trace of a smile quivered on Louisa's lips. "You are
perfectly reprehensible, you know," she said.

"Know? I beg to inform you, Miss Rosy-Cheeks, that
reprehensibility is my stock-in-trade!" He grinned.

And then his eyes grew troubled, the depth of concern
in them startling her. "This town is not a safe place for a
young lady to go about alone," he said with a gentleness
of which she would never have believed him capable on

the basis of their brief and somewhat irregular acquaintance. "No! Listen to me for a moment, rather than informing me that I am much too forthcoming a lout for
your tastes, and am involving myself in your affairs in a
most unpardonable manner—which is what I am certain
you were about to say, given the expression on that pert
little face of yours!" He looked at her steadily, and slowly
her eyes fell before his. "There—that's better." He
reached over, covered her hand with his where it lay on
the pommel of her saddle. "Promise me you will go nowhere unattended—and I do not mean by your aunt, no
matter how charming she may be."

"Why should I promise you anything?"

"A footman, at the very least, and a young, strong one.
Promise me."

"This is ridiculous! I don't even know you! Why should
I listen to you?" she spat, eyes flashing. She stared at him
a moment, coloring. "Oh, very well, but I will only *consider*
your words. I *never* make promises I have no intention of
keeping."

"Do more than consider them, for both our sakes.
Heed them! I don't want to spend my days and nights
worrying about you. I've other concerns, and cannot
watch over you as I would like . . . Well, off with you. Join
your brother directly, if you please." And then he smiled,
touching the brim of his battered beaver. "Conversing
with strangers in the Park is not to be encouraged—
myself excepted, naturally. Perhaps Beckenham will come
to his senses and see to your welfare now the first moments of ardor have passed, rather than making a cake of
himself over that hell-born chit."

Unable to concoct a sufficiently barbed retort on the
spur of the moment, and greatly confused both by his
words and his manner, Louisa gave him a curt nod.
"Goodbye, Mr. Morrison," she said, and turned Commendatore's head down the alley. *He knew Harry . . .*

"Oh, no, Miss Rosy-Cheeks," he called softly after her, "this is only *au revoir.*"

Insufferable, *insufferable* man! The last word his yet again, and that "last word" every bit as insulting, as unpardonable as on the first occasion. And, such a disreputable appearance! He needed someone to take him in hand. Poverty did not excuse slovenliness! Amazing that his employer did not hold him to a higher standard . . . Still, perhaps when one was but a glorified groom, and only employed as a charitable act, it wasn't as serious as when one sprang from the lower orders—especially if one were an old friend or acquaintance of one's employer, and had fallen on hard times. Maintaining a proper appearance in the ton did not come cheap.

Behind her Louisa heard heavy hoofbeats steadily receding. At least he was gone, and from the look of Harry—deeply occupied with the Glorious Gwendolyn— he had not noticed her delay. That was a mercy! She had no desire to be catechized on her encounter with James Morrison, nor to be instructed to cut his acquaintance should he approach her again.

Like him she might not. Approve him? Not likely! But, she would reach her own decisions as to the suitability of any acquaintance, no matter how unconventional.

She came up to Harry, still deep in conversation with his diamond, at a sedate walk. Gwendolyn's escort hung back from the lovers on a restless, showy hack that had done well to make it out of the stableyard unwinded. Louisa drew rein while still a few yards from them, waiting to be noticed. The stranger, a scrawny, foppish scarecrow with the profile of a fish and shoulders which sloped like a cottage roof beneath his wasp-waisted, buckram-wadded lilac coat, attempted a halfhearted bow in her direction, sawing at his mount's reins and shifting his seat precipitously, greatly discomposing the uneasy beast. From his shoulders a seven-caped purple velvet cloak edged in white fur and lined with white satin trailed to spread across the hack's croup.

"Oh, Lord," Louisa muttered.

"Help! He's wild!" the would-be fop yelped, slipping precariously in the saddle as the hack grabbed at the bit, sidling with amazing spirit.

Harry's head snapped around.

The hack's ears slammed back. His head jerked down, muzzle almost touching his knees, as he lashed out with his back hooves. Harry crammed his reins beneath his saddle flap, urged Thunderer forward, grasped the hack's bridle and jerked his head up without breaking the flow of his conversation with Gwendolyn. The action seemed automatic, almost habitual. The stranger flushed to the roots of his sparse carroty hair, cursing steadily—if un- imaginatively—under his breath as he attempted to loosen Harry's grip and wrench the horse's head away, stirrups lost, high-crowned white beaver flying.

Louisa stifled a giggle. Gwendolyn gasped, raising a trembling hand to her heart.

Either horse or rider succeeded in his goal, and they parted company—the hack to tear down the alley as if pursued by the fiends of hell, the man to land ignomini- ously on his rump, still cursing, his soaring shirt-points close to poking out his eyes.

Harry swore, shaking his bruised hand as he main- tained balance and seat with knees alone. Gwendolyn shrieked, her mount dancing, and gave every indication of preparing a faint. Louisa burst into laughter.

"See to them!" she called to Harry, and took off in hot pursuit of the hack, blue velvet habit streaming in the wind as she galloped *ventre à terre* through Hyde Park at last, Commendatore bugling his triumph.

Trees flashed past as she pelted down the alley. Horri- fied nursemaids held hands before their mouths and pulled their charges out of harm's way, convinced they were witnessing a fatal runaway. Children pointed and laughed, delighted to see such unaccustomed sport on a placid spring morning. Great gobbets of damp turf flew through the air as the anonymous hack tore from the bridle path, charging across sedate lawns and through pristine flower beds. Louisa followed, damning the fool who had caused the contretemps, terrified one of the scrambling children would be injured, flying across the beds and leaping obstacles as if she were leading a hunt. Far ahead two more riders enthusiastically gave chase, hats lost to the wind of their passage, gaining rapidly on their target who was by now quite clearly past his endurance. And then, suddenly, she could see it was over—the horse's flying reins plucked from the air with consummate skill, his bridle seized, the beast brought to a shuddering halt.

She gave a sigh of relief, collected Commendatore, took him over one last glorious celebratory hedge for the sheer joy of it, then brought him to a sedate trot, commiserating with him over the end of their romp, hand stroking his glossy neck as she complimented him on his speed, his manners, his beauty, his grace.

The two riders turned to watch her approach as she became uncomfortably conscious of lost shako, wind-whipped hair, and flushed cheeks.

"By Jove, but you can ride!" one of the men called admiringly as she trotted up. "Captain Quentin Heath at your service, Ma'am. And that mangy fellow who's got your horse is Captain Stephen Gracechurch—though the horse ain't yours, I take it," he concluded, inventorying Commendatore's points with a practiced eye after throwing a disparaging glance at the trembling nag. "My guess is, you'd not be caught dead near such a commoner unless you was forced to it."

Louisa laughed, eyes darting from one wind-blown man to the other. It was the pair who had passed her earlier, exactly as she had imagined them to be in every detail. "No—he's not mine," she agreed. "You have that right." She extended her hand, which Heath adroitly saluted. "I'm Louisa Beckenham, but I haven't the foggiest idea of the identity of the clunch who was attempting to ride him." She beamed at Gracechurch. "Thank you so much for capturing him! I was in dread of an injury to some helpless bystander. If I'm not mistaken, I've heard my brother mention your names, gentlemen. Harry Beckenham?"

Gracechurch broke into a grin that rivaled hers. "Thought that was him back a bit. Didn't look as if he wished to be disturbed. Your most obedient, Miss Beckenham!"

"He might have blessed you for disturbing him, had he foreseen *this*"—her gesture included her hair, her habit, the hack—"was going to happen. What a bumblebroth!"

"Not Harry's, I trust?"

"Oh, the bumblebroth's his right enough, but not the hack. Harry would no more be caught on such glue-bait than I! They're back that way. If you wouldn't mind, I'd be grateful for your assistance in reuniting horseman with horse."

The men chuckled, pointed out the nearest path as they fell in beside her. They proceeded at a sober walk, the hack being incapable of anything more, sides heaving, left fore sprained. They chatted as they rode beneath the fresh green canopy of leaves, sun-dappled, caressed by the soft breeze—of Harry and his release from hospital, his selling out, and the inconvenience of his lost arm; of the Peninsula, and how they had come to know Harry, value him as a friend and trusted comrade in arms. Louisa glowed as if it were her praises they were singing rather than her brother's, delighting in their company and charmed by their easy manner. This was a ride on a spring morning as such an excursion should be, replete with light banter and warm laughter—a great contrast to what she had anticipated when Harry "noticed" Gwendolyn Fortescue lurking in the alley with some man in tow who was plainly a prospective candidate for Louisa's hand.

When they came up at last with Harry, there was a wide-eyed knot of children gathered around two recumbent figures, a pair of nursemaids ministering to the casualties' needs with *sal volatile* and handkerchiefs moistened with lavender water. The erstwhile rider was moaning for a physician, the lady for her mother, and Harry appeared ready to tear out their throats—or, perhaps, his own—if they uttered another sound.

"Thank God you caught him!" he exclaimed when he noticed Louisa, then broke into a surprised grin at the sight of Gracechurch and Heath. "Wouldn't you know it—the pair of you, no less, rising Phoenix-like to pull me from the brambles as usual! How d'you come to be in London? The last I knew, you were stuck in Lisbon."

"Five months ago, Harry?" Gracechurch laughed. "What's needed here?"

"A hackney—possibly two," Harry said, pushing his hand distractedly through his hair. "I can't determine whether Norval wants to be taken to Fortescue House, or directly to a sawbones."

"So—that's 'Cousin Norval,' " Louisa said, looking at her brother through narrowed eyes. "No, I thank you! It's best the introductions weren't even performed—saves you a deal of trouble."

"Louisa, for God's sake—" Harry began.

"*One* hackney," Heath interposed, sizing up the looks on brother's and sister's faces accurately. "Bring the physician to the hillock, rather than the hillock to the physician. I'll see to it."

He wheeled his gray, cantered up the alley, leaving Stephen Gracechurch in possession of the livery hack, Harry, the nursemaids and children, the invalids, and

Louisa. It had every aspect, Louisa chuckled to herself, of a strategic—and highly intelligent—retreat.

Gracechurch glanced around him, spotted where Harry had tethered Thunderer and Gwendolyn's mare, handed the hack over to Harry, and swung from the saddle.

"There's nothing we can do for that pair," he said, indicating Gwendolyn and her cousin with a jerk of his head. "Well attended, from the looks of it. Best we play least-in-sight for the moment. See to the brute, Harry—if proximity to such a bag of bones won't sully you forever!"

Harry chuckled wanly, led the limping and dejected hack across the alley to a separate tree as Gracechurch tethered his gray, then extended a hand to Louisa.

"I believe, Miss Beckenham, that our stay here is likely to be indefinite—Quentin being more experienced at foraging on bivouac than in the centers of civilization. You would do best to dismount while we wait for matters to sort themselves out."

Louisa smiled back and slid gracefully from Commendatore's back, resting her hand only lightly in the mustachioed captain's.

"Permit me to—"

"Oh, no—I always see to *this* gentleman myself," she said with a twinkle that took any possible sting from her words.

"Mustn't confuse the 'gentleman,' " Gracechurch said with an answering smile. "Gentlemen in a confused state are apt to be dangerous—to themselves, and to others." His eyes flicked to where Harry once more hovered distractedly over the apparently semi-conscious Gwendolyn. "Who's the lady-fair?"

"Miss Gwendolyn Fortescue, escorted—if you can call it that—by her cousin, Norval Quarmayne, if I recall the name properly. A diamond of the first water, believe me!

Harry counts himself fortunate that she will tolerate his presence on occasion."

"Fortescue? I've heard her mentioned, now and again. This isn't likely to raise his stock," Gracechurch chuckled. "Too bad we ain't in Spain—he'd fare better there."

Louisa cocked her head. "He noticed the pretty *señoritas*, then?" she asked, eyes on the Fortescue diamond, who had of a sudden gone rigid.

"Harry? No—passed 'em by, the more fool he! They noticed *him* right enough, though, the graceless dog."

"Indeed?" The diamond had relaxed, still gracefully *évanouie*. "How odd."

"Sisters are as incapable of judging the attractions of their brothers as brothers are those of their sisters," Gracechurch said with a wink. "Don't feel put out—it's a natural condition, familiarity, as they say, breeding contempt. *Hi, there*—I say, Harry!" he called softly, yet his voice had a carrying power which spun Harry around. "Come away from there, old fellow. You might be of some use if that was a Light Bob spilling his life's blood on the field, but delicate females with the vapors ain't in our line."

Harry looked doubtfully first at Gracechurch and Louisa, then down at the diamond and Cousin Norval, and hesitantly retreated a step or two. Norval's head rose on the instant, peering first at the children, then beyond them at Louisa, her brother, and Gracechurch.

"Shoot the brute," he moaned. "Tried to *kill* me!"

"What—right here in the Park?" Louisa laughed. "Don't make more of a cake of yourself than you already have, Mr. Quarmayne! The entire thing was your fault."

"Louisa!" her brother hissed in an agonized whisper. *"Please!"*

"He's nothing but a cow-handed man-milliner," she said flatly, surveying the mired lavender riding coat, the purple unmentionables and tangled cloak, and the white

Hessians with distaste, not particularly troubling about how far her voice might carry.

"That's no reason to say so!"

" 'Cousin Norval,' " she muttered. "I might have known . . . 'Bang-up-to-the-mark?' I'll say he is. Couldn't see past his shirt points if his life depended on it!"

The diamond uttered a delicate moan, waved the smelling salts aside, fluttering her lashes prettily. Harry was at her side in a shot, all tenderness and concern, Louisa temporarily forgotten. The diamond struggled to sit, leaning weakly against a plump nursemaid's shoulder, gazing confusedly at Harry, rosebud mouth in a pout.

"I want my mama," she said plaintively.

"I know, my darling. Heath's gone for a hackney. He'll have one here directly."

"I want my mama *now!*"

"Don't be an idiot!" Norval spat next to her, now attempting to sit also. *"You* ain't been thrown by a wild horse, and severely injured. Told you it wouldn't fadge, you little fool! I *ain't* a horseman, and that's the plain truth. If a horseman's what the bitch must have, find her someone else. My cloak's *ruined,"* he moaned. "First time I've worn it, too! I *ain't* gettin' up on that nag again—not if her fortune's ten times what you say!"

"You see how it is," Louisa said softly to Gracechurch.

"I do indeed!" he chuckled. "May I offer my services— as escort, suitor, major domo, groom, champion, or anything else you require?"

"It's as well for you I'm not literal-minded, or you might find yourself at point-non-plus! As it is, I'll accept your offer in the spirit in which it is intended."

"I can think of worse fates than being leg-shackled to Harry's sister," he returned with a grin.

"On less than half an hour's acquaintance?"

"Men have been known to reach such a determination

on the basis of very little more," he responded, glancing at Harry and his diamond.

"True," Louisa agreed, "but that does not necessarily ensure their greatest happiness. We've had quite enough of *that* in this family, without my continuing the tradition!"

"I take your point, Miss Beckenham. Your *servant*, then—now and forever, in any way and at any time, and if more is to come of it, we'll leave that in the hands of the gods. Acceptable?"

"Highly!" she twinkled. "At least *you* can sit a horse!"

"I should hope so!"

Miss Fortescue was standing now, clinging to Harry's arm as he led her over to Louisa and Gracechurch.

"Miss Beckenham," she said tremulously, tears sparkling in her eyes, "what a disaster! We had planned *such* a pleasant outing for you."

"I thought as much," Louisa muttered.

"I beg your pardon? I did not quite catch your words. All this upset has strangely discommoded me."

"It was not to be," Louisa said more clearly, as Gracechurch burst into laughter and Harry threw him a furious glance.

The diamond smiled wanly, forgiveness and forbearance writ on her perfect features, lending them an almost saintly look. "Did I not notice you conversing with a stranger before you joined us?" she inquired archly. "You appeared to be having trouble with your mount, just like poor Cousin Norval. *Much* too large and spirited a mount for a lady," she said in gentle reproof, ignoring Harry's soft-voiced cautions.

"Yes," Louisa returned curtly, "a groom exercising one of his master's horses, and treating the Park as if it were a steeplechase. Commendatore took it in his head to emulate the black."

"But, you were *conversing* with the man!"

"He noticed my problem, and lent a hand. Commendatore would never have behaved so had he been given proper exercise over the last weeks." She threw a meaningful glance at her brother, who reddened slightly.

"Indeed? I thought I recognized the horse, you see. Did the 'groom' happen to mention the animal's name?"

"El Moro," Louisa said between clenched teeth.

"Then His Grace of Rawdon must be returned to town . . . You are certain it was not he? By report, he permits none but himself to exercise that particular mount. It is notorious—a vicious, ill-natured, evil-tempered beast, just like its master."

"No," Louisa grated, "I'm sorry to disappoint you. The man was merely an ordinary, somewhat presumptuous groom, and a slovenly one at that. His Grace should be more strict with his servants; but then, perhaps he is indisposed, which would account for someone else exercising his horse, as well as for the appearance of his groom," she said in a tone that signaled the end of the topic. "Are you feeling a bit more the thing now, Miss Fortescue?"

"Indeed—so silly of me!" she simpered. "I am no use in an emergency, I fear—so unlike you, taking off in *such* a way across the Park after that dreadful commoner without a thought to your own safety! Not that there was the least need," she continued, throwing Gracechurch a winning smile, "when there were brave gentlemen in plenty to see to the problem. That *was* brazen, I am afraid. We must put it about that your horse ran away with you, or there will be talk of the most unpleasant kind. I have always found," she dimpled, "that when *I* have need of a gentleman's services, one is *always* at hand."

Louisa clenched her teeth and took a deep breath, as the diamond fluttered her lashes impartially at Harry and Gracechurch.

"Permit me, Miss Fortescue," Harry said quickly,

brought to a sense of both the niceties and the dangers of the morning.

He performed the introductions, and the conversation became general except for Louisa, who maintained a stony silence. Gwendolyn inquired about their Peninsular service, shuddering prettily at the slightest mention of the dangers and privations. Gracechurch smiled down at her, a hard light behind the amusement in his eyes.

"I do not wonder at your interest," he commented, "given that you are well acquainted with one of our brother officers." Then he turned to Harry, face clouding, as he continued blandly, "Did you know poor Fotheringham took a ball shortly after you were hit? Within the week, I believe. Strange incident, that . . ."

Gwendolyn went rigid. Harry scowled at the mention of such a thing in front of his diamond.

"Fotheringham?" Louisa asked, interest roused. "I don't believe Harry's ever mentioned him, and I thought I knew all your names. How is the poor man?"

"Man? Barely more than a boy! Hadn't been with us over a month when it happened. Home now, and furious that he's been invalided out."

Miss Fortescue made a small sound, hand rising to her face as Gracechurch turned.

"Don't distress yourself overly, Miss Fortescue," he said, voice level. "Heath and I brought him home safely to England as soon as he could travel. He'd been butchered enough on the field, and we wanted to get him in the hands of his own physician. It was a near thing . . . Ball's out now. Badly weakened, poor lad, but he'll recover, which is more than can be said for many."

The Fortescue diamond turned white, crumpled at their feet.

"Oh, Lord—you ass!" Harry exploded. "She's been gently reared, can't bear the mention of suffering. Whatever did you think you were doing?" He dropped to his knees beside the delicate damsel. "Hi! You, over there!" he called, cradling her in his arms, "We need your salts again!"

"Now, whatever caused that?" Louisa exclaimed. "I would have sworn she was totally recovered—if indeed she was incapacitated to begin with."

"How uncharitable of you," Gracechurch murmured, drawing her slightly aside. "You are observing a rare and precious blossom of English femaledom. *Naturally* she was incapacitated."

"No, you're wrong. *Before,*" Louisa said, flushing slightly, "her cheeks were pink. *Now* she is white as a snowdrop. The look is unmistakable. I have it on good authority that a white face is a sure sign of a genuine faint."

"I bow in deference to your superior knowledge of female indispositions," Gracechurch responded, eyes never leaving Harry and his diamond. "Perhaps she has had a shock," he suggested after a moment.

At the far end of the alley Louisa espied a hackney proceeding at a careful pace, guided by a rider on a gray mount.

"At last!" she exclaimed. "Captain Heath appears to be returning. *Now* we will get this sorted out. What a morning! I hope, once everything is seen to, you and Captain Heath will call on us. You will have earned a cold collation at the very least. This has all been a bit more than any of us bargained for."

"Indeed it has," Gracechurch agreed with a look of grim satisfaction, eyes still on Harry and his inamorata. "A great deal more."

Seven

In the event, it was several days before Captains Grace-church and Heath found time to call, and by then Lady Daphne was most anxious to speak with them.

Matters in the Park did not sort themselves as Louisa anticipated, though Harry did see his unwell love and the much abused Cousin Norval to Fortescue House, remaining long enough to ascertain that Gwendolyn, while sadly weakened and not at all herself, was in no imminent danger, and Norval's injuries were more to pride and raiment than person.

Just after the hackney pulled away, bearing its precious burdens with a highly harassed Harry in attendance, Colonel Winthrop and Major Lord Percy Fenton cantered up, drawn by the curious plethora of horses and paucity of riders. They subsequently lent a hand with the matter—once greetings on the part of the military contingent were seen to, complete with much laughter, slapping of backs, and effusions of delight and surprise as headquarters staff were not often granted home leave.

Louisa was forthwith escorted to her aunt's by Captain Heath while the others saw the assorted mounts safe to their respective stables.

Neither Heath nor Gracechurch was in regimentals—a puzzling detail which had not at first struck Louisa in the confusion. War-time regulations stipulated that all military be uniformed, whether on leave or active duty. Now, with a moment to consider less dramatic matters than an overset fribble and a young lady whose faints at first seemed to come and go to suit her convenience, then quite suddenly and inexplicably became genuine, Louisa's brows rose in surprise.

"Have you and your friend sold out, then?" she inquired after commenting on his and Gracechurch's severely cut but definitely nonmilitary garb as they rode slowly through the busy morning streets, picking their way between carriages, hawkers pushing barrows, drayer's carts, and pedestrians.

Heath's face grew blank as he stiffened in the saddle. Then he threw Louisa a smile at once rueful and self-deprecatory, eyes twinkling.

"Nothing left," he informed her. "We've permission to go about like this for a time. Not something one talks about in the general way, especially to a lady, but since you ask—and I *should* have realized any sister of Harry's would be conversant with regulations, and—well—ah— what little we'd got left that was vaguely presentable was on our backs when we arrived in England, and even that was disreputably tattered and verminous. My batman burned it all soon as we landed—ours, Fotheringham's, everything," he explained glibly. "Won't go into details, but Stephen and I were cowering in a sodden hedgerow garbed as nature intended—which was demmed unpleasant, let me tell you, nature not being all it's cracked up to be—because no self-respecting innkeeper would let us past the door in our lively condition. Private Crawley's a good forager—first requirement for a Peninsular batman—and he procured us some lye soap and some rather rough togs to last until we reached civilization. We're in Scott's hands now, but we're only a pair of lowly captains, you know—" He shrugged. "He'll get round to us eventually. There's time enough . . ." he concluded his involved and rather lengthy explanation.

"But, poor Lieutenant Fotheringham! Surely, in his condition—"

"Farm wife took pity on him," Heath interjected quickly. "Not us, though. Demmed uncomfortable situation, I can tell you."

When they reached Lady Daphne's elegant little town house, Heath refused Louisa's repeated invitations to meet her aunt, and join them in a nuncheon which she was certain could be stretched to feed three more than adequately, as enough for six was invariably presented them. The dashing young captain was profuse in his apologies and regrets, but firm on the fact that while he would have liked nothing better, he had made arrangements to join the others at White's. Should he not appear, they would wait for him and eventually become concerned. And, he had smiled, she must understand—they had much to discuss, coming upon one another unexpectedly so far from Spain.

He assisted her in dismounting, turned Commendatore over to the patiently-waiting Ben Cullom, and tipped his hat, vanishing from Louisa's ken with a smile and a promise that he would call soon.

Harry, while the others were lightheartedly seeing to the aftermath, waited anxiously at Fortescue House until the physician sonorously pronounced the victims of that morning's debacle safely on the road to recovery—if every care were taken of the gentle girl, with no upsets to startle her into a brain fever, and the gentleman concerned would but wear less form-fitting unmentionables and confine himself to a soft cushion for a few days. Harry then took himself off to Lady Daphne's, intent on forcing the issue of Louisa's habit, the flirtations she appeared to have set up with both Gracechurch and Heath on barely a few minutes' acquaintance, her conversing longer than was proper with a strange groom no matter what the circumstances, as well as her inappropriate and unnecessary gallop through Hyde Park when she was the sole cause of the series of mishaps to begin with, given she had not properly kept pace with him when he joined Gwendolyn Fortescue and Norval Quarmayne. Harry's list of her indiscretions for the one morning was bitterly long.

He had every intention of hinting to Quentin Heath and Stephen Gracechurch—whom he fully expected to find ensconced in his aunt's drawing room—that they were least wanted, and had best make their departure so he could get down to cases with Louisa. If need be, he planned to take them aside, and inform them Louisa was about to become betrothed to a wealthy Yorkshire widower with a hopeful family—this invention on the advice of Lady Fortescue.

"*That* will put a stop to *all* undesirable attentions," Gwendolyn's redoubtable mother had explained, the image of efficiency and determination, while they awaited the physician's verdict. "You must understand, my dear Lord Beckenham—should your sister form a connection of which we cannot approve, it will be as if she had not wed at all. There are standards to be maintained!"

With this stricture Harry firmly agreed.

Gracechurch and Heath—and the rest of his friends— might be well enough in themselves, and the best of companions for a soldier in Spain or a bachelor on the town, but as connections for the peerless Gwendolyn, they clearly would not do. The disgusting incident with Dickie Fotheringham, of which Lady Fortescue had informed him in strictest confidence when he explained that mention of the cur's name and injuries were what appeared to have overset Gwendolyn, was proof enough of that.

The damnable lecher!—Harry raged as he summoned

a hackney. Forcing himself on an unsuspecting and innocent girl in the most horribly debauched fashion, coming close to compromising her, and this while Harry was in Spain risking his life for King and Country! No wonder his poor darling had fainted dead away. Subject her to potential contact with such a rakehellish care-for-nobody by selfishly maintaining his military friendships? Not likely! A small price to pay to assure Gwendolyn's security and peace of mind. No real sacrifice, when he came down to it. Indeed, if Fotheringham were not already flat on his back from wounds received in battle, Harry would have felt forced to call him out—even at this late date, and no matter what the difference in their ages and experience. Unfortunately, the Frogs had done the job for him . . .

As it was, he intended a few choice words with Heath and Gracechurch concerning their taste in boon companions and protégés. Not that he could explain his reasons as clearly as he would have liked, for Gwendolyn's name must remain unsullied, which did pose a few problems in plain speaking.

Perhaps, for her sake, the best solution would be to give Fotheringham the cut direct the moment he showed his callow, filthy face, and Gracechurch and Heath as well, without reasons or explanations. He owed them nothing—nothing! The thought of Gwendolyn being mauled by the jug-bitten, randy young lout made Harry's blood boil. And *this* was the type of man Aunt Daffy considered suitable for Louisa? No wonder Gwendolyn had cautioned him about his aunt's reputation among the ton! A procuress, that was all she was—nothing but an abbess in disguise. As for the criticism of his intimacy with former fellow-officers, that made perfect sense once he learned of Fotheringham's assault. His poor darling couldn't bear the sight of a red coat after her terrible experience, and no wonder!

He would get Louisa out of there now, *today*, and under

the Fortescue roof where she would be safe from such insults as Gwendolyn had endured! And, get the stubborn girl married off, the sooner the better, no matter to whom. And, marry Gwendolyn out of hand so he could protect her from all the evils the world held. He might have only one arm, but he would manage somehow . . .

By the time he arrived at his aunt's, Harry was in fine fighting trim. Unfortunately, Hoskins informed him, the ladies were out paying calls, and had left no word as to their anticipated hour of return. And, no, none of the military gentlemen were with them. Harry fumed on the stoop, stymied.

"Can't you keep a better eye on them than that?" he finally snarled at the startled butler. "You're no better than they are!" He whirled, but the hackney had already departed. "Get me a damn carriage, and hurry up about it!" he spat, stormed past the stunned old man to throw himself in one of the reception area chairs, legs thrust in front of him, hand crammed deep in his pocket, chin on chest, stump throbbing.

By the time Hoskins had summoned a footman and the footman had summoned a hackney a half hour had passed, and Harry's mind was made up.

It was imperative that he go to Marleybourne soon— urgent letters from steward and bailiff detailing depredations of poachers, slates off the roof which had the marks of vandalism, and a flooded field and burned barn on the home farm all demanded his personal attention. He would go now, today, this minute. He would see the damnable business taken care of—What were stewards and bailiffs paid for, anyway, except to see to just such things without inconveniencing their employers!—and return to town as fast as he could, and then the fur would fly. He'd settle with Fotheringham, wound or no, and Gracechurch and Heath and all the rest of them. He'd take Louisa in hand, beat her into submission if he had to, but she would select from among Lady Fortescue's candidates, be married by special license within days of his return. A man still had some rights!

And Gwendolyn?

His face softened. Obviously, if Fotheringham had been given the opportunity to accost her as he had, her parents were not to be trusted to guard her from harm. He would brook no opposition there, either. He'd get *two* special licenses while he was about it. Gwendolyn and he would follow Louisa in front of the padre, and it would be over and done with. And, high time . . . He'd waited three long years. Being forced to wait even one day longer to make her his wife was intolerable. Lord and Lady Fortescue, Louisa, Aunt Daphne, even Gwendolyn, were all totally unreasonable and insensitive. It was up to him to put them in their places, and he would do it—just see if he wouldn't!

"I want paper, pen, and ink," he snapped when Hoskins informed him a hackney was at the steps. "Pay the fellow off, or give him something to wait—I don't care which."

The much-tried Hoskins saw to the pen, ink, and several sheets of Lady Daphne's heavy, patchouli-scented paper, while the upper footman guarded the door and the under footman commiserated with the jarvey over the fits and starts of the ton, sweetening his sympathy with a pint of ale and several coins.

Harry complained about the frivolously scented paper, its feminine color, the excess of light in the morning parlor, the lack of a fire, and then settled down to business, scowling. Of the essential note to Lady Fortescue he made quick work—he had been unavoidably called to Marleybourne, would be gone upward of a week, and insisted on being granted a private interview with Lord Fortescue upon his return, at which time certain matters would be discussed in their entirety and accommodations reached. With every wish for Gwendolyn's speedy recovery, he remained, and *et cetera*.

Then, clenching his jaw, he scrawled rapidly across the next sheet:

Madam—

I am regrettably called to Marleybourne, and shall be forced to absent myself from London for a period not to exceed a fortnight. During my absence, you will oblige me by remaining within the confines of your home. Neither you nor my sister are to attend any social functions whatsoever, nor receive any guests beyond Lady Fortescue and her daughters.

In the event, it has devolved that you are lamentably lacking in that good sense and judgment required to guide my sister, and are totally unsuited to act as her chaperon and sponsor among the ton. That you follow my instructions is mandatory to safeguard her welfare and good name. Your influence is not only detrimental to both, but conducive to friction between my sister and myself, for which reasons I shall be removing her from your household immediately upon my return and placing her in the care of persons more suited to the trust which you have so basely abused. These are not requests, but orders which I issue as Head of the Family, and with which I expect you to comply without protests or attempts to justify that which can never be justified.

Please understand that I hold you responsible not only for my own lamentable situation, but for those unfortunate traits of character in my sister which you have fostered against all customary concepts and accepted standards of decorum and female propriety. Your libertine propensities and lack of good judgment have rendered a once sweet and innocent girl little better than a harlot—in dress, in manner, and in choice of companions. Until such time as you have remedied those traits of character and personal habits which render you an unfit influence on—and companion for—my sister, all contact between you shall be severed.

Henry Beckenham, Viscount Marleybourne

That put it plainly enough, he decided after reviewing what he had written. There could be no doubt as to the issues involved, his understanding of them, or his determination that Louisa should suffer no more from their aunt's pernicious influence than she already had. That things had come to such a pass was damnable, but then so was the schism their aunt had fostered between them. As for the Cyprian into which their aunt seemed determined to transform Louisa—

He grunted, seized another sheet of paper. His aunt disposed of, it was time to turn his attention to his sister—a far easier task, and far less unpalatable, as he knew his strictures would be rescuing her from a situation which she did not herself understand.

It was quickly done: She was to have absolutely no contact with his former military associates, of whose perfidy to the last man there could no longer be any doubt; nor was she to so much as step beyond their aunt's door during his absence—not to ride in the Park, not to attend social gatherings, not to gad about shopping (The inexcusable expenses of her entirely unsuitable wardrobe were to stop on the instant! Such frivolous and wordly garments were not fitting for a woman of her age and station, and would be discarded and more suitable toggery procured upon his return. Any items awaiting delivery were to be countermanded immediately. Her fortune was not hers to fritter away as if it belonged to her personally. It was rather the property of her future husband. As such, she had no right to squander it, since she merely held it in trust for him. Indeed, her current actions were little more than those of a common thief, and if there were any justice in the world, would be subject to prosecution in a court of law.); nor was she to have contact with any individual, in person or in writing, beyond Lady Fortescue and Gwendolyn and those they might introduce to her notice—all this on pain of his displeasure as Head of the Family. She was, moreover, to prepare herself for instant removal to Fortescue House on the day of his return, and to hold herself ready to make a selection of spouse immediately thereafter, with nuptials by special license to follow within a matter of days.

Well satisfied with these three epistles, he left two propped on the parlor mantel, gave the third to Hoskins, instructing that it be delivered immediately to Fortescue House, and made his departure.

"Whatever can he be thinking of?" Louisa gasped when she read the tender effusion on returning home. "He's all about in his head!"

Lady Daphne started to crumple her letter as she turned toward the fireplace, thought better of the matter and smoothed it carefully. Poor boy . . . but *now* was not the time for heart burnings or pity.

"Let me see yours," she said curtly, proceeded to compare the two. Then she folded them, went to the small, deceptively fragile-looking desk between the windows, and locked the letters away in its single drawer, a thoughtful expression on her face.

Her eyes flicked around the parlor, coming to rest on the mantel. "We never received those," she said. "If it is necessary, we shall say they were misplaced amid a jumble of invitations, and were only discovered the very day they are mentioned. You understand, Louisa? We shall otherwise ignore their existence."

Louisa sank down on the small settee across from the fireplace, staring at her aunt.

"I didn't see yours," she said, voice hollow, "but I know what mine was like, and from the look on your face, yours was not much better."

"Better?" Her aunt gave a harsh laugh. "No, it wasn't better."

"What *is* the matter with Harry?"

" 'Love,' " Lady Daphne retorted, "along with a virulent attack of self-consequence and Fortescue-*itis*." She crossed to the door, opened it. "Hoskins?" she called, "Come here, if you please."

The elderly butler followed her into the parlor, closing the door behind him, reluctance writ large on his sober features. Lady Daphne turned to him, examining his face carefully, an expectant look in her eyes.

"Well?" she said.

"I beg your pardon, my lady?"

"Come now, Hoskins! We have been together too many years for milk-and-water, so no roundaboutations, if you please! What happened here this morning after Louisa and I departed?"

"Master Ha—Lord Beckenham called," Hoskins admitted, clearly unsettled.

"I am well aware of that. *What happened?*"

Hoskins swallowed, looking anywhere but at his employer. "He was informed you were from home," he offered hesitantly.

"And then?"

"He requested a hackney."

"And *then?*"

Hoskins took a deep breath. "His lordship requested writing materials."

"With which you provided him. I am able to recognize my own paper," she said tartly. "I assume he proceeded to write some letters. How many?"

"I do not know, my lady."

"Of how many are you aware?"

"Three, my lady."

"The ones addressed to Miss Beckenham and myself account for two. To whom was the third directed?"

"To Lady Fortescue." The starch seemed to drain from Hoskins of a sudden, leaving him an old and troubled man. "Lord Beckenham instructed me to see to its delivery, and then departed."

"Thank you, Hoskins," Lady Daphne said gently. "I know this conversation is not what either you or I are accustomed to or can approve. Just one thing more: Should the matter arise, you noticed the letters the viscount left for his sister and me on the mantel had fallen over after his departure, their having been insecurely positioned. Fearing we would not see them, you placed them with a stack of invitations on my desk, knowing it is my custom to review the post and any messages placed there upon returning home." She paused a moment, eyes boring into Hoskins', nodded. *"Was* the letter delivered to Fortescue House?"

"Naturally, my lady. Matthew was dispatched immediately," Hoskins said more firmly, drawing himself up to his full dignity.

"Too bad. I would have given a deal to know what it said." Lady Daphne smiled, her face softening. "Thank you for assisting the viscount in my absence. And, Hoskins—my thanks also, to you and the rest of the staff, for any forbearance which was required during Lord Beckenham's visit."

"That is not necessary, my lady."

"Perhaps, and perhaps not. Relay the message all the same." There was sympathy and understanding in her eyes as she studied the old man. "One thing more—I returned this afternoon suffering from an atrocious *migraine,* and so never reviewed the items on my desk. I am sure you will corroborate my unfortunate and painful indisposition, should anyone inquire. That will be all, Hoskins, except that my niece and I could do with some tea."

Hoskins bowed, equanimity partially restored, and departed. Lady Daphne removed hat and pelisse, placed them on a chair by the windows, then stood staring abstractedly at the desk as her niece sat shivering by the small fire.

"Has Harry ever before been subject to wild fits of temper?" she inquired at last. "I have not been much in his company since he came down from Harrow."

"Rarely," Louisa responded after a moment's thought, "and when he *has* been infuriated, it has generally been with good cause."

"Until now . . . I wondered, for those are the letters of a dangerously angry, irrational, and desperate man."

Louisa shivered from a cold unrelated to the warm, sunny day. "I know," she said, "and an unhappy and confused one as well. I am thankful he is not now in London."

"As am I," Lady Daphne sighed. "Customarily even-tempered, like his father, you would say then?"

"Excepting the usual flights when he was thwarted in some project he held dear, yes, and those were long ago when he was little more than a boy."

"But, the *man* is a reasonable one?"

"Always," Louisa agreed, "until now, and invariably sensitive to the feelings and wishes of others, often placing them above his own convenience and desires."

Lady Daphne turned from the desk and took a chair opposite Louisa, a slight frown marring her aristocratic features. She remained there, staring at the embers of the fire that had been lit for Harry until Hoskins returned with the tea. She indicated he was to place the tray on a table between Louisa and herself, waited for him to depart with the under footman, then looked piercingly at her niece.

"I want you to tell me what transpired from the moment you left with Harry this morning until you arrived home," she said, deliberately lifting the heavy silver pot. "Everything. Every word, every gesture, every look as you observed them. Leave nothing out, no matter how seemingly insignificant. I am already aware," she said wryly, "that Harriet Fortescue holds me in no very high esteem, so you need not fear shocking or surprising me."

Only the sudden reappearance of James Morrison diverted her momentarily from her single-minded inquisition, and then she only raised her brows, asked two apparently inconsequential questions and appeared satisfied. That the superior groom had cautioned Louisa against the diamond she found interesting, but little more, declaring tartly, "The lower orders often know more of what transpires among the ton than Sally Jersey herself." Louisa did not trouble to inform her aunt of his other, more personal comments, feeling these were of too private a nature, and too susceptible to misinterpretation, for casual recounting. Indeed, she was not certain how she felt about them—or him—herself.

Louisa's sketch of Norval Quarmayne had Lady Daphne chuckling. Of the gallop across the Park she said only that she was certain the wild career had done both horse and rider a deal of good. Her interest peaked when Captains Gracechurch and Heath made their appearance, and that not in military garb. "Headquarters, you say? Arthur Wellesley's own staff? And here on leave at such a time, escorting a wounded boy of no particular distinction? Interesting." But, she would not comment further, beyond indicating they had probably been assigned to courier duty. Louisa completed her recital with a description of Gwendolyn's second faint, the arrival of the hackney, and Harry's departure with the wounded.

After some consideration, Lady Daphne decided it would be proper for them to send a note of cheer and a basket of fruit and restorative jellies to young Fotheringham, as he was a friend of Harry's and—she believed—the son of a lady who had made her come-out the same year she herself had. She instructed Louisa to send a note to Colonel Winthrop's lodgings, begging the boy's direction or, should he not have it to hand, the direction of Captains Heath and Gracechurch, who were sure to. Then, satisfied with that day's work, she turned the conversation to the rout they were to attend that evening, and which gown would at once show Louisa to best advantage and withstand the inevitable crush most successfully.

No response arrived from Colonel Winthrop that day or the next—most unusual in a man of such punctilious courtesy, Lady Daphne grumbled. The rout on the night of the eventful day Harry departed for Marleybourne was every bit the sad crush Lady Daphne had anticipated, but of those she was most interested in encountering—Lady Fortescue, Gwendolyn, and Harry's military friends— there was no sign. She passed her time among the other dowagers, first watching the dancing and then in the card room, gently steering the conversation to the exquisite Fortescue diamond. No one knew the reason for her absence. All lamented it as rendering the occasion somewhat flat. As for Louisa, her bevy of admirers pursued her unrelentingly, Donclennon, per usual, treading on her feet, tearing her gown, mangling her fan, and spilling punch on her shawl. The self-important Peter Sackett's rescue was timely, and almost welcome despite his unpleasant breath, roving eyes, and damp hands.

The next morning the customary flowers—forget-me-nots, this time, framed by deep green leaves and haloed by delicate ferns—arrived bound by their customary silk stocking, but with an additional pair of gifts: a riding crop and a curb bit. Louisa swore softly, then colored as she remembered Morrison's sallies regarding teasing. She would, she decided, be best served by ignoring what was clearly intended to annoy—and him, if ever she saw the pernicious, encroaching—

But, she admitted to herself, she had been remiss in not

protesting the flowers at the outset of their recent encounter. His income could not be great, and he was wasting what little blunt he had on them, and now on what was an exquisite and clearly very costly crop, its handle inlaid with nacre and silver. This had to stop. A little economy on his part, and he would be able to afford a new coat, perhaps even a man to see to his needs. She dreaded to think where he might be living—over a stable somewhere, probably, or in cheap lodgings in the worst part of town. The flowers, under such circumstances, were inexcusable. She would, she decided, bring him to a proper sense of his best interests the next time she saw him. Time enough to cut him if he refused to heed her wise counsels. She instructed Hoskins to have the flowers placed by her bed, the crop with her riding habits, and the bit sent round to where Harry was stabling his cattle.

That day passed in peaceable fashion, with the usual flood of dutiful morning callers consisting of Louisa's partners of the previous evening, some shopping, and an evening at the theater organized by pompous, tippling Lord Peter Sackett, of whom Lady Daphne had high hopes for Louisa. Certainly his attentions were becoming particular, if always in keeping with the best of taste and never overstepping that invisible boundary beyond which a man was forced to declare himself or be considered beneath contempt. The girl could do worse should her inclinations tend toward him, and he wanted only a little encouragement to bring him along nicely. It would be a pleasant triumph to have Louisa betrothed prior to Harry's return from the country, and certainly Sackett was preferable to Donclennon or any of the Fortescue tribe . . . Kean was in fine form, the farce following the tragedy witty and amusing—if a trifle warm. Taken all in all, a satisfactory day—except for one factor: Nowhere, at any time, had Lady Daphne caught sight of Harry's military friends, or of any of the company from Fortescue House.

Still, there had been news. A visitor to Sackett's box during one of the intervals imparted the information that the diamond was rumored to be seriously indisposed, and likely to remain so for the rest of the season. There was much coming and going between Harley Street and Fortescue House, and straw had been laid on the cobbles to deaden the sound of passing carriages. Iniquitous it might be to be actively pleased by such an eventuality, Lady Daphne admitted to herself, so she would only concede to not being actively displeased . . .

The next morning she sent off a second note to Colonel Winthrop, requesting the direction of Captains Heath and Gracechurch, then left Louisa laughing over her latest flowers—an unusual arrangement of snapdragons, thistles, and sprigs of bramble—in the breakfast parlor. She was about to ascend the stairs when a sharp rap at the street door made her pause in puzzlement and glance down to the ground level. It was an unusual hour for a morning caller, though not unheard of. She nodded to Charles, on guard by the door, saying they were at home to visitors—especially any of Lord Beckenham's military friends.

Giles Fortescue jittered on the stoop, stuffed into a wasp-waisted lilac coat, unmentionables of palest primrose and gleaming purple-tasseled yellow Hessians, his shirt points soaring well above his rosy cheeks, his neckcloth a desperate attempt at the *Trône d'Amour,* and a lavender high-crowned beaver perched at a daring angle on his gleaming ginger locks—a veritable Pink of the Ton. He clutched a cauliflowerlike posy so tightly compacted that neither air nor water could have penetrated its dense fastness.

"Well!" Lady Daphne exclaimed under her breath. "Will marvels never cease?" Then she smiled, came down, extending her hand graciously as Charles struggled to relieve the boy of his gloves, hat, and cane. "Mr. Fortescue—how delightful to see you!"

Giles juggled uncertainly with posy and gloves, attempting at the same time to bow over Lady Daphne's hand, instead plunging his head into the flowers and thrusting gloves and cane at her rather than the harried footman.

"Coffee, I think, in the drawing room," she said, throwing a significant look at Charles while giving Giles a chance to regain his equilibrium, "and perhaps some Madeira and biscuits as well. And be so good as to inform Miss Beckenham we have a caller, and I expect her to join us as soon as may be."

Charles, once more the perfect picture of an impassive servant, finally succeeded in capturing the impedimenta of the Honorable Giles, and Lady Daphne herself led the flushing and stammering youth up the stairs, past the breakfast parlor, and into the more formal drawing room they used for callers of ceremony rather than intimate friends.

She ushered the boy in, indicated a seat opposite her, and gracefully sank into a low Queen Anne chair, fanning her skirts and settling her flounces.

"Been meaning to call before," Giles mumbled as he perched uneasily on the delicate Chippendale side chair after carefully disposing the tails of his coat, "but m'mother's been keeping me rather on the hop, don't you know."

"Indeed, I can understand her desiring the escort of such a handsome son," Lady Daphne twinkled.

"Don't know about that. Ain't it, anyway. Has me running hither an' yon 'til I don't know where I'm at," the boy explained. "If it's not one fool thing, it's another."

"How fortunate you can assist her, and how charming in you to come to us when you were able. Has not the recent weather been delightful after all our rain?" she said, smiling encouragement. If this was not the first morning call the boy had paid lacking the eye of censorious maternal vigilance to show him the way, it was very close to it, Lady Daphne decided. Well, best make things as easy as possible for the lad, since Harry had taken him in such liking. They all had to start somewhere. "The flowers are positively bursting into bloom in my garden," she suggested.

"The weather has indeed been clement," Giles proffered after a moment's indecision as to what to do with the clotted posy he still clutched as a man will a spar from a sinking ship, finally depositing it on the floor beside him and clearing his throat vigorously. "I understand the experts say we shall have no more rain."

"Yes, and the cold is quite fled—only a slight chill to the air requiring small fires in the grates morning and evening. The season is in full career at last."

"Fires are very pleasant and cheerful," Giles returned, still struggling. "I have read that the aborigines consider them an inducement to socialization, as well as of worth for the warmth and light they afford. Indeed, in many ancient religions, there are gods of fire and light, proving—ah—proving—"

"That the sun, and its dependent fires, have always been of greatest importance to mankind," Lady Daphne kindly finished for him. "You no doubt refer to Prometheus, Azhur-Mazda, and the rest. How very acute of you to recall such a thing." Her eyes sparkled mischievously. "How *very* smart you are. Such a lovely shade of lilac!"

"D'you think so?" He examined his coat doubtfully, as if seeing it for the first time. "Wasn't certain, you see. Rather different from m'father's general style, or Lord Beckenham's, come to that. Wasn't quite sure, but the

man at Nugee's said—That is, m'mother usually—But
they are so occupied at home that I didn't like to—"

"And how is your poor sister after the sad upset of the
other day?" Lady Daphne interposed smoothly.

"Gwennie? A lot of fuss and feathers over nothing, *I*
think! Won't come out of her room, cries all the time.
Haven't seen the watering pot m'self, you understand.
Ain't permitted to. No visitors allowed—not *any!* Beyond
m'mother, that is, and some Harley Street quack she's
called in. Not even Soph and Belle. Puts their noses out
of joint, I can tell you." He coughed nervously, not certain
he should have said so much. "Wanted to say what an
out-and-outer I thought Miss Beckenham was—going
after Cousin Norval's nag like that—no matter what anyone says. Too courageous by half!"

"How kind in you to say so," Lady Daphne returned.
"Certainly there was some danger to pedestrians, and so
my niece acted without regard to the proprieties."

"Miss Beckenham could never do anything improper!"
Giles protested. "She would render any act in the best of
taste just by performing it."

Goodness! Lady Daphne sighed resignedly—he *did*
have a case. Well, the hotter the fire, the sooner it would
burn itself out.

"We heard only yesterday evening of your sister's unfortunate indisposition, and intended to call later today to
offer our best wishes for her speedy recovery," she lied
baldly. "I take it such a call would not be welcome at this
delicate juncture?"

"Doubt it," Giles said, shedding his formal tone as he
would an uncomfortable coat. "M'mother's at sixes and
sevens, and the entire household's in an upset. Meals're
late—if you get 'em at all—and burnt half the time. M'father's threatening to remove to one of his clubs until the
fracas is over an' Gwennie comes to her senses. Hysterical

flights ain't much in his line, or mine either, come to that!"

"Oh, dear—as serious as that?" Lady Daphne returned blandly. "Perhaps a note and some flowers sent round by a footman would be in better keeping with the distress you are all suffering."

"Ain't suffering at all—not in the usual way," Giles said without thinking. "Gwennie's throwing tantrums, m'mother's mad as a hornet, m'father's not much better, and the girls're in the sulks—that's all. Thought I'd play least-in-sight for a bit. Don't like having 'em pick at me just because I'm ready to hand. Bad enough when there's a reason for it, but I ain't involved in this!"

"How distressed Lord Beckenham will be when he learns he was called out of town just when Miss Fortescue most needed his support," Lady Daphne essayed.

"Don't believe they'd let him near her," Giles objected, shaking his head. "Been screaming she never wants to— Never mind that!" he cut off nervously. "Never said it!"

"I have forgot it already," Lady Daphne purred.

Louisa appeared, followed by Hoskins, Matthew, and one of the upstairs maids bearing trays of refreshments. Giles leapt to his feet, almost knocking over his chair as he grabbed the cauliflower posy and thrust it at Louisa while babbling his disjointed greetings. Louisa maintained her gravity, accepting the flowers and his awkward salute to her hand with praiseworthy sangfroid, and requested Hoskins to see the flowers placed in water and returned to the drawing room.

Giles was provided with Madeira and a plate of biscuits placed at his elbow. Lady Daphne and Louisa accepted coffee as a matter of form, and the servants departed.

Giles sipped too nervously and quickly at his wine, made crumbs of the biscuits schoolboy-style, and struggled to follow the conversational ball wherever the ladies sent it flying while constantly referring to his pocket watch to ensure he did not overstay his prescribed fifteen minutes. Punctilious to the dot, he jumped to his feet at the correct instant with obvious relief, rather distractedly begging Louisa to go driving with him in the Park the next afternoon as he made his adieux. Louisa, remembering only too well the accident to Harry's chaise, began to demur when Lady Daphne interrupted to say Louisa would be delighted, and herself arranged the exact hour at which he would call for her niece. Hoskins appeared to usher him out, the door closed behind them, and Lady Daphne helped herself to a celebratory glass of Madeira, very well satisfied with how the day had begun.

"Will you have me accused of robbing the cradle?" Louisa exploded as she watched her aunt. "*That* is the noddy who ran into Harry's chaise! What's more, I shall look a complete fool in his company—*if* I survive the experience!"

"Just think how little Lady Fortescue will like it, should it come to her ears," Lady Daphne said smugly.

"I care nothing for what Lady Fortescue thinks—good *or* bad!"

"How very short-sighted of you. Come now—just when things begin to be interesting, you climb on your high ropes. *Not* wise, not politic, not *intelligent.* They're in a rare mess at Fortescue House, if I understand the lad correctly. You will drive out with him tomorrow, and you will garner the latest information as to how they go on. I shall tell you *exactly* what to ask, and how to ask it. A shame to impose on him in such a manner, but there you have it—it's Harry, or the lad, and with *me* Harry comes first! You *do* want to help your poor benighted brother, do you not?"

At that Louisa subsided, sinking into her chair. "What ever are you up to?" she asked.

"Nothing that need concern you at the moment. Primarily, keeping my finger on the pulse of matters—or, at least *attempting* it. You can be very useful, if you are willing, or you can leave it to me to render Harry what assistance I can without you. Those are your only choices. If you want to help Harry, you drive out with young Giles—tomorrow, the next day, and every time he invites you."

"That *puppy!*"

"Have your eyes on a man, do you? No—don't answer that! Puppy the boy may be, and a graceless scamp into the bargain, but there isn't a mean bone in him, which is more than I can say for the rest of his tribe. I suspect he's in a fair way to idolizing Harry. Talk to him about your brother, if the weather gets heavy. Besides, he'll tire of you soon enough. I just hope you maintain his interest long enough."

"Long enough for *what?*" Louisa demanded, exasperated by her aunt's cryptic pronouncements.

"Long enough for *me,*" Lady Daphne returned, offering no more insight into her thinking and plans than before.

Eight

They abandoned the drawing room for the cozier confines of the little parlor, Lady Daphne to take up her stitchery and Louisa—after a few futile minutes of wishing Harry had not whisked Ben Cullum off to Marleybourne with him, thus leaving her without a groom to play propriety should she wish to indulge in solitary excursions with Commendatore—to pursue humor and romance between the covers of a witty and irreverent just-released confection titled *Pride and Prejudice* which she had acquired at Hatchard's. Families, she chuckled to herself as she delightedly sped into the eleventh chapter, could be the very devil—sisters as much as brothers, if Misses Mary and Kitty were anything to go by . . . As for the good Mrs. Bennet and her machinations, she and Aunt Daphne were sisters under the skin, however much more subtle might be her own dear aunt's ploys.

Silence stretched between them, more or less comfortable in its nature, though Louisa repeatedly lifted her head to glance in puzzlement at her aunt, even Mr. Darcy's hauteur and Mr. Bingley's charm failing to entirely capture her attention. Lady Daphne met these unspoken inquiries with a bland, innocent smile when she noticed them. Mostly she managed to keep her silvered head, crowned by a delicate passementerie cap, bent industriously over her tambour frame, the perfect picture of a lady of the ton engaged, with mind unencumbered by such uncomfortable baggage as the ton might not approve, in a pastime of which the ton highly approved. That the pose was not indicative of the true state of affairs Louisa had not the slightest doubt, but if irritated demands for explanations had not served in the drawing room, petulant pleas would not serve here.

They had not been thus engaged above half an hour when Hoskins appeared at the door, eyes questioning.

"Major Lord Fenton, Captain Heath, and Captain Gracechurch are below, my lady," he informed them. "You instructed Charles—"

"Good heavens," Lady Daphne smiled. "If *this* keeps up, we shall have *nowhere* to put more flowers! Show them up, of course. We'll receive them here—no need for the drawing room."

Louisa set her book aside, wondering if being accompanied on a ride through the Park by *three* gentlemen would constitute proper chaperonage, and decided reluctantly it would not. Why the great difference between horseback and an open carriage she would never understand. Of course, with a carriage there was generally the gentleman's groom or tiger in attendance, and that did constitute chaperonage of a sort . . . What a bother! She rose as the officers entered, a smile of delight on her face.

"Thank you all again for your assistance in the Park!" she said, beaming. "Which of you to greet first is the only question. I suppose it must be done by strict precedence of rank—such a bore among friends!"

Compliments were exchanged, introductions made, Lady Daphne and Louisa put in possession of bouquets of spring flowers; wine, tea, and biscuits were ordered, and the company disposed itself about the sun-filled room, Captain Gracechurch to sit near Lady Daphne, with Heath and Fenton flanking Louisa.

"And how is your nephew keeping himself?" Gracechurch inquired as soon as refreshments had been served
and the servants retired, leaning back in the comfortable
Queen Anne wing chair he had selected and smiling. "We
haven't seen him these last days and feared he might be
indisposed."

"Not a bit of it," Lady Daphne responded, needle
poised above her tapestry. "Harry was called to Marleybourne most unexpectedly on urgent business, but we
anticipate his return within a reasonable time."

"Marleybourne? Upon what pretext?" Fenton
frowned, clearly puzzled. "I cannot call to mind his mentioning any problems which required his presence."

"I haven't the slightest notion," Lady Daphne returned, brows rising at the improper question. "The 'lad'
is now a man, and does not keep me apprised of his
business. Tell me—how does your friend, Fotheringham,
go on? Louisa mentioned his unfortunate experience in
the Peninsula."

"As well as could be expected," Gracechurch replied,
setting aside his glass of Madeira. "I wonder what can
have called Harry out of town at this particular time? We
had counted on seeing something of him, and our stay is
cursed brief. Do you have any notion, Miss Beckenham?
Being until recently responsible for the running of the
estate, you must surely be *au courant* with affairs there, and
so able to at least venture a guess."

"Not now," Louisa replied, smile a trifle too bright.
"Since my coming to London, I have had no contact with
anyone at the Court."

"I do not take it kindly that you did not inform me of
the Fotheringham boy's direction, Captain Gracechurch," Lady Daphne threw in with a stern look. "I did
ask Colonel Winthrop to refer my inquiry to you, were he
not aware of the lad's whereabouts. I assume you must

have seen the colonel since the sad imbroglio in the Park with Miss Fortescue and her cousin?"

"Yes, I have seen him," Gracechurch replied shortly. "Did your nephew inform you of the exact date of his return, Lady Cheltenham?"

"Hardly! He would consider *that* beneath his dignity. It is for we poor females to sit and wait, with what patience we can muster, while the gentlemen disport themselves as they wish for as long as they wish. Did not Colonel Winthrop relay my request?"

"He did indeed. We have been distressingly busy in the interim. No disrespect was intended." Gracechurch smiled disarmingly, eyes traveling the delicate painted paper, the graceful furnishings which combined the best of the current and previous periods. "What a charming room you have here—the perfect setting for two such lovely ladies," he said, rose to examine a small watercolor of storm-tossed seas, mist obscuring the horizon, a shaft of light glowing through turbulent clouds to shatter in golden spangles on sullen waves. "A Turner! I suspected as much." He turned to Lady Daphne, remaining by the fireplace, from which vantage he could easily observe all the room's occupants. "You are to be highly commended. Not everyone is astute enough to recognize his worth. Was the decorating done at your direction, Lady Cheltenham?"

"Thank you—it was. It is eclectic, but then I am an eclectic person. How delightful that you recognize the artist! He is one of my favorites, though there is too much to him for many. One always likes to have one's treasures appreciated." She paused, smiled. "Isn't Fotheringham the Marquess of Breigh's heir? A charming lad, not much above twenty years, with curling black hair and ice-blue eyes and the smile of an angel?"

"I believe so," returned Gracechurch, glancing around the parlor. "Are these all family pieces, or—"

"Then I have known him since he was in short coats!" Lady Daphne interrupted, eyes sparkling. "Handsome fortune he'll come into one of these days, along with the title and estates. Not that the boy's exactly poverty-stricken, even now. Comfortable personal fortune from a great-uncle on the distaff side, as I recall."

Heath, who had been watching this exchange through narrowed eyes, turned to Louisa. "You find all this stuff about Fotheringham a dead bore, don't you." he said sympathetically. "Can't stand nattering about people I'm not acquainted with, either. Actually, we came to inquire whether you're attending Lady Stoking's masquerade to-morrow. I hope you are. I plan to go myself, and look to you to give me a pair of dances."

Louisa glanced at her aunt, coloring. The event had been the subject of numerous bitter altercations with Harry—surely nothing exceptional these days—Harry maintaining that such entertainments were grossly im-proper and conducive to licentious behavior, Lady Daphne that they were great fun for all concerned, and Muriel Stoking well up to skirting the proprieties without overstepping them.

"We depend on being there," Lady Daphne answered firmly.

"I'd appreciate a hint as to how you'll appear," Heath said with a plaintive smile. "Impossible to find you other-wise. Terrible crush it'll be, they say—event of the Sea-son."

"Let the cat out of the bag? I should say not!" Lady Daphne exclaimed with a laugh. "You'll have to take your chances along with the rest of the young bucks. Tell me, now you are here," she said, turning back to Grace-church, calmly maintaining his post at the fireplace, "what *is* Dickie Fotheringham's direction? I had thought to send him a note, along with such gifts as would be appropriate to an invalid, perhaps even call if he is up to a visit from an old lady."

"I am afraid I am unaware of his current whereabouts. You might apply to the Horse Guards, if you wish, or possibly the medical department."

Lady Daphne leaned back in her chair, looking at him steadily and maintaining an equally steady silence. Slowly he flushed.

"Will you let us know if you hear of your nephew's plans," he requested after an uncomfortable moment. "We *are* rather anxious to get in touch with him."

"Mentioned he was on the lookout for a hunter or two," Heath explained. "Fenton thinks he's found one as'll suit. Good price, too. Tell her, Percy."

"Ah . . . Magnificent bay," Major Fenton said quickly after an uneasy pause. "Gelding not unlike his Thunderer." Then, warming to his subject, "Strong in the field, superior fencer—always throws his heart over—and well up to Harry's weight."

"Wouldn't want him to miss out," Heath threw in.

"Perfect for the Quorn," Gracechurch added as the clincher.

Louisa's head spun, her eyes darting from one man to the next, a puzzled expression on her face. Lady Daphne watched both her and the men, more than amusement in her slight smile. She let the silence hang for a moment, as if to see what more they might find to say in explanation or encouragement.

Finally, taking pity on them and tiring of her own game, she exclaimed, "That *does* indeed sound to be the sort of mount Harry would appreciate—and would appreciate him! I shall, naturally, inform you if I hear of his plans, so that you in turn may inform him of this magnificent hunter as soon as possible."

"Thank you, Lady Cheltenham," Gracechurch returned, and smiled at the much confused Louisa. "And how is your Commendatore faring?" he asked. "Have you been able to take him out since your adventure in the Park?"

"No, unfortunately," Louisa replied ruefully, her face clearing. "Harry departed so suddenly for Marleybourne, taking old Ben Cullum with him, that no arrangements could be made for a substitute. As my aunt considers Harry's stableboys unequal to the task of keeping up with me, and her own as too well-along in years, I'm at point-non-plus. I only became aware of Commendatore's arrival the day we first met, you see. Harry had been otherwise occupied, and had not thought to inform me of his exceptional kindness in bringing my favorite mount to town."

"Must near kill you," Heath laughed.

"I am not best pleased," Louisa admitted.

"Perhaps something might be arranged by way of a groom of your own, at least on a temporary basis," Grace-church suggested.

"I should like nothing better, but Harry would not take it in very good part. He was distinctly put out when I hired an abigail without consulting him—though why a man should want to concern himself with ladies' maids leaves me mystified." Though not so very mystified as all that, she admitted to herself. Lady Fortescue, Harry had informed her in high dudgeon, had already seen to the matter for her, and would not take it kindly that her candidate had been rejected without so much as the courtesy of an interview. "A groom *is* a different matter, however, and there he would be justified in his displeasure should I act without his counsel," she added.

"So *many* things dependent on Harry's return," Lady Daphne threw in. "It might almost be best for someone to go to the Court and fetch him back."

"I hardly think that is necessary—only a groom, and a horse for him to ride, after all," Percy Fenton responded.

"But, what of the hunter?" Lady Daphne queried innocently.

"See to it ourselves, if we have to," Heath explained. "Harry's sure to want it."

"How kind in you! It would be a crime were he to miss out on acquiring such an ideal addition to his stable."

"My thought exactly! What friends're for," he smiled.

"Have you heard how Miss Fortescue does since the accident?" Fenton inquired courteously as he leaned forward, arms resting on thighs, clasped hands dangling between knees. "I have not seen her about town, and must admit to a degree of concern."

"You admire the beauty, too?" Lady Daphne asked. "Be on your guard, then. I doubt Harry would be pleased should you show too marked a preference in that direction."

"I am certain he would not. How does she do—have you heard?"

"The lady is currently indisposed, I believe."

"Nothing serious, I hope?"

"I doubt it. Apparently an exalted fit of the vapors. The incident was trying to her delicate sensibilities."

"Terrifying experience for a young girl," Heath agreed.

"And yet, from Louisa's account, it was news of young Fotheringham's injuries that did the most damage," Lady Daphne insisted, setting aside her tambour frame, eyes flying from one man to the other. "I was not aware they were even acquainted, let alone so well that such news would totally overset her. How did the poor boy come to be hit? His family must have been distracted with worry."

"No way to be certain," Gracechurch responded after a moment, deep in thought, then abandoned the fireplace to regain his seat by Lady Daphne. "We didn't come across him until he was in hospital, well back from the lines."

"Indeed? And immediately took him under your wing, I believe Louisa said?"

"He wanted assistance," Heath said flatly. "Couldn't leave the poor lad like that."

"Such is often the case, I have heard. So lamentable! Conditions are not of the best for our brave wounded, with never enough surgeons or medical supplies. The privations under which you are forced to suffer protecting us from That Monster while we sit comfortably at home making merry are shocking!"

"If only more people felt as you do," Stephen Grace-church smiled, "we would be in much better case. As it is, we survive quite well for the most part, in spite of the shifts we are put to." His eyes twinkled as he glanced at Heath and Fenton. "Remember Harry Smith's hares?"

"How could one forget," Fenton grinned. "But we ate, and he recovered."

Gracechurch turned to Louisa. "Some of the officers hunt hares from horseback," he explained, "if you can believe such a thing. Helps fill out the larder when times are lean and supplies fail to keep pace. Old Hookey won't have us raiding the countryside the way the French do, you see, though we're free to purchase what we can—if there is anything to be had, and we've the funds."

"More sporting than you'd think," Heath joined in. "Hares're demmed fast!"

"Are they indeed?" Louisa asked faintly. "Was my brother ever involved in such an *unusual* pastime?"

"Harry? He wasn't the time we're speaking of. Other times, yes. Harry likes to hunt, you know. Hares'll do when there's nothing better."

"How serious are poor Fotheringham's wounds?" Lady Daphne interrupted, exasperation coloring her voice. *"He* is of more account than *hares*, I should hope! At the very least, I should like to write to his mother expressing my concern, and I shouldn't care to make an unforgivable gaffe."

Silence stretched as the three men exchanged glances.

"Serious enough," Gracechurch admitted finally, "but he'll recover."

"I *am* so glad! It would be a terrible thing if he did not. A late-in-life child, you know, and so doubly precious. And, the only son . . . Is he perchance with his mother at Greytrees?"

Gracechurch looked at her blankly. Fenton and Heath shifted in their seats.

"You do not know, then? What a shame! I had *so* hoped you could give me his direction! Some more wine, gentlemen? Or, given the hour, perhaps you would prefer brandy. I know that was invariably my late husband's choice."

Gracechurch chuckled, and declined for them all.

Lady Daphne turned to Fenton. "I believe you were first on the scene when dear Harry was hit," she continued smoothly. "How speaking of poor Dickie brings it back to me! *Please* don't think me morbid, but I have *always* wondered exactly how Harry came to be wounded. We worried about him, of course, but he always seemed to lead such a *charmed* life, even as a boy! And then, that *dreadful* letter, telling us of his face and arm . . . It was not a *major* engagement, was it?"

"Salamanca? Depends on what you consider 'major.' Twasn't Agincourt, but twasn't a skirmish, either." Fenton smiled at Louisa. "I'm certain Miss Beckenham would rather not hear the details. Come—will you not give us at least a hint of your costume for tomorrow?"

Louisa laughed, disclaimed, refused, protested, and finally admitted as how royalty—of a sort—might figure in her plans.

"Disguises and masquerades are all very well," Lady Daphne interjected tartly, *"but how was Harry wounded?*

Come gentlemen—Louisa ain't *missish*, and neither am I, but Harry won't speak of it."

"Such incidents aren't pleasant to recall," Heath said, face serious "Possibly he doesn't remember much. My cousin never did. Confused time, don't you know?"

"I am not asking *Harry*, however"—Lady Daphne's voice remained sharp as her bright eyes bored into Heath—"so what he may or may not remember is not at issue. I am asking Major Fenton, who *was* there and, so far as I know, not suffering from fits of absentmindedness!"

"Most officers make it a policy never to speak of such things in the company of ladies," Gracechurch interposed smoothly. He hesitated as Lady Daphne looked expectantly from him to Fenton. Then he gave the barest of nods.

"Hostilities had more or less ceased," Fenton admitted. "The night was dark. Harry became separated temporarily from his companions. Probably an angry Frog with a last ball to spend in honor of *La Belle France*. Common enough occurrence, unfortunately."

"Enough of Harry," Gracechurch said firmly. "Your interest is perhaps natural, but the incident is over and done with."

"Is it?" Lady Daphne asked, looking at each man in turn.

"How could it not be? Your nephew is home in England, safe and well."

Shortly thereafter the three men took their leave, promising to let Louisa know if they came across a candidate for the position of groom of whom they thought her brother would approve, and swearing to uncover the secret of her identity on the morrow, no matter how many obstacles she threw in their way.

* * *

"Now, *that* was interesting," Lady Daphne said consideringly as their footsteps faded down the stairs.

"*Interesting?* Most of the time we all seemed to be talking at cross-purposes," Louisa complained irritably. "A more disjointed conversation I do not believe I have ever endured—at least among those who are supposedly rational. One would have thought we were all candidates for Bedlam."

"*Exactly!*" Lady Daphne returned with satisfaction. "It was all quite clumsily done, too, so they must be in a great hurry," but what she meant by that she refused to explain.

Instead, she sent Louisa in search of some colored wools she believed she had misplaced in her bedchamber, and then called for the upper footman to be sent to her. She looked him over when he arrived—a strapping man, as all footmen were supposed to be, with broad shoulders and fine calves, and a look of strength to him which she suspected was genuine. No dandified milksop, this one! Good . . . The eyes were intelligent, and the dignity was not something pasted on. It was inherent. That was good, too. The poor man was uneasy, and trying not to show it. No wonder. Employers rarely *looked* at their servants. They merely issued orders, and then only to those who appeared above stairs. Beyond Cook, she had not the slightest notion of the appearance of those who served in the kitchens—nor any need or desire to know.

"How long have you been in my service, Charles?" she asked after a moment.

"Nineteen years, my lady," he answered rigidly, certain dismissal for some fault, real or imagined, was in the offing.

She smiled. "Don't be distressed. Nothing is amiss. You have given me faithful service in that time, I know."

Charles remembered a certain Boxing Day, and a certain bottle of claret, and a flush crept over his lean, hard features, reddening his ears and nose as it pinked his cheeks in colorful contrast to his gray livery with its silver facings.

"Thank you, my lady," he strangled.

She nodded absently. "Now . . ." She hesitated, wondering how to phrase it without insulting him. "Now, I am in need of a very different kind of service. One of a special sort I suspect you are uniquely able to render me." Again she hesitated. "You were born in London, were you not, within sound of the Bow Bells?"

He swallowed hard, nodded.

"Come, man—it's nothing to be ashamed of! None of us can control the conditions of our birth. The essential is to make the most of the hand one is dealt. You've done very well for yourself."

He nodded, more ill at ease than ever. Whatever the old tabby wanted—and a liberal employer she had been—he hoped it was not something too out of the common way. A refusal might mean the door—and without a character. At his age, he couldn't afford that.

"Tell me," she continued, "have you maintained any of your childhood friendships?"

"Yes, m'lady, I 'as," he admitted grudgingly, shaken.

"Good!" She smiled conspiratorially. "I want you to find me a man you trust completely. Small, nondescript, able to vanish in a crowd—even when there isn't a crowd at hand. You understand the sort I mean?"

The old gentry-mort was known for fits and starts, but she was also known to have a good head on her—not like some as he'd heard mentioned. He nodded.

"Bring him to see me. If he is the type of individual I seek I will pay you five pounds, and him another five just for coming to speak with me. If we reach an accommodation, there will be an additional ten pounds in it for each of you."

Charles' eyes boggled. Five pounds was standard wages for a year.

"It is nothing underhanded, believe me—or, at least, not *very*. Illegal it most definitely is not. Of that you may both rest assured. I am not about to take to the High Toby, or any such, at *my* age. Newgate is *not* my idea of a comfortable residence."

"No, Mum," he muttered, completely undone.

"And do not speak of this to *anyone*—is that clear? Not to Hoskins, not to my niece, not to any of your friends among the great houses, or in the less affluent parts of town. I am paying for *silence* as well as service, and I believe you will admit I am paying most generously."

She did not permit herself to grin until he had closed the door behind him, a much puzzled and distressed footman. Now she felt as if her face would crack. Harry, marry the Fortescue diamond? Not likely! Not while she had breath in her body. He might curse his dear old aunt for a time, but he would bless her in the end if what she suspected were true.

As for Louisa, well, she would see . . . The possibilities were beginning to multiply. Definitely a *most* interesting season, unlike those of the past few years when the rounds of socialization, the faces, the gowns, and the gossip all seemed to melt into one another. She had, she decided, been becoming distinctly *dull* until Louisa came to town.

"I'll take good care of 'em *both*, Rockford," she whispered, thinking of her quiet, gentle, scholarly brother with deep affection, and not a little longing, "and I'll make a better job of it than ever you or Isabella could have! It's someone like me they need now, reprehensible though I may be at times."

There were flowers in plenty the next morning, but none bound by a single silk stocking, and all sported large calling cards and messages. Lady Daphne's brows rose as a secretive smile flickered at the corners of her lips, but she made no comment.

And Louisa?

She was strangely discomposed. Of course she had intended the foolishness to end—for Morrison's sake, if for no other reason. Perhaps his funds were at low tide. Perhaps he had merely tired of the game. Well, that was what she'd wanted, wasn't it? For the disagreeable man, with his commands and his jokes and his pranks and his arrogance, to disappear into the hole from which he had emerged?

The best thing was for her to put the aberrational episode out of her mind, forget there ever was a rider with warm laughing eyes and a devilish grin who almost ran her down in the Park on a huge black horse.

She looked up with a bright smile of satisfaction. "Well, at last!" she caroled. "No more of those dreadful flowers with no card to them. Such an infantile prank, really. I am so thankful the joke has outworn the jokester's pocket and patience. Such a relief!"

Lady Daphne uttered an inarticulate, rather abstracted sound, all her attention apparently claimed by the *Morning Post*.

"Shocking lot of tattle here," she chuckled with relish, "much of it delightfully warm! Listen to *this*, Louisa: 'Miss F-, glittering Diamond of the Ton, said to be dulled to Paste, languishes in seclusion behind drawn blinds. Be she weaving Willow Wands after five years' polar isolation, or only Straw?' *That* must have the Fortescue beldame tearing her hair out—and the Dulled Diamond's as well, if I know the harpy! We'll see your brother's nonpareille reappearing after this bit, mark my words, if only to give lie to such rumors. Your ride in the Park with Giles should be *most* productive this afternoon." She returned to the paper without waiting for Louisa's opinions. "Oh, what fun! He must be *furious*. 'It is rumored His Dashing Grace of R-, recently arrived in Town, is setting his House to rights with many Modern Improvements of inordinate expense. Is His Grace's Handkerchief to be flung down at last? And which Fortunate Fair will be given an opportunity to seize the Cambric if he forsakes the Muslin?' Rawdon'll ignore the piece, naturally—only thing one *can* do—Such impertinence!—but I wouldn't want to be on *his* staff today!" She glanced up, twinkled, went back to the *Post*. "I see here that Dickie Fotheringham's mother has come to town. It *must* be she! 'Lady F-, Relict of that Distinguished Diplomat of Continental Fame, the Honorable G. E. F., adds glitter to the current Season from her rooms at the C-, but appears to prefer the austere environs of the Horse Guards to the delicate bowers of that fashionable Hostelry. Is it Senior Staff which has all the Lady's devotion, and is an Interesting Announcement soon to be anticipated?' Well, really! I wonder who inserted *that?*" She glanced up, eyes wide. "You said something, my dear?"

"No—nothing to the purpose," Louisa snapped, collected herself. "Aren't these primroses from Lord Sackett lovely? Such a beautiful shade."

"They're well enough, I suppose. Anything of interest among this morning's crop of invitations?"

Louisa shook her head. "The usual, from the usual people," she replied in a bored tone, sifting through the stack. "Balls, routs, a Venetian breakfast, a turtle dinner, assorted evening parties. Oh—and a musicale at Lady Tentree's, complete with Italian soprano. *That* I hope we can avoid. The rest are the usual sort of thing—what will eventuate as dinners with too many diners, too much food and punctilio, too little intelligent conversation, and various insipid damsels begging to display their wares *à la Fortescue* at pianoforte or harp for the delectation of those idiots who believe musical aptitude equates with childbearing potential."

"Louisa!"

That young lady shrugged, tossed the invitations aside. "It's true, you know." She drew herself up, expanded her chest. " 'Dear Miss Blither-Blather,' " she intoned in a deep and penetrating voice, " 'will you not favor us upon the harp, accompanying yourself at the pianoforte with your toes while warbling a delightful ditty composed by your incomparable self in your superior soprano? The gentlemen have been most importunate in their requests to experience these proofs of your fecundity.' " Lady Daphne chuckled reluctantly. Louisa seemed to shrink, losing her air of matronly formidability, lips pouting, voice rising, lashes fluttering, as delicate hand rose to suppress palpitations of maidenly breast. " 'Oh, Lady Fiddle-Faddle,' " she simpered, writhing with becomingly modest ecstasy, " 'you wish *me* to display *my* poor little talents before these *illustrious* and *wealthy* gentlemen? I am *overcome!* ' "

"Sickening—I agree. Still, that's the way of the world as it is currently constituted, and if games must be played, it is best to play them *well.*"

"I refuse to play them at all!" Louisa spat.

"That has become more than obvious over the past weeks. You are quite the little fool, you know, Louisa. What *are* you expecting—for a Prince of the Realm to tumble to his knees upon glimpsing you, begging for the privilege of showering you with diamonds and emeralds? Won't wash, you know, even if you *could* manage it. The royals may spend money like drunken sailors, but they are always more or less in dun territory, and are better known for cartes blanches than honest proposals."

"I don't know *what* I expect," Louisa sighed. "Better than I've seen to date—that's certain! They're all very well for a cotillion or a country dance, but across the breakfast cups for a *lifetime?*" She shuddered. "The *best* of them would be insufferable—tyrants or opinionated bores, mostly, with no conversation beyond their own self-consequence and the glory of continuing their family lines."

"Surely you don't include Lord Sackett in that indictment?"

"He *is* less objectionable than most, but only by contrast," Louisa retorted. "A self-important, prosing bore, forever striking an attitude to ensure one notes his superior profile. His hands are *clammy*, and his breath? *Faugh!*"

"Oh, my! I had no idea . . . And poor Donclennon would be impossible! You'd need a new wardrobe each day, and new feet rather more often than that. Major Lord Fenton, then? He has been most attentive. Or *any* of Harry's friends, for that matter?"

Louisa smiled warmly, indignation evaporating. "No—there you are right. Harry's friends are delightful, every one. Intelligent. Personable. Conversable. Witty. And, *Harry's friends*. They see me as an extra sister, and I am afraid I see them as extra brothers. Friendship, yes—long, and lasting, I hope. But, a deep attachment, or something even warmer?" She smiled sadly. "I wish it were possible, but it isn't."

"Captain Gracechurch—"

"Is a hardened flirt," Louisa retorted. "Delightful as an afternoon's companion, but he was already pretending to make his proposals less than a quarter hour after we met. All that is charming, but I pity his wife, once he acquires one, for she will never know where her husband's eye will next roam, and where his eye roams he will be sure to follow."

"You *have* changed since you arrived. I remember your saying a convenient husband was all you desired. Now you require sincere attachment *and* fidelity! And wit, and intelligence, and conversability, and a slew of other virtues and qualities bound up in one unlikely package."

"And humor," Louisa interjected. "That, too."

"You must not become *too* particular, my dear. I suppose even *personal* attractions enter into it now: broad shoulders, and a tall frame, and curling hair, and speaking eyes, and elegance of manner and address, and I know not what all!"

"*Especially* the 'what-all,' " Louisa laughed. "Perhaps I was foolish then, and perhaps I am too demanding now, but I will not spend the remainder of my life dealing with a prosy bore with nothing more in his brainpan than name, title, and fortune."

"You do not require much," Lady Daphne sighed. "Only perfection, or as close to it as this poor world can offer. *All* men have feet of clay, my dear, no matter what appearance they first present. As things stand, I don't know *who* might be good enough for you."

"No one," Louisa chuckled, "so let us not concern ourselves overly with the matter. In the event, I suppose I shall be forced to settle for that which I at least do not actively despise—something rather on the order of Harald Donclennon, perhaps. He, at least, is inoffensive. For now, let us fiddle while Rome burns, shall we? When I mount my pyre, I promise to perform my self-immolation with grace and style!"

Lady Daphne said nothing, but her eyes had a decided twinkle to them as she turned back to the paper.

The day was half gone when Hoskins announced Captains Heath and Gracechurch, and an "individual."

The individual turned out to be a former trooper whose wounds, combined with a severe bout of fever, had forced him to quit the army. Sergeant Hobbs, according to Heath, was now reduced to doing such odd jobs as fell in his way to keep body and soul united, and was existing on the edge of starvation. That he had not turned to crime, as so many in his situation did, was testimony to the man's superior character. The story was a pathetic one, winning Louisa's instant sympathy, and she readily agreed to interview the former soldier—who was waiting in the hall—as a prospective groom. A Peninsular veteran would *have* to meet with Harry's approval. And if he didn't? Well, Harry wasn't God, no matter what he might think!

"How did you ever find someone suitable so quickly?" Lady Daphne asked, once more at her tambour frame plying colored wools.

Gracechurch smiled. "You know how it is in any tight society, Lady Cheltenham," he said. "You ask one individual, and in doing so you have asked an hundred. Sergeant Hobbs, and his story, surfaced within an hour of our first mentioning the need for a man down on his luck, experienced with horses, and deserving of assistance."

"Thing is, there's a problem," Quentin Heath threw in. "Poor fellow has no billet. Been living on the streets. There isn't room where Harry's got his cattle quartered, unfortunately. One of us'd be glad to oblige, but there isn't a one of us as has set up his stable since we're just visiting the village for a bit, and the expense isn't worth it."

"And so you want him to be lodged here," Lady Daphne said slowly, looking from Heath to Gracechurch, face politely inquiring.

"If that is possible," Gracechurch responded. "A pallet behind the cookstove would be palatial compared to what he's endured."

Lady Daphne's lips quivered, but she managed not to laugh outright. "I am certain it would be," she agreed. "Very well—have the man brought in. Then we shall see what we shall see."

But what she saw was in no way what she expected. Hobbs was thin to emaciation, below average in height, with a beak-nosed craggy face so pale his skin resembled

crumpled parchment. He was clean, neat, but his old
uniform was in rags, his ancient boots cracked, one of the
soles half unstitched. One great rawboned, callused paw
clutched a frayed cap. The other opened and closed nervously, both dangling from knobby wrists that hung far
below his tattered cuffs. Only his eyes seemed alive—
snapping black orbs that darted around the parlor, then
settled on the infinity of a soldier at parade rest.

"You are Sergeant Hobbs?" Louisa asked gently, eyes
stinging at the picture of proud, indomitable destitution
he presented.

"Yes, miss," the man responded in a rasping voice.
"Sergeant Willie Hobbs. I was a trooper, afore."

"On the Peninsula, Captain Heath said. My brother
saw service there, also."

"Yes, miss. Cap'n Gracechurch told me."

"And you know horses?"

A slow smile spread across his seamed features. "Like
a mother knows her babes," he said, looking directly at
Louisa for the first time.

"I believe the gentlemen also told you I am in need of
a groom, at least temporarily, and perhaps permanently," she said, convinced of her aunt's tacit approval
by that lady's silence. "Would the position be of interest
to you?"

"To see to your horses, miss?"

"Currently there's only one, but as my primary reason
for desiring a groom is to have someone available to
accompany me when I wish to ride in the Park, there
would ultimately be at least two."

The man nodded, clearly too overcome to know what
to say.

"You would lodge here," Louisa continued. "You
would be provided with clothes, a horse, and a saddle.

You would take your meals in the servants' hall, and there would of course be the customary salary."

He nodded again, disbelief and hope warring in his eyes.

"Do you have a family?" Louisa asked tentatively. "A wife? Children?"

Hobbs shook his head. "No, miss—there's just me."

"All right, then—do you wish the position?"

He drew himself up to his full height of little more than five feet. "Please, miss, very much."

"Then it is yours." She beamed at him. "I am positive we shall deal excellently, for I am neither a difficult nor an unreasonable employer. Earn my Commendatore's liking and respect, and you will have mine. We shall discuss your exact duties later." She turned to Heath. "If I provide you with funds, could you see Sergeant Hobbs outfitted, take him to Tattersall's to purchase a mount? Nothing shabby—one I might ride myself on occasion. I refuse to waste money on inferior cattle." She smiled bitterly. "Were we at Marleybourne I would not be forced to impose on you in this manner, but in London so much is not permitted me."

"Glad to," Heath grinned. "No imposition at all. Can't have you setting 'em by the ears, showing up at Tatt's. Wouldn't *do*."

They chatted for a few minutes—about the masquerade that evening, Hobbs' needs, the probable date of Harry's return to town—while the former sergeant waited in the hall. Then the captains bade Lady Daphne goodbye, and Louisa escorted the three men to the door after assuring they had sufficient funds to see to clothing and a mount for Hobbs. When she returned to the parlor, she found her aunt staring thoughtfully at her tambour frame, fingers poised in mid-stitch.

"You appear abstracted," she said. "Is there a problem? Do you not approve of Hobbs?"

Lady Daphne shook her head, looked up, then completed her stitch.

"I always think I am *so* clever," she said ruefully. "This time I think I've been an utter *fool!* That, or I've been royally diddled, and I can't decide which."

Nine

"How did it go?" Lady Daphne inquired later that day, eyes dancing, when Louisa entered the parlor following her drive in the Park with Giles Fortescue.

Louisa threw her aunt a baleful glance, indicated her wind-blown hair and tangled ribbons. "I believe," she said, "I am in need of a restorative. A *strong* restorative! For your information, I intend to have a fit of the vapors, palpitations, and a superior case of the hysterics—not necessarily in that order—but have them I will! I've *earned* them!"

"As bad as all *that?*"

"Don't look so innocent, my dearly beloved aunt! You know very well it had to be, and you don't care a jot. Summon minions bearing burnt feathers and lavender water!"

"I'm always ready to be entertained," Lady Daphne twinkled, patted the settee beside her. "Come—smooth your ruffled plumage and tell me all about it."

The excursion, from Lady Daphne's point of view, had been an unqualified success. Giles, resplendent in a startling eight-caped puce driving coat, bilious lime-green inexpressibles, and scarlet-tasseled purple Hessians of extreme cut and mirror shine—"Really," that lady had noted softly to Louisa before she departed with the dashing blade, "Harry *must* return to town soon, if only to take the poor boy in hand!"—was punctual to the minute, face closely matching coat in hue as he proudly handed Louisa into a red racing curricle of outré design with butter-yellow upholstery and wheels of livid green picked out with orange scrollwork.

The appearance of boy and conveyance had been only the first disaster, Louisa fumed as Hoskins discreetly deposited tea, wine, and ratafia biscuits on the small table in front of the parlor fireplace. Sally Jersey actually *guffawed* as she waved in passing. Mrs. Drummond-Burrell raised her impeccable brows and sniffed as at the detection of an unpleasant odor. Lord Sackett had—

"That's all very well," Lady Daphne interrupted tartly, "but what did you learn?"

"Never to go driving in the Park with puppies!" Louisa spat. "If you had been forced to endure the looks I received, the tittering, the—"

"What did you learn?"

"Nothing to the point. Did you truly expect me to? The Honorable Giles was all overblown compliments and convoluted Etonesque literary allusions of dubious provenance—when he wasn't battling a team far too strong for his capabilities. That we didn't come to grief an hundred times is only due to Divine Providence. I was finally forced to take the ribbons, or we would have overturned—Is that *all* the boy knows how to do in a curricle?—*and Emily Cowper into the bargain!*"

"An uncomfortable afternoon?"

"Uncomfortable? Next time, *you* drive out with Giles Fortescue, and see how you like it!"

"Oh, I believe I'll leave that part of our project to you. My heart isn't as sound as it once was, and I shouldn't like to think of the boy having my demise on his conscience."

"Your heart is as sound as it was when you were sixteen!"

"Of course it is—but it makes a *wonderful* excuse not to do things I don't care to, don't you think?"

Louisa laughed, eyes still glittering, and came to rest on a chair across from her aunt.

"There isn't all that much," she said more calmly. "What you are about I cannot conceive. I asked the questions you suggested, but none of Giles's answers makes any sense, except in a vague sort of way. It's as if they had all gone mad of a sudden."

Lady Daphne, however, made very good sense indeed of the erratic and disjointed information Louisa had pried from Harriet Fortescue's son. While the diamond might not appear that evening at Muriel Stoking's masquerade (such an event not being sufficiently refined to meet with Lady Fortescue's elevated standards), it was certain she would soon be forced by her mother to show her dulled visage among the ton—so long as that lady did not change her mind yet again as to what it was best to do. One moment she declared they must give a ball, bring Sophronia out a year early. The next she was demanding an immediate removal to Fortescue Lodge, with house in town closed and shuttered, door knocker taken down, and servants sent on unpaid holiday. Then, without pause or apparent consideration, she would demand departure posthaste for the Continent, only to batter herself against the unbreachable walls of the Corsican adventurer's having rendered that haven of distressed damsels impracticable. "Never seen m'mother in such a dither," Giles had proclaimed. "Not like her at all. Usually knows what she wants. Gets it, too."

And, dulled indeed the fair damsel's visage was, according to Giles. "Watering pots ain't generally pretty sights," he had informed Louisa, "and m'fool sister's just like the rest. *First* she has the vapors, *an' then* she cries 'cause her eyes're red an' her face's gone blotchy, the silly twit! House reeks of burnt feathers an' *sal volatile*. Don't know what Lord Beckenham sees in her—or any of the rest of the gudgeons, for that matter. Buttered eggs in their cocklofts, that's what!"

Lord Fortescue had not been permitted to decamp, and spent his time defending a house besieged by importunate well-wishers who were invariably refused admittance. "M'mother's afraid they'll hear Gwennie," Giles had said forthrightly, "but stap me if they can't hear her from the street! Sounds like one of them new contraptions run by steam, once she gets going. That, or she whimpers. Can't hear her then, so it's not as bad."

"Mark my words," Lady Daphne chuckled, "they'll never recover from this. Oh, they'll hold their heads up and pretend nothing's gone amiss, and Harriet Fortescue will play the *grande dame* as usual, but *this* time the termagant's gone too far, and she knows it. How perfectly delightful!"

"But what of Harry?" Louisa pleaded, for the moment ignoring her aunt's intriguing comment. Gone too far in *what?*

"Harry? What of him?" she shrugged. "He's safe at Marleybourne, *miles* from his precious Gwendolyn and her charming mother. What more could you ask?"

"But what will happen when he returns to town?"

"We shall pray he does not do so for a very long time."

Charles interrupted them at this juncture, bearing a small and exquisite, intricately enameled silver cloisonné coffer on a silver salver. Lady Daphne's brows rose as she glanced puckishly at Louisa.

"High time!" she muttered, and then, at full voice, "Whatever is it *now*, Charles? Not more callers, I hope. If it is, show 'em the door. We must dress soon."

"No callers, m'lady," he said. "Only a messenger, who has departed. I was instructed to present this item to Miss Louisa."

"Well, *present* it!" the old lady directed tartly, eyes sparkling.

Louisa accepted the box with all the reluctance of a lady afraid of heights about to embark on a balloon ascension, and set it quickly aside.

"Well, aren't you going to look inside?" Lady Daphne demanded as Charles retreated, closing the doors behind him. "Is there a card?"

"No," Louisa returned curtly.

"Oh, dear," the old lady exclaimed with every evidence of satisfaction, "another of *those.*"

"So it would appear."

"Not opening it won't solve anything. Don't be *missish*, Louisa! Here, give it to me, if you're so reluctant."

"James Morrison is nothing but a superior groom, no matter what he may once have been," Louisa said, "and this trinket must have set him back ten years' wages! I will not encourage his foolishness by so much as *touching* the thing! The only possible explanation is that he is a gamester in addition to the rest, which is reprehensible."

"*Most* reprehensible," Lady Daphne agreed, "but aren't you the least bit curious?"

Resignedly Louisa took up the box, unfastened the delicate clasp, gasped. Inside, on a tufted bed of deepest blue velvet, nestled a glittering silver-shot satin mask, its frilled borders, eyeholes, and brows picked out with diamonds, pearls, and sapphires. "Oh, dear Lord!" she whispered, color draining from her face. Beneath the mask reposed not one, but a pair of stockings of the finest silk, intricate clocks worked in silver thread at the ankles. "I can't accept this . . ." Numbly, hands trembling, she passed the box to her aunt. "Whatever am I to do? I don't even know the man's direction!"

"Very pretty," Lady Daphne returned, picking up the mask and examining it carefully. "*Excellent* taste. It will be perfect with your costume."

"Have you taken leave of your senses? I *cannot* accept such a gift! It is far too valuable. The crop was bad enough. This is *far* worse. It looks," she shuddered, "like a *payment* of some sort."

"Oh, I don't think so," Lady Daphne returned. "The gems are sure to be paste, you know. Don't be more of an idiot than you can help."

"The box alone would render—"

"You'll wear the mask," her aunt said firmly, "and no argumentation about it. The one you have isn't half so pretty."

"Aunt Da—"

"Enough! You'll wear it, and there's an end to the subject. The colors and style are absolute perfection. I wonder how the man knew?"

"Morrison? He has a spy in the house—or hadn't you realized? If I could determine who it is, I'd kill him!"

"And risk a trip to Tyburn for the sake of a *groom?* Don't be silly!"

"You're behind-times," Louisa spat. "They don't use Tyburn anymore. Besides, it would be worth it."

As they were ascending the stairs to don their costumes for the masquerade Louisa paused, suddenly remembering a curious incident when she was returning from her drive with Giles Fortescue. She had noted a little man, she informed her aunt, dressed like a vagrant leaving the area way, seeming to glide as if riding the air, hat pulled low over his face, scarf twisted well above his mouth. Had Lady Daphne been aware of such an individual calling on one of the staff? She would have mentioned it immediately, Louisa apologized, but first her ire at the disastrous expedition with the Fortescue sprig and then Morrison's gift had put it completely out of her mind.

"Keep it there," Lady Daphne returned. "There is no need I am aware of for you to know *all* my business!"

* * *

The evening was refreshingly cool, blessed by the playful breezes which occasionally swept the capital free of its kennel stench before the leaden weight of summer laid its hand impartially on mansion and stew. The sky was a clear spangled blue-black, the air redolent with pastoral warmth and green vitality, making the country-bred Louisa long desperately for Marleybourne and the freedoms it had once offered, the security and love.

Miserably uncomfortable in the stiff, tightly-laced ball gown of an earlier generation, the heavy powdered wig with its plumes and flowers and miniature fans and garlands of pearls, she watched the merrymakers tiredly from her refuge in a small alcove across from the main ballroom of Lady Stoking's Palladian mansion, tapping her fan absently against the ballooning panniers of her sweeping brocaded skirts. Around her marble pillars soared, gleaming like satin in the soft light of hundreds of candles. Her alcove, the hall, the ballroom, were sylvan glades overflowing with trees and flowers, with grottoes and meandering streams through which fish darted, silver and gold flashes of light. Before her kings and queens, jesters and milkmaids, and pirates and fairies whirled in an improbable juxtaposition of times and places and personages. Banners and canopies of striped silk and satin caught with golden ropes festooned walls and ceilings, lending an air of oriental decadence to the overwhelmingly opulent scene. And yet, she conceded, it was beautiful in a nightmarish sort of way, the swirling kaleidoscope of colors like a stained glass window set in motion—if one admired such things. She did not.

Louisa turned with a sigh, and picked her way through a compacted jungle of palms and ferns decorated with miniature Chinese lanterns to doors giving on the terrace which ran the length of the back of the house overlooking

the Thames. The gardens were invitingly dark and secluded after the overperfumed and overcrowded ballroom, sweeping down to the river's edge in moonlit
peace. The setting was gemlike, the city merely a dream
on the horizon, yet close enough that an hour's carriage
ride had brought them to the gates.

Louisa slipped onto the terrace, sinking against the cool
stone wall with thankfulness, ice-blue skirts and silver-shot
white velvet overdress caught with knots of crystalline
leaves and silver roses shimmering in the dark, spangled
shoes twinkling. From within a minuet lilted, threading its
way through the house and into the gentle night—a
ghost-tune, bearing with it memories of simpler festivities
at Marleybourne during her parents' lifetime when she
would hide behind the balusters to watch the sprightly,
graceful dancers.

Marleybourne, for her, no longer existed, she admitted
sadly, vanished as surely as those long-ago revelers. Harry
was determined on his diamond, and his diamond was
determined on her permanent expulsion. What Lady
Daphne thought she could do to remedy the situation—
brave words aside—Louisa could not imagine, nor that
Harry's return to town—and his diamond—would be
longer delayed than absolutely mandatory.

She thought with despair of Harry's letters, still hidden
in the locked drawer of her aunt's elegant desk in the
parlor. That he had every intention of forcing her removal to Fortescue House upon his return she had not the
least doubt. Even if he did not succeed, the brangles
between them might well force a permanent rift. Her only
hope at this juncture was a speedy marriage—preferably
before Harry's return—and of that there was no possibility.

Not that the evening had not gone well in that respect,
if one were not overnice concerning the manner or nature
of the proposal or the man making it, but a soddenly

incoherent offer from a Lord Sackett so deeply indentured that once he fell to his knees it took all Louisa's efforts to drag him back to his feet was *not* what she had in mind. Gracechurch, too, had cornered her—in one of those ubiquitous dark grottoes sprinkled about to encourage just such romantic encounters. *His* words, at least, had been graceful, and delivered with such consummate artistry that she had almost regretted giving him his congé. Young Giles Fortescue's ardent approaches she had managed to forestall by her precipitous retreat to the alcove. As for indecent suggestions, those she had received in superabundance from amorous bucks who found courage behind a mask and permission in civility. Her arms and cheeks ached as much from pinches as her feet did from the assault of clumsy-gaited septuagenarians with the illusion they retained the graces of their youth. Even Donclennon, deeply in his cups, had managed to overset her, suddenly extolling the glories of the Highlands while declaiming bloody Scots ballads in incomprehensible Gaelic.

Harry, for all the ridiculously toplofty notions he had acquired from his diamond, might be in the right about events such as this. And, if right about Lady Stoking's masquerade, perhaps about much else as well . . . She *had* made a mull of things, one way and another, and was no closer to the altar than when she came to town. Time might not be gone, but it was fleeing on swift feet.

She gazed out over the gardens, barely seeing the fairy lights which glimmered in the trees through tears that sprang unwanted to her eyes. It had seemed so simple at Marleybourne! Nothing was simple at all—not that Aunt Daphne had not done her best. Louisa had entry to the most glittering homes. The cards of invitation were endless. Her escorts were of elevated birth and fortune. That didn't help—not if she were unwilling to accept a life of boredom with a self-consequential cipher whose only claims to her affections were lineage and respectability. She needed a clear, practical solution, and she could not think of a one—she, who had run the Court for the year and a half since their father's death, settled the tenants' disputes, increased the harvests, and for ten years had been the social arbiter of their corner of the county! It was ludicrous . . .

She gave herself a shake, pulled off her mask, and dashed the tears from her eyes. They were a self-indulgence she could ill afford.

From below came a raucous laugh, a high-pitched giggle, then a screech that cut off abruptly. Concerned, Louisa started toward the sweep of stone steps leading to the garden, a silver road into the darkness, as she replaced her mask.

"I wouldn't, if I were you," a deep voice came from behind her. "In such an instance, you would not be the least wanted, and, indeed, very much in the way. Or, if wanted, you could not be of use, being inexperienced in the ways of the fancy. In either case, your presence would definitely be *de trop.*"

Louisa froze, then slowly turned. A black silk domino loomed in the doorway, impenetrably dark against lesser darkness. Her hand rose to touch the mask covering the upper half of her face, eyes widening as she shivered in the light night wind. Then she raised her head high, a queen about to mount the scaffold.

"I suspected I might see you here tonight," she said carefully. "The coffer and mask are most beautiful. Thank you."

"No more beautiful than their recipient, and the mask, at least, most becoming," the voice came warmly back. Then, with a hint of laughter, "Do you sport my other offering as well?"

She colored, suddenly understanding the forwardness of the young blades who accosted her in the ballroom, trapping her in darkened corners to whisper suggestions they would never have broached in daylight. There was an intoxication to the anonymity of having one's face partially hidden which lent boldness and made possible things that, under other conditions, would have been unimaginable.

"As a matter of fact, I do."

"Fortunate gift," came the bantering voice, "in what it encompasses!"

"You have been uncommonly perspicacious as well as generous," she retorted. "Who, in my aunt's house, is in your employ?"

"No one," Morrison said, stepping out of the shadows and onto the moonlit terrace to stand beside her, gazing first across the gardens, then smiling warmly into her eyes. "Don't be so prickly! I possess imagination, you see, and so have no need of spies." A chuckle lit the night. "You make quite a charming courtesan of the *Ancien Régime*," he said.

"Courtesan, indeed! I am supposed to be a character from one of Perrault's tales."

"Not the *Capuchon*, certainly. No red hood, though I would be delighted to play the wolf to your sweet innocence. *Cendrillon*, I'll wager then, or the *Belle au Bois Dormant*—one or the other. Much more appropriate than a courtesan, now I think on it—especially the latter." He scowled down at her, the furrowing of his brow visible above the mask, glanced around the terrace. "You came out here alone?" he questioned, voice sharp.

"Good heavens, Mr. Morrison—why ever not? A select gathering, people of the highest respectability—what could happen to me here?"

"Exactly the same thing that could happen to you in any stew, my love. The only difference would lie in the probable cleanliness of your attackers—though even that is not certain. There are extra servants everywhere, hired for the occasion. Who knows who or what they are? I *told* you not to—" He paused, and she sensed dark eyes studying her face with rare concern. In a flash her mask was whisked away. "What is the matter?" he said abruptly, voice losing its angry tone. "You have been crying."

"You are mistaken, sir. A trick of the moonlight only."

"Indeed? I think not." His hand came up and wiped away a telltale stain, lingering a moment against her cheek. "Come—we are friends, are we not? Here—if it makes you feel better, put this back on."

He handed her the mask, which she accepted gratefully. She had been right about its sheltering properties, and the courage they gave. The beginnings of an idea were circling in her mind—an astonishing, improper, unheard-of, and very logical idea brought on by his tone and her desperation. A solution to the problem of Harry. A solution to the diamond. A solution to Morrison's impecunious state. A solution to everything. Carefully she looped the fine earpieces through the curls of her elevated coiffure as she faced herself bluntly, reviewing the past months with a candor that made her blush behind the mask's satin and lace. So *that* was why even Aunt Daphne's candidates had appeared such bores . . .

"I would like to discuss your situation," she said at last with great care, "and I would rather go where we cannot be overheard for both our sakes. Would it be highly improper to walk by the river?"

"Highly—but don't let that concern you. You are safe with me, I assure you."

The voice was smiling again, though the laughter had fled. Instead there was that same concern which had struck her the day of Gwendolyn Fortescue's faints in the Park, and again just a few moments ago. She was right, then . . . She had to be! That, or she had lost all understanding of human nature. Of herself, her own sensations, she did not dare think overly much. Somewhere in some deep and hidden recess of her heart and mind she knew the truth, but it was too startling, too unanticipated for open admission. She was, apparently, not at all the person whom she had always thought herself to be. That was something she would consider later—in a year, perhaps, or ten, or twenty. Or, perhaps, never. By then, consideration would be meaningless . . .

Morrison pulled her hand through the crook of his arm, guided her down the sweeping stone steps to the path below. "Though what about my 'situation' concerns you so much that you desire to discuss it I have not the slightest notion." His voice seemed to smile. "Perhaps you had best explain."

"You have entry to Lady Stoking's," Louisa returned tentatively. "I had begun to suspect something of the sort might be the case."

"Indeed?" The laughter was back now, full-blown and merry. "And this entry concerns you? You fear I might pollute the glittering throng?"

"Don't be ridiculous!" she snapped, then continued more evenly, "That you might have social contact with the gentlemen of the ton would not be astonishing. They choose their friends where they wish—even among such individuals as pugilists and race course touts, I understand. That you might have entry even now into the best homes, however, only makes your current predicament the more distressing."

"I see."

But, from the puzzled tone, she could tell that he didn't—or else did not desire to acknowledge the anomalies of his situation. She would have to tread gently here. There was enormous pride—of that she was certain—and careful courtesy which probably masked a considerable temper, as well as a streak of unusual sensitivity for one who presented himself to the world as an impoverished devil-may-care prankster. If she were to accomplish her goal, it would be essential to leave that pride intact, to make it clear that it was he, and not she, who was conferring a boon.

"I do not want to know your personal history—at least not now," she said, words coming slowly and with painful effort. "That you have in some way suffered extreme reverses of fortune is clear. It does not matter to me whether they were of your own doing, though I shall be thankful if they were not, as you will understand in a moment." She took a deep breath. "Your knowledge of horseflesh must be extensive if you are employed by His Grace of Rawdon," she continued carefully, feeling his arm stiffen beneath her hand. "I understand he is known for the superiority of his cattle and the extent of his stable."

"He has that reputation," Morrison returned after a moment's reflection. "I believe the reputation to be justly earned. How did you arrive at the conclusion that I am in his employ?"

"There is no need to go into that now," Louisa protested, face burning. "It is sufficient that it provides a high recommendation. Such a man would not entrust his favorite mount to just anyone."

"True. I take it someone has been speaking to you of El Moro."

She nodded as they came to the foot of the path and stopped by the moon-spangled river. It flowed past them, gently murmuring, willows sweeping down to touch the rippled water with tender fronds. From across the way a bird called, voice hesitant in the night air, as if it knew the hour for its morning song had not yet arrived. Faint strains of a popular waltz floated from the house, more a dream of music than music itself.

"Would you care to sit?" Morrison asked. "I believe there is a bench to our right, and it appears you intend our discussion to be a lengthy one."

"Thank you," Louisa replied in a small voice. This was far more difficult than she had anticipated, mask or no mask. How the gentlemen ever managed it unless well above-par she had no idea, and she had not that advantage. Sackett, in his cups and sullenly maudlin, no longer seemed quite so iniquitous.

Morrison led her along the bank until the path vanished around a bend. A curving marble bench sparkled in the liquid moonlight, high dark shrubs shielding it from view of the house and gardens. He doffed the black silk domino, whirling it through the air to settle in soft folds over the bench, and gave a slightly mocking bow. Biting a trembling lower lip, Louisa seated herself as far to one end as she could, settling her cumbersome skirts about her, and peeked up at him through her mask.

Morrison was dressed in the height of simplicity—stark white linen and waistcoat against stark black coat. Something gleamed in his snowy neckcloth, sending flashes of light like the uncertain beam of a star through the clouds. His hair was neatly swept back, his eyes invisible behind a black mask he did not trouble to remove. However improper his deshabille in the Park, tonight his appearance was all that was elegant—at least in the moonlight, which probably masked shoddy fabric and inferior cut unless his sartorial splendor was thanks to the Duke of Rawdon's castoffs. So bitterly unfair . . .

Morrison sat—not precisely crowding her, but not at what she had planned to be his end of the bench either—and looked at her expectantly.

"Well?" he said. "We were going to discuss my—ah—*situation*, I believe?"

"I am an extremely wealthy woman, you know," Louisa said, rushing her fences.

"What has that to do with anything?" he responded indifferently.

"I am also in something of a predicament, just as you are, though its nature is entirely different."

"The Fortescue diamond?" he asked after a moment.

"In part, and in part my brother."

"Damn his stupid, priggish hide!" Morrison muttered, then turned to face her. "Don't let Beckenham's tantrums overset you. They will pass."

"I think not," Louisa sighed. "He is determined to have her, and—Please understand, what I am telling you is in strictest confidence. Should it become known among the ton, that public knowledge would destroy every hope my brother has of what he believes to be his greatest happiness. And should I be instrumental in destroying that happiness, I would never be able to earn his forgiveness— nor could I forgive myself."

"All right—what you tell me is between we two only, no matter how difficult or unwise I may find it to keep your confidence."

"Thank you." She hesitated. Above them an owl whispered through the branches, feathers barely stirring the air. She started, looking up, the hint of a smile on her lips. How beautiful and serene the night was—so unlike her own tumultuous situation! "There is an understanding between them, and has been for three years and more," she resumed reluctantly. "Miss Fortescue remained faithful to my brother throughout his service in the Peninsular Army, and following his return sans arm and with scarred face. For this, if for nothing else, I must honor her."

"Indeed a particularly touching example of female fidelity," he remarked, a touch of acid to his voice.

"I do not care for her either," Louisa admitted, "but in the end it is neither your affair nor mine. It is Harry's. She has laid a precondition to the announcement of their betrothal, and if that precondition is not soon met, or if word of their attachment leaks among the ton, she will show him the door."

"I see. She will then become unofficially betrothed to yet another young idiot, no doubt waiting anxiously in the wings at this very moment," he said wryly, "and your precious brother will blow his poor, addled brains out."

"More likely mine," Louisa chuckled hollowly.

"And this precondition set by the incomparable Miss Fortescue—what is it?"

"I am to be wedded and bedded prior to any announcement," she said tonelessly. "She does not want me at Marleybourne."

"Up to her usual tricks," he muttered. *"Damn the vixen!* Listen to me, Louisa—" He grasped her hands tightly in his, their pressure warmly reassuring. "There is no way your brother is going to marry that virago in angel's guise. Don't concern yourself about it."

"You don't know Harry," she said sadly, his use of her name unnoticed. "When once he takes a notion—"

"Yes, I do. This notion he will lose, and soon."

She shook her head. "Even if he does, it doesn't matter," she explained, gently pulling her hands away and staring blindly at the river. "I've promised, and I've never broken a promise in my life. I'm not about to begin now. Moreover, should he decide against her, I want there to be no other impediment than his improved understanding of her character. That's what I wanted to talk to you about." She turned, facing him with a combination of determined pride and desperation. "Harry has been trying to force me into marriage with anyone in sight— mostly connections of the Fortescue family. I have met none of them, but from what I observed in the Park only a few days ago—" She shuddered. "My entire reason for coming to London for the season was to find a husband," she said baldly.

"Nothing unusual in that. Same reason every girl comes."

"I am *not* a girl. I was mistress of the household at

Marleybourne for ten years, and I managed the estate in every particular between the time of our father's death and my brother's recovery from his wounds."

"My apologies. You are definitely not a green girl," he responded, a hint of laughter in his voice.

"No, I am not . . . Which brings me to the point."

"I wondered when we'd get there," he murmured.

"This is *not* easy!" she snapped, then went on with more dignity, "Your origins, clearly, are good. To be trapped acting as a glorified groom for some overweeningly prideful rake of a duke whose only recommendation appears to be his wealth and station must be galling to you, for you are worth a thousand of him, and yet trapped you are. Given your manner, even taking into account the relatively few times we have actually spoken—"

"Three," he tossed in. "Once on the day of your arrival. Once in the Park. And, now."

"That's not very much, is it," she admitted faintly.

"No, it isn't."

"Even so, I have sensed you are not . . . *indifferent* . . . to me."

"No, I am not indifferent," he grinned, "though I will admit to a rather constant state of bemusement combined with occasional irritation."

Louisa choked back that she was not the only one who could be irritating, took another deep breath. "Neither am I indifferent to you," she blurted, "however much I may wish I was."

"And *now* we reach the point," he chuckled.

"Yes, we do. You have an apparently insurmountable problem. *I* have an apparently insurmountable problem. The solution to both our problems is identical. I want you to—It is that—If we were to—Please, will you marry me?" she blurted. "No—wait! Listen to me! I know *you* cannot ask *me*. No gentleman reduced to the status of a groom *could* ask a lady to marry him, especially if she is wealthy, but that is no reason why—"

"A fortune hunter might. How d'you know I'm not?" he inquired gently.

"Some things are possible in this world, and some are not. A gamester you certainly are, and probably a rake into the bargain, but never—"

"What makes you think I'm a gamester?" he asked in surprise.

"That's the only way you could have sent all those flowers, or the crop, or any of the rest of it," she returned matter-of-factly. "I paid the wages at Marleybourne. I could probably tell you your annual income within a few pence."

"I suppose you could at that, given such a circumstance," he laughed. "What a delightfully unpredictable little baggage you are under that starched veneer! And so, you want me to marry you . . . Of all the things I suspected you might ask of me, *that* was not one. I am clearly lacking in imagination and foresight. At least life with you would never be dull! And what is it you offer me as inducement—beyond your own sweet self and your considerable fortune, of course," he asked, lightly teasing.

"That's all," she admitted, voice trembling. *"Please* don't laugh at me! I do not deserve your contempt, whatever else I may deserve. With your knowledge of horseflesh and my money, I thought we could find a farm with a pleasant house, and—"

"And turn me into a horse trader!" He threw back his head and the laughter rolled forth, at once delighted and joyous and rueful. Then sensing her gathering herself up for flight, he whirled, sobering on the instant, to pull her into his arms. "This is all very wrong, you know, if quite delightful," he said gently. "It's not the lady who generally asks the gentleman."

"But, I explained why—"

"I know you did, and I am more grateful for your courage than you will perhaps ever comprehend. You have answered a question which has long troubled me, for clearly you see past *what* I am to *who* I am, and this lapse from convention cannot have come easily for you. You are very certain? I am some years your senior, you know. Forget Harry, and his problems, for once in your life, and consider yourself!"

"I'm certain," she whispered, hiding her face against his shoulder, heart pounding at what she had done this night, the irrevocability of it, the brazenness, and yet curiously satisfied and at peace. "I've never been more certain of anything in my life—if you will only promise to give up gaming. I am wealthy, yes, but my fortune won't run to that kind of extravagance—not if we're trying to establish a stud—and many fine properties have been lost to the throw of a die or the turn of a card. If that is what happened to you, I don't want it to happen again."

"I promise not to be too expensive," Morrison choked, "so long as you will permit me the indulgence of an occasional game of copper loo." He removed his mask, then tilted her chin to remove hers. "I think we can dispense with these now," he said huskily, and bent his head to brush her lips tenderly with his, crushing her against him as the world spun away. "Dear Lord, but I adore you!" he whispered. "I love you so much it frightens me. Louisa—look at me." She lifted her eyes to his, blushing furiously, heart pounding. "Never permit the rapidity with which this has seemed to happen, or its unconventionality, to trouble you. Hearts have their own logic which no logician will ever comprehend . . ."

"I could have saved you all this," he said ruefully much later as they stood to leave their secluded haven and the river's muted murmur, "or most of it, but for reasons of my own I preferred to permit things to continue as they had begun. I hope someday you will find it in you to forgive me."

"There is nothing to forgive," Louisa answered gently, a sense of wonder in her voice, her hands resting lightly on Morrison's broad shoulders. "We were both in the suds. Now we are not."

"You are wrong, my darling little baggage," he said seriously. "There is a great deal to forgive. Far more than you have any notion."

"You have *what?*"

Lady Daphne sank into her favorite chair by the parlor fireplace, staring at her niece with a mixture of bewilderment and laughter. Slowly, with an indication of ponderous resolution, the clock in the hall struck the hour: four o'clock of a fine spring morning. Before her Louisa stood proudly, still garbed in her antique ball gown, cloak discarded, bewigged head high and chin determined.

"I have asked James Morrison to marry me, and he has agreed."

"You are not bamming me? You are serious?"

"Completely serious."

"Oh, my Lord . . . And when is this event to take place?"

"As soon as possible. I shall give him the funds to procure a special license tomorrow. We plan to spend our wedding journey searching for a suitable property on which to establish a stud. I want everything decided and accomplished before Harry returns, you see."

"I do, indeed. You asked Morrison, and he agreed . . . This is indeed an age of marvels," she said with slow wonder. "I am not often given to female fits, but I think either hartshorn or a glass of wine is in order. Wine, preferably, given the taste *and* the event. Ring for Hoskins—he is sure not to be abed yet, and you would never find where he keeps the champagne. This *is* a cause for celebration, I presume?"

"*I* believe it to be," Louisa responded tartly from the bell rope.

"And just how did all this come about?" her aunt asked weakly.

"It seemed the ideal solution to both our predicaments."

"I understand yours, but what is his?"

"A man of gentle birth forced to seek employment as a groom due to reverses of fortune? What could be more horrible! And that he is of gentle birth there can be no doubt—he must have entry everywhere, as he was at Lady Stoking's."

"Not quite everywhere, perhaps," Lady Daphne responded, still staring at her niece bemusedly as she thought of the denizens of Fortescue House. "Have you considered properly, Louisa? You can forget Harry, and his ridiculous demands. That will soon be at an end."

"Strange—that is what James said, as well."

"So it's 'James' now, is it, and not *that turnip?* Well, you can trust his opinion," Lady Daphne returned tartly, "even if you refuse to trust mine. He would have your best interests at heart, and methods of informing himself unavailable to you or me." She paused, clearly seeking to find the precise words she wanted. "We are not speaking here of a dinner partner who can be discarded after a few hours' boredom, but of a lifetime. This bears a strong resemblance to the determinations you voiced when you first arrived."

Louisa's face took on a brilliant scarlet hue. "I was a fool then," she admitted, "but I am a little wiser now. He is intelligent, conversable, personable, kind, and possessed of a lively sense of humor. I will never be bored, though I may often be irritated. And, he has promised to give up gaming for his sake as well as mine. Besides," she continued in a small voice, turning away, "I love him to distraction. I don't know how *that* happened in such a ridiculously short time, but it did. I shall never be able to say anything to Harry now concerning the length of his acquaintance with Miss Fortescue when he asked for her hand. I am royally hoist on my own petard."

"You are indeed. Who is to make the announcement?"

"There will be none—only a notice in the *Gazette* after the fact."

"Bride clothes? Trousseau?"

"I have no need of either. The gowns purchased for the season will do well enough. Besides, I have better uses for my money now."

Hoskins, resplendent in blue satin dressing gown embroidered with golden phoenixes and improbable pink foliage, hurtled through the door, candle in hand.

"My lady?" he gasped, glancing anxiously around the room.

"Champagne—the best we have in the cellars, Hoskins," Lady Daphne said, turning to him. "Miss Beckenham has just announced her betrothal—to the gentleman of the silk-stocking bouquets. A *groom* currently in the *employ* of His Grace of Rawdon," she said with a significant look, "by the name of *James Morrison*. A gentleman, according to my niece, who suffered reverses for fortune, and now appears to have come about. Be certain you inform the staff."

Hoskins stared at her in bewilderment for a moment. Then his face cleared, taking on a look of unalloyed delight combined with not a little amusement.

"May I be the first to wish you happy, miss?" he beamed.

"Indeed you may," Louisa responded. "And you are the very first," she added, throwing a speaking look at her aunt.

"Oh, I wish you happy, my dear—I do indeed! And, I

think you very well may be, once the first hurdles are past."

Hoskins vanished silently on soft-footed slippers as Lady Daphne continued to study her niece, a slight frown drawing down her finely arched brows. Louisa moved restlessly around the room, touching objects, straightening pictures, adjusting cushions and draperies in no need of adjustment. The girl was as bad as Harry! Was this pacing, then, the characteristic Beckenham response to emotional turmoil?

"When is Morrison going to discuss his personal circumstances with you?" she inquired finally. "I should think that would be a wise step prior to any nuptials."

"When he is ready," Louisa responded defensively. "I have no desire to question him, and thus cause a rift between us. He is a very proud man, and I cannot think the discussion will be pleasant for him."

"No, it probably will not," Lady Daphne returned thoughtfully, "but if he is wise, he will face up to the issue as soon as possible—preferably tomorrow."

"I am content to wait his pleasure in this," Louisa said firmly, "and so must you be. While he is a man who may be led, I do not believe he is a man who can be *bludgeoned.*"

At this sally Lady Daphne chuckled, admitting as how Louisa probably had the right of it, and the subject was dropped as Hoskins reappeared with a chilled bottle and two fine Waterford glasses on a silver tray, livery properly in place.

Ten

The next days passed in a joyous haze for Louisa.

Harry remained safely ensconced at Marleybourne, secure from the importunings of his diamond and spared the sight of a Louisa by far too content with her lot to portray that air of cool detachment he would have considered mandatory given her advanced age, limited prospects, and improperly acquired—and definitely questionable—fiancé. Lord Sackett disappeared from her circle of admirers, proposals unrenewed following the failure of his inebriated declaration. Giles Fortescue haunted Lady Daphne's town house, but he seemed to sense something had changed with Louisa, and so contented himself with the ready and undemanding friendship offered, along with refuge from his mother's lashing tongue and irrational fits. Lady Daphne cultivated the boy assiduously for what information he could give, in return dropping hints concerning his current mode of dress which were surprisingly well received and instantly acted upon. Of Captains Heath and Gracechurch they saw a great deal—both at home, and among the ton—but Colonel Winthrop had deserted London for the bedside of an aged and ailing uncle, dragging Percy Fenton and Hugh Malfont into the country with him for companionship, intent on securing a potential inheritance to himself.

The flowers bound by silk stockings were replaced by single daily roses, each in an exquisite container of porcelain or crystal, of silver filigree or enamelware. Louisa attempted to remonstrate with Morrison at the first's arrival when he appeared traveling shank's mare while she and Lady Daphne were still chatting over the breakfast cups the morning following Lady Stoking's masquerade.

"We are not yet married," he informed her firmly, "and until we are you will permit me to employ what funds I have at my disposal in any way I see fit without comment."

"Tyrant," Lady Daphne muttered, at which he grinned.

"Naturally. A characteristic of the men of my family. We are known to be a determined and hardheaded lot."

"You'll need that hard head," Lady Daphne retorted, "there's a rare peal due to be rung over it soon," then subsided at the glare he threw her.

"I've instructed Hoskins you are not at home to callers this morning," he tossed into the sudden silence. "No need to let our secret out before it's necessary."

Lady Daphne returned glare for glare.

The sun flooded through the windows that morning as if intent on invading every cranny of the room, lighting the farthest corners with a radiance which, to Louisa, partook of the mythic—the sun of Mount Parnassus miraculously shining on pedestrian London, with the Serpentine become a wine-dark sea, sturdy oaks and beeches transmuted to lemon and mimosa and olive. She knew not where to rest her eyes as Morrison pulled up a chair, dropped a casual kiss on the top of her head, and sat beside her as if he had been doing so all his life, nodding to Hoskins for coffee. With time might come ease, but she doubted it. There was so much reckless vitality to the man that she suspected he would disturb her as easily after fifty years as he did now.

"I'm afraid I'll be forced to leave town for a few days," he informed Louisa with a rueful smile. "You took me rather by surprise last night, you know, and there are certain matters which I must see to in advance of the event." He turned to Lady Daphne, dark eyes suddenly hooded and serious. "We face a delay of upward of a se'night over the schedule your niece proposed—regrettable, but unavoidable. If this causes problems with Beckenham, I'll settle with him when I return. Should worse come to worst, refuse him the door until then. Even one such as I has affairs which must be regularized prior to such a major and permanent step."

"Yes, indeed," that lady snapped, "though perhaps you should have said *above all* one such as you!"

"Possibly," he smiled, unruffled.

Not even the unwelcome news of his departure could dull Louisa's glow—half pleasure at seeing this most unlikely of men at her aunt's breakfast table, half dismay at the role she acted the night before. She sat taller in her chair, attempted to appear at ease, a flush of confusion lighting her features. Moon-madness it might have been, but it wore well in the daylight. The doubts of a sleepless pillow and tangled sheets had been banished the instant Morrison strode into the breakfast parlor.

"Have you given notice to the duke?" she inquired, not quite certain how far she dared press anything with this man she was suddenly and surprisingly to wed. "It is advisable you treat him with a modicum of civility, if he is such a fancier of horseflesh as I have been led to believe. We might find an excellent client in him one day."

"The arrangement between us has always been of a rather informal nature," Morrison replied evenly, avoiding the fulminating glance Lady Daphne threw him. "I have done all that is necessary. Do not concern yourself overly with His Grace. Should we establish a stud worthy of the name, he will be our first and most faithful patron."

Lady Daphne snorted. Morrison ignored her, pulled a small object wrapped in yellowed tissue from his pocket, and placed it before Louisa. Lady Daphne's brows rose. Morrison smiled slightly, nodded. Again Lady Daphne snorted. Again Morrison ignored her as Louisa's eyes flew from one to the other in puzzlement. Though nothing had been said, there was no question but that the two were acquainted, and that Lady Daphne did not entirely disapprove either the man or their betrothal—though how much she approved was debatable. Of Morrison's antecedents or history she had refused to give Louisa the least notion, stating categorically that this was Morrison's business, and not hers. Now, Louisa shook her head, looked doubtfully at Morrison.

"Open it," he said. "You need something to remind you of me while I am gone."

"I require no reminders," Louisa retorted, "or, if I do, I have all I need," nodding at his single rose. "What foolishness have you indulged yourself in this time?"

"No foolishness, miss. Hold your tongue, and do as you were told."

"Tyrant, indeed!"

But she smiled, and picking up the informally presented gift, played the childhood game of feeling through the wrapping to guess the contents. Of divination there was no need. The brittle paper fell away at a touch to reveal a heavy gold ring sized to a delicate hand. Louisa stared up at Morrison, consternation and dismay in her eyes. He took it from her and slipped it on her finger.

"I thought it would fit," he smiled. "The last to wear it had a hand very much like yours, and was no less lovely."

"This is an old family piece, isn't it?" she scowled much later as she turned her finger, studying the rainbowed shattering of light from its pavéed diamonds and single glowing ruby, the heavily carved band in the form of a chain of gracefully linked hands, two more hands rising to cup the stones.

They had retreated to the parlor, leaving Lady Daphne to go over menus for the week with Cook, risen Lazarus-like on her weekly pilgrimage from below-stairs. Morrison watched Louisa carefully, his face an unaccustomed blank, ill-fitting shabby coat clearly several seasons past its prime stretched too tightly across his shoulders, scratched boots polished by an inexpert hand braced as if against a pitching deck, lending him an almost piratical look.

She turned from the window to face him where he stood by the fireplace—Was that the only place a man ever came to rest?—arm stretched along the marble mantel.

"You've saved this through everything, haven't you?" she accused.

He nodded, then shrugged. "It's not such a great thing, Louisa, but it is a tradition in the family. One . . . ah . . . salvages what one can."

"Your boots are worn, your cuffs frayed. God alone knows what stew you currently call home, for you refused to give me your direction last night, and again this morning. This could have bought you comfort, decent clothing, food, respectable lodgings, and you—" She shook her head to rid her eyes of tears which had sprung to them. "You foolish, idiotish, wonderful man," she whispered huskily. "How damnably Quixotic you are! What am I ever going to do with you?"

He smiled wryly, crossed the room to seize her shoulders, and shook her not entirely gently. "If you'll love me, that's quite enough," he said, closing his arms tightly around her slender form. "I'm not everything you puff me up to be. Certainly no self-sacrificing hero. Indeed, I am more to be held in contempt than admiration at the moment. Keep that in mind, or you will suffer bitter disappointment. I am a man, nothing more, with but a smattering of the few virtues and all the failings of the breed."

"*Why* won't you accept funds from me before our wedding day," she wailed despairingly against his worn coat, "except for what is needed for the license? Then you could tell me where I might find you, at the very least."

"Because I have no need of extra shillings or pounds," he whispered into her golden curls. "Even the license is not beyond my means, though I considered it best to give way to you in that one thing. *I will not* be your chattel or your plaything, Louisa—understand that clearly. Whatever I am, poor or wealthy, good or bad or indifferent, Peer of the Realm or lowliest dogsbody—you must take me as I am, without the least thought to changing me. On that road lies disaster for us both."

They had parted soon after, Morrison cautioning her that the ring might be recognized, and she would do well to wear it on a chain around her neck rather than on her finger until his return. Louisa then disappeared into her bedchamber to draw up improbable lists of linens and household furnishings which she discarded half completed as being totally useless until the size and style of their future home was known. Morrison stepped into the back parlor to exchange sharp words with Lady Daphne, then vanished into the anonymity of London's teeming streets, still traveling afoot. The next morning a note arrived with his single rose, bidding Louisa a fond temporary farewell and charging her to relay his deepest respects to her aunt.

That a dullness pervaded the town in his absence there was no doubt, at least to Louisa's mind, and yet the mere fact that he existed, that he would return, made it impossible to be actively miserable. Marleybourne, she decided, had been as much a state of mind and atmosphere created by two deeply loving people as it had been a place. Together she and Morrison would create a new Marleybourne, call it what they might.

And Harry? The old Marleybourne? It would be up to him to create it anew. Whether he would be successful or fail miserably would depend in great part on the one he chose to assist him in the task. If it were to be the Glorious Gwendolyn, Marleybourne might slip for a generation or two, but it would recover. The essential was that nothing was ever permanently lost. This Louisa understood now with a certainty which she found at once comforting and startling, a visceral knowledge which had nothing to do with logic and which nothing the future could bring would shatter—of this she was convinced. In the event, all depended on one slightly rakehellish, slightly disreputable and down-at-the-heels reformed gamester of respectable origins who had turned her world upside down as easily as he had lifted her through the window of Harry's overturned chaise.

The Fortescue diamond made a tentative reappearance three days after Morrison's departure—a ride through the Park at the fashionable hour of five o'clock in her mother's landau. So pulled was her appearance, so dulled her sparkle that the ton were convinced she had weakened into a decline. "She's wearing the willow—mark my words!" Lady Jersey informed her gossips, to which opinion Mrs. Drummond-Burrell graciously added, "Overbred and inbred never does well. Consider Caroline Lamb. The Fortescue gel's rendering her home equally hideous," which, from a lady who had been one of the diamond's greatest admirers (if that self-important lady could be said to admire anyone beyond herself), indicated a disastrous fall from grace indeed. The diamond retreated to the fastness of the family mansion, and left the beau monde to titter or sympathize as they would.

" 'S come to a pretty pass," Giles informed Lady Daphne one afternoon over a glass of Madeira. "M'father's taken off for White's, swears he won't be back until m'mother's got Gwennie in form again. Don't see much chance of that. *She's* down pin again, and m'mother's tearing the house apart—won't say why. An' Soph an' Belle? M'mother swears she's takin' 'em to Brighton, bringin' 'em *both* out this summer, if you can credit it! They're *babies!* Why, Soph's not seen her sixteenth yet, and Belle's not a minute over fourteen, and they're both spotty as they can stare with lumps in all the wrong places. All they know to do if a fellow so much as *glances* at 'em is *giggle!* Fine mull *they'll* make of things, but m'mother claims they'll do if they starve themselves a bit—plump as partridges, don't you know—and put cucumber slices on their faces at night. *Do!* Every man with ears an' eyes'll run like sixty—t'other way.

"M'mother's lost her wits, that's what," he continued, "even if I shouldn't say it—don't try to tell me different! Ever play at billiards? She's like a ball you hit a glancin' blow without knowin' the trick of it—careens all over the place accomplishin' nothing. Make me look a cake, the lot 'em do, even m'father. Been playin' deep enough to drown mountains, an' losin' an abbey a night, I'm told. Haven't seen it for m'self—can't stand the hells, an' that's where he goes mostly—but that pays no duns. Can't look m'friends in the eye, an' *that's* the truth of it! Almost considerin' goin' on a repairin' lease 'til quarter day. I'm at low tide, an' m'father won't speak of an advance."

To this rather long-winded diatribe Lady Daphne made gentle murmurs of comfort, allowed as how young girls growing up was as hard on older brothers as on parents, and mentioned that buttonholes the size of cabbages were not quite the thing.

Hobbs proved a gem, much to Louisa's delight. The diminutive former sergeant and the formidable Commendatore achieved companionable understanding on first encounter, and early rides in the Park became a welcome beginning to each day. In one respect only did Hobbs fail to please: He kept such a stern eye on Louisa, and was so quickly at her side or only a few feet behind should any gentlemen join her, no matter how respectable, that it was as if Harry, and not she, had employed him. Nothing she said could dissuade him from his anxious hovering.

"It's this way, Miss Louisa," he explained with that instant familiarity of one who feels himself an old family retainer and specially privileged, no matter how long his period of employ, "Cap'n Gracechurch said as how I was to look arter you, no matter what, an' so, no matter what, I'm lookin' arter you. Take it up with the cap'n."

Take it up with "the cap'n" she did at the first opportunity, with lamentable lack of success.

"London isn't safe for beautiful, wealthy young women," he told her bluntly. "You may not be willing to accept any closer relationship between us, but you must let me stand your friend in this, and a poor friend indeed I would prove did I not see to your welfare and safety with your brother absent for an indefinite period. When some other man takes on the responsibility of you, I'll step aside. In the meantime, Hobbs will ride close—though not so close as to cause you embarrassment. There, perhaps, he has erred."

That Lady Daphne had Louisa's safety and welfare well in hand made not a jot of difference to the captain or the groom and so matters continued the same, with Hobbs dogging her every step beyond the house, even to constituting himself chief parcel bearer and escort on shopping expeditions, his wiry frame suprisingly strong, his pace indefatigable.

Regular meals and decent clothing had gone far to improve the man's appearance, but he remained scrawny as a starved chicken—to the great dismay of Cook, who had undertaken to fatten him to her size with bridals in mind. Courteous Hobbs invariably was to all, but for him no one appeared to exist but Louisa—a fact that at once touched and dismayed her. The man was so excellent at his assigned tasks, however, and so willing to help out even the pot boy (whose hero he had become, supplanting an aggrieved Charles), that she could not find it in herself to protest further. His devotion was obvious and total. A reprimand only brought a sorrowful look to his eyes and a stubborn jut to this chin. Louisa gave it up. When Morrison returned matters would rectify themselves. Hobbs she intended to have continue in her employ following their marriage. He was far more than a stablehand or simple groom—his knowledge of horseflesh encyclopedic, his judgment at least as good as her own, given his pithy comments on the mounts of the ton encountered on their rides—and would be of infinite use in establishing their stud. Hobbs had found a permanent home, if he wanted one. Morrison, she knew, would concur.

During this period Lady Daphne twice had a private caller. A small man, nondescript, quiet, and self-effacing, he slipped to and from the house with only Charles the wiser. Tom the Toff—he could mind his aitches and gees when he wished—was as satisfied with his temporary employer as she was with him. The only thing that didn't satisfy him in the beginning was his lack of success in the task she had set him.

"Well?" Lady Daphne inquired on his first visit, after seeing to it he was well supplied with ale and thick sandwiches of beef and cheese.

"I ain't found nothing," he said shamefacedly around enormous bites of bread and meat, "nor I ain't found nobody. I follers them officers, an' I goes where they goes,' an' they don't go *nowheres* but where they's suppose ter go. Divil-a-bit I've learnt, an' there's the truth with no bark on it. I ain't never seed nothing the like of it! Swells as they is usually goes on the town, but not *these* swells. No better 'n Bible-thumpers . . ." he concluded morosely. "Ain't natural."

"Exactly what are these places they go where they *should*," Lady Daphne asked, much intrigued and not entirely disappointed.

The Horse Guards, the Park, Almack's, the Clarendon (where they'd a friend staying who joined them regularly), some private homes, a "coupla boozin' kens," Vauxhall once with a large party, the theater, Manton's, Gentleman Jack's, White's—the list was innocuous enough. Lady Daphne considered the problem as the little man ate deliberately, making his way through the sandwiches as a fisherman would slog through mud. She felt as if she were engaged in much the same type of slogging, but with notably less success. The Clarendon was hopeless, the Horse Guards ditto, as were the traditional male haunts. But, were they? She could have him watch each of the private homes in turn for the comings and goings of a man who looked to be a physician, of course, but . . .

"How often do they go to Gentleman Jack's?" she asked. The former champion's sparring establishment was a favorite rendezvous with young, active gentlemen of the ton.

He shook his head. "Oncet," he said.

Clearly that wasn't it. "Cribb's! Is that one of the . . . ah . . . 'boozing kens?' "

Tom the Toff nodded. "Usually crowns the night there," he said.

And *that* was it! she smiled. Clever . . . A ring of protection could be woven about the Fotheringham boy in such a place so dense no one could penetrate it. But why had her thoughts turned in *that* direction? It had not been *protection* she had first thought of regarding Fotheringham—or at least not *that* sort of protection.

"There are private rooms, aren't there," she said consideringly.

"Ar," Tom answered around the last sandwich, imbibed a slug of ale. *"Wery* private, some on 'em."

"Are you familiar with Cribb and his place?"

"Good ken fer a pint."

"Wonderful! You shall have *many* pints there. Do you know the servants? Is there anyone new?"

He considered, eyeing the empty plate and pitcher thoughtfully. Then he nodded. "There be a old mort," he said, "kind o' finicking, waits in back."

"What does she look like?"

"A old mort," he shrugged. "Gentry-make, mebbe, wrong side o' the blanket."

"Could you take me there?"

"You? Wouldn't do," he said stiffly. "Wouldn't do a'tall."

She let it go regretfully. When they were girls it had invariably been hoydenish Daphne who fell into scrapes, composed Heather who rescued her. The idea of facing down Heather Fotheringham, posing as a superannuated serving wench in such a place, was positively delicious. And it *had* to be she, with Dickie sequestered somewhere within those "private" rooms. But, *why* . . . ? In the beginning she had merely wanted to find the boy to annoy the stiffly uncommunicative Gracechurch, and in passing confirm that it was to the lad the Glorious Gwendolyn had given what heart she had to give, the betrothal to Harry all her mother's doing.

"Would it appear strange if you went there several nights in a row?" she asked.

He shrugged, shook his head.

"Very well, then. Go for the next five nights, and then report to me. I will provide you with additional funds, for it won't do to have your pockets to let." He voiced a vigorous protest, pride insulted and manhood demeaned, at which she shook her head. "*My* responsibility," she insisted. "*My* orders *and my funds.* Do not be foolish, man! I want to know who accompanies Heath and Gracechurch, and who goes to the private rooms. *Every name!* It is no sinecure I'm handing you. You will have to follow them, learn their identities if you do not know them already."

The second meeting was more to Tom the Toff's satisfaction. If the old gentry-mort had been pleased the first time, now she was ecstatic.

"Winthrop, Fenton, and Malfont," she said smugly.

"But not fer the last two nights," he warned.

"That's understandable. They are no longer in town. And, His Grace the Duke of Rawdon . . . Now, *there's* an interesting one. He is supposedly gone from town also."

Tom the Toff shook his head. "Ain't gone nowhere," he said. "*And,* his man what calls hisself Jasper Foote." He looked at Lady Daphne dubiously, shrugged. She wanted to know. "An', yer gel's groom, Hobbs, only, if he be a groom, I'm the Prince o' Whales."

"I *wasn't* diddled!" she crowed with delight. "You, my dear Tom, are worth your weight in gold! Not that I *really* believed he was a *groom*. Or, *just* a groom, for he is an excellent one, you know. Is he *truly* 'Sergeant Willie Hobbs,' late of His Majesty's Forces?"

To this Tom could give no sure answer. Sergeant Hobbs was Sergeant Hobbs, so far as he had been able to determine. The man had no existence prior to entering Louisa's employ, but this wasn't all that unusual. Tom would see what he could learn if she wanted, but it might not be much, and certainly not worth the time or expense. There were too many like him, returned from the Peninsula with no future, no matter how heroic their past. Lady Daphne agreed. To have Hobbs confirmed as part of the strange group surrounding Louisa and Harry was enough.

But . . . *Rawdon!* With his unexpected presence, the pattern she had anticipated had been destroyed. If the cursed fellow had been playing fast and loose, she would have his liver for dinner *en brochette* . . .

That same night Marleybourne slept, breathing quietly under a liquid spring half-moon which transformed graveled paths to soft snow-drifted ribbons of dappled lace, and silvered leaves and trunks impartially. The shadows in the woods were thick and deep, night-rustlings of small creatures going about their private business only intensifying the sense of timeless peace.

Within the ancient house all was silent, servants and master abed, fires banked and dawn but a dream on a horizon many hours distant. A gentle night wind ruffled the surface of the ornamental lake and stirred the heavy draperies at Harry's windows, pulled back on his orders with casements thrown wide to allow the perfumed air and warmth of the season to flood the house with renewed life.

Harry tossed restlessly, sleep flown and mind churning. He was no closer to returning to town than he had been the day he arrived. Solve one problem and a dozen sprang up in its place, each demanding his personal attention. He seemed to have to do with idiots as the days hurtled toward the hour Lady Fortescue would show him the door, Louisa unwed and Gwendolyn lost to him forever. Lady Fortescue had been clear on the point: Gwendolyn had reached an age where further delay was unthinkable. If he missed his opportunity, he had no one to blame but himself.

Harry had been stunned, on the few occasions he was permitted the house, to discover the number of men of wealth and breeding who flocked around his diamond, civilians and officers alike. He had imagined nothing approaching it while in Spain, though he had admitted reluctantly to himself that she would not be sitting alone at home anxiously awaiting letters which, by parental decree, could never be sent. Malfont now formed part of her court, and Fenton had been dancing attendance since well before the disastrous morning in the Park, traitors both. While he might be effectively gagged by Lady Fortescue's commands, only a fool would not have seen how it was between him and Gwendolyn! For them to play at fixing their interests with her was sheer popinjay mischief. And he had counted them among his friends . . .

Harry wearily abandoned his bed and the futile task of finding rest there, pulled on a light silk dressing gown, and went to stare out the windows across his fertile acres. How barren the place would be without his darling, with her presence what a paradise on earth! Did Louisa have any concept of what she was doing to him, the despair and anguish her intransigence caused? As for the interfering old busybody who was his father's elder sister, she should have been locked away years ago. When he returned to London he would rectify everything—if he arrived in time. The question was, would he . . .

Something moved at the edge of the woods by the lake. Harry's eyes narrowed as he peered into the moonlit night, trying to distinguish form from shadow, similar sightings in the Peninsula stirring a *frisson* of unease at the back of his mind. No one had legitimate business out there at this hour. But, search however he might, he could spot nothing more. Whatever had lurked at the verge, it was gone. A deer or a poacher, he finally concluded, or else his own overactive imagination playing tricks on him in the suggestible hours before dawn. Any one of the three could account for the ambiguous sighting.

The next morning he walked the area, examining the undergrowth and the muddy lake banks with care. There were prints aplenty, both animal and human, as well as freshly broken branches, their green pithy hearts still bleeding sap. Crushed leaves littered the ground, adding a sharp tang to the softer scent of woodland flowers. It proved nothing, but he summoned Wharton that afternoon, warned the gamekeeper to be on the lookout for more poachers. Times were hard, hungry men not overly concerned with niceties of law and ownership. Should Wharton surprise anyone, Harry instructed the man be brought to the house. He would want to interview any miscreant personally before a formal complaint was lodged with Squire Worth, the local magistrate. Were the lawbreaker a returned Peninsular, or any other with equal right to his sympathy, he would do his best to render assistance.

Then he forgot the incident, caught up in the seemingly endless problems to be found on an estate the size and complexity of Marleybourne. Tenants' quarrels, missing stock—not only poachers appeared to have invaded the neighborhood—the depredations of urchins in trout stream and orchard, the illness of a pensioned servant now residing in the village, all had their claim on his attention. He gave it unstintingly, courtesy equal to that he remembered his gentle father showing, and if there were moments when his more ready temper longed to break forth, those who came to seek him never knew. The roofer arrived, complete with workmen and carts of slates and wood for scaffolding, and the spring peace of the house was destroyed. Forbearance expended, Harry strode down to the stables that afternoon, ordered Ben Cullum to saddle Thunderer, and took off across the fields at a wild full gallop, intent on outrunning his seemingly endless troubles.

He did not return until the sun was sinking behind the woods, casting long shadows across the sweeping lawns and flaming the Court's upper windows scarlet and gold and brilliant orange. The ride, he knew, had been the tonic he required, though guilt nibbled at the edges of his pleasurable exhaustion in acknowledgment of responsibilities self-indulgently abandoned.

He walked the lathered Thunderer slowly toward the stables, a gentle amble which hinted at no great desire to return to the confines of the house and the tedious, vexatious concerns that awaited him there even at this advanced hour.

Ben Cullum was sitting on the top paddock rail, shoulders hunched, staring moodily into the middle distance when Harry rode up. The elderly groom eased himself to the ground, spat, took hold of Thunderer's bridle, looking horse and man over with detached care, ferocious gray brows drawn down.

"Gone a fair piece, has you, sir," he said neutrally.

"A fair piece," Harry agreed, a twinkle in his eyes. "You don't approve?"

"It ain't for me to approve or disapprove, your lordship," the groom returned sourly, by which Harry knew he was in for a solid scold if he did not cut the man off at the outset. "If you're bent on breakin' your own fool neck, and foundering poor Thunderer here into the bargain, 'tis your business, and none of mine—though takin' your temper out on a poor defenseless beast ain't in no way what I can approve of, nor ever could!"

"True," Harry agreed amiably, dismounting with the care of a child on its first pony. "Give this old friend an extra measure of oats—he's earned it."

"And you'll be having an extra measure of oats at t'house, as well? You've been off-feed, they says."

"At least today I've appetite enough to do justice to Mrs. Preeble's cooking, which can't be said of the last few dinners she's had set before me—you're right there."

"You're peckish? Good. Then twon't worrit you none

to know there's guests come." Ben nodded at the stable door. "Full house, t'night."

"Guests?" Harry scowled. "There's no one expected."

"That's as how they said it was—that you wasn't in no way expecting 'em. Military gentlemen, three on 'em. Said as how you'd no notion of their bein' in the neighborhood, which was how they planned it. Wanted ter surprise you."

"Such surprises I can well dispense with," Harry snapped. "Out with it, man—which ones are they? You know them all from London."

"Seein' as how you asked me so polite-like, your lordship, it happens they're Colonel Winthrop, an' Major Fenton an' that Cap'n Malfont."

"Stop calling me 'your lordship,' " Harry spat, exasperated. "Just because I'm in your black books is no reason to treat me as if I were still in short coats."

"Sometimes that's where you belongs, your lordship," Ben grumbled. "Them's as fine a set of gentlemen as you'll find in a month o' Sundays. You treat 'em civil-like, or I'll not be lettin' you ride Thunderer tommorer."

Harry stared at Ben, caught his twinkling eye, and broke into a roar of delighted laughter. "A sprain mysteriously acquired in his stall during the night, no doubt?"

"Mebbe. Now, up to the house with you," Ben grinned in response, "an' don't you be forgettin' you ain't growed up so great an' grand I can't take a birch to you if needs be!"

The men were comfortably ensconced in the library when Harry joined them, apologizing for being absent when they arrived and then appearing in all his dirt.

"Your inn," Malfont smiled. "They give excellent service here, I'll have you know. Don't have to ask for anything above once! Not like Spain, thank the Lord!"

"Better not be," Harry grinned in response, "or I'll have sharp words with those who should know better.

Louisa had 'em well trained. What brings you all here?" he asked, turning to the colonel. "Not that I'm not delighted to see you."

"Are you?" Colonel Winthrop returned, a measuring look in his eye. "That's as well then, for we intend to bivouac here until you return to town. Reports that an uncle of mine was hanging by a hair were grossly exaggerated—nothing more than a flare-up of his gout, which always makes the old fellow cross as a bear, and declare he's about to stick his spoon in the wall. We pelted up posthaste, only to find we were least wanted—except as butts for his temper-fits. Poor old gaffer's not at his best at these times. Since we were in the general vicinity, we thought we'd make the best of a bad tale and impose on you."

Harry looked levelly at his former commanding officer, brows slowly rising. It was the longest speech he'd ever known the colonel to make.

"Imposition? Don't be absurd. Delighted to have you," he said, only partly lying. "No problem keeping you occupied. There's rabbits and rats in plenty, and the trout are rising nicely, even if there's no hare or boar. The squire's giving a birthday romp for his youngest girl—seventeen now, and a rare handful—tomorrow, so you'll have a chance to examine what the neighborhood offers in the way of fair companions, as well."

"You don't have to entertain *us*," Percy Fenton threw in with a grin. "A corner of your barn'll do, so long as the hay's dry and clean. Better billet than many we've known."

"If Mrs. Cruickshank hasn't seen you comfortably settled, and your men as well if you brought 'em, I'll stand on my head and sing 'Rule, Britannia'!"

"She's seen to us most delightfully," Colonel Winthrop smiled, more certain of his ground here. "Delightful lady—reminds me of my Aunt Amelia. Put us in rooms near yours to save the servants trouble at my suggestion. I hope you don't mind?"

"No need for the State Apartments," Malfont tossed in, "and that did seem her first intention."

"Wouldn't know how to act in 'em," Fenton grinned, "not even George here, and he's the highest rank among us."

"Oh, I say now—" the colonel returned, flushing.

The rest burst into laughter as Harry helped himself to wine from a decanter on his desk, then raised his glass.

"To dry billets," he chuckled, "with no fleas and no lice and no bedbugs, smoke that goes up a chimney as God and man intended, and a sound roof over our heads—or a partially sound one, at any rate. Missing slates brought me here, among other things," he added at their questioning looks, "vandals, apparently—though how they managed it I've no notion. Repairs are in hand."

It wasn't that Harry was truly pleased to see the three officers, but he wasn't exactly displeased either. Unrelieved doses of his own company, broken only by two invitations to dine at the local squire's and one at the vicarage—all the other neighbors being in Town—had begun to pall. If he was to be stuck at Marleybourne, and it appeared he was for the moment, better to have congenial companions than not. The Court was far enough from London that Lady Fortescue's caveats need not apply. If he were successful in wedding Louisa off, this might be his last opportunity for such masculine indulgence. Furious though he had been when he learned of Fotheringham's attack on Gwendolyn, he could not in fairness blame these men for the young lout's disgusting behavior. He had been overly hasty there—fortunately only in his mind, but he still felt a twinge of guilt at his almost irrational fury with all men in uniform because of the failings of one. They might not know it, these three old comrades-in-arms, but he owed them the deepest of apologies. He hoped his actions would speak for him, had they an inkling of his earlier sentiments, for raise the subject he could not.

Harry cornered Fenton later that evening, desperate for news of his Gwendolyn, and certain Lord Percy had made the most of his enforced absence from the city.

"Don't rightly know," Fenton replied to his hesitant inquiries after a thoughtful pause. "George got word of his uncle shortly after you left, and I can't say paying court to the diamond was uppermost in any of our minds. We thought we were going to attend a deathbed, you see, and other matters were submerged in the larger issue."

Harry looked at him askance, brows rising.

"Why don't you ask George," the major suggested reluctantly. "He might be aware of something I am not."

But, Colonel Winthrop knew no more of the diamond's state of health or recovery from the unfortunate morning expedition to Hyde Park than Fenton, and Malfont was equally ignorant. It shocked Harry to realize these seemingly kindly men felt no more concern toward a lovely and delicate young girl after whom they had dangled only days before than they would have toward a stranger. He finally accepted with a disillusioned shrug that they might be incapable of judging her true worth, and had merely been amusing themselves at her expense. It was a common-enough failing.

The evening passed pleasurably, billiards succeeding whist, brandy liberally lacing both, remembrances of shared Peninsular adventures and mishaps growing with the retelling. When Harry retired for the night he found himself yawningly sleepy—whether from his wild ride across the fields or the generous potations in which he had indulged following an enormous and delicious dinner he was unsure—not that it mattered. It was enough that, for the first time since his arrival at Marleybourne, he was content to seek his bed. Sleep, hard and deep, came quickly that night.

He never knew what woke him.

It may have been that uncanny sense, developed in the Peninsula, which had saved his life more than once. Even the ball that found him had not done the damage it might, for he had whirled aside an instant before it struck, arm rather than heart taking the blow. Perhaps it was an attack of biliousness—certainly they had all indulged themselves at dinner and after. The only thing of which he was ever certain was that he roused to full and instant wakefulness, conscious of another person in the room.

Harry froze. The darkness was relieved by a single tentative shaft of moonlight striking through the window to silhouette a burly figure looming over him, little more than an amorphous shape that blended with the bed curtains he never closed.

There was no time for thought or conscious action as a pillow slammed over his face, choking off breath. Grunted words that made no sense rang in his ears. *"Got ye this time, me fine lord!"*

The man was pressing a knee against his chest, rhythmically expulsing air from his lungs, simultaneously crushing the pillow against nose and mouth. Harry forced himself to relax beneath the suffocating weight, then exploded, almost convulsing as he grabbed one-armed at his assailant, legs flailing. A twisting wrench brought him to his feet, pillow and attacker flung away. He lunged for the cursing, elusive figure as he roared for Fenton, Winthrop, Malfont—someone to come to his aid. There was a handful of dark rough fabric in his hand, and then that was all there was—cloth trailing to the floor and tangling in his legs as his muscular attacker leapt to the sill of his window, swung over the ledge, grabbed a rope hanging there and slid down. The sound of receding hoofbeats echoed in his ears as Malfont, Fenton, and Winthrop tumbled into his room, nightcaps askew, hair tousled, eyes sleep-rimed.

"What's to do?" Winthrop glanced around the dark room. "Nightmare?" Then he spotted the rope tied to a heavy chest beside the window, glistening in the moonlight, and the cloth dangling from Harry's hand. He touched Malfont's arm, pointed.

"Not exactly," Harry croaked, knees shaking. "Damned housebreaker. Light some candles, will you?"

He sank onto the edge of his bed, clutching the fabric in a death grip. A golden glow rose before him. He stared numbly at Percy Fenton, dressing gown slung hastily over elegant shoulders, burst into high-pitched laughter. The man's hair was in spikes.

"Some brandy, I think," he heard Winthrop murmur, and footsteps receded.

A hand was on his shoulder, shaking him. He was relieved firmly of what proved to be a heavily worn and filthy brown frieze cloak. A glass was thrust in his hand, his hand forced to his lips. He gulped fiercely at the stinging liquor, gasped, shuddered, and the room took on a semblance of normality. Malfont was at the window coiling the rope. Winthrop loomed over him, Fenton at his side, decanter in hand. He glared at his friends, held out the glass, hand still unsteady. It was refilled. He took another gulp, then a deep breath.

"I don't know what's the matter with me," he rasped. "Never reacted like this in the Peninsula."

"It's different when it's personal," Winthrop said gently. "I think it's time we talked."

"*Personal?* There's nothing personal about a housebreaker," Harry protested, standing with slow effort. "I've made a fool of myself, is all. First I leave my window open as clear invitation, and then I can't even manage to overcome the bloody bastard! Fine husband I'll make some poor benighted woman . . . Useless, plodding—"

"Enough of that!" Winthrop snapped. "We can talk here, or we can go downstairs if you'd prefer, but talk we will."

"Don't be an old woman," Harry snarled.

"Leave it be, George," Percy Fenton cautioned, grasping the older man's arm. "Isn't the time or place for it. *Wait.*"

Winthrop glanced at Malfont, a question in his eyes. The young captain looked long and hard at Harry, still shivering by the bed, most of the second glass of brandy gone.

"Leave it," he agreed. "There's always tomorrow, or the next day."

"Am I then to be permitted to return to my bed, find what rest I can?" Harry snapped with an edge to his voice. "This ain't the Peninsula, you know, and we're none of us under orders. It's *my house!*" The words had an insulted, petulant ring to them, as if he couldn't decide which were the greater offense—the invasion of his home, or the fact that another man dared attempt to issue orders there.

Malfont's hand descended heavily on his shoulder. "It's late, Harry, and you've had a bit of a do. Dawn, soon. Sleep if you can. If you can't, I'm only across the hall and always eager for an early ride."

Harry nodded, tight-lipped, refusing to relinquish what little control he had regained. It was not the attack that horrified him so deeply, but his shuddering reaction to it. He watched, hollow-eyed, as the three men filed from his room. It appeared he had lost more than an arm at Salamanca.

Eleven

They were about to abandon the breakfast table a few hours later when a clattering rose from the gravel which paved the circular drive in front of the Court.

The meal had been strained, Harry looming at the table's head like a sepulchral visitor as he brooded over the night's events, eyes the murky color of slate, voice curt and forbidding, scar livid in his haggard face. Repeatedly the colonel had attempted to raise the issue of the night intruder. Repeatedly Harry scowled him down as the two younger officers exchanged concerned, uneasy glances.

A man had been born during the small hours, sour and reclusive in his thoughts, taciturn—not precisely uncivil, but ill at ease as much with himself as with his companions. Harry Beckenham was in a state of shock, denying what had occurred except for his own inglorious part in it, and *that* he dwelt on with morbid, self-denigrating fury if he spoke at all. For the rest, he snarled "Leave it!" to Winthrop's mildest attempts at discussion of circumstance or intent. He was beyond reason, refusing to listen or analyze or consider—the diametric opposite of the keen-minded young officer of the Peninsula. More time was needed, the three officers realized—likely more than would be granted them, if events of the previous night were anything to judge by.

Now Harry rose from his place, food almost untouched, to investigate the unexpected arrival, his friends watching anxiously as he stalked to the open windows overlooking the drive, face thunderous, hand rising to grip the frame. He paused there, scowl deepening, body taut. Then a reluctant grin cracked his rigid features.

"I'll be damned," he said softly. "It's the puppy!"

A dust-covered dun horse trembled wearily just beyond the steps, legs splayed, sides heaving, muzzle almost touching the ground. Giles Fortescue, ginger hair bare to the morning sun, sagged in the saddle—as filthy and disreputable as his mount, and equally past caring about his surroundings or appearance—whatever color his coat and leathers might once have boasted hidden under layers of road-grime. Slowly he raised his head as if drawing on some last reserve of strength, and peered uncomprehendingly around him. A groom was dashing up from the stables, cramming a chunk of bread in his pocket as he hastily wiped his mouth with the back of his hand, several others pelting behind. He skidded to a halt, gravel flying beneath his thick boots, and reached up to assist the boy in dismounting. Giles shook his head and swung out of the saddle, wavering slightly as his feet met the drive.

"I'll do," the young voice floated to the house, harsh with exhaustion. "See to m'poor nag, will you? Done yeoman service." He pulled a portmanteau from where it dangled on the rawboned mare's rump, unbuckling the leather straps which held it to the saddle, and handed a stableboy a shilling. "Give her a good rubdown, an' extra feed. Might be well to walk her, if she'll stand for it. Doubt she will. Pushed us both unmercifully."

"Whatever can that young make-bait have been about?" Concern and amusement warred in Harry's voice as Colonel Winthrop joined him at the window. "He looks like he's been on a forced march!"

Winthrop's eyes narrowed as he stared incredulously at

the boy, now staggering up to the house as Bedloe opened the heavy door and a brace of footmen hastened down the steps to relieve him of his bag.

"Damn!" he muttered. "Of all the impertinent gall." He threw a worried glance at Malfont and Fenton. "It's the Fortescue sprig," he cautioned.

The captain and the major returned his look, faces grim. Harry was already striding into the hall, shoulders back, head up, eyes sparkling, showing the first signs of returning to himself since the night's upheavals as his voice rang out in amused welcome, cares thrust aside for the moment. The officers quickly gathered by the table, conferring in low tones as they glanced apprehensively at the open door, Winthrop issuing orders, Malfont and Fenton nodding agreement and throwing in occasional suggestions.

"What devilment have you been up to now, you young jackanapes!" Harry's words floated back to them. "Is that any way to treat an innocent beast?"

"Wanted to see if I was up to it," the immature voice cracked, touched with pride. "Know all about Wellington's forced marches. Did it! Not a bite to eat all the way from town—just water. That's how *you* did it with Moore at Corunna, ain't it? Did better by m'nag, but not much. Came straight through, night an' day, except when we slept by the road, an' we didn't sleep much, let me tell you! 'Course, we didn't have Frogs shootin' at us, so it wasn't *really* the same . . . We walked, or we jogged, an' sometimes we trotted if she was up to it, an' we never stopped 'less she couldn't go on. Even led her part of the way—to give her a rest, you know. Strange experience— sleepin' under the stars. Don't know how you stood it. I imagined all *kinds* of things!"

"You young fool!" Harry laughed. "Whatever are you doing here?"

"Thought I'd bear you company. Things're black-and-blue grim at home."

The three officers appeared in the arched stone doorway of the dining chamber, eyes narrowed, faces cold and uncommunicative, hesitating as they reviewed the cavernous great hall's layout. A sweeping oak staircase rose in the center to divide into paired galleries at the second level, guarded by suits of ancestral armor on pedestals. On either side soared twin fireplaces large enough to roast an ox. Harry stood by the heavy Jacobean refectory table in the middle of the hall, hand resting on its gleaming dark surface, Giles in front of him, battered portmanteau at his feet. Winthrop eased to the side, from which vantage he could observe the tableau of boy and man. Fenton and Malfont moved to flank Harry, a derisive smile on Malfont's lips, contempt and hatred flaming in Fenton's eyes.

The boy stared at the three men in consternation.

"Odd—we had the same thought, as you can see," Fenton said with acid sweetness.

"I'm sorry." The boy turned to Harry, shamefaced, shoulders sagging, the laughter and triumph of his great surprise evaporated. "You've no need of me at all. Of all the blundering clunches—I'd no idea—"

"How could you, cawker?" Harry grinned. "*These* idiots only appeared on my doorstep last night, determined I turn innkeeper. Come, Giles—it's no disaster! We'll be glad of your company." He threw his arm around the dejected boy, and pulled him toward the dining chamber. "See to food for young Mr. Fortescue," he called to Bedloe, lurking by the staircase. "Lots of it! He's sure to be ravenous. And have Mrs. Cruickshank put him in the rooms I had as a boy, and tell her to have a bath readied. He wants at least one—if not three or four! Now," he continued, forcing Giles to a chair beside his own at the heavy oak table which was mate to the one in the hall, "what's all this about things being 'black-and-blue grim' at home? You look like the very devil! Here—clean the worst of the grime from your hands with this." Harry tossed him a handkerchief and shoved the bowl of pansies in the center of the table toward him, first removing the flowers and pitching them in the cold fireplace. "Use the water in there. Have they sent you for me? Gwendolyn's not ill, is she?"

The boy flushed, scrubbed at his hands, shook his head, discarded the handkerchief after a few swipes, reached for an apple. "A bit vaporish is all, but m'mother's at sixes and sevens, an' the house's all torn up. Uncomfortable. So, I thought I'd play least-in-sight for a bit, 'specially as m'pockets're to let an' m'father cut up stiff over an advance on m'allowance. They don't know where I am, an' they won't care," he added, slightly defensive. "Left a note, but no particulars—just said I'd gone on a repairing lease to visit a sick friend."

"Dun territory again?" Harry scowled. "I thought I warned you the last time—"

" 'T'ain't my fault!" Giles protested around his apple. "Not this time. Wasn't the last time, either, only I didn't like to tell you. M'mother's forever wantin' most o' m'blunt for the housekeeping—says havin' me at home's an expense she can't meet—an' m'father's always demandin' part to pay off his cursed vowels. Belle an' Soph an' Gwennie usually filch the rest for some demmed female doodad or other when m'back's turned. Only one ain't had his hands in m'purse this quarter's Cousin Norval, an' *that's* only 'cause he sold off his cattle. If I ever get to spend a crown on m'self these days, I'm doin' well. Wasn't like that at first," he conceded, munching disgustedly, "but it is now."

"I'd no idea . . ."

" 'Course you didn't. Ain't the kind of thing one likes to talk about. Easier to let you think I'm a fool with no notion the worth of a coach-wheel—one has *some* family pride, after all—but not *this* time! M'mother made me sell up m'curricle two days ago, y'see," he explained indignantly, *"and* m'team. Said Belle an' Soph need new dresses for Brighton. So, I held back a couple pounds for m'self and lit out from town on Gorgon—she ain't pretty, but she gets me places—before m'mother made me sell *her* as well. Gorgon wouldn't've brought much anyhow, but it'd've been useless to tell m'mother that. No way she'd've listened," he added, discarding the core. "Always gets what she wants, m'mother does—*always!*"

The three officers had been standing in the doorway listening to Giles's candid recital of how things stood at Fortescue House. Now they resumed their places as Bedloe and four footmen entered with fresh platters of cold beef and bread, chunks of Double-Gloucester and crumbly yellow Cheddar, boiled eggs, the remains of a game pie, and more foaming pitchers of ale. Harry winced at the stately procession. Fenton refilled his tankard and leaned back, measuring Giles unwinkingly as the boy piled his plate high and dug in with the gnawing appetite of youth.

"River Tick, eh?" he commented.

Giles looked up, nodded. "Whole family's at point-non-plus," he mumbled around his sirloin. "No reason not to say so. Whole town'll know soon enough. Lodge's mortgaged to the hilt. M'father sold off what land wasn't entailed years ago, an' what's left's in bad heart 'cause he bleeds it dry. Reason they want Gwennie to get hitched. Can't understand what you out-an'-outers see in her, m'self. Mewling chit if ever there was one, an' so stuck on herself she don't *need* any other admirers—but then, I'm only her brother."

"Dear God . . . No, you wouldn't understand," Harry said, voice hollow. "She is everything of which a man dreams."

"Be a lot prettier if she didn't pout so much," Giles

retorted sagely, "an' a lot nicer to have around if she didn't think she's so perfect everybody has to bow an' scrape if she lifts her little finger, but then if I can't see what you do in her, you're not likely to see what I see, either."

"Oh, wisdom of youth," Fenton murmured. "As bad as all that," he asked aloud, wincing at the pain and horror in Harry's eyes.

"Worse," Giles returned baldly. He shrugged. "It's none of my doing, but I do feel sorry for Belle and Soph. It's none o' their doing either, even if they are silly twits with their noses in the air and giggling all the time, and they're the ones likely to have to pay the piper. Gwennie's had her chance, and a fine mull she's made of it. *Now* m'mother's talking of emigrating if the Brighton thing don't work."

"I see . . ." Malfont said. "Why Brighton?"

"Lots o' fools in Brighton," Giles grinned. "Big military camp, too. M'mother insists Soph an' Belle're sure to snag a few hearts, an' that'd get us out of dun territory for a while, what with the marriage settlements. Me, I think she's muddle-headed."

"Surely you can't be serious!" Harry exploded, ignoring the edict of silence and the presence of his three friends in face of the disaster Giles so matter-of-factly detailed. "There was no sign of any of this when I left, and once Gwendolyn is my wife, everything will be regularized. There's no need for—"

"She'll never marry you," Giles stated flatly. "Never marry anyone, come to that. Ain't made for parson's mousetrap. You wait an' see."

"It's all a boy's exaggerations," Harry insisted later to the silent Winthrop.

They were returning to the Court after a leisurely tour

of the nearer parts of the estate—an excursion requested by Winthrop, who claimed he had no notion of land management, and had best begin to learn as his uncle might only have suffered from the gout this time, but wouldn't last forever. His request had been strongly seconded by Fenton and Malfont, who suggested the best person to escort them might be the bailiff as Harry was sure to be occupied with estate matters. Harry had scoffed at the idea, delighted with the excuse to escape the house and his viscountial responsibilities for a day in the open, using tenant visits as his pretext to both them and himself.

The day had been just what he needed—no demands on his time or purse, and no opportunity for brooding on his personal concerns. He had played tour guide with verve and charm, landlord with unerring skill and warmth, but now, homeward bound with face pleasantly sun and wind burned, muscles just short of complaint, body and mind relaxed, he felt able to turn to pressing matters set aside in the morning.

Ahead of them Fenton, Malfont, and a clean and revived Giles rode together, Giles mounted on one of Harry's hacks, eagerly prying every imaginable scrap of information about Wellington, the Peninsula, and above all the Light Bobs from the two amused officers. "Army-mad," Harry had winked earlier, once the strange tension he had sensed in his friends at the boy's unexpected presence had eased. "Don't let him tease you overmuch."

They still watched the puppy with latent wariness, but the curt rejoinders, the barbed comments, the sarcastic tones seemed done with. Harry was thankful. What had come over them he could not imagine, for these were men well accustomed to the impetuosities, the erratic fits and starts of young sprigs suddenly released from parental restraint, and more than capable of dealing with high-spirited antics without sour snubs. The boy had done nothing to earn their dislike or contempt, and yet even now their bristling was merely subdued, hackles ready to rise at the most innocent question or statement. Harry found it not a little irritating, as well as deucedly uncomfortable.

"That there may be minor temporary problems of some sort, I'll grant," he continued now as their mounts ambled peacefully up a gentle rise, the sun warm on their backs. Thunderer snorted, tossing his head. Harry brought him to book with a firm word as the trio ahead vanished into a small spinney of oak and beech and elm through which the farm track they were following meandered. "Nothing unusual in that, even among the best families—and the Fortescues are certainly *that*. But, a catastrophe of the magnitude Giles implies? Impossible! Minor reverses on the 'Change, most likely, with Lord Fortescue foolish enough to inform his wife, and that poor lady with no more understanding of financial matters than any female, and so envisaging the wolf at the door. Lads of Giles's age—He's barely eighteen, after all!—have a penchant for disaster and drama. When we return to town, we'll find it's all a tempest in a teapot rather than the Cheltenham tragedy he regaled us with earlier—mark my words."

"Likely you have the right of it," Winthrop returned noncommittally, eyes sweeping the country through which they passed. "You have greater knowledge of their circumstances than ever I could." He stiffened of a sudden, squinting against the sun as he studied a low grassy hill crowned by gorse and stunted trees to their right and slightly behind them, dropping back to form a barrier between Harry and whatever he had glimpsed. "Thought I saw movement in that coppice," he pointed. "Anyone supposed to be up there?"

Harry shrugged. "Have to ask my bailiff," he said disinterestedly. "I've nothing to do with daily assignments . . . Still, it might be best to put forward our return—though

Giles will be in high dudgeon after his dramatic flight to rescue me from my own company."

"The lad will survive." Winthrop's narrowed eyes remained fixed on the hill, his face blank.

"You're right there—made of iron under all his silly fopperies, but Gwendolyn lacks the strength to suffer any reverse, no matter how minor, unsupported."

"What of your roof, and the rest of it?"

"My damned steward can see to it. If he can't, I'll find another steward."

They were approaching the spinney now, following the same bend in the track around which the others had vanished minutes ago.

"By far too late to set out today," Winthrop objected, considering the level of the sun with a practiced eye. They entered the spinney, the little hill now blocked by thick trees. The others reappeared ahead of them, waiting in the center of the track as they talked. Winthrop's shoulders visibly relaxed as he eased abreast of Harry. "I've no desire to pretend I'm haring for Corunna again."

"There's Squire Worth's do tonight, in any case. Promised I'd go, and I wouldn't let little Patsy down for the world. She sets some store on my being there, you see," Harry grinned, troubles temporarily forgotten. "I've pulled the minx from more trout streams and rescued her from more brambles and apple trees—Including my own!—than you can count since she was the size of a grasshopper, and she insists I'll never believe she's 'all grown up and a real lady' unless I'm there. She's right—I won't believe it, even then."

The men ahead of them broke into a slow canter, vanishing around another bend in the irregular track.

"What are you going to do about the boy?" Winthrop asked after a moment.

"Giles? Take him with us, if you can bear his Peninsular -*itis* all the way to London," Harry chuckled. Then his face turned serious. "What I'd really like is to purchase the lad a pair of colors, but Lady Fortescue would never stand for it. Despises Wellington, the army, all of it. Our faces are disfigured by exposure to the elements, you see," he explained wryly. "She feels even more strongly about the navy. *Not* proper vocations for *gentlemen*."

"Keep it in mind, once we're in town. If young Fortescue is everything you claim, I'll see to him when the time comes."

"A generous offer—especially as you didn't appear to care for him overly much at first meeting."

"It's possible I misjudged him. If I did, he might be glad of those colors one day."

"He'd be glad of them now."

"All the more reason . . ."

The gunshots came just as they were exiting the spinney—two in rapid succession, then silence, then a third.

The vouchers had arrived. Far too late to impart any cachet, and long after Lady Daphne had given them up as a lost cause, but they *had* arrived. Almack's had opened its hallowed portals at last, Louisa's gallop across the Park forgiven, provinciality and lamentable bookish tendencies overlooked in favor of face and fortune and name.

Louisa tossed the heavy cream cards aside, lip curling, and reached out to touch the delicate white rose in its cloisonné container at her place, dawn-moist fern fronds embracing its perfection. Her eyes softened. Seven days would have been an eternity just now, and Morrison had outstayed his anticipated absence by an additional three. Was he *never* returning . . . ?

"What was that you discarded with *such* disgust?" Lady Daphne inquired, glancing up from the *Morning Post*.

"Proof I was not conspicuously born to the wrong side of the blanket, am possessed of the customary limbs and sensory organs, and am not noticeably lacking in either hair or wit—though the latter is not a prime requisite."

"*Almack's!*" Lady Daphne breathed. "*At last!*"

"I have no need of their condescension," Louisa protested, smile lingering in her eyes.

"No? Think of your daughters!"

"The Drummond-Burrell will not live forever."

"Don't count on it. She is *exactly* the sort who will, just to confound us all." Lady Daphne stretched out her hand. "Let me see!" she commanded.

Reluctantly, Louisa handed the missives over. Lady Daphne seized them and examined them joyfully, eyes aglow.

"Sally Jersey, no less! And, today is *Wednesday.* How fortunate! Tonight, we *go!*"

"Attend the Marriage Mart? Don't be idiotish! I'd be flying in false feathers."

"Fly featherless, if you wish. You're *going!*"

"Nothing but weak tea, stale cake, dry bread-and-butter, thimbles of lemonade, and every impossible female in London staring down her nose at me? No, I thank you! I've better things to do with my time."

"Such as mooning over roses? Morrison would expect you to go, given the opportunity," Lady Daphne insisted, resorting to tactics her contemporaries would have recognized on the instant. "Think of the stud!"

"*At Almack's?*"

"Absolutely! Contacts," Lady Daphne explained, certain of her ground. "The gentlemen who lead you out tonight will purchase horses tomorrow. Well, not quite *tomorrow,* perhaps, but *soon.*"

"I do not desire to exhibit myself in that place," Louisa declared with a flash of her old temper. "To this moment I have gone everywhere you suggest. I have comported myself as you direct, dressed as you command, chosen my acquaintance where you dictate. But, Almack's? *No!* Demeaning, cheapening, disgusting! James would *never* expect it of me, and you should not, either. I *will not* expose myself to inspection by every rake and fortune hunter in London, my 'points' reviewed as if I were a prime bit o' blood to be broke to bridle. There is no need for it now, and *I won't do it!*"

"Yes, I remember—'Tatt's is more honest.' Don't be *missish*, Louisa. It ain't becoming. Besides, it'll be you judging the bloods against your precious Morrison, if I've any knowledge of you. Am I right, or am I wrong?"

"You'd be right, of course, if—"

"I am *always* right," Lady Daphne declared with a twinkle, "or hadn't you noticed? No more foolishness, miss, and no more argumentation. What your Morrison expects of you may prove a shock once you know a bit more of him. Tonight we go, and there's an end to it!"

She dragged a protesting Louisa to her bedchamber, summoned Holfers, inspected every gown and declared only one—fortunately previously unworn—suitable for a first appearance in Almack's august precincts. Then it was the Pantheon Bazaar for new kid gloves and slippers, a quick stop by Hookham's to exchange a book, another at Gunter's for ices to revivify them, and Lady Daphne swept Louisa home to be teased by the coiffeur, pestered and poked and prodded by Holfers, and admired when she descended the stairs at last by Hoskins, Charles, Matthew, and Hobbs, the supper she had hastily consumed from a tray in her room a leaden weight on her stomach, her hands and feet ice, and a headache promising to grow to gargantuan proportions already in fine fettle behind her brows.

There was no denying Louisa presented a stunning picture despite her irritation with the entire ritual and the almost superstitious reverence with which Lady Daphne regarded not only the event, but the preparations preceding it.

Only one gown of traditional debutante-white had found its way into Louisa's colorful wardrobe, but such a gown! Virginal it was, as tradition dictated—a filmy sar-cenet confection over a slip of white satin, with innocent clusters of delicate blue silk forget-me-nots at shoulder, high waist and relatively demure neckline emphasizing the simple, elegant lines, but the effect was regal rather than chichi or girlish. Her golden curls were dressed à la Sappho, feathery tendrils permitted to escape at random to soften her face, ice-blue and silver ribbons twining through her hair, caught here and there by still more forget-me-nots. Her mother's pearls, a gauze scarf of ice-blue silk and ice-blue gloves, completed the toilette pre-scribed by her aunt.

"The fabric and touch of color elevate you from the schoolgirl, thank Heavens," Lady Daphne proclaimed after inspecting her carefully, twitching skirts and adjust-ing draperies until she was satisfied. "I was never certain about this gown . . . You'll do."

"I should hope so!" Louisa snapped. "I do not expect to expend this much time or effort on my wedding day, and to endure all this merely to impress a set of unpleasant old harridans is ridiculous!"

"You will learn I *never* expend effort needlessly." Lady Daphne handed her a delicate fan, the lacy spokes of creamy carved ivory linked by the finest gauze on which had been painted still more forget-me-nots touched with diamond dust, her eyes unexpectedly misting. "For luck," she said softly. "I was carrying this at the ball where I met your uncle. The spokes are the same, though the fabric is new. Now, a pleasant expression on your pretty face as the final ornament, if you please!"

Louisa complied with poor grace. The result was not exactly what Lady Daphne had in mind. She sighed as she shepherded her niece to their waiting carriage, Hobbs trotting behind them to ride beside the coachman. Was there *ever* such a contrary girl . . . !

They arrived at Almack's well in advance of the hour the doors were closed, but late enough they did not form part of the initial crush. Lady Daphne swept Louisa through the ceremony of greeting the patronesses—only gentle Lady Cowper and acid-tongued Countess Lieven were in evidence by the entry—and to chairs at one side of the main room.

The orchestra was holding forth from its balcony, a spirited mazurka that had the couples whirling in the well-lit ballroom like parti-colored leaves caught in a high wind. Knots of chaperons lined the walls, tiny chairs clumped together. Unfortunate wallflowers gathered protectively, chattering as if gossip and exchanges of compliments on each other's toilettes were the sole reasons for their presence. Blades scanned the room, quizzing glasses raised in lordly hauteur, examining potential partners as they would cattle at a country fair and belittling most as being either of insufficient beauty or fortune. The atmosphere was moist, stifling, redolent with the aroma of overheated bodies and the cloying sweetness of too many clashing scents too liberally applied. Louisa's nose wrinkled in distaste.

"Are they expecting Prinny, that they will not permit a breath of air?" she complained, then looked about her more carefully, determined to be displeased and finding it no difficult endeavor. "So, this is the holy of holies," she commented with as much disdain as interest as they sat. "It's not much, is it? Even the room is poorly proportioned, and the orchestra only tolerable. What fools people are!"

"Yet, it serves its purpose," Lady Daphne smiled. "If a gentleman of substance searching for a suitable wife encounters a girl *here*, he can be certain her *antecedents* are impeccable, whatever her *character*. As for the gentlemen, they are in such demand even your Morrison would not be shown the door should he present himself—so long as he kept the mark, naturally."

"Morrison? Here? Never!" Louisa said sourly. *"He* would know better. Tell me—what would he have in common with *those?"* She indicated a gaggle of preening fops as they drifted past ogling the season's crop, quizzing glasses active, lisps and drawls rendering their speech fashionably incomprehensible. "Or, heaven forbid, *those!"* tilting her head toward three girls in overly decorated muslins whose affected simpers, baby-talk, gushes of shrill laughter, sidelong glances, and fluttering lashes were rendering them both conspicuous and ridiculous. "He would never hold himself so cheap!"

"You select the worst possible examples, and offer them as a paradigm. Unjust, Louisa! Those poor little geese are only what their mothers made them, and *exactly* what a certain type of gentleman finds *most* attractive."

The set came to an end. Tabitha Brassthwaite bustled up, exclaiming delight over their unexpected presence. Louisa relinquished her chair and was instantly claimed for the next set by the Honorable Gordon Dinsmore, dun-colored locks artfully plastered across his ruddy skull to mask an unfortunate lack of hair. Of similarly disguising his pomposity and lack of wit there was not the least hope. Louisa threw a despairing look at her aunt. Lady Daphne beamed innocently, reminded her to refuse all waltzes until presented with a suitable partner by one of the patronesses, and turned back to her friend, barely missing a beat in their flow of gossip.

From that moment Louisa was swept from the arms of one buck to the next, feet trodden on, sense and sensibility assaulted, a smile pasted across her face with the same determination as Dinsmore's hair ornamented his cranium, and with equal lack of believability. Of relief there was little—a set with Captain Gracechurch, another with the younger brother of a heavy-lidded Pink graced with the improbable name of Heironymus Excelsior Coddington-Smythe. The captain was a delight, the sprig a pleasant surprise. At the end of their set he escorted Louisa to a chair, then hurried off to procure her a glass of lemonade.

The floor cleared, the couples melting away as Louisa watched absently, wishing young Coddington-Smythe had deposited her rather closer to Lady Daphne. The orchestra shuffled sheets of music, adjusted seats and tunings, and the unmistakable rhythms of a waltz washed over the room. Louisa sighed wistfully, preparing herself for another half hour discussing pointer bitches, Aristophanes, and the esoteric art of fly-casting.

Then, cutting straight across the floor toward her, swept Sally Jersey. Her plump hand rested lightly on the arm of a tall, broad-shouldered man whose curling dark hair was lightly dusted with silver at the temples. Lady Jersey's face was upturned to his, her chatter gushing as she flirted shamelessly.

"James . . ." Louisa breathed in disbelief, heart racing.

Strange—it was he who looked to belong here, the others who seemed out of place. The easy pride of his carriage and the perfection of his stark evening dress turned every head. Simpers and fluttering lashes swirled in his wake, fops and fribbles blanching at the picture of heedless masculine power he presented. Heads nodded in his direction, smiles flashed, greetings were called. They were halfway across the floor, couples parting before them like the Red Sea for Moses. Three quarters of the way. Then they were almost treading on her skirts, Sally Jersey giggling and simpering like a girl fresh from the schoolroom, rapping Morrison's knuckles with her fan, calling him a naughty man for having stayed away so long, commanding him never to do so again. Across the room Lady Daphne surged to her feet, eyes staring, mouth open, poised as if she intended to charge across the floor. Tabitha Brassthwaite grabbed her arm, holding her back. Sally Jersey was on top of Louisa now, eyes snapping, mouth drawn up in a perfect bow. Behind her Morrison loomed, dark and substantial, a slight smile twisting his lips.

"Miss Beckenham," Lady Jersey trilled affectedly, all flutters and graces, "this gentleman has most particularly requested that I present him to you as an excellent partner for the waltz. I am sure you are aware of the honor he does you."

Louisa rose slowly, eyes locking questioningly with Morrison's. She read amusement there, delight, supreme confidence, the wonderful warmth that had drawn her to him against her will, as the beginnings of dread stirred in her heart. He *belonged* here . . .

"His Grace, James Edward Fitzmorris Debenham, Duke of Rawdon, *et cetera.*"

She froze, color draining from her face as he bowed over her hand, uttered some inanity concerning his delight at making the acquaintance of the loveliest woman in the room, and offered his arm, eyes laughing merrily into hers at their private joke. Puppetlike, she curtsied stiffly, face blank with horror, and permitted him to lead her onto the floor, unable to breathe or think as her world came crashing around her ears.

Lady Jersey stared after them, slightly puzzled. If there was one thing she would have sworn, it was the Beckenham girl had better manners than *that*. Not a smile, not a word—just a cold offering of her hand. Then she shrugged. She'd sent the chit vouchers as Rawdon requested, presented him. On his head be it.

Out on the floor, Rawdon circled Louisa expertly,

amusement and devilment in his eyes, chuckling at her pale averted face and lowered lids.

"Out of charity with me again?" he teased.

She maintained her stony silence as the room turned around her, unrelenting in its gyrations, the lights so glaring she felt exposed naked on a pillory.

"Come, Louisa—say something! Aren't you going to welcome me back?"

She lifted her head then, and looked directly in his eyes, her own yielding nothing. "How can I welcome you back," she inquired evenly, "when I could not possibly have been aware of your absence, Your Grace, having only now made your acquaintance?"

"So that's how you're going to play it," he laughed. "At least thank me for acting the gallant Galahad, and rescuing you from sitting out the waltz with feet tapping and soul awash in a sea of jealousy while some popinjay bored you to tears with tales of his prowess on the field of sartorial honor! Why," he chuckled, "I may have just saved your soul from eternal damnation, love, looked on that way. Strange—to think of salvation being found in a ballroom, though I suppose there's no reason it couldn't be. You look very fetching, you know," he added after a moment, hand tightening at her waist. "Rather like a woodland sprite. I can see I've been remiss in not permitting myself the luxury of attending more of these tedious functions. With you at my side, they will all be the most delightful of scintillating festivities. If boredom threatens, I'll only have to look at you to regain my sense of the beautiful and wondrous."

"You are babbling, Your Grace."

"Out of charity with me, indeed," he grinned. "What a tongue it has! Come—don't be so foolish. Nothing has changed."

"No, I suppose it hasn't. That is perhaps the worst of all," she murmured.

"Sorry, love—I couldn't hear you."

"Nothing, Your Grace. I was merely remarking on the size of the room, or the excellence of the orchestra, or some such."

"Vixen! While your idea of a stud is excellent—I should have thought of it myself years ago!—I think we should wait to establish it for at least a year. Other things to occupy ourselves with at first."

"Do what you will, Your Grace. Your business is no concern of mine."

They circled the room, the faintest glint of annoyance showing in Rawdon's eyes now, Louisa's determinedly averted. He smiled mechanically at acquaintances and friends, avoiding the languishing looks thrown at him, the inviting sidelong glances, by habit.

"Aren't you in the least bit glad you're not about to marry a pauper?" he asked finally, her silence driving him beyond exasperation.

"I am not aware that I am about to marry anyone," she returned coldly. "You'd best mind your steps, Your Grace. That's the third time you've gone wrong, and I would prefer not to be trampled. Perhaps you should return me to my aunt."

"Enough, Louisa! Don't be a child," he snapped. His eyes flew around the room, ignoring the curious glances now being thrown their way. "If you mistook me for something I am not, that is your own fault, and none of mine. I warned you, but you refused to listen." He spotted Lady Daphne, a look of horrified fury on her face. Rawdon flashed her a saucy wink and steered Louisa toward a small curtained alcove beyond the dance floor. "There are explanations for everything, my love," he said more gently, taking firm hold on the temper that was about to break forth at her idiocy. "Quite evidently you refuse to speak with me, but speak we must."

Around her dancers whirled, faces seeming caught in

the rictus of death, voices shrill with laughter. Wave after wave of disillusionment and mortification washed over her. Pride alone held her determinedly erect, when she longed only to crumple to the floor, or flee sobbing to hide where none could find her.

"I cannot think of a thing you might have to say that would be of the least interest to me, Your Grace," she responded icily.

"No? Try this: I have no intention of releasing you from our agreement." Rawdon whirled her into the alcove, and jerked the curtains closed. "You are begging me to put you across my knee and paddle you," he growled, pulling her into his arms and attempting to kiss her. She averted her face, so that for his pains he received a mouthful of hair and ribbon. He grasped her chin, forced her head up. "Look at me, damn you!" he said sharply.

She met his eyes, cold contempt in her own, her head high. "Will you be so good as to release me, your grace? I do not care to be mauled, and I would rather not make a scene in this place for both our sakes."

"*Mauled?* What is the matter with you, you little termagant? Don't you understand it's preferable not to be having your pockets forever to let, if you can possibly avoid it? I've done you no injury, and yet you—"

"*Done me no injury?* You arrogant, egoistic, insufferable—" She was shaking, neck and jaw muscles contracted so tightly she could barely speak, in an effort to regain some control of voice and body. She stood there a moment, staring at him, then took a deep breath, expelling it slowly. "I met a man once who offered me his friendship," she continued more calmly, eyes stinging. "He stated there was to be complete honesty between us as a precondition to that friendship. I gave him the honesty he demanded. I gave him honesty beyond anything commonly acceptable for a lady. I demeaned myself for his sake. I laid myself at his feet, to accept or reject. I offered him my heart, and he repaid my trust and honesty with lies. I have since learned he is deceased—no great loss, given the magnitude of his betrayal. I will not mourn him, Your Grace, for the man I loved never existed. And now, if you will excuse me, I find I am unwell, and wish to return to my aunt. You will find other partners in plenty, I am sure, to play your games. I do not care for them, you see, having not been acquainted with the rules at the outset."

"Your pride is hurt," he said with dawning understanding. "You foolish child—I am the same person I was a week ago, and I love you every bit as much. Nothing essential has changed, I tell you."

"My thanks for the waltz, Your Grace."

Her skirts swept the floor in a deep, mocking court curtsy. Then she stumbled from the alcove, blinking back tears, pausing as she searched desperately for her aunt, heart hollow, throat aching. Behind her Rawdon was framed by the alcove's graceful arch.

"My name *is* James, Louisa," he said softly. "I only altered the Fitzmorris slightly and omitted the Debenham—for good reason. I'll explain it all, if only you'll listen. It's time you knew, and you'll approve completely—believe me! Now, come back here and accept my apologies for having wounded you, and let us get on with our lives."

She turned to face him, the look of horror deepening. "My aunt knew . . ." she whispered. "My aunt knew all along. How you must have laughed together over the fool I have made of myself!"

"Louisa—" he pleaded, hand outstretched. *"Please . . . !* I never intended—"

"Don't touch me!" she hissed, backing away from him, not caring who saw her or what they might think. "There is no way you could have loved me, and done this to me! It was a lie—all of it. Don't you understand? You and my

aunt, between you, have made a complete fool of me! *A groom?* How could I have been such a blind idiot! *I loathe you!*"

A hand grasped her arm. She looked up in mute appeal, trembling, face cold and numb. It was Stephen Gracechurch, glancing from her to Rawdon, puzzlement giving way to understanding.

"So *this* is who—Of all the damn-fool pranks I've ever known you to play," he said quietly, "this one takes the prize for sheer lunacy, Jamie. You should be horse-whipped! Now, leave well-enough alone. This young lady deserved better of you."

Around them couples no longer pretended to dance, their feet stilled as they watched and listened in fascination. Gracechurch pulled Louisa around, started for the entry.

"No—wait!" Rawdon called, following them.

Louisa turned back, torn between despair, fury, embarrassment, and hope. "Yes?"

"Lady Cheltenham knew, but she didn't approve," he said haltingly, face as white as Louisa's, eyes as stark. "She combed my hair until my head ached, but I insisted on proceeding in my own manner. You must in no way blame her."

"Very noble," she returned. "And now, if you will please excuse me—"

A quick look passed between the two men. Gracechurch gave the slightest of nods.

"Please," Louisa begged, looking up at the captain, "will you get me *away* from here before I further disgrace myself!"

Almack's, naturally, recovered. It was not a place for high drama, and therefore high drama had not taken place. It was not a venue for intimate personal tragedy, no matter how many were played out in its sedate precincts, so none had occurred. Neither was it a stage for comedy, but rather the rendezvous of those with the most serious of intentions—the perpetuation of family lines, with suitable *obéissance* to the uniting of rank and fortune. Therefore a farce could not have just been presented for the dancers' delectation.

Within minutes the tale of the confrontation between Miss Louisa Caroline Beckenham, spinster, and His Grace, James Edward Fiztmorris Debenham, Duke of Rawdon *et cetera*, had become so garbled not even Lady Jersey—who had introduced the principals and was highly skilled in the art of unscrambling—could unscramble it.

By morning the majority held the duke, after demanding to be presented to the young woman, had so grossly insulted her that a stalwart friend of her brother's—a Peninsular Hero of high rank and immense fortune without whose sage counsel Wellington dared not so much as select a bottle of claret, let alone commit to battle—had been forced to rescue the damsel and call the notorious Corinthian out. One version had it they met daringly at dawn in Green Park, Rawdon to delope in belated admission of heinous guilt, the Peninsular Hero to wing the blackguard as a warning to mend his rakish ways. The other favored swords and Hounslow Heath, with much the same results.

And the fair, abused damsel? Horrified by the Wicked Ways of Men, she was held to be cloistered within her aunt's home, resorting to vinaigrette, *sal volatile*, the vapors, and restorative jellies in a courageous effort to regain her equanimity. Unlikely parallels were drawn to Saint Joan, the Lily Maid of Astolat, and Eleanor of Aquitaine. Sympathetic messages flooded the house for two days, Charles and Matthew hard pressed to find sufficient containers for the effusive floral tributes to injured purity. Callers left cards innumerable, unwilling to impose on the sacred rights of hysteria, but equally unwilling to be caught among the ranks of those not *au courant*.

And, the reality?

The reality was Louisa, after they returned from Almack's, slightly disheveled, head flung back, arms akimbo, declaring, "He thought he was the Frog Prince! He *lied* to me from the day we met, and *then* he had the audacity to expect me to *prostrate* myself before him in humble gratitude, *marveling* that he would *deign* to so much as cast an *eye* in my unworthy direction in his new incarnation! Can you credit it? The despicable, lying, arrogant—I *despise* him! With no aspersions cast on his actual parents, 'His Grace' is an unmitigated *bastard!* No—he's worse than that! And, No! I will not apologize for using the word. It fits perfectly, and to blazes with propriety! What good did propriety ever do anyone in any case—tell me that!"

To her aunt's tentative suggestion that, while she did not condone Rawdon's actions, it might be wise to listen to any explanation he might offer before condemning him out of hand, Louisa retorted, "Lies—that's all he'd have to offer! All he knows to do is *lie!*" Then, voice choking, "How could I ever trust him again in *anything?*"

The other side of reality was a sodden pillow, replaced without comment or report, by a young housemaid who returned to the nether regions with tears in her own eyes. It was an elderly lady of impeccable breeding and subtle humor, indomitable through every other trial of her life, who found this one trial too much.

"A pox on them both!" Lady Daphne declared after Louisa stormed from the room for the tenth time in a single day. "I am definitely too old for such histrionics!"

Then a worse reality took hold. The fits of temper ceased. The pillows remained dry. The famous ruby betrothal ring of the dukes of Rawdon, carefully wrapped,

256   *Monique Ellis*

was sent by messenger—sans message—to a certain mansion in Grosvenor Square. Louisa, eyes hard, demanded a return to Almack's. She had, she said, business to conduct there.

Twelve

"I cautioned you, but you wouldn't listen," Lady Daphne retorted tartly, looking James Edward Fitzmorris Debenham, Duke of Rawdon, *et cetera,* straight in the eye, her own flashing with unmistakable anger. He had the grace to flush, and drop his gaze to the tea tray reposing between them.

They sat in the smallest drawing room of his Grosvenor Square residence, its lack of personality unrelieved by the slightest concession to anything but luxury and exquisite taste, two stiff figures on opposing Sheraton chairs, not quite adversaries, not quite allies. Brilliant sunlight filtered through gossamer silk curtains, flooding the room, glinting on hard surfaces, reflecting from polished mirrors, echoing the lemon-yellow watered silk wall coverings and gold and teal tapestried upholstery. Two days had passed since the debacle at Almack's. Given what she faced at home with Louisa, Lady Daphne was not in the best of humors.

"You bring me the damnedest luck with the girls you take under your wing," Rawdon muttered.

"No bad luck is involved *this time*—only your own stupidity! The other was an aberrational fugue, as well you know. Marianne may have *attracted* you, but that little partridge could never have *held* you. *That* would have been a union created in hell . . . much as I would have delighted in having you as a son-in-law." Lady Daphne sighed, poured out, handed Rawdon a delicate Sèvres cup ringed in yellow roses, not troubling to ask whether he wanted sugar or milk. "I will grant you this—you're every bit as miserable as my niece, for what comfort that may afford either of us. Louisa insists you be forbidden the house. As I wish to avoid being strangled in my bed, I have agreed."

"I know—I've made a perfect mull of everything, but . . . There are excellent explanations for everything. It *wasn't* just a lark, you know. I'd no choice. She *must* speak with me." He looked up, exasperation and hurt battling on his face. "Whatever has made the damned girl so intransigent? I never intended harm!" he exploded.

"No—you played your usual tricks, and when the game became serious, you had no notion how to end it. But, *Almack's?* With all of London there to watch how it went, like a public exhibition? I could have throttled you when I saw what you were about!"

"It was not the wisest thing I have ever done."

"Wise? What *did* you expect her reaction to be, pray tell? Joy? Delight? Rapture?"

"I expected her to laugh at herself, at me, at all of it, I believe," he mumbled. "A delightful tale to tell our grand-children on a cold winter's night."

"Men! *Think!* She asks you to marry her, believing you an impoverished gamester who spends his last ha'penny on flowers and trumperies for her. *Then* she discovers she's landed one of the biggest catches on the mart—so wealthy he makes *her* fortune look like *pin money*. There isn't a fond mother or simpering miss among the ton who wouldn't accuse her of cream-pot love, should the facts ever sur-face. She's mortified, and with good reason. You've made her look every kind of a fool. She won't forgive that easily."

"She must—for both our sakes." He eyed Lady Daphne almost coldly, eyes hard, a tormented glint lurking in their dark depths. "She won't relent?"

"Eventually. Perhaps. After she's worn herself to the bone with crying by night and throwing tantrums by day. A pretty pickle you've placed her in, as well as cutting up *my* peace quite unconsionably."

"There's nothing I can do?"

"You've done *quite* enough. You *could* abduct her, I suppose . . . She might forgive you *that*—in fifty years or so."

Lady Daphne watched the duke carefully. He had lost a touch of his devil-may-care air. All to the good . . . But, the determined underlying strength remained. That, too, was good. The cold separateness, the essential privacy of the man usually masked by his genial bonhomie and antic escapades had begun to erode. *That* was eminently satisfactory. The insult he had offered Louisa at Almack's might be the making of them both, once pride was found a cold bedfellow . . .

The interview was at Rawdon's instigation, just as she had planned, and in *his* home—again, as planned. This room, however, was not quite what she would have wished—obviously one of those austerely perfect areas that bore no relevance to the duke or his life—a spotlessly gleaming cheerless chamber in whose anonymity the *title* might receive creditors and debtors and old ladies with a tendency to meddle and pry, while the *man* remained imperiously unreachable. Still, just because this was where she had been ushered was no reason to *remain* there. She needed him where the *man* took his comfort and ease, and the *title* never intruded.

"It *was* rather arrogant of you, you know," she said conversationally, "expecting her to fall into your arms, crowing with delight. She has *that* right, at least. You've played at love so long, I doubt you know *how* to be serious—but you may learn. Enough of this," she sighed, and sat more erectly. "There's naught to be done for the moment, and it's best you accept the fact. You may win yourself back into her good graces, but it won't be easy, and it won't be soon."

She again reached for the teapot, absently took another cup, made as if to pour, face downturned, eyes flicking to his beneath lowered lashes. "There's a question I've been wanting to ask you, only all this silliness caused me to forget. Louisa mentioned"—she tilted the pot slightly—"that you cautioned her regarding the Fortescue chit. A very *pointed* caution. I was not aware you were acquainted with the paragon—or her family."

"I'm not," he replied curtly. "Nor with the family. But, if one is on the Town, one hears things."

"How vague you are! What *sort* of things? I'm *most* anxious to disentangle Harry, you know." The pot tilted a bit more, as if her wrist were tiring. "The gudgeon has been making Louisa's life a misery since his return from the Continent, and it's time and more *that* foolishness came to an end!"

"Yes, I know—it's what forced her to approach me," he said with a bitter smile. "Not to worry. I think he'll come to his senses soon."

"You think! On what basis?"

"Men generally do come to the realization they've made fools of themselves, given sufficient time," he rejoined wryly, "or, hadn't you noticed that characteristic?"

"They may *realize* it, but they rarely *admit* it," she replied tartly. The pot tilted still further. "I greatly fear he will continue to pursue the chit even when he understands she isn't worthy of his attentions. Indeed, unworthiness might provide an additional goad. A misplaced sense of chivalry runs through the Beckenham line—witness Louisa's begging an impoverished gentleman-groom to wed her because *he,* given his poverty, could never in good conscience approach her!"

"Harry Beckenham has been played for a fool," Rawdon said evenly, "but he is in good company. Have a care—you are about to pour tea all over the tray."

"I *am?*" Lady Daphne stared down at her hand, eyes widening. "Oh, my! How *very* clumsy of me! I *do* beg your pardon."

She made as if to replace the pot. Rawdon was never quite certain how she contrived the rest, but of a sudden the tray overturned, pot, cups, saucers flying, as his unmentionables received a liberal baptism of scalding amber liquid. He leapt to his feet, stifling an oath, and grabbed the bell pull as Lady Daphne made little noises of concern and consternation, dabbing at her skirts with a dainty lace handkerchief. The door opened, revealing his butler, glassy-eyed as he surveyed the disaster.

"Send Gersten to my rooms, and have Mrs. Chilton see to Lady Cheltenham's needs." Rawdon glowered, storming toward the stairs. "And get that mess cleaned up!" he barked over his shoulder, taking the steps two at a time, legs tingling. "I'll be back directly."

"Don't worry about me, my dear boy," Lady Daphne called after him. "We ladies are so much better protected, you know! So *many* layers . . ." she trailed off helplessly, glancing from her skirts—which were barely spattered— to the debris-strewn floor. "I am *so* sorry," she said to the parlor maid who materialized behind the butler. "One gets clumsy in one's old age, I suppose, and one's wrist *does* weaken. I really have no need of the *housekeeper*. Is there some out of the way corner where I might await the duke while you see to things here? The library, perhaps? Or His Grace's study? I have heard the paneling is remarkably fine, and I have *always* been interested—"

In the event it was the library, which did not suit Lady Daphne half so well as the study would have, but was not totally unrewarding. A portrait of Charles Christopher Debenham, Viscount Lindley, hung over the gleaming oak fireplace—a stunningly handsome youth with his older brother's curling locks and humorous dark eyes, full regimentals lending him a self-conscious dignity that underscored the charm of his open, candid expression.

She studied the glowing face, trying to recall when the boy had last been in London. He had been, she remembered, about to depart for the Peninsula. Rawdon was absent until just the end, the lad conspicuous in every haunt of the ton where young girls might be found. And then Lindley had departed, not for some sunny Spanish clime of castles and orange groves, but to an early grave in a mountain pass with an outlandish name. And then she saw him as ghostly music from a ball long past echoed in her ears. He was leading out a delicate young girl with a cloud of russet hair, head bent to catch her words, a tender smile on his lips, the girl's face hidden by other dancers. Lady Daphne shook her head. The connection might be there, but she could not swear to it.

The door opened behind her.

"It is very like," she said, not bothering to turn, voice infinitely gentle. "A charming young scapegrace if ever there was one. You must miss him dreadfully."

"I do," Rawdon returned gruffly behind her. "Why did they put you in here?"

"I requested it." Lady Daphne turned, standing beneath the portrait of Rawdon's younger brother, killed in the retreat to Corunna. "This room speaks of you far better than the other, and your study was not permitted me. Old Mathers was definite, if delicate."

She glanced about her, eyes cataloguing the massive volumes and sturdy, antiquated furniture which conceded little to style and everything to comfort. Heavy green velvet draperies were looped back from windows whose glass almost vanished, so clean it was. She might have been in the library at Marleybourne, so distinctive was the air of sanctuary the room exuded. A room to give a man confidence when that was needed, and to welcome him uncritically in moments of despair. A small case by the window held what appeared to be young Lindley's medals and honors—a jumble of schoolboy prizes mixed indiscriminately with the more serious awards of an all too brief adulthood. A hint of satisfaction gleamed in Lady Daphne's eyes as she sank into a chair by the fireplace. This just might be the right room after all . . .

She looked at Rawdon challengingly where he maintained his position barely within the golden oak doors, as if poised for flight. *For God and Saint George,* she swore silently, *and Harry, Christo, Dickie, and all the rest . . .*

"It is time, I think, that we talk seriously," she said deliberately, indicating the massive red leather chair opposite her. "If you do not mind, I would prefer *this* room, as it is so much more pleasant than that arctic audience chamber you reserve for the importunate, and a thimble of ratafia to the sop your cook claims is tea—if you would not mind?"

"I find that I am unexpectedly—"

"I knew you in short coats," Lady Daphne snapped, voice hardening. "Do not try to play me for a fool, James Debenham. Many things I may be, but *that* I am not!"

A slow, rueful smile broke on his face. "No, you never were," he sighed. "What is of such great importance that you wish to discuss it here?"

"Your brother. Dickie Fotheringham. Harry. Louisa. A duo of *most* unlikely captains. A Peninsular trio which has disappeared on a repairing lease, ostensibly to attend a comatose octogenarian uncle whose identity and direction I have *not* been able to discover. A *most* unusual groom by the name of Hobbs. A 'boozin' ken' known as Cribb's Parlor. But, primarily, a Peer of the Realm whose crest is so well known as to be *unmistakable,* and yet was encountered driving through London not long ago in a carriage which lacked markings of *any* sort—this not only according to my niece, who is so country-bred and naïve she would not have known the difference, but according to my own *very* superior butler, who would have recognized your arms on the instant."

Rawdon stared at her blankly. "You mystify me. What have all these subjects to do with one another?"

"That is the tack you intend to take?"

"Tack? The carriage is easily explained, God knows. My own was in for some repairs, and I was given the loan—"

"James Debenham! What kind of fool do you take me for?"

"It's quite true. You may inquire of—"

"Oh, I'm certain it's true enough, as far as it goes. Clever . . ."

"As for the rest, I haven't the slightest notion what maggot you've got in your brain, but—"

"The maggots have names," she returned. "Christo Debenham. Harry Beckenham. Dickie Fotheringham. What a plethora of '-hams'! Presumably other names I have not uncovered, but would recognize on the instant. Young men of military profession and independent fortune whose fathers were notable either for their untimely deaths, or their total unworldliness. Each bears a diamond in his arms—or whatever it is maggots employ for arms. Don't look at me like that, my boy. I'm *not* in my dotage yet! You've diddled me fairly, the lot of you, longer than I'm willing to permit. Louisa is trapped in your machinations through no fault of her own. One *cannot* hold *her* to account for being her brother's sister—only my late brother and his wife can be called to book for that contretemps, and *they* are beyond your reach. As for Harry being a fool, he *is* in good company—beginning with your own, if you think I have yet to cut my wisdoms."

"You are feeling the heat," Rawdon said dispassionately, reaching for the bell pull. "Permit me to summon your carriage."

"You would do better to send posthaste for 'Captains' Gracechurch and Heath. I am deeply concerned for the safety of my niece and nephew."

When Lady Daphne returned to her tall, elegant town house, far from satisfied with the results of her morning call, she found Louisa in conference with Holfers. Louisa's wardrobe littered her sleeping chamber—settee, chairs, bed, sporting frothy rainbows of à la modality. Armoire and dressing room doors gaped. At least, Lady Daphne noted, there were no trunks in evidence as yet.

"What's all this?" the redoubtable old lady asked, removing her maroon pelisse and handing it to her dresser. If she was not exactly in favor of a retreat to the country, neither was she entirely adverse to the proposition. Marianne and her nabob would welcome a visit, and as Marianne was increasing again, social activities would be limited. Plenty of leisure for Louisa to brood over Rawdon, and come to her senses. "Decamping?"

Louisa looked up, a brittle smile lighting her features. "Regrouping," she responded. "I find a pressing need for new ball gowns now we are permitted Almack's. No one remembers one's wardrobe half so well as those harpies who line the walls at such places, waiting for one to appear in something furbished up to eke out the season."

"I see."

"New colors, new styles—that's what is wanted," Louisa said gaily. "Something the slightest bit outrageous to attract the gentlemen's eyes."

Lady Daphne ran a quick inventory from where she

stood by the door. "The idea is well enough in itself," she agreed. "Replace all this for the moment," she instructed Holfers. "No need to turn my home into a silk warehouse." She took Louisa firmly by the arm, led her away. "You and I," she said, "will retreat to a less encumbered place, and confer."

"Brighton, I think, for the summer," Louisa trilled as Lady Daphne guided her into her private sitting room, rang the bell. "I understand it's all the crack to take a house there. I'll stand the nonsense, if you'll accompany me."

"And then?"

"If I can't snare a husband in Brighton, I shall succeed nowhere and must hie me to a nunnery. Lady Fortescue ought to accept that as a suitable substitute for wedlock."

Lady Daphne refrained from response, instead instructing the young upstairs maid who appeared at the door to bring them tea, then sank gracefully into a small Queen Anne rosewood chair by the flower-decorated hearth. Louisa paced the room restlessly, picking up and replacing objects, her stride more suited to Marleybourne's open fields.

"Two days of mourning are sufficient, then?" the old lady finally asked.

"Mourning? Whatever can you mean?"

"I understand you informed Rawdon he is dead."

"How do you know that?" Louisa whirled, eyes flaming.

"He told me himself," Lady Daphne said placidly. "Just because *you* won't receive the idiot doesn't mean *I* must forego a friendship of long standing."

"So *that* is where you went this morning on your mysterious errand. How *could* you!"

"Easily. I summoned my carriage at the appropriate hour, gave Merton the appropriate instructions, and within fifteen minutes was—"

"You know very well that is not what I mean!"

"Just because a man makes a complete ass of himself is no reason for women to make the identical error," Lady Daphne retorted tartly. "You may cut off your nose to spite your face, but I *refuse* to permit you to perform the same office for me. I *like* my nose!"

"You do not understand—"

"I understand very well," Lady Daphne returned. "Your role of Lady Bountiful has been taken from you, and out of pride you are prepared to whistle happiness, fortune, your entire future, down the wind. I don't know *which* of you is the greater fool, but at the moment I am inclined to award you the honors."

"Not a matter open to discussion," Louisa countered.

"I suggested to Rawdon that he whisk you off to Gretna Green," the old lady remarked after a moment. "Wouldn't have it, unfortunately, though he was quite willing to put the other part of my suggestion into immediate practice."

"Oh? And what was *that*, pray tell?"

"A sound beating, on general principles, twice a day. You are quite the fool, my girl, and I've had more than enough of your mopes." The less sympathy *either* of them received at this point, the better—though of the two of them, Louisa was definitely more deserving of gentle treatment. First Harry and his ridiculous demands, and now Rawdon, with his insufferable love of high jinks. Of all the caper-witted—One thing was certain: Louisa did not have much luck with the men she chose to love. "I take it you have decided, unlike Harry's diamond, it is time for you to show your face once more? Where and when shall it be?"

"Lord Donclennon calls for me at five for a drive in the Park, and I have accepted the escort of Captains Gracechurch and Heath to the theater this evening on both our parts, to be followed by supper at Grillon's."

"What of *my* plans? Tonight is Mabel Delaford's rout."

"The theater will serve much better," Louisa retorted. "I have no desire to face down the impertinent yet."

Louisa's reappearance among the ton after only two days' seclusion was a nine days' wonder for but one. Then, with its customary fickleness, the beau monde turned to fresher fodder, the affaire Beckenham-Rawdon declared a hum.

The first drive in the Park was the hardest for Louisa, the appearance at the theater scarcely less so. She wore her most daring gown, complete with her mother's diamonds, and if a slight sense of guilt at the way she was using Harry's two Peninsular friends tickled her conscience, she ignored it. She needed to be seen, and seen she would be—in the company of as many admiring and prepossessing gentlemen as possible. Lady Daphne gave her her head; if she felt Louisa's gaiety was a little forced, she kept her own counsel.

The party returned from their late supper at Grillon's to find Colonel Winthrop ensconced in the little back parlor awaiting their arrival. He rose as Lady Daphne entered, followed by a Louisa whose brittle laugh shattered against the windows. Behind her Gracechurch and Heath froze on the sill, taking in Winthrop's serious face. The proprieties were quickly dispensed with, Lady Daphne sending Hoskins for brandy and tea.

Louisa lingered by the door, amber velvet cloak trailing from her fingers, gold reticule discarded on the chair beside her. Gracechurch moved forward, pantherlike, eyes glued to Winthrop as Heath eased to the door's other side, a silent presence in the shadows.

"Back so soon?" Gracechurch asked, tone politely welcoming. "I hope your business was successfully concluded?"

Winthrop smiled lazily. "Yes and no," he responded.

"Tales of imminent death were grossly exaggerated—nothing but gout, poor old fellow. Miserable with it, and of course we weren't the least use, so we joined Harry at Marleybourne. Seemed the most sensible thing to do, since we were already three-quarters there."

Yes, he conceded, they had barely been gone before they returned—quite a sudden decision. And, yes, Harry had returned as well.

"Where's Harry?" Gracechurch asked, an edge to his voice.

Currently in Fenton's quarters, Winthrop told them, but insisting on returning to his own lodgings instanter. Giles Fortescue had appeared at the Court the morning after their arrival, borne them company on their return to London. By this time the puppy should be in the bosom of his family.

Gracechurch's jaw clenched.

Then Winthrop turned to Louisa and Lady Daphne. "I don't wish to alarm you, but we met with a slight delay on our way to town," he said gently. "Better you hear the truth from me than an exaggerated account from one of your acquaintance. Some discharged troopers who had taken to the High Toby, from their cursing. Harry was winged. The Fortescue lad took a ball in the shoulder—quickly extracted, thanks to Fenton. Little more than a flesh wound, really, but it could have been serious."

Lady Daphne sank into the closest chair, eyes flying from Gracechurch to Winthrop.

"And, Harry?" she asked hollowly.

"He insists on returning to his own billet," Winthrop repeated, eyes flicking briefly to the stone-faced Gracechurch. "May be there already, for all I know. Fenton will keep him company for this one night at least—you need have no fear." A slight smile creased Winthrop's serious face. "Harry insists too much of a pother has been made already. Could be, though he was fit for broiling when he discovered the Fortescue lad had taken a hit. Quite a bit of confusion at such a moment, you know. Darkness, small hours, everyone half-asleep. We were fools to attempt a night journey, I suppose—even with a partial moon to give us light—given the reputation of the roads once the sun falls, but Harry was most insistent we press on." He turned to Gracechurch. "Young Fortescue had brought word of his sister's indisposition, you see," he explained. "While Harry didn't see his way free to leave instantly—the country come-out of a neighbor's daughter which he had promised the young lady to attend—once we did make our departure, it was with all speed."

Gracechurch nodded, indicated a chair as he looked from Louisa to Lady Daphne. "By your leave?" he requested, then sank down, a slight frown drawing dark brows over steely blue eyes. "Tell us more," he said. "I am particularly interested in the Fortescue sprig."

"He's all right," Winthrop insisted firmly. "No question there. Sound as they come, and resilient beyond the ordinary. No one suspected he was injured until he fell at our feet from loss of blood while we were attending Harry after the fracas was over. More bottom than sense, that boy has. A thick bandage and a good draught of brandy set him to rights, and we spent the night at the next respectable inn we found, mostly thanks to Harry's concern for the lad."

"Why ever didn't the boy let you know he had taken a hurt?" Lady Daphne demanded.

"Said he had two good arms. If he hadn't already been on the ground, I think Harry would have planted him a facer. Clunch kept insisting we see to Harry first. I was sorely tempted to lay him out myself by the time all was done."

"Harry is returning to his lodgings." Gracechurch scowled.

"Nothing for it," Winthrop replied, an edge to his voice. "He insists."

"I would like to see my brother," Louisa interrupted from the doorway, reaching for her discarded reticule with a trembling hand.

"At this hour?" Lady Daphne inquired tartly. "Do not be more of an idiot than you already are, if you can possibly help it. Harry would no more welcome your precipitous arrival than I would permit your going. If he has the sense he was born with—which I often doubt—he is asleep, and Major Fenton as well. We have been assured his injuries are negligible. Tomorrow is time enough."

She threw a quick glance at her desk, framed by the pair of windows at the end of the room. Louisa followed her eyes, paling slightly.

"Give Harry a chance to regain his equilibrium," Lady Daphne said more gently. "A call from you at this hour after his recent ordeal would be in no one's best interests."

"But he was wounded *yesterday,*" Louisa protested uncertainly.

"All the more reason not to go rushing to his side like a demented maiden aunt," Lady Daphne returned. "He wouldn't thank you for it—believe me!"

"Lady Cheltenham has the right of it," Winthrop agreed. "Ladies do not belong around bandages and bloody basins."

"Of all the *missish* statements!" Louisa snapped. "I am not likely to have a spasm at the sight of my brother with an excess of padding on his shoulder."

"Sticking plaster on his brow, actually," Winthrop corrected. "Parted his hair."

"I see . . ." Gracechurch said slowly, words drawn out. "And he insists on returning to his own lodgings."

"Nothing we could do," Winthrop bit out, "short of hitting him over the head and abducting him. I will admit to having been tempted, but as the possibility for profitable discussion is yet to arrive, we were more or less helpless."

Gracechurch's eyes flew from Louisa's puzzled face to Lady Daphne's more shuttered, yet curiously satisfied expression. Captain Heath, this while, had been keeping to the shadows, silently observing and listening. Now he stepped forward, laughingly apologizing for turning Lady Daphne's parlor into the next best thing to a bivouac. The gentlemen made their departures, Captain Heath promising to return on the morrow with news of Harry, and Lady Daphne and Louisa wearily made their way to bed.

The next morning Harry, hair carefully arranged to mask the sticking plaster on his forehead, and with more than usual care taken as to raiment, presented himself at the Fortescue doors as early as propriety permitted, having sent an enormous bouquet ahead of him to announce his return from Marleybourne. Now that he was in town, only four things were of importance—to have it out with Lord Fortescue, shift Louisa's residence to Fortescue House, see her properly wed at last, and get on with his life. He had already taken the first step: Two special licenses reposed in his coat pocket—one bearing his and Gwendolyn's names, the other only awaiting determination of the groom to be completed—a courtesy for which he had been forced to make a considerable additional donation to the bishop's (unspecified) favorite charity.

He was left pacing the marble entry with its en-niched copies of classical statuary for fifteen interminable minutes, during which time he could hear sounds of hasty comings and goings above him accompanied by voices raised in heated altercation. Finally he was shown into the unused downstairs reception room that served as a cloakroom when the Fortescues entertained, there to resume his pacing. Another half hour passed before anyone put in an appearance, and then it was neither Lord nor Lady Fortescue, nor even the supremely regal butler who ruled over the household, but rather a burly under footman who informed Harry, face frozen, that the family was not at home, then pointedly escorted him to the door and watched him down the steps.

Harry turned to stare at the house when he reached the pavement. There was a fluttering of curtains at a second-floor window which he knew to be the young ladies' parlor. He thought he caught a glimpse of Belinda's carroty ringlets, but the front windows were sealed as if against infection, not a sound filtering from house to street. And, the salver on which invitations and calling cards were usually deposited had been empty save for his solitary note sent with that morning's flowers—which meant that Gwendolyn might have no idea he had returned.

Mystified and not a little angry, he made his way to White's hoping to find Lord Fortescue at his usual place at the tables. Fortescue was nowhere to be seen, and indeed had not appeared at White's—nor any of his other customary haunts—in over a week according to one of his sycophantic circle. After enduring some mild quizzing regarding his wound from various humor-minded friends—"Sabers at dawn, eh? Who's the ladybird?"— Harry departed for his lodgings with the beginnings of a superior headache which, by the time he reached his chambers, had developed sufficient intensity to make him seek his bed with curtains drawn, trying to pretend it was night. Of Percy Fenton there was fortunately no sign, nor of the rest of the interfering marplots who had joined him at the Court.

Lying rock-still, Harry went over the brief uncomfortable time he had spent in Fortescue House that morning, trying to make sense of it. There could have been no misunderstanding the intent of the letter he sent Lady Fortescue just prior to his departure for Marleybourne. They *had* to have been expecting him. They *had* to have known he would brook no more interference from them or Louisa or his encroaching aunt. They *had* to know all Gwendolyn's demands were about to be met.

And met they would be—of that neither his precious sister nor his unsavory aunt could retain the slightest doubt. There, too, he had been supremely explicit.

With a groan he turned on his side, laying his face gingerly on a pillow that seemed fabricated of river cobbles.

Marriage to the woman he loved should have been such a simple thing. After all, missing arm or no, he was wealthy, titled, far from his dotage, and of reasonably personable appearance despite the unfortunate scar, and—he had been informed on numerous occasions—possessed of not inconsiderable charm. Instead, it had been a confusing nightmare from the moment he set foot in England, stump still aching, body weak from all he had endured. His sister and his aunt conspired against him. His damnable friends insisted on turning up at the most inopportune of moments. Just when he was ready to settle things he was called unavoidably to Marleybourne.

The only unalloyed pleasure he had known in months, he admitted wryly, had come when little Patsy Worth, playing the grown-up lady to impish perfection, had insisted she would open her ball with him and no one else, missing arm or no, and Harry had discovered to his delight that he could still dance. What a wonderful surprise to bring back to Gwendolyn! While she never complained, the poor darling had quite clearly found it tedious to sit out with him when she might have been more entertainingly employed on the floor with a sound partner. And yet, perhaps not so unalloyed at that . . . When he had attempted to thank Patsy for the unexpected gift she had given him, haltingly explaining what it would mean to another lady, the little minx had looked him up and down, proclaimed him less of a gentleman than she had believed, then whirled away to join some young, heavy-footed county buck in a rompish country dance. A woman grown? Perhaps not, but already with all the irritating, unfathomable characteristics of the breed . . .

From the sitting room came the sound of doors opening and closing, of low voices, of a decanter unstoppered, the clink of crystal against crystal. Percy, probably, and maybe the rest of them as well. They were welcome to his brandy, so long as they didn't insist he join them. Harry, confused and unsettled, sank uneasily into a sleep peopled by unlikely footmen, night marauders who appeared more intent on blood than gold, and accusing female faces among which little Patsy's, his sister's, and his aunt's were prominent.

Louisa Beckenham, with a party consisting of only the best of the young of the ton, had departed for a day's outing at Richmond Park, complete with *al fresco* dining provided in hampers from Gunter's. It was not that Louisa had truly wanted to form part of the outing, but again it was a place to be seen enjoying herself in a carefree manner, and Lady Daphne had convinced her— with very little effort—that it would be wiser to wait for Harry to approach them than for them to go in search of her temperamental brother.

Hobbs, stolid in his insistence that—no matter how many young Corinthians and members of the Four-Horse-Club formed part of the group—his services were required, had saddled up his own strong hack as well as Commendatore. While he had agreed to hang back closer to the carriages which carried those ladies too delicate to ride such a distance, he informed his Miss Louisa that no matter how much *she* might think customs had changed, it hadn't done in his day for a young lady to gad about unescorted by her groom. Until Captain Gracechurch informed him otherwise, he would form part of any party she joined—if only in a peripheral manner. That her brother had returned to town made not the least difference to the determined groom.

Lady Daphne had come in on the argument just before Louisa's setting out, ignored her niece, thanked Hobbs for his care of her, and told the redoubtable groom that if Miss Beckenham gave him the *least* bit of trouble, he had only to refer to *her* for support. It had been an unaccustomedly sullen Louisa whom Lady Daphne had watched depart to join the Richmond Park expedition, a self-effacing and almost apologetic Hobbs who followed discreetly behind.

With a sigh of relief Lady Daphne found she had her home to herself for once, and retreated to the breakfast parlor and rang for a fresh pot of chocolate. Indolence appealed—some hours spent with *La Belle Assemblée* to determine the latest styles for a seaside summer, perhaps a morning call on a friend of *her* generation and interests rather than all the simpering misses and posturing bucks with whom Louisa now seemed determined to surround herself, a quiet nuncheon uninterrupted by the knocker, a decorous drive in the Park at five, perhaps, followed by a peaceful evening at her own fireside—even if the weather were too warm for a fire. If she had been dullish prior to Louisa's descent on London, Lady Daphne could not help but wonder if *this* Season might not be proving too much of a good thing.

She barely had time to turn to the tattle page and take a first sip of her chocolate when the knocker sounded. And she had—*Stupid, stupid neglectful woman!*—failed to inform Hoskins that she was at home to no one. With a sigh she straightened the lace cap perching jauntily on her silver curls, settled the diaphanous gray and rose muslin morning gown with its deep burgundy flounces and ribbons into more fetching folds, when Giles Fortescue was shown in, arm reposing interestingly in a sling, his clothes of a miraculous sobriety which lent maturity to his customarily eager puppy's face.

He bowed, placing a small posy of lily-of-the-valley in Lady Daphne's hand. "Just came by t'see you weren't worried 'bout Harry—Lord Beckenham, that is. All right an' tight," Giles said after accepting a cup of chocolate and a place at the table quite as if he were a member of the family. "Didn't want Miss Beckenham to worry, don't you see."

"How very kind," Lady Daphne murmured. "You seem to have had the worst of the encounter. Colonel Winthrop informed us of what happened. Very exciting it must have been?" she ended on an inquiring note.

Giles cocked his head, studying her for a moment. "Miss Beckenham ain't here?" he asked finally.

"No—I'm so sorry," Lady Daphne twinkled. "An expedition to Richmond Park. You will have to make do with me."

"Make do? I say, now——" Giles flushed, shook his head. "You don't understand at all," he protested. "*Glad* she ain't here. Wanted to talk to *you*. Funny thing about t'other night," he said, face taking on a thoughtful seriousness that hinted at the man he might become, "I've been accosted by highwaymen before. More'n once, come to that."

His eyes flew from Hoskins, imperturbable by the sideboard, to the footman lurking by the servants' door, back to Lady Daphne. Deliberately he helped himself to more chocolate from the pot Hoskins had placed before him.

"Still, it ain't a subject fit for ladies," he said, sipping slowly. "Shouldn't have brought it up. Only thing that matters is, nobody's permanently damaged. Beautiful day, ain't it? Miss Beckenham should enjoy her jaunt. That groom fellow of hers go along?"

"Hobbs?" smiled Lady Daphne. "Her ever-patient shadow."

"Good. Can't be too careful these days," Giles returned. He leaned back gingerly in his chair, looking steadily and patiently at Lady Daphne. "Learned that t'other night. Never know who's lurking about."

"That will be all, Hoskins," Lady Daphne said after a startled pause.

As soon as Hoskins and Matthew had disappeared Giles leaned forward intently, free forearm on the table, chocolate forgotten.

" 'Twasn't like they say it is in books," he informed Lady Daphne earnestly. "In fact, 'twasn't like books at all. Nothing romantic about having someone take a shot at you. Even less romantic being hit. Hurts like the very devil."

"You poor boy . . ." she whispered.

"Don't think I'm a boy anymore," he said flatly. "May've been when I left town. Not when I came back. Thing of it is—don't think it was accidental, if you see what I mean. There was an incident at the Court, too. Poachers, Harry claimed, shooting wild. I don't know. Odd time o' day for poachers, and an odd place, too, 'specially with so many people about. I think Harry's in some kind of trouble. Don't realize it himself, the silly gudgeon. Talked to Colonel Winthrop. *Tried* to talk to Major Fenton an' Captain Heath. Wouldn't listen to me, any of 'em. Said I was imagining things—and *they're* supposed to be his *friends!* Didn't know where to turn. Then I thought of you. Don't want to frighten Miss Beckenham. Don't want to frighten you, for that matter, but there it is—someone's *got* to know. I can't be responsible for *everyone*. 'Nough trouble lookin' after m'self. Don't do a very good job of it, either," he said ruefully, indicating his shoulder.

"I think you've done a magnificent job," Lady Daphne said huskily. "How did you come to be with Harry and his friends?"

"Went up to Marleybourne to bear Harry company. Not in the *least* necessary, as it turned out." A slow, self-deprecatory smile broke on his face. "Damned officious, in fact. Colonel Winthrop and the rest'd arrived the night before. No way to take off immediately. M'poor nag was tuckered out, an' so was I. Pulled a silly trick, you see—rode straight through, just to see if I could. Caperwitted!"

"Whatever did you do that for?"

Giles shrugged, winced. "Always hearin' about Wellington's forced marches. Wanted to see if I was up to snuff. Maybe I can't have a pair of colors, but I'd like to know I could do 'em honor—or at least not be an inconvenience."

"Suppose I were to make you a present of those colors—which regiment would you want?"

"Don't even think of it!' Giles protested, flushing. "M'mother'd kill us both. 'Sides, couldn't accept a gift like that. Couple thousand pounds at the least, an' *that's* only the beginning. There's mounts, an' uniforms, an'—well, it's not to be thought of," he concluded firmly, "so don't you think of it. Didn't come here about *me*, in any case. Came about Harry. What're we to do? *I* can't mount guard on him day an' night. Managed to keep an eye on him 'til we reached London, but Major Fenton insisted on dumping me on m'father's doorstep. Not much use after that."

"I imagine your wound must have set the household by the ears."

"M'mother screamed a lot, an' Gwennie had her usual vapors. Then m'father sent 'em out of the room, and asked me what happened. So, I told him. Didn't like it above half. Said I'd no reason to be chasing off to Marleybourne. Said whatever happened served me right. Correct about that, but not for the reasons *he* gave," Giles said angrily.

"Things continue uncomfortable at home?"

"*Uncomfortable?* Downright impossible, if you ask me. No idea *what* bee m'mother's got in her bonnet now. Don't matter—normal state of affairs these days. Thing of it is, if Harry's in trouble, could be Miss Beckenham is, too. Wouldn't want anything to happen to either of 'em."

"I suspect you're making a great to-do over relatively little," Lady Daphne said, mentally excusing herself as best she could. "Being accosted by footpads is not that uncommon, as you indicated."

Giles shoulders slumped. "You don't believe me, either," he said.

"It's not a question of belief," Lady Daphne returned gently. "If Colonel Winthrop and the rest see no danger, experienced as they are, you may trust their judgment."

"Didn't *feel* right," Giles protested, sighed. "I'll do what I can, but there's not much I *can* do."

Lady Daphne rose, bringing the unusual morning call to an end. "Let me know if your suspicions are further aroused," she instructed the boy as she saw him to the door. "I am not saying you are entirely wrong—only that at this juncture I am every bit as helpless as you are. And, thank you so much for the beautiful flowers."

Fifteen minutes later, garbed in a stylish ashes-of-roses town robe and superior hat, she rapped on the roof of her carriage. "Grosvenor Square," she said sharply, then leaned back in the seat, lips firmly compressed. If Rawdon wasn't there, she'd follow him until she ran him to earth—even if it meant entering such a place as Gentleman Jackson's.

Thirteen

The shadows were lengthening as the Richmond Park party turned homeward, faces caressed by the dying breeze. There was a pleasant somnolence to the advance group on horseback. Total lethargy had descended on the open carriages trailing behind—a landau, a barouche, and two sporting curricles driven by blades with greater desire to escort specific young ladies than ambition to display their prowess on horseback. Far to the rear rumbled the victual wagons, exhausted maids and footmen napping away their first moments of leisure since well before dawn.

The sun's warmth lingered, touching the woods with gold and painting shimmering highlights on the horses' flanks. Low voices drifted through the trees, mingling with the rustle of leaves, the jingle of harnesses, the soft sibilance of bird wings feathering the air on their own homeward journeys.

Louisa rode slightly apart, observing the desultory flirtations, and the more pointed courting rituals with casual interest. After a full day in their company, the girls were unendurably vapid behind their alluring attitudes and pretty poses, the bucks of a universal greenness that rendered them dead bores. Why she had agreed to come—

But, of course, she knew why. She had, once more,

been "seen"—that prime requisite without whose aid she could never hope to live down the scene at Almack's. The comments, the snide whispers had been pointed enough, the uncivil gigglings and sly questions setting her teeth on edge even as she feigned misunderstanding the pointed barbs. And, wound those barbs did—though perhaps not in the way her lively young tormentors intended. The ultimate insult had been finding herself relegated to the position of chaperon, treated as such with condescending deference by the girls, and by the gentlemen of the party with a casual camaraderie which indicated she was far beneath their touch given her advanced years—for all the world as if she were a governess or a maiden aunt.

Harry had had it right after all. She was an ape leader, on the shelf, invited this day only to play gooseberry to males barely her senior and girls much her junior. A widower would have to suffice, or a roué with sudden intimations of mortality and no heir. Why she had ever imagined something more was possible she would never know.

With a sigh she dropped her hands, Morrison's crop threaded loosely between her fingers. Commendatore broke into a steady, mile-eating trot at her signal, quickly outdistancing the others scattered in small groups along the lane. The way ahead twisted gently, skirting oak and beech whose immense girth and rough bark spoke of ancient roots deeply set in the rich dark loam. The air was soft, gentle, filled with woodland scents. Her seat automatic from years in the saddle, lulled by the unaccustomed peace and privacy, Louisa's lids drooped.

An alternative to her present course would have to be found, and soon. Harry, if he persisted, must be permitted his diamond, however small his chance of happiness with her once the vows were spoken, but too many days like this and she would be accepting the whuffling vicar and his superior cellar as an excellent bargain.

Did it matter, in the end? You lived for a while, and were young. Then you grew older. At last, decrepit in mind and body, forgotten by friends and an inconvenience to family, you died. The trees surrounding her had seen generations pass beneath their highflung canopies. In such a continuous stream of lives, her personal heartache was laughable in its lack of consequence to anyone but herself. And the man to whose life she would join hers? The management of a household was the management of a household, whether vicarage or ducal seat. The only difference lay in scale and degree of comfort. Either way she would be consigning control of her life and fortune to a stranger whose wisdom and good will there would be no judging before the fact.

From behind her came the steadily approaching beat of heavy hooves. Damn Hobbs and his single-minded persistence! Not a moment alone to think, to sorrow, to decide what she must do. Tonight she would have it out with Gracechurch, dismiss her infernal groom, send him back to whatever stew he had sprung from. Enough was enough!

Commendatore reared, his scream shattering the evening calm. Louisa flung herself against his heavy neck, crop and reins lost, fingers digging into his thick black mane as her eyes flew open. A dusky gray gelding barred the way, burly hooded rider shouting orders. Two dun-colored hacks crowded Commendatore, masked figures reaching for his bridle, the reins, wrenching her arms, her shoulders, tearing at her habit, attempting to drag her from the saddle. Her screams rose over the chestnut's as she clung desperately to her perch, Commendatore's flying hooves and flashing teeth wreaking havoc wherever he found a target. A shot rang over her head as Hobbs thundered around the bend. A second pistol appeared in his hand, barking to send the gray wheeling, the hooded rider bent low in the saddle. The heavy horse crashed into the undergrowth, vanishing through trees.

Hobbs bore down on the remaining pair of horsemen, second pistol discarded for a knife pulled from his boot, another gripped in his teeth, reins loosely twisted under his thigh, a wild ululating cry rising from his throat. The brigands threw one look over their shoulders and fled after their leader.

As suddenly as it had begun it was over, the trembling Commendatore alone in the center of the road, eyes rolling, as Hobbs skidded to a halt beside them. He assessed the young woman with a practiced eye—habit torn, hat lost, eyes wide with terrified shock, hair in bedraggled streamers around her white face. He reached over and gently loosened her death-grip on Commendatore's mane. Her fingers came away reluctantly, cut and bleeding from the coarse horsehair. But, she'd do. Her head was coming up, her shoulders squaring. Made of good stuff, the Beckenhams were.

"What—what was that?" she implored, voice shaking.

"Now d'you see why I won't be having you traipsing off on your own, Miss Louisa? England ain't a safe place for a young lady by herself these days."

"Dear God . . ." she said haltingly. "Were they—"

"Only too right, they were!" Hobbs returned, a bite to his tone, pistol and knives vanishing. "But, you've taken no serious hurt, and mayhap you've learned a pair o' valuable lessons. Next time you be riding, wear your gloves, silly girl! And, don't be heading off on your own again—you hear? Not by an inch!"

Shouts echoed in the sudden calm as the lead riders of the picnic party rounded the bend, mounts at full gallop.

"Get me out of this," she whispered. "I can't face—"

"Commendatore didn't like the looks of a badger and took off with you—understand?" Hobbs's tone permitted no opposition. "Nothing more. This ain't in the way of being all that uncommon, but you wouldn't be wanting more tales spreading among the nobs, and spread they would!"

Louisa nodded as the riders bearing down on them slowed.

"You'll ride in one o' them carriages, an' I'll lead the fellow home," Hobbs continued firmly, gripping Commendatore's bridle as he turned to the young bucks gathering round in clouds of dust with much jockeying for position. "Deal o' pother over summat little," he told them, eyes twinkling. "His Honor ain't accustomed to bein'—"

"See here—we heard shots," Chuffy Goffington panted. "You can't tell me—"

"Sure to have, m'lord, lessen' you're deaf. Fired over the silly bonesetter's head, I did," Hobbs explained soothingly. "Stops 'im every time just like a charm, but Miss Louisa here's a bit shaken. Badger spooked the beast. Not accustomed to such things, he isn't, an' didn't take to it kindly a'tall. If she could ride with the young ladies in one o' them carriages, now that'd be just the ticket."

"My crop." Louisa stared blankly from her empty, bloodied hands to the young men whose mounts shifted nervously around her. "I've lost my crop."

"Now, don't you be worritin' yerself about a silly crop, Miss Louisa," Hobbs said sternly. "There's many another in this world just like it."

She shook her head, tears filling her eyes, as Hobbs pulled Commendatore's head around and started to lead him back toward the approaching carriages at a sedate walk, the young riders falling in behind them.

"No there isn't," she said despairingly.

An hour and a half later a grim-visaged Hobbs stood in front of Lady Daphne, feet braced, hands clasped behind his back. No vestige of the groom remained beyond clothes suited to a menial.

"How much have you guessed?" he demanded without preamble.

The old lady studied him, eyes twinkling. "More than any of your confederates would care to admit, I suspect." Then her face turned serious. "What *did* happen today?"

"No more sorties for your niece to places such as Richmond Park," he said firmly. "Handle the girl any way you like, but see to it." He sighed, gestured to a heavy and ornate silver tray on which decanters and glasses reposed. "By your leave, Lady Cheltenham?"

"Certainly." Lady Daphne's amusement was audible. "How should I address you? 'Lieutenant'? 'Captain?' "

"If you want the full thing, it's Major Lord Jason Ventriss, at your service—but 'Hobbs' is still wiser for the moment. We won't be disturbed?"

"Louisa is above stairs, repairing the ravages. She's requested a tray in her room. We won't be seeing her again this evening. She was well and truly overset by whatever happened."

"Good. It may be the saving of her." He turned to face Lady Daphne, glass in hand, a visibly shaken man, heavy scowl drawing down his lean, hawk-nosed features. "A few seconds more—How much have you ferreted out? I've not had the opportunity to meet with Heath today, but I understand you sought out His Grace of Rawdon shortly after a visit from the Fortescue boy."

"So—now I'm to be taken seriously?"

Hobbs/Ventriss shrugged. "By me, at least. Nothing less is justifiable."

"It's quite simple, really," she said hesitantly, "once one admits the possibility of the impossible. At first I began to suspect I was only fit for Bedlam, but—"

"Hardly that," Ventriss returned with a rare smile.

"It would appear the Fortescue beldame has been betrothing her diamond to sprigs of independent fortune and military persuasion." Lady Daphne's voice was unnaturally tentative, her face pale. Until now she had been able to find comfort in telling herself she was a fool—at least part of the time. "Dex Fortescue convinces them to make out wills in the girl's favor as a pledge of sincerity using *his* solicitor. He demands absolute secrecy from the lads on pain of the informal understanding being brought to an immediate end, the diamond lost to them forever. The young officers depart immediately for the Peninsula, and if fate does not lend a helping hand, are transformed into fallen heroes by more deliberate methods whenever Newgate threatens—a form of fortune on the hoof. *Please* tell me I'm wrong."

"I can't. Go on . . ."

"I presume the lads all lack living male parents," she sighed, suddenly exhausted, "or else their fathers are more or less *non compos mentis*. A distraught mother or bereaved sister is unlikely to make uncomfortable inquiries. Harriet Fortescue has, however, made some serious miscalculations." Lady Daphne watched Ventriss pace the room, turn, pace again, absently clutching his forgotten brandy. "The first was Christo Debenham."

Ventriss whirled to peer narrowly at Lady Daphne, brows rising. "His Grace was suspicious," he agreed. "You have come far indeed on very little."

"Not so little as all that! I have always enjoyed conundrums. In this case there was an added inducement to deduction. I do *not* enjoy being frightened—for myself, or for those I love . . . Rawdon went to the Horse Guards?"

"Not exactly. He initiated extensive private inquiries which became rather troublesome. In the end, we came to him. His Grace was treading on rather sensitive toes."

"Such suspicions would be difficult to prove."

"Damnably difficult. He had written to . . . one who exceeds him in influence, if not of so elevated a rank

. . . stating a suspicion that well-breached bachelor officers were being murdered to feather the nest of a virago and her offspring. Official interest was aroused, His Grace of Rawdon having a reputation for a clear head, and being personally known to . . . ah—"

"To Arthur Wellesley, Marquess of Wellington," Lady Daphne said with a hollow chuckle. "Don't be so damned *careful—I'm* not the enemy!"

"Yes, well . . . Orders were issued. We became involved." Ventriss paused by the windows, watching the darkening mews beyond the long narrow garden for signs of unaccustomed activity. Then he set down his glass absently, released the rosy draperies, pulled them closed. "Wouldn't do for the curious to see you entertaining your niece's groom. Even you can carry eccentricity only so far, and there's irregularity enough as it is." He stood there a moment, staring at the floor. *"Damnably* difficult," he muttered, and resumed his restless pacing, brandy forgotten.

Circuit after circuit of the room melted beneath his rough boots. He paused occasionally to light one candelabra, then another, until the cool penumbra turned warm and golden. There was an anticipatory atmosphere, a tensile sense of events drawing together at last, of resolutions not only possible, but likely.

"Then someone bungled," Lady Daphne threw into a stillness punctuated only by the sound of Ventriss's heels meeting the parquet floor, tired of waiting for him to continue. "First Harry, and now Dickie Fotheringham return—quite against all expectations—definitely wounded but definitely alive, and *each* expecting the Fortescue chit to become his bride. Lady Harriet's second major miscalculation. I didn't have it at first, you know," she conceded. "I thought the girl had formed a *tendre* for Fotheringham and was being forced into Harry's arms by her mother. *Then* I realized she had to be Dickie's senior by at least a year—a not impossible attachment, but *highly* unlikely given her character. Mathematics are not my strongest suit," she apologized.

He glanced up, nodded. "You have it," he agreed, "or most of it," resumed his silent pacing, finally coming to rest in front of the graceful Adam fireplace. "You don't happen to have such a thing as a dagger—or a pistol or swordstick—about you, do you?"

"No . . ."

"Good," he sighed, scrubbing his chin, watching the diminutive old lady carefully. "We're using Major Beckenham as bait," he admitted finally. "Lieutenant Fotheringham volunteered, but it was out of the question. His wounds are not healing properly in spite of the most devoted care."

"I know." Lady Daphne's expression became almost puckish. "His mother's own. How *is* Lady Heather dealing with the other wenches at Cribb's?"

Ventriss stared at her incredulously. Then a wry grin broke on his stern face. "You are everything I was warned," he congratulated her. "How did you determine that?"

"I have my ways. Don't be concerned—as soon as I began to understand what might be transpiring, I called my man off. I would *never* knowingly endanger Dickie merely to indulge idle curiosity, or what my brother always considered a lamentable penchant for mischief. He *is* being well guarded?"

"We know our business . . . It's been a near thing, and he's not out of the suds yet. Weeks more before he'll be able to leave his bed, longer still before he can attempt relearning to walk. The paralysis may be permanent, but he *will* live."

"Oh, dear God . . ." Her eyes closed at some inner vision. Slowly, effortfully, she swallowed. "I don't know which is worse—Christo, or Dickie," she whispered, "but I do know I now understand our ancestors' predilection for such things as whips, boiling oil, and the stake—barbarities I have always held in utmost repugnance. No punishment would be sufficient . . ."

Then her head rose as if under the command of some external manipulator, eyes looking out on a world permanently metamorphosed. Ventriss paused, flushing slightly under Lady Daphne's steady, unwinking stare. Her face was expressionless now—at what cost he did not dare venture a guess. He met her eyes determinedly, unwilling to grant himself easy quarter. The old lady was making it all the more difficult by her very courage and lack of complaint. Vapors and spasms he had expected despite the duke's cautions, and could have dealt with more easily. Raw determination was a thing he had never before seen in a female. It was close to unmanning him.

"Fotheringham was the first real hope of proof we had," he explained when her silence became too much for him. "The lad was still in Spain, barely off the battlefield, and convinced he was dying. He begged a friend to pen a farewell message to the diamond. Devotion beyond the grave, all the rest. Pleaded with her not to mourn, insisted she love again, that he would watch over her forever—her guardian angel. The correspondence edict didn't matter then, you see, as he'd never live to claim the prize. The letter fell into our hands—never mind how. With *that* to lend substance, we intensified our investigation of other instances, but it took months to get the lad in shape to return to England. A near thing. A *very* near thing . . . Your nephew? The circumstances had always been questionable. Winthrop and the rest were sent home to get close to the major, spotted the tangible connection, and we were off."

"The unusual groom. The 'captains'. The precipitous trip to a dying uncle's bedside." She nodded, neither surprised nor incensed. "You *are* keeping careful watch over Harry?"

"He is so well guarded no attempt could succeed."

"Marleybourne?"

"One certain, one problematical. It *could* have been a careless poacher's stray bullets. On the road, once—no question."

"You don't appear to be very efficient. The perpetrators invariably escape, and the attacks continue."

"Two didn't, but . . ."

"But, they are dead? A bullet in the kneecap is *quite* incapacitating, I have heard, but definitely not lethal, thus permitting you the luxury of asking pointed questions. You might try it . . . Two fortunes just beyond her grasp. Harriet Fortescue must be *rigid* with fury."

"And desperate. And, exceedingly dangerous," he cautioned. "Do not underestimate her determination. She has had men killed, and will have no compunction eliminating Major Beckenham just as ruthlessly and seizing his fortune if she can. We will stop her in the end, but with what we have now? No hope. We'd be laughed out of court."

"Not necessarily a case for the courts," Lady Daphne said judiciously. "The notoriety would not sit well with the victims' families, and would reopen so many painful wounds to no purpose. Nothing will bring the lads back, besides which, *how* do you go about proving it was the Fortescues' agent, and not a French bullet . . . I think I'll take some of that brandy, if you don't mind. I could do with it. While I have always detested the woman, to have such suspicions confirmed—"

She watched Ventriss snap out of his abstraction, and cross to the drinks tray to fill two more glasses with amber liquid. The wiry major was still on edge, anticipating a peal rung over his head. She hadn't the heart for it. It was as if a game of lottery tickets had become a corpse-strewn battlefield.

He handed her a glass, took a chair opposite her, and leaned forward intently.

"Questions?" he asked as she sipped at the biting liquor.

She was grateful for the warmth that flooded her. It might be damnably difficult to obtain the absolute proof they required. It was equally difficult to refrain from the histrionics the middle-aged officer clearly expected. *Damnably* difficult.

"Louisa?" she said after a moment. "You are here for her benefit."

"They seek a double sweep—that is our conclusion. Your niece to wed someone under their control, subsequently to die in childbed or of some fortuitous accident."

"Then they should not be seeking Harry's death," Lady Daphne retorted. "No possible hold over the girl without Harry."

"They are no longer thinking clearly. Lieutenant Fotheringham has altered his will, and they have been permitted to learn of the alteration."

"If Harry were to amend *his* will?"

"He'd be safe enough, and we'd lose our best chance of catching them. Lord knows how many other young men would die merely to feed the Fortescue maw before we'd have another such opportunity. Do you want those deaths on your conscience?"

"Hardly, though what you ask is mightily difficult for me to accept."

"We are increasing the pressure, hoping they will make a fatal misstep. Duns are constantly at their door. We have arranged for certain debts to fall due. A . . . ah . . . *gentleman* of our acquaintance has been encouraged to join Lord Fortescue in games of chance, with lamentable results for the Fortescue fortunes. The house of cards is crumbling."

"The two younger girls? The boy, Giles?"

"Trapped. The girls are definitely not involved—too young to be of any use in such a game until they make their come-outs. The boy?" He shrugged. "Some think one way, some another. He appeared most fortuitously at your nephew's door the morning after the first attack at Marleybourne. He is carefully watched. Involved or not, the younger ones'll pay the penalty when the time comes, just like the others."

"Unjust! You can call off your dogs. Giles is himself concerned that something underhanded is occurring. He came to me—"

"We know. Honest? Possibly, and possibly only *very* clever. There's a strong streak of self-preservation in that family."

Lady Daphne sighed, shook her head. "I would wager my nephew's life on the lad's innocence," she said. "He is nothing more than an engaging, bumbling puppy. Some things are within the realm of the possible. Some are not. And Rawdon? He seeks to avenge Christo, I suppose."

"Not so much that as to obtain justice, and assure the deaths end—a form of living memorial to his brother. His grace has been in town incognito—or as incognito as such a man can ever travel—for months. An appearance here and there as himself, the rest spent masquerading as— well, your niece encountered him," he said with a wry smile. "Damnable situation *that's* created, but he's close to laying his hands on one of the Fortescue agents."

"Is Louisa also 'bait?' " she inquired acidly.

"No . . ." Ventriss smiled then. "We, too, are desperate, but not desperate enough to endanger a lady. Major Beckenham, though he does not know it, remains on full pay, serving King and Country—however reluctantly— until this matter is concluded. We have attempted to lay the facts before him. The little witch is in it as deep as her parents, but it's not a matter for discussion as yet. The time will come."

"You have that wrong. Harry is besotted. He will maintain her innocence to the end." Lady Daphne sighed, straightened her shoulders. "Tell me what I can do to help. At the least, I would like my man to become part of your group if that is permissible. If you didn't tumble to him, neither will the Fortescues, and he is very clever. About tomorrow evening—there may be a slight problem . . ."

Harry protested pressing business with his aunt and sister, but after a leisurely and excellent early dinner at White's accompanied by equally excellent wines and much unusually frank discussion, he finally agreed to join Heath, Gracechurch, and Fenton in a rubber of whist, succeeded by another, and yet another. He kept his eye warily on the time as hand followed hand, determined to arrive at his aunt's as she and Louisa were gathering around the tea tray and in no way expecting him—the element of surprise in his favor. If he couldn't settle the matter of Louisa's future with Lady Fortescue for the moment—and it appeared he couldn't—at the very least he could ascertain that she and his aunt were obeying orders. They had better be! He'd made his position clear enough, God knows . . . If they weren't, he'd remove Louisa this very night, batter his way into Fortescue House if he had to, start demanding explanations and a little cooperation. *Anything* was preferable to this damnable, mist-fogged limbo in which he currently floated!

Harry stared at the jumble of cards in his hand, their import escaping him, and cursed softly. He couldn't even keep his mind on a simple game these days! And no wonder . . . Head still protesting from the crease of two nights ago. Gwendolyn incommunicado, hiding herself from him in the most perplexing manner. Giles, with his wild tales of conditions at Fortescue House. Louisa playing the fashionable impure. Was it any wonder he was at the end of his tether?

"Harry!"

The former major's eyes lifted from his cards as he shook his head to clear it.

"Sorry—wool-gathering, I'm afraid."

Gracechurch eyed him narrowly, a slight frown drawing flaring brows down over hooded eyes. He gave every appearance of an officer on the battlefield assessing the enemy. Odd, that . . . Now he thought of it, Percy and Quentin had much the same look to them, and the room seemed muzzy, as if clouded with those same mists that trapped him wherever he turned. His world was most definitely spinning off its axis. He needed a Copernicus or a Galileo to set it right, but those savants were beyond mortal reach.

Harry tucked his cards under his stump, reached for his glass, drained it. The mists swirled closer, hiding all but what was directly in front of him. Devil take it—how much brandy had he consumed? He'd never felt like this, even when most deeply jug-bitten.

"It's your play, Harry," Fenton prodded gently.

Harry tried to nod. His head continued to sink forward until his chin was touching his chest. His torso followed in an amazingly graceful slow bow, coming to rest on the baize-covered table, glass knocked to the floor, cards spilling from under his stump.

Heath reached over, lifted an eyelid.

"Done," he said tersely. "I still don't like this."

"None of us does," Fenton returned. "Unfortunately, the poor blasted idiot hasn't left us much choice. He eluded your men twice today. If it hadn't been for that light-fingered cutpurse *cum* agent of Lady Cheltenham's, we'd've lost him completely, and then those supposed

Mohawks would've had a perfect chance at him—broad daylight or no. Cribb's, or his rooms?"

"Neither," Heath said softly, scowling as his eyes flicked to nearby tables. Harry's indisposition was going unremarked. Good. "And not our billets, either. Rawdon's, I think. In the morning we can claim we thought he'd taken a bad turn, and needed to get him settled the soonest possible, have a doctor take a look. Head wounds can do strange things to you . . . Probably shouldn't've been drinking," he commented with a meaningful look at the other two. "Our faults entirely—encouraging him to have dinner with us and then stay on half the night. Rawdon'll agree to the fabrication."

"Perhaps, but he's not—" Gracechurch began.

"They've never tumbled to him," Heath insisted. "Safest place available, given Cribb's is out of the question. Harry doesn't know Rawdon's household, as they're the barest of acquaintances. We'll be able to add some footmen without his being any the wiser, slip a little something in his food to keep him under the weather for the next se'night or so."

"I want him on the streets," Gracechurch countered firmly, low voice masked by the raucous laughter of a party of young blades at an adjoining table. No one was paying them the least attention. A man taken in drink was too common a sight here to be remarkable. Sometimes the most public places could be the safest for this kind of thing, but it always bothered him. Incapacitating Harry had been unplanned—if provided for—and clumsily done, but when the fool started to storm about removing his sister to Fortescue House that very night, or the next morning at the latest, he'd *had* to intervene. Ventriss might have lied to Lady Cheltenham about using Louisa Beckenham as bait—and very attractive bait that young lady was proving, which put him in the most damnable of situations. How did one justify placing a woman one would have liked to marry in such danger—to oneself, or to anyone? And yet, it *had* to be done, but there was a point beyond which he refused to go. Permitting her to be forced into the Fortescue household was one of them. If nothing else, it was impractical. They couldn't watch over her there, and once inside those doors—"Rawdon's for the night if you insist, but no more. I'll have our men form a floating box around him if you're that concerned," he conceded, glancing briefly at Heath, "but he's got to be out in the open or we're wasting our time. I *want* that witch and her little angel!"

The men's eyes met briefly over Harry's slumped body. Heath nodded.

"Time to move along," Fenton said, rising slowly. "Give me a hand, will you? Harder to shift this kind of dead weight when you've only one good arm to grab hold of, and Harry's off gathering rosebuds at such a distance I doubt his feet will respond."

The ninth Duke of Rawdon sprawled in the old red leather wing chair by his library hearth, coat and waistcoat unbuttoned, neckcloth cast aside, a glass of amber liquid in his hand, scowling abstractedly at his impeccable, mirrorlike Hessians.

The heavy green velvet draperies were drawn against the night, their deep folds almost black in the feeble light cast by the small blaze sputtering on the grate and the branch of candles at his side. The evening had turned unexpectedly cool, and there were a few more hours to pass before he would have to leave for Cribb's. The fire was welcome—as much for its reassuringly companionable glow as for the warmth it provided. Above him his younger brother smiled enigmatically from within his gilded frame, brilliant regimentals lost in the gloom. Ovid's *Metamorphoses* lay splayed on the floor by Rawdon's chair, cast aside when the messenger had arrived, and now forgotten. His gaze shifted broodingly to the crumpled note in his other hand, its words only too clearly emblazoned on his mind.

Your Grace—

Knowing of your keen interest in matters of Natural History—which interest I share—I take the liberty to inform you that a specimen of a rare and lovely Species of butterfly (Societatis louisiensis according to Linnaean binomial classification), discovered by you only recently to be extent within the purviews of this great City, was almost netted this day by avid collectors near Richmond Park.

The specimen they sought to entrap is currently at liberty, but as the Species is in danger of vanishing from England—its only known habitat—some form of discouragement should be offered these determined collectors, and every effort made to protect this rare and beautiful Species of Lepidoptera from further depredations. My understanding is, given the Species' migratory patterns, excellent examples may be anticipated in the vicinity of Vauxhall Gardens—an undeniable attraction to most Fauna of the Societatis' Genus—tomorrow evening. It is probable the collectors will trace them there.

I feel secure in placing the challenging problem of protecting these lovely creatures in your infinitely capable hands, more customary recourse being unavailable to me within the Royal Lepidopterian Society.

Your Most Obedient Servant,
Charles Glendenning, Esq.

So—Louisa had almost been kidnapped at Richmond Park, and she would be attending the revelries at Vauxhall tomorrow. Of all the damnably dangerous places for her to set foot—Given her oft-stated suspicions, Daphne Cheltenham deserved to be horsewhipped for permitting such foolishness!

The hastily scrawled note was a naked plea for assistance.

Glendenning was, of course, Ventriss of the Horse Guards—or, if one preferred, "Hobbs," Louisa's groom. Inane the seemingly innocuous note might appear to most. To Rawdon it was a blatant admission of incompetence on Ventriss's part, of the Horse Guards' inexcusable, indeed *criminal,* negligence in failing to protect Louisa, and *that* he *would not* countenance. Why he had *ever* agreed to their continued use of her—

What the devil did Ventriss expect him to do? He couldn't dog the girl's footsteps night and day! That was what was needed, of course—and not just him, but an army of protectors so thick not even the damnable Fortescues could touch her—but Lady Daphne had made it plain he was to stay clear until she saw signs of Louisa relenting. There was absolutely no way he could safeguard the girl himself—not as things stood. Ventriss would have to find assistance elsewhere. Bow Street, perhaps—he undoubtedly had connections there—or else among the cronies of Lady Daphne's little cutpurse. And yet, Ventriss had indicated his hands were tied. *None* of those might be available to him, which placed the problem back squarely on his own shoulders.

And then his eyes narrowed. A *married* Louisa would be useless to the Fortescue harpies, her fortune become her husband's property, and thus permanently beyond their grasp. They'd have no more interest in her. She would be safe.

The notion was insane! Was he fit only for St. Mary's after these last months? There were some things a gentleman might do and retain that designation—among them send a delightful baggage flowers bound by silk stockings. There were others that were beyond the realm of the possible. But, she would be safe . . . As to his own position, his part in the matter—

Ventriss had intimated there was protection only he could offer. Was this what the runty little genius at dissimulation meant?

The tiniest flicker of a smile quirked the corner of Rawdon's mouth.

He could do it. No—he *would* do it!

An abduction, by damn, at his age . . . !

He'd explain exactly why once he had her safe, with his ring on her finger and their signatures in the registry book of some out-of-the-way parish. Angry she might be at first. Furious, even. That wouldn't matter. Foolish she was not—except where it concerned the two of them, and—perhaps—her graceless brother.

His smile broadened as he shifted in his chair, glancing apologetically up at Christo.

Ventriss . . . *This* had to be what he meant. That enough was enough. That a moment came when personal considerations must outweigh all else. It was time Louisa understood what had been happening, knew *why* he had done the things he had done, why he'd been *forced* to. It hadn't all been a game, no matter what Daphne Cheltenham might think . . . He'd tell Louisa about Christo, about Fotheringham, about the others of whose deaths they were suspicious—there were an even dozen—and about her own brother. If necessary, he'd even take her to see Fotheringham, and be damned to secrecy and security! He'd sacrificed enough already in the attempt to trap Christo's murderers. There came a time for living again, once the first acid fire of grieving was past. The fury and despair over what had been done to his brother would never ease, but giving up on the almost four-year struggle in order to safeguard her would make Louisa see reason as nothing else could. And, she would forgive him. She had to—if not for her own sake or his, then because of her damned fool of a brother! He'd been trying to safeguard

Beckenham's worthless, ungrateful hide as well, even if he *was* being used as bait.

Arthur Wellesley, the Horse Guards, Gracechurch, Heath—they could all go to the devil! The entire thing had been begun at his instigation, and if they weren't sufficiently clever to stop the old beldame, then eventually he'd do it himself in the most direct manner possible. Was Ventriss intimating that might prove necessary, as well? Possibly. The prospect of killing a woman didn't necessarily sit well with him, but then Harriet Fortescue was not a conventional female. She was a spider, arms scrabbling in the dark to snare whatever unwary prey might wander within her reach. Call it the eradication of vermin, then . . . A public service.

From the front of the house came a violent pounding at the door.

Rawdon rose slowly, setting his glass on the small table beside his chair. He looked at his brother's likeness steadily, brought his hand up in a half-salute. He could almost have sworn the portrait winked.

Christo would have been the perfect accomplice, a thousand impossible plans spilling pell-mell from his fertile imagination, each one more inventive than the last. His own mind was a hopeless muddle at the moment, stuck in the pedestrian paths of what he could only suppose was called middle age. *An abduction? That,* for all the pranks he had played at one time or another, was something he had *never* considered. Lord, but he needed Christo! But then, if Christo had been here to help, there would be no need for any of this.

Besides, he grinned reluctantly, still staring at his brother's portrait, to be seriously contemplating the abduction of a young woman of wealth and beauty and rank at his age—even if the goal were to ensure her safety—must mean he wasn't ready for the pasture yet! How Christo would have laughed . . . The greatest prank of his inglorious career, and it would be played out in deadly earnest and total secrecy.

Voices penetrated the library's quiet. Rawdon shrugged. He'd manage to snatch Louisa somehow for the simple reason that, according to Ventriss, he had no choice. By this time two days from now she'd be his wife—if only in name.

He'd need a special license, but that presented no problem, and his black domino would suffice for Vauxhall. They were common enough that she wouldn't suspect his identity until too late, and if she did it wouldn't matter. He'd be in control—not Louisa.

With a smile still lingering on his lips he went out into the hall to investigate, cursing softly under his breath when he spotted a sodden Beckenham sagging between Heath and Fenton, Gracechurch standing a little aside conferring with Mathers. Quickly he crammed Ventriss's crumpled note in his pocket, strode forth to take charge. First order of business—get rid of them, and that as quickly as possible. He was through with it all!

Fourteen

London never slept, and so it cannot be said the city found peace or forgetfulness in oblivion that night. And, as a city is, in a very real sense, merely the reflection of its denizens, neither did certain inhabitants of stately mansions and elegant town homes scattered along the more fashionable streets and squares of Mayfair seek the customary peace of their beds, while in the stews a ferment of activity erupted unusual even for those noxious environs.

Thus, as the sun tipped the horizon it found Louisa perched on the window seat in her bedchamber, clad only in a thin wrap and with a light coverlet pulled around her shoulders. She had spent most of the night huddled there, shivering as she watched the slow-wheeling progression of stars and moon through the night sky. Her palms and fingers still stung from cuts that reopened at the slightest movement, and there were great hand-shaped bruises on her arms and shoulders, blue-black prints edged in red which throbbed dully in reminder that London, as Hobbs had informed her, was no safe place for a young lady of independent tendencies.

She longed for Marleybourne. Even more, she longed for the time when Rawdon was known to her only as a handsome gamester down on his luck, and employed as a groom in a noble household. The few days of her betrothal had equalled the happiest periods of her childhood, perhaps even surpassed them. Never had she felt such a deep contentment combined with such blinding anticipation. And then, with a few unknowing and careless words, Sally Jersey had swept away her illusions. The tattered remnants of her dignity were all she had now, and cold comfort indeed they were offering—even less than the thin coverlet gathered around her shoulders . . .

The terror of the moments in the woods-rimmed lane remained as a cold hard knot which she dared not examine too closely for fear of falling into an hysterical fit—an indulgence that would have served no purpose except to relieve overwrought emotions. As Hobbs had pointed out only too accurately, the contretemps had been her fault from beginning to end. Foolish to protest what she herself had caused through her own stubborn independence of spirit, her own maudlin desire for privacy to mourn that which had never truly existed.

She sighed, resting her head against the soft curtains bunched at the side of the window as the sky lightened, the scattered puffs of high-flying cloud as yet untouched by the sun strangely dark against the diaphanous blue, the stars winking out one by one.

Tonight's excursion to Vauxhall was being hosted by Harald Donclennon, that son of an old bosom-bow of Lady Daphne's who had married a wild Scotsman and abandoned the ton to reside in domestic bliss far to the north of Hadrian's Wall. If Dugald Donclennon had been the impetuous and devilishly handsome young laird Aunt Daphne described, Lord Harald had proved his diametric opposite. Stolid, parsimonious of word and purse, congenitally incapable of completing a thought or sentence unless the sentiments expressed were of the most trite, of barely medium height and more than medium girth, and with understanding and interests limited to the concerns of his acres and ancestral pile of rubble, he had taken a strong liking to Louisa, pursuing her with dogged determination from ballroom to rout, spilling champagne on her gowns and treading ponderously on her toes since the night of Lady Daphne's first dinner party months before, his weak blue eyes gazing on her with an approval of which this pleasure party, planned in her honor, was the ultimate proof.

Donclennon was, Louisa knew, quaking on the verge of a declaration. For all his thin sandy locks and air of judging everything by the coin it might take to acquire it, he was not a bad man. Indeed, he could have rare flashes of genuine kindness—witness this evening's excursion, which had been planned solely for her amusement. That he took no pleasure in rack punch or shaved ham or fireworks was a simple matter of character definition. Would this thoughtfulness carry past the altar? She suspected it might, and she did not actively dislike him, as she did so many of the men of fashion she had encountered during the season. Dull Donclennon might be, and unprepossessing in the extreme, but he had only one face to show the world, being too unimaginative to have fashioned a second for social purposes.

She would bring him to the point tonight. A stroll to watch the fireworks from a more advantageous location than the box he had certainly secured, and then a gentle guiding toward the Dark Walk—which she doubted he even knew existed—would turn the trick. Scotland, and the isolation it offered, as well as the freedoms that isolation would mean, had become a great attraction since yesterday—perhaps Donclennon's greatest attraction. Many marriages began so, with at best only a mild liking as their foundation. Such a relationship would engender peace, and peace—given her experience of James Morrison—was a thing she found she now craved above all. No heights of ecstasy, perhaps, but no depths of despair, either. Merely a succession of gray days, each indistinguishable from the ones preceding it, as youth faded through middle age into decrepitude, identical in character and tone to the future she had been contemplating moments before the burly, hooded abductor and his masked confederates interrupted her ruminations.

By this time tomorrow she would be betrothed. Given Donclennon's oft-stated desire to return to his ancestral acres, the marriage would follow quickly—preferably by special license. It could not be too soon for Louisa. She wanted the tumult of the past weeks behind her, her future decided, and with no opportunities left for choice or repining. A long betrothal, where there was love, would be torment enough. Where it did not exist, such a delay—even of a few weeks—permitted too much opportunity for a change of heart.

And Aunt Daphne? She would, in all likelihood, protest. Violently. And vociferously. She had adored Donclennon's mother, would have set her own cap at Donclennon's father had Sophy Brightwell not been so clearly enamored of the dashing blond giant. Young Donclennon, however, was not his father.

"How *they* could have produced *him* I shall never know!" her aunt had declared times beyond mention. "Harald is a changeling. He *must* be, as Sophy would *never* have played Dugald false! What a disappointment he must have been to his poor father, and what an embarrassment to dear Sophy."

Still, it was her decision, and not her aunt's. She would quietly clear the field for Harry and his diamond. She had already made the point with her admirer, subtly if definitely, that she was her own mistress and residing under her aunt's protection by her own choice, with no one to answer to but herself. Donclennon would not approach Harry first seeking permission to address her, and if she had her way she would be wed and on the road to Scotland before her brother had the slightest notion of her intentions.

And, James Morrison?

Louisa sighed. He didn't exist, or else he was the figment of a moon-struck imagination fed on a too-steady diet of Minerva vaporings. There was only His Grace of Rawdon—wealthy beyond the dreams of avarice, sophisticated, rakehellish, and endowed with a streak of malicious, mischievous masculine cruelty such as she had never before encountered. Marleybourne was not the proper direction from which to approach London if one wished to survive.

The sun tipped the earth, glinting off chimneys, painting the world with light. Beyond exhaustion, almost beyond feeling, Louisa came to her feet, stumbled across the cold floor to her bed, collapsed on top of it without seeking the warmth of the covers, and curled in a tight ball beneath the thin coverlet that had served her as a shawl during the long night.

From his study on Grosvenor Square, Rawdon watched the same sun paint the tops of the trees, turning them first a rosy lavender, then deep blushing pink, and finally a flaming gold. Too restless for sleep, nerves too jangled at the prospect of what he planned, and—admit it he must—too joyfully anticipating the coming night when all problems would be resolved and his life take on the tenor he intended rather than swinging from depths to heights like a leaf caught in a March gale, he had spent the night alternately pacing the floor and making lists of what he must accomplish before taking off for Vauxhall.

He had decided to whisk Louisa to Rawdonmere for the ceremony, keep her there in safety and seclusion for the first weeks of their marriage. Time enough for a honeymoon when she was resigned to her fate, or perhaps rather more than that, he had concluded with a sparkle in his eyes that had been absent since the disastrous evening at Almack's.

The practical aspects of the coming adventure had occupied his thoughts through most of the long cold hours, Louisa's comfort and convenience his first concern once the initial and unavoidable upsets of forced abduction and hasty journey were past. The anticipatable problems were now resolved to his satisfaction. Food, money, transportation, even clothing were accounted for.

With a smile his fingers sought the waistcoat pocket where he had carried the damnable ring ever since Louisa returned it to him. It was still there, waiting for him to put it back where it belonged. Certainly it would never grace any other hand in *his* generation . . . Come to think of it, he needed to acquire something in the way of a wedding band. That, if nothing else, should convince Louisa he was not about to accept any silly demurs on her part.

He snuffed the guttering candles on his desk, pulled several sheets of paper from a drawer, sharpened two fresh pens, reviewed the lists. First order of business for the new day: A letter to his solicitor, announcing his change in status, and instructing that the marriage settlement documents be completed as originally detailed, and forwarded to him for signature.

Rawdon paused, scowling slightly as he stared at the ruby ring he had placed on the desk in front of him. Then he grinned. And, he'd have the man send an announcement of their nuptials to all the appropriate papers. So much for Louisa's potential recalcitrance! She'd never be able to fight an official *fait accompli,* and the announcement would ensure her safety as nothing else could— along with the patrols he would establish at Rawdonmere. The Fortescues had robbed him of his brother. There was no way he would permit them to rob him of the woman he loved as well.

* * *

Harry regained consciousness on toward noon, his head of a size he would never have thought it possible to attain through the ordinary expedient of downing a few glasses of brandy—once he was capable of thought. Gersten, Rawdon's valet, stood by the bed, proffering a salver on which reposed a tankard containing a dark-brown brew of his own contriving. Percy Fenton lounged on a tufted sofa by the fireplace, neckcloth loosened, a tray holding the remains of a substantial breakfast at his elbow, the morning papers scattered about him.

Sunlight flooded the room, blinding in its intensity. Harry groaned at the brilliant assault, and gestured toward the open draperies.

"Close 'em!" he tried to protest, but found his mouth so dry, his tongue so thick and furred that only an unintelligible croak emerged. His very throat ached, as if dust-parched from a day-long march at the height of Spanish summer.

Gersten extended the salver. Harry stared at it blankly for a moment. Then understanding dawned. He seized the tankard, sniffed the contents, groaned, shuddered, and gulped them down.

"Close the demmed curtains!" he pleaded as Percy came to his feet. "Have some pity, man!"

"Making indentures last night?" Fenton quipped, whisking the damask draperies across the window, cutting off the worst of the glare.

"You ought to know. You were there," Harry grumbled, sinking back against the pillows. "Oh, Lord—my head! Where in hell are we? Don't recognize this place."

"Not surprising. You've never been here before," Percy returned as the valet glided to the door, admitting a string of maids carrying cans of hot water to pour in the copper bath in front of the fire. "Brought you to Jamie

Debenham's place. You were in no condition to make suggestions."

"Debenham?" Harry protested weakly. "Duke of Rawdon? Don't know him well enough to impose like this."

"We do."

Harry closed his eyes wearily, but it didn't help. The bed continued to spin, tilting one way and then another, like a rudderless boat on a wave-tossed sea.

"What the devil did I consume to put me in this condition?" he complained.

"Brandy, just like the rest of us," Percy replied with a certain mental reservation. "Our fault you swallowed a spider. Shouldn't't've kept filling your glass, not with that lump on your noggin. A delayed reaction, probably. Heads're odd things. Stephen and Quentin requested I tender their apologies."

"Much good their apologies'll do me now!" Harry moaned. "I don't think I'll live out the morning."

To his surprise—and Fenton's unabashed amusement—he did. Gersten was a forceful man when the need arose. Harry was pulled protesting from his bed, thrust into the steaming copper tub, soaked and soaped and scrubbed and forced to drink scalding black coffee until he complained another cup would bring it all up, and then that final insult was forced on him. Once his retching subsided he was made to stand in the now-emptied tub as pannikins of first blistering hot and then icy-cold water were poured over his trembling frame. After that the world seemed a little brighter. The room stopped behaving like a giant pendulum, and by the time he was dressed in fresh clothes fetched from his lodgings, neckcloth properly—if simply—tied and mirrorlike boots encasing his feet and legs, he felt rather more the thing. A generous—if carefully selected—breakfast completed the process. At two-thirty of a still-blinding afternoon, Lords Harry Beckenham and Percy Fenton emerged from the austerely classical mansion on Grosvenor Square without having once set eyes on His Grace of Rawdon, which was exactly as both Fenton and Rawdon had planned.

They sauntered toward Brook Street, two young bucks on the strut, coats hugging their shoulders in smooth sweeps of Bath superfine, inexpressibles clinging to muscular thighs like second skins, linen snowy and waistcoats, if not aspiring to the heights of Tulipdom, at least not dowdy. Fenton swung a walking stick casually in rhythm with his stride, a fob twinkling at his waist, quizzing glass at the ready to inspect any vision of pulchritude which met his eye. Behind them a strapping flower seller in voluminous skirts and a heavy shawl completed her transaction with a jarvey whose hackney now sported a clot of marigolds in the whip socket. She tucked the ha'penny in a capacious pocket, sauntered after the two young men, hips rolling like barrels broken loose from their lashings in the hold of a ship. The jarvey started his horse off in the opposite direction, hooves clattering on the cobbles.

"Where to?" Fenton inquired as they turned off the square.

"My aunt's," Harry responded tightly, his plans of the night before unforgotten, "and I'd rather do without your company, if you don't mind."

"But I mind very much. Besides," Fenton said complacently, "she isn't home, and neither's your sister. Gone shopping—I have it on the best authority. Big do at Vauxhall tonight, and they're hunting up some special doodads for Louisa."

Harry's jaw clenched. Then he took a deep breath. Percy, after all, wasn't responsible for Louisa's or his aunt's ignoring the instructions he had left them—nor for their plans to attend some highly-improper festivity at the noisome and déclassé Vauxhall, where cits rubbed shoulders with lords, the muslin company paraded its wares, and the veriest shabster with the price of admission could tread on the toes of his betters and ogle their ladies. No, in that he could see his aunt's fine Italian hand. Whether she was intent on ruining Louisa, or Louisa was bent on a course of self-destruction, didn't matter. The result would be the same once Lady Fortescue caught wind of it, and hear of it she would. Lord knew what her sources of information were, but it often seemed neither he nor Louisa could take a breath without her being apprised of the fact.

"Fortescue House, then," he said. "I've some unfinished business there. Then I'll run Louisa and my demmed aunt to ground. I don't care where they've got to—enough is enough! And for *that* endeavor, old friend, you are definitely not wanted."

At the next corner they flagged a hackney sporting marigolds in the whip socket, and rode in questionable comfort to the diamond's home. There the same burly under footman answered Harry's impatient knock, informed him curtly that the family wasn't receiving, not a one on 'em *including* the young miss, and that he'd best be getting himself away from where he wasn't wanted. Infuriated, Harry first protested, then attempted to force his way past the supercilious and crude lackey. He ended on his posterior in the area way, staring up at the house's blank white facade just as the filmy curtains of the second-floor parlor fell back into place. This time he could have sworn it was Gwendolyn's perfect features he glimpsed—except that he would also have sworn the expression on those angelic features was a combination of terror and contempt. Had the world taken leave of its senses?

The door slammed as Percy came down the steps to join him on the flags and extended a hand.

"Might as well forget her for the moment," Percy said gently, pulling Harry to his feet and dusting him off. "It's clear whatever understanding you had before, it's off."

"Be damned to you if I will!" Harry growled.

He started back for the door, fist clenched, jaw working. Percy Fenton grabbed his arm, spun him away.

"Come on, now," he insisted, pulling Harry purposefully down the street. "That won't do any good. I hear she's been down pin ever since that morning in the Park. Probably just doesn't want you to see her until she's looking her best. Females're funny that way. Could be she's blaming you for the entire mess, too. When they're like that, it's best to leave 'em to themselves, I've found. Get over their megrims sooner. Winthrop mentioned a spanking team of grays coming on the block at Tatt's in a few days. What say we go take a gander? Might be on view, and I'm of a mind to set up a stable if we're to be here much longer. Dashed nuisance having to part with the ready to hire inferior cattle every time I want to go somewhere."

He dragged the protesting Harry down the street. Their hackney had gotten no further than the corner, where the jarvey waited patiently for a pause in the traffic, whistling between his teeth as his nag's head sagged listlessly toward the pavement.

"Changed your minds, have you, gents?" he inquired laconically as Percy drew abreast, now propelling the reluctant Harry slightly ahead of him, gripping his arm with a force that permitted no escape. "Any other destination in mind, seeing as how that one ain't to your liking?"

"Yes, Tatt's," Percy stated flatly.

"Over my dead body," Harry grunted through clenched teeth, eyes flashing. He wrenched his arm from Percy's incautiously relaxed grip, planted his friend a facer, and whirled to storm back down the street.

"Now, now, gov'ner," the jarvey protested, whip lashing out, " 'at's no way to treat a cove what's your friend."

Before the words were fairly spoken, Harry was flat on the pavement once more, feet tangled in the thong. The jarvey sighed resignedly, clambered down from his perch, retrieved the whip, pulled Harry to his feet, and gave him a light but scientifically placed tap on the chin, then caught him as he crumpled.

"Be damned glad when this is over," the jarvey grumbled, opening the door, hoisting Harry within, and dumping him unceremoniously on the vehicle's none-too-clean floor. Then he leaned over Percy, who remained slumped in the street against the carriage wheel, blinking and delicately feeling his chin. "Now what, sir?" he asked.

"Damned if I know, Sergeant," Percy admitted. "Lord, but Harry's handy with his fives! That, or I'm becoming an old woman."

"Come on now, sir—let's get you inside afore someone starts asking questions."

"You shouldn't've laid him out, you know," Percy grumbled as the sergeant helped him to his feet. "How in blazes am I supposed to explain that?"

"Didn't want him goin' in that there house without you, did you, sir?"

"You can wager your last groat on that! Chances are he'd've ended up food for the fishes."

"Well, there you have it, sir." The sergeant practically shoved Fenton into the hackney, slamming the door after him. "It was stop him, or let him go," he said softly through the open window. "I figured as how you'd want him stopped, and you weren't in no case to be giving orders or lendin' a hand. I stopped him quick as I could, and with least fuss. You can tell him as how I thought he was assaulting you, sir, and determined on holding him for the Charlies, if he complains too loud. You can even tell 'im," the sergeant grinned, "that you gave me a regular bear-garden jaw for popping him one, which I didn't like a'tall. Still want to go to Tatt's?"

"Lord, no!" Fenton sighed. He looked at Harry, now sprawling in the filthy straw, with something akin to disgust. "What the deuce am I supposed to do with you now, you great lummox?" he muttered. "Was there ever such a nodcock!"

"You, sir?" the sergeant intoned. "Or him?"

They arrived from Westminster via the watergate, rowing across the Thames as the last vestiges of a late spring twilight faded from the sky. Donclennon, if he were going to do a thing—no matter how distasteful to him personally—was clearly determined to do it properly.

Vauxhall was at its best—if indeed it could ever be anything else. Thousands of fairy lanterns twinkled in the trees, and from the giant kiosk the strains of a spirited polka filtered to where Louisa, Harald Donclennon, General Sir Garth Maitland, and Lady Daphne strolled along the alley toward the box Donclennon had reserved. Vauxhall, even at this relatively early hour, was more than crowded, the brightly colored throngs eddying past groups paused in conversation and lighthearted greeting. Though this was not a special masquerade night, there were masks and dominoes in plenty—revelers with no desire to be recognized—at least with each other.

Louisa paced sedately at Donclennon's side, thankful that this evening, like the previous one, was cooler than customary. The sleeves that hid her bruised arms and shoulders were unremarkable, her gloves and delicate silk shawl at one with what seemed to be the uniform of the evening for all the ladies—if not the high and low-priced bits of muslin who felt they had to display their wares no matter what the weather. Head high, hand lightly resting on Donclennon's fleshy arm, she walked as if in a fog, refusing to think of the past or the future. Her gown of palest gray silk shot with silver threads and embroidered with clusters of pearly flowers at shoulders, bustline, and vandyked hem, floated around her, lending her a wraith-like appearance, as if she were no more substantial than smoke trailing into the darkening sky. Even her glorious golden curls had lost their vibrancy in the uncertain light, transmuted to a soft silvery gray. The only color came from her vivid blue eyes, and night had darkened these to a hue so deep as to be almost black.

She murmured an unintelligible acknowledgment to a comment of Donclennon's, trying to drag herself from the mists in which she seemed to have existed since she took her decision that morning to bring him to the point, and with him as her husband flee London and the disasters and heartache her time there had engendered.

Behind them Lady Daphne giggled at something General Maitland said, and Maitland broke into a belly-rolling roar of laughter.

Louisa's face remained blank, her eyes barely registering the colorful scene around her. In her befogged state she passed a crestfallen Giles without acknowledging his surprised and delighted hail, completely missed the presence of Fenton, Heath, and Gracechurch, lounging with her brother not far up the alley from where she walked. She never even noticed them, or saw that after spotting her they had drawn her brother's attention to a party disappearing in another direction. Of Hobbs/Ventriss determinedly dogging their steps, his slight wiry form swathed in a deep green domino several sizes too large for him, she was totally unaware. Lady Daphne, attention captured by Maitland—a charming rake in his time, and a delightful and witty raconteur ever—had eyes and ears only for her husband's old friend and schoolmate, invited by Donclennon for her entertainment. None of them noticed the tall, broad-shouldered figure in a black domino who observed them from a slight distance, nor his shorter, stockier brown shadow. Nor did any of them particularly notice the jack-straw in a sweeping purple satin hooded cape with spangled lining, the cape's hood pulled low over his forehead, the wings of a mask extend-

ing its sides like oversized ears, nor *his* trio of Sancho
Panzas, clad in nondescript dull brown coats and gray
pantaloons, caps pulled low to hide their features.

Harry disappeared with Fenton, Gracechurch, and
Heath down one of the side alleys, efficiently whisked
from sight and sighting. The black domino and the purple
cape moved through the crowds, never quite out of sight,
never quite near enough to stand out from those swirling
around them. Donclennon handed Louisa into their box,
seated her as Maitland puffed his way up the few steps,
technically supporting Lady Daphne, but in reality accepting rather more assistance than he rendered.

Donclennon murmured something about the crush.

Louisa nodded abstractedly, toying with the gloves
which hid her lacerated hands, winced at the sudden flash
of pain as one of the cuts reopened, resignedly folded her
hands in her lap and pasted a smile across her lips.

Donclennon signaled the hovering waiter that light refreshments and punch were to be brought. Arrack punch
and biscuits appeared as if by magic, accompanied by
platters of shaved ham, bowls of new peas dressed in a
cream sauce, lobster patties, mushroom fritters, and
dishes of quivering, jewellike jellies—quince and currant
and wine—and delicate, frothy fruit syllabubs.

Maitland helped himself and Lady Daphne liberally to
ham, fritters, patties, and punch, and began a highly
expurgated version of a barracks-tale going the rounds of
the clubs. Lady Daphne chuckled, sipped the punch, and
toyed with the food, eyes sparkling. Donclennon scowled
at Maitland. Louisa turned her most determined smile on
Donclennon, drained her glass of punch with a shudder,
expressed a desire for it to be refilled, ignored the food
Donclennon had piled helter-skelter on her plate despite
her protests, and embarked on a determined and subtle
course of flirtatious flattery that left his lordship red-faced
and delighted, his height—at least in his own estima-

tion—increased by several inches and his rather corpulent body and fleshy features adonized. Pot-valiant, he asked Louisa if she cared to dance. She acquiesced with such gay alacrity that Lady Daphne threw her a puzzled look, Donclennon's toe-bruising habits well known to her from Louisa's previous descriptions—as well as her own sad experience. Louisa beamed at Lady Daphne as she rose from her seat, gesturing impatiently for Donclennon to join her. He surged upward, jostling the table, sweat dewing his face in a fine shining film.

The country dance that had been in vigorous process when they quitted the box drew to a close as they approached the floor. Donclennon puffed his chest out as the musicians broke into a waltz, laying his hand possessively over Louisa's where it rested gracefully on his arm. He smiled proudly at her, dragged her into the whirling throng, seized her in his arms, and ponderously trod on her foot as he lurched into the dance. The faintest tremor of a wince flitted across Louisa's features. Donclennon made no apology, unaware of her freshly injured status.

By the time the dance was half over, Louisa ached in every muscle and bone. Her hands screamed. Her head pounded. Her face seemed frozen in its gay smile, ready to shatter if so much as touched. Of her abused feet, trampled at almost every turn, she dared not think. They *might* carry her as far as the Dark Walk, but only if she brought this charade to a rapid conclusion. One more tromping would leave her crippled for life.

She wavered in Donclennon's arms, raised her hand to her forehead, then seemed to wilt before his eyes—a delicate flower seared by the heat from one of the new infernal machines installed against much protest in midland factories.

"I'm a little faint, I think, my lord," she quavered. "The heat . . . The press of people. I'm so sorry. I was *so* enjoying our dance!" She looked at him pathetically, eyes on a level with his. "If we could but walk for a bit—?"

"My dear Miss Beckenham!" His concern was clearly profound, which gave Louisa only the slightest twinge of conscience. She was, after all, about to give him the opportunity to acquire that which he had given every evidence of desiring. At least *this* time she would not say the actual words, but men appeared to require an inordinate amount of encouragement combined with ideal opportunity to bring them to their knees. So much for traditional conventions of courtship! "Our box! Permit me to escort you—Or should I call for assistance? Or perhaps your aunt—?"

"No—no! A momentary indisposition only, I'm sure." She gazed at him appealingly. "If we could just walk for a bit, away from all these crowds, I shall be rapidly restored."

He had his arm around her shoulders now, ignoring the proprieties in face of her obvious disability as he bludgeoned their way through the dancers, paying no heed to those whom he threw off balance, leaving a trail of scowls and curses in his wake. He blundered past a tall figure in a black domino, trod on the toes of a lanky effete in a swirling purple cape, at last gained an untenanted patch of ground by an empty bench, forced Louisa to sit, seized her fan, and began plying first her and then himself with it.

"Uncommon warm!" he puffed into the breeze he created. "So sorry! Wouldn't put you out of frame for the world. Not my intention. Not my intention at all!"

He blathered on in much the same vein, alternately apologizing for the unseasonable heat as he fanned away in the unusually cool evening air, and inquiring of her whether she did better now, and desperately urging they regain their box where her aunt could minister to her with such appropriate female remedies as hartshorn and *sal volatile* while he summoned his carriage.

At last Louisa rose in desperation, retrieved her fan—rather tattered from his vigorous application of it—and placed her hand on his arm.

"Really—what I need most is to walk," she insisted. "I'm a country mouse, you know, and walking always sets me to rights." She smiled winsomely. "That appears a pleasant path." She pointed to one of the less well-lit walks in a direction opposed to their box's location. That way, if she remembered correctly, led in the proper—or improper—direction.

Determinedly she guided his footsteps, bringing them ever closer to the infamous Dark Walk with its secluded benches and intimate romantic arbors designed with assignations in mind, ignoring his protests that he suspected that to be promenading unchaperoned in such places was definitely not the thing, that he should return her instantly to the protection of her aunt, that this was not at all what he should or could countenance as a place to escort a lady of delicate and refined sensibilities.

The crowds thinned as they approached this most daring area of Vauxhall. There were rustlings in the underbrush, low-pitched laughter, sudden squeals.

"My head aches," Louisa insisted, blushing at sounds that were blatant rather than suggestive, but never for a moment relaxing her grip on his arm or permitting him to turn their steps toward better-lighted and more frequented paths, "and my senses are whirling. I need peace such as one finds in the country. I need to rest my eyes on this blessed darkness. They have been blinded by all the brightness." Her cajolings sounded fatuous, even to her, but she refused to permit Donclennon to deflect her from her goal of reaching the most secluded and romantic spot she could find before her determination gave out.

She tottered artistically on battered feet, thankful the penumbra hid the pain that was sure to have flashed across her face at this uncalled-for additional abuse. In response, Donclennon trod heavily on her instep. She drew her breath in, masking a grunt of agony. If he had not broken a bone, he had done his best. From behind them came a low chuckle. Limping now, leaning heavily on Donclennon's arm even as she clutched it and propelled him further down the almost-empty Dark Walk, she refused to give up. She could never face another such evening. Either she brought him to the point now, or she would be forced to accept one of the Fortescue connections, and that she would never do.

"Can we not sit a moment," she quavered, fluttering her lashes and simpering with all the flirtatious enticement she could muster—actions lost on Donclennon in the almost nonexistent light. "Is that not a little grotto just beyond that big tree? It's sure to contain a bench, and I find myself unaccountably wearied."

"My dear Miss Beckenham!" Donclennon expostulated. "Not the thing! Not the thing at all. I insist we—"

Whatever Donclennon had intended insisting the world was never to know. There was a scrape of gravel behind them, as if from furtive but rapid steps. He gave a sudden startled grunt, stiffened, and crumpled at Louisa's feet, almost dragging her to the ground with him. She whirled, the beginnings of a scream muffled by a strong hand covering her mouth. The force of her turn spun her into a thick dark cloak, stifling her as the hand vanished and her head, her body, her arms, her legs, were trapped in the cloak's voluminous folds. She was grasped tightly for a moment against a hard and unyielding chest, then slung unceremoniously over a broad shoulder, unable to decipher the meaning behind the rapid low murmur of voices. She tried to wrench free, to kick, to pound the firmly muscled body with her fists, to scream. It was no good. She could barely breathe, let alone capture enough air to make herself heard, and the cloak had been wrapped around her so tightly that there was no moving.

With a weak sob she collapsed, sagging beneath arms that held her forcefully in place far above the ground, one wrapped firmly around her neck and shoulders, the other gripping her calves and ankles against the man's waist and side so that she was painfully wrenched. A faint would have been welcome. One refused to come.

Her captor began to stride purposefully down the Dark Walk as she jounced uncomfortably against his hard shoulders and hips within the woolen cloak. Objects struck her rump, her back, her shoulders, grabbed at the cloak. She suspected they had broken into the trees beside the alley, and were lounging it now, out of sight of any potential rescuers.

And then she was tumbling to the ground, hitting it with the combined force of two falling bodies, helplessly entangled in someone else's limbs which seemed to still cling to her, now with the force of desperation rather than arrogant confidence. She gasped for breath as the enveloping cloak was torn from her face, a thin lantern beam blinding her as her eyes snapped open. She blinked. Four dim shadows loomed above her.

"Thank you!" she quavered, tears of relief trembling on her lids. "I'll see you're well rewarded for your timely assistance, whoever you are. Now, if you will just disentangle me from—"

"That's the bitch!" a voice hissed triumphantly. "Kill the bloody light!"

There was a flash of blinding pain as something struck her skull, and then nothing.

Fifteen

Rawdon groaned, gripping his splitting head between shaking hands as he attempted to struggle to his knees, then collapsed back among the leaves and twigs littering the woods just beyond the Dark Walk.

"He's coming 'round, now," Jasper Foote's voice rasped at his side. "Give me a hand here, if'n you would, Major. His grace is no light-weight."

"What in bloody hell've you two been doing?" Ventriss spat.

Rawdon felt his shoulders seized, and he was unceremoniously pulled to a sitting position. The world swam around him, the darkness populated by fireflies which he suspected had no substance or reality. His hand traveled laboriously to the back of his head, found the anticipated lump, and came away wet and sticky.

"Devil take it!" he muttered. "I might as well be jug-bitten, the use I am now."

"Stop feeling sorry for yourself," Ventriss snapped. *"What have you been up to?"*

"Tryin' to see to Miss Beckenham's safety," Jasper responded after waiting a moment for the duke to express his version of events. "We was goin' t'take her to Rawdonmere. No way those damned Fortescues could've got their paws on her there."

"Civilians!" Ventriss groaned. "Of all the stupid, asi-
nine—"

"After the fact—not before," Rawdon mumbled.
"Before the fact it looked to accomplish all you wanted,
and more."

"I told you to *guard* her—not abduct her! This has torn
it fair and well. What am I to tell Gracechurch—"

"I'll do the telling," Rawdon muttered, still nursing his
sore head. "My fault—all of it." The world seemed to be
regaining its customary axis, and the dancing points of
light had almost vanished. The dull throb he could ignore
for as long as he had to. "How'd you know to come
hunting for me, Jasper?"

"Saw a bunch of unlikely citizens headin' for a traveling chaise well down the way, lugging a bundle. They was
gone afore I could reach 'em, but I didn't have no doubt
as to what that bundle was," Jasper responded tonelessly.

"Damn!" Ventriss spat. "See anything else? How many
were there? Did you recognize the chaise? Which way did
they go?"

"Hold on there, Major. One question at a time," Foote
protested. He scowled in the darkness, trying to remember. It had all happened so fast . . . "They were just blots
in the dark—like ink spots on black cloth. I *think* there was
four on 'em, maybe five, not counting the ones on the
box. Two there, one to drive an' one riding guard. Lamps
warn't lit—just a little lantern a skinny runt in a cloak was
holding."

"Could you tell anything about the rest?"

"There was one bigger 'n the others—burly-like, thickset," Jasper said, desperately trying to recall details as he
replayed the scene in his mind.

"The famous Fortescue under footman?" Rawdon
threw in, gradually registering what his groom was saying.

"Can't be sure, Your Grace. Built like him, but there

warn't enough light t'see faces. Be logical if it was him, though."

"The chaise—any markings?" Ventriss interrupted impatiently.

"Some kind o' crest, or maybe it were just the lantern light glinting off the paint—can't be sure."

"How many got aboard?"

"The burly one, the skinny runt in the cape, an' the bundle. T'others took off, headin' every which way. There wasn't no blasted way to follow 'em, Your Grace," Jasper apologized, ignoring the major for the moment, "so I come after you. Knew somethin' untoward had happened, and I figured the soonest I found you the soonest we could get help."

"Too bad that wasn't your initial philosophy," Ventriss countered. "Of all the irresponsible—"

"Didn't seem like it at the time," Rawdon protested weakly, regaining his feet with his groom's assistance. The world continued to dance around him, but the gratuitous fireworks had ceased, and the ground beneath his feet seemed solid enough, even if it had a tendency to wobble a bit. "I had the entire thing well planned out. Incidentally, there should be a lump of lard back that way coming to life just about now."

"Donclennon?" There was a hint of an unexpected chuckle in Ventriss's cold voice. "Already being seen to. Who tapped him—you, or Foote?"

"Does it matter? Person or persons unknown . . ."

"Oh, you're safe enough," Ventriss grumbled. "No time to be wasted on fruitless investigations at the moment. Think you can walk?"

"Just about."

"Let's be going, then. We'll accomplish nothing here."

They broke into the Dark Walk, paused, looking down its length to where a more brightly lit path crossed at its end. Rawdon, head balanced uncertainly on his shoulders and leaning heavily on Foote and Major Ventriss, wavered as he spotted an unlikely couple stumbling its way unsteadily up the alley—one short and rotund, the other with the shambling and awkward gait of a youth grown too quickly into his height.

"What the devil?" he muttered.

"Young Fortescue," Ventriss said tonelessly. "He's been dogging Beckenham and his sister all evening, alternating his attentions according to which one seemed least protected at the time. Very persistent. Pure blind luck he spotted Donclennon and Miss Beckenham coming off the dance floor, and followed. *I'd* lost them in the crowds. So had the others. Boy stayed well back when they started down the Dark Walk—not wanting, so he said, to interfere in anything that wasn't his concern—but not too happy about their being so isolated. Saw the whole thing: Donclennon accosted, Miss Beckenham abducted by a ruddy giant and a pernicious little gnome of a man—his words, not mine. Went tearing off to find Major Beckenham. Fenton got to him before he could say anything damaging in Beckenham's hearing, whisked him over to me, and here we all are."

Ventriss sighed, eyes flicking over the duke. "Think you can make it to your carriage? I'd rather not have you seen in this condition in public. The less attention we attract tonight, the better."

"Then what? I insist—"

"You're in no position to insist on *anything!*" the major seethed. Then, as Foote murmured something placating and explanatory in Ventriss's ear, he sighed again. "Oh, very well. Get yourself patched up, and join us at Cribb's. They haven't tumbled to the place yet, but for Lord's sake use a hired conveyance, and get yourself well away from your own home before you flag one down."

"I am well acquainted with elementary precautions," Rawdon said stiffly.

"Not so's an unbiased judge could tell!"

Ventriss dropped the duke's arm, strode purposefully down the aisle after Donclennon and young Fortescue, shoulders squaring as he contemplated various courses of action.

First on the agenda—And to hell with the others and their opinions of whether he was ready for it or not!—was a full and frank recounting of the history of the Fortescue diamond's serial and simultaneous betrothals, and the fates of her betrotheds, to that ass of a Harry Beckenham! Oh Lord—he had to inform Lady Cheltenham . . .

Louisa was first conscious of an intolerable ache in her head. She was being jostled unmercifully, which wasn't helping matters, and somehow it was impossible to move. Something was cutting into her already abused wrists and ankles. Ropes? That made no sense. Who would have the need, let alone the temerity, to bind her hand and foot? And her mouth tasted and felt vile—as if crammed with a filthy scrap of cloth. She gagged, dry throat raw and protesting, then moaned as her eyes flickered open.

At first she could make no sense of what she felt and saw.

Beneath her were boards, slick and highly polished, cool against her cheek—moving boards, rising and dropping again and again with an irregular lurching rhythm to strike her burning face and assault her aching limbs.

Faint light filtered from above, catching the edges of something just beyond the limit of her vision. Folds of cloth? Dark, soft, and shimmering, like heavy silk. And something shiny, like the edge or lip of an object. And, something heavy on her back, pressing her down, holding her in place. Many somethings. She attempted to count them, gave it up as hopeless.

There were creakings and rumblings, and a sound as if

of muffled drums. Insubstantial, sourceless, a slurred voice seemed to fill the tiny space with a hollow roar even though it was soft, the barest hint of a whisper.

"She's coming 'round, Aunt Harriet."

She knew that voice! High-pitched, peevish, petulant, complaining . . .

Dear Lord! What had happened to her? She could remember Vauxhall, and Harald Donclennon treading unheedingly on her toes, crushing her instep under his heavy foot. She could remember the Dark Walk, guiding him there, simpering like the most sickening of debutantes as she plotted and contrived her way into forcing a declaration from him. And then? Donclennon grunting, falling at her feet, but not in the way she had intended. Not at *all* in the way she had intended!

Being stifled in a dark woolen cloak—she remembered that all too clearly, and being slung across some brute's broad shoulders. And then, hurtling to the ground. And then—

"I say—Aunt Harriet," the voice came again, louder this time, terrifying in its unidentifiable familiarity, "she's coming 'round, don't you know?"

"Indeed? See to it, Bratchett."

Louisa attempted to raise her head. The sudden pain was shattering, nauseating. She slumped nervelessly as darkness overtook her once more.

Harry Beckenham glared from the men gathered around him at the table to his aunt and the elegant, white-haired woman beside her standing by the bed, then to the wasted frame and haggard face of Dickie Fotheringham, propped against a thick stack of pillows, a thin coverlet draped over his motionless legs.

"*NO!*" he roared, focusing on Jason Ventriss. "No, damn you, you Horse Guards wonder!" Then, as they watched him expressionlessly, "No," he said more quietly, if with equal determination, eyes meeting each man's in turn, "I refuse to believe you. It's impossible. Absolutely impossible."

" 'Tain't at all," Giles Fortescue spat into the silence that followed Harry's protest. "In fact, it's the only thing that makes sense, once you think about it. Saw Cousin Norval there tonight m'self, tried to talk to him. Fellow in the purple cloak with the silly spangled lining, I keep telling you. Wasn't best pleased to see me—I can tell you that! Cursed me up one side and down the other for comin' up to him. Saw Bratchett, too—m'mother's hulk of a footman what never knows how to put the covers right or pour wine, an' is as rude as a Charlie to anyone what comes to the door. Is *that* any kind of a proper footman? What else would she *keep* him for, I ask you? You know what m'mother's like about proper servants, Harry! She'd *never* put up with that lout if she didn't have some special reason. And he had two others with him, big and mean-looking as the dogs in Seven Dials."

"Bratchett's the one whom you say keeps disappearing for irregular periods?" Gracechurch asked, voice level, more stating than questioning.

"Only too right, he does." Giles turned to the others, ignoring Harry now, desperate to explain and convince. "And, when he's gone, he's gone for weeks. M'mother once said she'd sent him up to the Lodge on an errand when I asked about it, but for a month and more? What kind of errand would *that* be, I ask you? Not too careful about what she said to me, either," he concluded on a triumphant note. "I had to go up for some books I'd forgotten—wanted the ride anyway, the town being what it is an' m'family what they are—and Bratchett wasn't there at all. Not anywhere. Never *had* been, according to the housekeeper! Considered asking m'mother about it, then thought better of the whole thing. Awful unpleasant woman, m'mother, when she wants to be."

"When was this?" Colonel Winthrop asked, eyes flicking from Harry to the boy, and then over to Fotheringham.

"Can't remember for sure," Giles said doubtfully after puzzling for a moment. "I was down from school. 'Bout a year and a half ago, I think. Little more, maybe. More likely a little less. Never have been able to stand the fellow, so I don't go looking for him in particular, if you understand me."

"Perfectly." His eyes rested briefly on Gracechurch, who gave a slight nod. Yes, the timing was right for one of the incidents. "And, after that?"

"Not sure. Something under a year, if you mean his being gone for a good time, but don't hold me to an exact date. Can't give you one."

"During the summer, possibly? Late July, say, and early August?"

"Could be, come to think of it. We was at the Lodge for a time, and I don't recall his sour phiz lurking about. What's so important about July and—Oh, Lord! Salamanca . . ."

"Damn you all!" Harry cursed softly.

Gracechurch ignored him, eyes still fixed on Giles. "What about more recently?"

"Been there one day an' gone the next ever since we came to town. No way of telling. Really!" Giles insisted as multitudes of eyes seemed to spear him where he sat.

"Let's take what you're most likely to remember," Heath interposed smoothly. "When did this Bratchett return most recently?"

"Most recent time? That'd be about a week ago, I think. Been coming an' going a lot lately, I keep telling you." Giles turned to Harry, who pointedly ignored him. "He was gone when I took m'nag an' went to join you at

Marleybourne," Giles insisted, "an' he wasn't back when you left me at m'parents, but he was there serving breakfast a few hours later, an' he was favoring his arm, like it hurt him. Don't you see, Harry—it's *got* to be him, an' if it's him, it's *them*, an' if it's them, there ain't any way Gwennie don't know and ain't cooperating! Only ones might not be mixed up in it're Soph 'n' Belle, an' I wouldn't risk a ha'penny on that. Even m'father's solicitor's got to be in it up to his neck, maybe even Cousin Norval and Cousin Gossmar, though it's deuced hard to think of a *padre*—"

"You disgusting little jackanapes!" Harry said, tone coldly level, refusing to look at the boy. "What do you expect to gain from spouting such lies?"

"They *ain't* lies, Harry! I may be a fool, but confound it, I'm *not* a liar! It's *my* sister and *my* parents we're talking 'bout here! D'you think I *like* it? But, it's the only thing that makes sense—that they've done all this. Just because they're my family don't mean I can stand by an' let 'em go around *killing* people and *kidnapping* your sister just to get their hands on some more blunt for m'father to game away! Don't you care about *her?* Don't you care about your sister at all? Or, is it just Gwennie you care about, an' yourself? Gwennie ain't what you think, you know—not by a long shot! And she ain't in love with you, an' she ain't going to marry you—I've told you that before!"

The small back room surrounded them as if they were encased in a cocoon, the low beamed ceiling darkened by the smoke of years of cheroots and pipes and fires. The furniture was sturdy, suited to men at their leisure, if not entirely graceless. The single small window was shuttered and curtained, an almost invisible patch of darkness against the dark walls. A lamp stood on the scarred round table, along with pitchers of ale, a platter of sandwiches—most of them gone—and tankards, battered but serviceable. The room was isolated at the end of a long corridor.

No sounds from tavern or parlor filtered through, and there was a subterranean feel to the place, as if they lurked deep within the earth, hidden from the sun, the sky, the stars—a place for hatching conspiracies, or foiling them. The heavy four-poster bed with its dingy velvet draperies, the commode, and the sturdy chair by its side were not complete anachronisms, nor was the pallet at the bed's foot.

Fotheringham studied Harry as he sat stubbornly silent at the table, face painted with deep shadows and glowing patches of soft warm light.

"I loved her, too, you know," he said gently. "I thought she was an angel come down to earth especially for me."

"I know all about you, and what you felt for Miss Fortescue," Harry snarled. "You should have been horse-whipped! I'm of half a mind to do it here and now." But his tone was slightly less assured than before.

"How much opportunity have you been given to be private with her?" Fotheringham asked patiently. "How well do you really know her?"

"That has nothing to do with it," Harry persisted. "*I* am a gentleman."

"This is getting us nowhere," Ventriss interrupted. "Beckenham, and what he does or doesn't believe, is not at issue. Finding his sister, and effecting her release before she is harmed—or worse—is." He signaled two short, heavily muscled men guarding the door. "Take the major upstairs. Gag and bind him, but make him as comfortable as you can. Don't leave him unguarded for a second. We don't want him escaping to raise the alarm."

Harry surged snarling to his feet. Lady Daphne started to raise a hand in protest, let it fall back to her side. Harry had made his position clear: Whatever had happened to Louisa, it was her own fault for not obeying his injunction to remain closeted in her aunt's home, receiving no one and going nowhere until he decided on her disposition.

The Fortescues were above suspicion, Louisa in their hands for her own protection—which was exactly where he had intended placing her himself, Gwendolyn a creature of air and light incapable of the horrors of which they accused her.

"Listen to me!" Fotheringham pleaded, wavering as he attempted to lean forward, stretching out a frail hand to grip Harry's coat. "How would I know about the arrangements if I had not once been a party to them as well? I went to Fortescue's slimy solicitor, too, and I signed the cursed will! Same terms. Same conditions. Same *everything!* Won't you understand? How much of a fool can you be! And Rawdon—he can tell you the same story, only his brother wasn't as lucky as we were, in spite of my legs and back and chest and your arm! And there were others. Dammit, Major Beckenham, we've *all* been played for fools! That doesn't mean we have to persist in self-induced blindness."

"You filthy, lying cockroach!" Harry whirled before anyone could stop him, features distorted by rage, and viciously knocked the gasping young Fotheringham back against the head of the bed.

Giles stared in horror at the man he had been so proud to call future brother, face draining of color, grabbed the tankard beside him and hurled it with deadly accuracy at Harry's head, then leapt to catch him as Harry stared blindly around him, eyes rolling, and started to slump to the floor.

"You can take him now," the boy said, tears streaming down his cheeks as he gently laid the stunned Peninsular hero on the well-swept boards. "He won't be giving you any trouble. I had a good arm at cricket, you see, and someone had to do something . . ."

He turned back to the others with immense dignity, ignoring his wet face as the guards moved forward on cat-feet, picked up the major, and carried him from the room.

"Now, about where they'll've taken her," he continued determinedly. "Pounds to pence it ain't the Lodge. Too public. Village's right outside the gates, you see, and there's too many servants about. You might want to send someone to check, but since Norval's involved, it's sure to be either his place, or else a hunting box m'father's got in Berkshire. They're both isolated. Berkshire'd be too far, though, I think. Besides, m'father's probably sold it off to redeem some of his blasted vowels donkeys' years ago— not entailed, you see. Most everything that isn't's gone now.

"Our best bet is Norval's place in Kent. It's tumble-down 'cause he hasn't the blunt to keep it up, an' if there's a caretaker, that's *all* there is. No close neighbors, an' no village nearby." He looked directly at Gracechurch. "I know how to get there," he said. "I could give you directions, but they're complicated, and you'd be sure to get lost. Can't afford the time for that. I know you don't trust me." He shoved his hands toward the captain. "Manacle 'em, sir, if that'll make you feel better, but let me guide you. *Please!* M'family can go to the devil, for all I care. Well, maybe not the little ones, but the only thing I want now is to get Miss Beckenham back safe. Whatever m'mother wants with her, it ain't likely to be pleasant, and she ain't likely to agree to it. There's no trusting m'mother when she's crossed. Doesn't happen too often, an' she don't like it a bit. Miss Beckenham's been crossing her left and right for weeks, an' she ain't likely to stop now."

"How far?" Rawdon asked. "How much time?"

"Less than a stage," Giles said eagerly, whirling to him. "That's why they'd go there. Wouldn't want to risk changing horses, don't you see? Too much chance Miss Beckenham'd raise a fuss, and questions'd be asked. And

there's shortcuts across fields. Couldn't take 'em in a
carriage, but if we ride—"

"Done," Rawdon said, rose stiffly to his feet. "You're
coming with me. Jasper, get directions from the lad and
follow as quickly as you can in the curricle. Use the bays,
and don't spare 'em. I don't care if they're ready for the
knacker when you get there. Just get there!" He turned to
the others as Jasper went into a huddle with Giles, conferring over routes and drawing sketchy maps on a crumpled
piece of paper the groom pulled from his pocket. "You
can stay here talking as long as you like," he said coldly,
"or you can come with us. Which will it be?"

"We're with you, of course," Gracechurch smiled.
"Give me ten minutes. No? Five, then. I want to know the
lay of the land, the best approaches, where Miss Beckenham is likely to be held, and devise a basic strategy.
Otherwise we'll be stumbling all over each other, and do
more harm than good. We could even get her injured or
killed, which is not, I believe, your goal. And, I want to
provide for search parties to head for the other properties
as well, just in case, and make arrangements to secure
Fortescue House. Show a little patience, Rawdon! We're
about to accomplish what you've been fighting for since
your brother's murder."

"I don't give a damn about my brother!"

The second time Louisa regained consciousness her
bonds had been released and the gag removed, and she
had just been doused with a jug of cold water to encourage her awakening.

Hands grasped her arms, jerked her roughly to her feet.
She spluttered, head swimming, heart pounding, as she
attempted to clear the stinging droplets from her eyes, her
hair straggling about her face and dripping onto her bod-
ice, her sodden gown clinging to every curve of her body.

Half-blinded, trembling from the icy draughts, she stared blankly at the people surrounding her—Norval Quarmayne, Lady Harriet Fortescue, a man whose height and breadth reminded her of her assailant of the day before in Richmond Park, and a corpulent white-haired cleric in full canonicals—then at the immense dark chamber. A single branch of yellowed candles flickered on the high stone mantel just beyond her, casting looming shadows over furniture which crouched like immense beasts ready to spring from beneath holland covers.

If only her head wouldn't throb so!

"What is the meaning of this outrage, Lady Fortescue!" she quavered with what force and dignity she could summon to the cause.

"The only outrage is your lack of sense of family," the older woman snorted, "combined with your wanton disregard of your brother's wishes! Now, we'll see just how independent you truly are. Lord Beckenham is in a bedchamber above, unconscious, gagged, and bound. Whether he sees tomorrow's sunrise—or the sun of any *other* morning—depends entirely on you."

"You're mad!" Louisa spat, hands gripping her elbows as she shivered helplessly in the dank, dust-laden air.

"I think not." Lady Fortescue smiled gently, adjusting the rosy Norwich shawl gathered around the shoulders of her maroon silk traveling costume into more pleasing folds. "Merely infinitely practical, and—unlike you—totally dedicated to my family." Then her head snapped up, the maroon bonnet with its frills and laces and ribbons and plumes nodding energetically. "You have a choice, Miss Beckenham. You may marry my nephew, and thus your fortune will come into his hands, and so into mine. Or, you may reject the holy estate of matrimony. That is your prerogative. In such case, your brother's body will be discovered along the high road, clearly the hapless victim of highwaymen, in a few days' time; you, my dear, shall be found floating in the Serpentine, your body recovered well before your brother's so that your fortune will have reverted to him, and so revert to my family through his will in my daughter's favor. Do I make myself clear?"

"Utterly mad!" Louisa hissed. "You sound like a third-rate actress in a third-rate melodrama!"

"How uncivil of you," Lady Fortescue intoned, voice and face devoid of expression, "when I have been so gracious as to escort you to my nephew's country seat." Her hand lashed out, beaded reticule swinging from her wrist. Louisa reeled from the stinging blow, hand flying to her abused face. "You must learn proper respect for your betters," the woman informed her caustically. "It shall be my pleasure to instruct you in proper decorum. You may curtsy, and kiss my cheek. *That* is the proper salutation for your future aunt."

"I'd die first!" Louisa gulped.

"Your choice entirely, but I do think you should reconsider. Death is quite, quite final, you know, and often rather sordid in its technical aspects. For you, I would make certain it was most unpleasant. Norval, the special license, please. Cousin Gossmar cannot proceed without it."

"I knew you were a fish," Louisa snarled at Quarmayne as he tore desperately through the pockets of his tight-fitting mustard and lime green striped coat, jangling multitudes of fobs as he attempted to locate the license, "but I didn't think you were such a *poor* fish!"

Lady Fortescue nodded to the man hulking in the background. He stepped into the light, seized Louisa's wrist, wrenched her arm behind her, and jerked. She gasped. He dropped her arm, and stepped back into the shadows.

"A lesson once taught does not require repetition," Lady Fortescue explained firmly. "It doesn't, does it? I insist you show your betrothed proper respect."

"I say, Aunt Harriet," Quarmayne protested weakly,

hands still scrabbling through his pockets, "it ain't at all the thing to treat a female like that, no matter what she's done. Fair sex, chivalry, an' all that."

"Don't be silly, Norval. She isn't a woman in the usual sense," Lady Fortescue informed him, "but merely an object that must serve its purpose, just like any object. You have located the license? Good—give it to me." She handed the document to Gossmar. "All is quite in order, I believe, Cousin?"

The white-haired cleric gulped, examined it, folded it, and placed it between the pages at the back of his prayer book, nodded helplessly. "Totally in order, Cousin Fortescue."

"Then, you may proceed. I am sure," she said sternly, turning to Louisa, "that you wish to see your brother released from his bonds as rapidly as may be, Miss Beckenham. In any case, the announcement of your nuptials will appear in the morning journals, along with a notice that you will be honeymooning in Scotland, as the Continent is currently beyond reach, so all these delays and protests are quite nonsensical."

"You've sent—?" Louisa's face reddened. "You unprincipled old harridan!"

"Hardly, my dear. Your affection for your brother is well known. Only one outcome is possible to this little scene, don't you agree?"

"No one will believe it—no one!"

"Of course they will." Lady Fortescue's voice was at once infinitely assured and infinitely reassuring. "A woman of your advanced years, youth gone and beauty faded, with nothing but a substantial dot to offer a potential bridegroom as enticement? Most natural arrangement in the world. Look at you!" she chuckled contemptuously. "You can't tell me you are presumptuous enough to believe you could hold personal attractions for any man! No—this marriage is all that is suitable in the eyes of the world."

"I—I refuse to be married in a sodden dress, and with my hair straggling in rat's tails around my face!" Louisa exploded, desperately playing for time as she fought wave after wave of vertigo.

"Norval doesn't mind, my dear, do you, Norval?" Norval shook his head. "There—you see? It doesn't matter at all to him. Why, to him, I am certain you are the perfection of all that is beautiful. He is aware of your lovely dot, you see, and so your features and raiment and character matter not a whit."

"I want to see my brother."

"After the ceremony *and* its consummation—not before."

"If I don't see my brother, there won't be any ceremony! How do I know he's not already dead?" Louisa demanded, certain of her ground here. They'd take her to Harry, or she'd throw every obstruction she could think of in their faces. And after she'd seen Harry? Well—she'd *still* keep throwing up obstructions.

"You'll just have to chance it," Lady Fortescue said softly, "won't you, my dear? Bratchett!"

The under footman whisked out of the shadows, grasped Louisa's arm, and began twisting. Louisa gasped, desperately trying to tear away, kicking at him with numbed feet.

"Not too much, Bratchett," Lady Fortescue cautioned, "or else use the other one. She must be able to sign the register when we're done."

Bratchett switched holds and gave Louisa's left arm a vicious wrench. She gave a gasping, indrawn moan as her arm leapt from its socket. A hand seized her right shoulder, holding her erect.

"Truly, Miss Beckenham, you are being most foolish," Lady Fortescue continued. "This is all so unnecessary. No one has any desire to cause you pain, but just as with any child, you must be corrected when you misbehave. Cousin Gossmar, you may proceed. Norval, please give Bratchett the ring."

There ensued another scrambling through pockets of coat and waistcoat, Norval muttering, Lady Fortescue regarding him with ill-disguised impatience. The ring was finally produced, a cheap thing of pot metal thinly washed with gold, its surface already marred by verdigris. With a chuckle, Lady Fortescue took the shawl which had somehow remained about Louisa's shoulders, and draped it over her dripping hair.

"Every bride should have a veil," she said maliciously. "It bespeaks her maiden status—which, at the present moment, is of no consequence to us whatsoever. However, let the conventions be preserved, by all means, since you insist on bride clothes. Cousin Gossmar, you may begin!"

"*Whuff*—In a court of law—*whuff*—"

"What do I care for courts of law!" his patroness thundered. "They are for the rabble—not for me."

"A Higher—*whuff-whuff*—Court, then," Gossmar protested weakly. "I am—*whuff-whuffle*—not certain this—*whuff*—marriage will be valid—*whuffle*— in the eyes of—*whuff-whuff*—God *or*—*whuffle-whuff*—Man."

"It'll be legal enough," Lady Fortescue snapped. "We'll all swear she entered into it willingly. An ape leader—it stands to reason! Besides, no one would dream of questioning my word. Now, stop your shilly-shallying. You know you'll perform the ceremony in the end, and the longer you delay, the longer the girl has to wait for Bratchett to put her arm back. A dislocated shoulder causes considerable pain, in case you didn't know."

Gossmar peered uncertainly from one to the other, cleared his throat, sighed.

" 'Dearly beloved'," he intoned resignedly, " 'we are

gathered together here in the sight of God, and in the face of this company—' "

It wasn't happening, Louisa insisted to herself. She was still unconscious, or she'd fainted from lack of air, tangled in a heavy cloak and lurching along slung across the shoulders of some uncaring lout. Or she was out of her mind from pain. Or perhaps, she'd died, and this was hell. It certainly felt like it . . .

" '—and, forsaking all others, keep thee only unto her, so long as ye both shall live?' "

There was silence, sudden and overpowering.

"Norval!" Lady Fortescue hissed warningly.

"I will," Quarmayne gulped.

" 'Louisa Caroline, wilt thou have this Man—' " The good vicar continued, voice deep and rolling with studied inflections, just as Harry had said it did, and with all the majesty of a mighty organ thundering in the vaults of a great cathedral. Certainly he looked the very image of a Man of God, she reflected as he droned on. And that was the problem—he was merely an image. " '—keep thee only unto him, so long as ye both shall live?' "

"I will not!" she declared, voice firm and resonant in the lofty chamber. "I-will-not—I-will-not—I-will-not—I-will-not—I-will—"

"Ignore her," Lady Fortescue instructed. "Keep going."

"But I—*whuff*—" Gossmar protested plaintively. "This is most—whuffle—irregular!"

"Keep going!"

" 'Who giveth this Woman to be married to this Man?' " Gossmar inquired, looking uncertainly from Bratchett to Lady Fortescue.

Bratchett grabbed Louisa's right hand, shoved it at Gossmar, stepped back. Louisa snatched her hand away. Bratchett clouted her on the side of the head, grabbed her hand again, shoved it back into Gossmar's.

"Hold on to 'er, dammit!" he snarled, then grasped her left shoulder, exerting a warning pressure.

Gossmar shoved Louisa's hand into Quarmayne's. "Hold on to her!" he pleaded. "Repeat after me: 'I, Norval Arthur Septimus take thee, Louisa Caroline, to my wedded Wife, to have and to hold from this day—' "

"*NO!*" Louisa flared with the carrying power of a Siddons. "NO! NO! NO!"

Quarmayne recited the words after the vicar, stumbling and repeating himself, garbling his name and Louisa's, and generally making a royal hash of the limpid prose of the Book of Common Prayer.

" '—according-to-God's-holy-ordinance, and-thereto-I-plight-thee-my-troth,' " Gossmar rushed, desperate to have done with it. "Repeat it, Norval! *Whuff!* Repeat it, boy!"

"—according to, and thereto, and by God's holy troth, and—*I can't remember it!*" Quarmayne squeaked, shrinking into himself. "You went too fast. Say it again," he pleaded, glancing in terror from his aunt to his bride.

"Get on with it!" Lady Fortescue snapped. "The intent was there, even if the words were not. We'll assume he said his part properly."

Bratchett snatched Louisa's hand from Norval's, forcing her to curl her fingers around Quarmayne's damp, quivering paw.

"She's ready," he informed the vicar.

" 'I, Louisa Caroline take thee Norval Arthur Septimus to my wedded Husband,' " Gossmar intoned hopefully, " 'to have and to hold from this day—' "

"I, Louisa Caroline DO NOT take this Norval Arthur Septimus to my wedded Husband!" she shouted at the ceiling, "Or to anything else! Do you hear me, God? I DO NOT! I will not marry this man! I am NOT marrying him!"

"Foolish, and quite rude," Lady Fortescue said into the

sudden ringing silence. "Poor Norval will think you don't care for him, and that's not true, is it, my dear? It's not true at all. You care for him very deeply, and are honored to become his wife because you care for your brother, and we are all going to be one family. Begin her vows again, Cousin Gossmar. And, Miss Beckenham, I will countenance no more sacrilegious desecrations of the marriage service! You *are* prepared to consummate this marriage as soon as the vows are completed?" she asked Quarmayne, now quaking by Louisa's side.

"If he ain't, I am, an' we'll say it war him," Bratchett chuckled from behind them. "Get on with it, preacher! I'm lookin' forward to tupping that dainty morsel, if'n his little nibs ain't got the stomach for it . . . Just reward, given the trouble her an' her precious brother've cost me, what with one thing an' another."

El Moro was flagging.

The others were far behind, hurtling through a darkness relieved only by the often cloud-masked moon with little regard to their own or their mounts' safety, but whatever was happening up ahead, they'd be far too late. Rawdon didn't know how he knew that, but he knew it with a terrifying certainty that almost stripped him of control, and had sent him rushing far ahead, demanding every ounce of speed and effort from his famous stallion, the sketchy map Giles Fortescue had drawn for Jasper Foote branded in his memory. Hills, fields, streams, clearings, vanished under the black's pounding hooves.

"Come on, old friend," Rawdon pleaded, leaning low over El Moro's powerful neck. "Just a little more—that's all I ask—and then you can spend the rest of your life cavorting in a pasture with as many fillies as you like!"

Whether the great horse understood the words is doubtful, but his speed seemed to redouble. Trees whipped past them, brooks vanished under his soaring jumps, fields became mere blurs, fresh young crops crushed in an arrow-straight line that bore no relevance to plow or furrow, and then the heavy stallion broke out of a patch of woods and came to a trembling halt above a miniature valley, sides heaving, skin quivering. Below them, in the hollow, huddled a group of ramshackle buildings. One, significantly larger, stood slightly apart from the others, a feeble glow coming from a bank of arched front windows. Quarmacorne Hall was exactly as Giles had described it, with the exception of a carriage at the side of the drive, the horses tethered to a baluster forming part of a low decorative railing along the front of the house. It was a fair distance—perhaps a third of a mile from the hill's crest—and the light was uncertain, but there didn't seem to be any guards posted. Why should there be? Company wasn't expected . . . Still, he'd have to be careful.

Rawdon felt for the knife in his boot, patted the new dueling pistols at his waist. All present and accounted for. Time to move on. He lowered his hands, guiding El Moro back into the sheltering trees in case unseen eyes were watching, then down the gentle hill, attention firmly fixed on the dimly glowing windows. The yards melted steadily away. Where the woods gave onto the overgrown drive he dismounted, tied the big black to a tree, still studying the main building—an old stone monstrosity overpopulated with crenelations, Gothic arches, gargoyles, and useless flying buttresses silhouetted against the night sky—now less than the length of a cricket field away. The lawns were billowing waves of grasses, the gardens choked with briars.

Swiftly, bent almost double, he crept forward. A horse whickered, one of the team tied to the terrace balustrade. El Moro answered, an ear-splitting bugle of defiance and challenge. Cursing, Rawdon gave up on stealth, pelting through the grasses and up the steps to the main door. A burly figure rose in front of him, barely visible in the dim light, a club in its fist. Rawdon sent it sprawling, and wrenched open the creaking portal. He glanced around the cavernous hall, reviewing Giles's description of the ground floor, then crashed through a pair of double doors across whose sill faint light streamed to pattern the dusty, mouse dropping–laden marble tiles. The brace of pistols leapt into his hands to train steadily on the little group in front of him. His eyes narrowed as his gaze flicked from Lady Fortescue to her tame padre and weak-chinned nephew.

"Louisa?" he said almost gently. "Where is Louisa Beckenham? What have you done with her?"

"This is private property," Quarmayne blustered at a nod from his aunt. "I'll have you arrested for trespass and up before a magistrate, and—"

"Where is Miss Beckenham?" Rawdon's voice had lost its gentleness.

"You are an uninvited interloper," Lady Fortescue snarled, eyes flicking to just beyond Rawdon. "Remove yourself, sirrah!"

"The devil I will!" Rawdon stalked toward the unholy trio, pistols never wavering. "These have hair triggers—a pair of Manton's best," he said conversationally. "You've heard of Manton, I presume? I am very tired, rather put out, and will not be too concerned should my finger twitch and one of them go off accidentally. It *will* be an accident, you know, but that won't matter to whomever the ball strikes. And, it *will* strike someone, I promise you. Now, I will ask you just once more—where is Miss Beckenham?"

"In there," Quarmayne croaked from behind his aunt, pointing to one of a pair of curtained alcoves flanking the fireplace.

Harriet Fortescue whirled on her nephew, eyes glint-

ing. "You fool!" she hissed. "You traitor! You unmitigated jackass!"

Her eyes flicked back to the doorway, and then she
gasped, sinking down in a timely swoon, drawing Rawdon's attention. Quarmayne and Gossmar separated,
leaving a wide path to the alcove. There was a hush of
sound. Rawdon's head exploded with a million fireworks
as he crumpled to the stone flags. Lady Fortescue opened
her eyes, surveying the room with a satisfied smile.

"Well done, Bratchett," she said, coming to her knees.
"If you will be so kind as to help me up, and then disem-
barrass us—*permanently*—of His Grace?"

The burly under footman took a step forward, then
seemed to hesitate, a look of startled incredulity on his
coarse-featured face as a hole blossomed in his chest, the
pistol's report deafening in the enclosed space. A pleased
Jasper Foote stood framed in the doorway, smoking pistol
in one hand, a knife in the other, Giles Fortescue panting
at his side. Bratchett stumbled forward and fell bonelessly
to the floor.

"It's over," Foote said matter-of-factly. "You, over
there—the skinny runt—get a cover over this one. Master
Fortescue, you know this place. Find us some water. His
Grace'll want to rejoin the living as soon as may be.
You"—he gestured at Gossmar—"get the old witch on
that chair, and tie her up. Use this." He shoved the
discharged pistol in his breeches, unhooked a coiled rope
from his waist, and tossed it to the vicar. "And, be quick
about it. Patience ain't my stock in trade, if you catch my
drift. Where's the girl?"

Quarmayne gestured toward the alcove, babbling inco-
herently. Lady Fortescue groped in her reticule as she
knelt on the floor, eyes glinting with febrile fire. Gossmar
was frozen in place, mouth opening and closing like a
beached fish's. Foote stooped over the duke, gently eased
the miraculously undischarged, fully cocked pistols from

beneath him, examined them carefully, grunted, nodded, uncocked them, shoved them in his breeches, and picked up the knife as he straightened. Giles, white-faced, stepped forward to assist his mother. She lashed out and jerked him to the floor. Clenching his arm, she jammed a miniature pistol to his temple.

"I am not exactly certain how this toy works," she said with deadly calm, "but I do know that if I pull the lever, a rather large hole will appear in Giles's head. It is no less than he deserves for his unconscionable action in bringing you here, so do not tempt me further than I am already tempted. You"—she continued, skewering Foote with her steely eyes—"drop the knife." The knife clattered to the floor. "Give Gossmar the pistols." Foote handed them over. "Now, go stand behind my worthless nephew, back to back. Cousin Gossmar, use the rope, and tie them up."

"My d-dear Cousin Fortescue"—Gossmar pleaded, whuffles lost in the drama of the moment—"all has been discovered. There is no p-possible course but to throw ourselves on the tender mercies of—"

"Do it!" she snapped. "Now!"

Tears of anxiety streaming from his eyes, the white-haired old cleric turned reluctantly from one man to the other. "Please . . . ?" he whimpered.

Behind them in the curtained alcove Louisa struggled desperately with the hastily contrived bonds that secured her wrists to her ankles, ignoring the dull ache in her shoulder. It had slipped into place accidentally under Lady Fortescue's rough handling what seemed only moments earlier when she and Bratchett had bundled her into the alcove after the coachman came to warn of a horseman on the hill, then tied her up, jamming the gag back in her mouth. Tears from the pain were close to blinding her, but she persisted with a determination that surprised even her. At last one end came free, then another. Panicking, she twisted back and forth fruitlessly, then forced herself to lie still, carefully unlooping one hank from another. At last the tasseled drapery cords fell away from her bleeding wrists and ankles. She stumbled to her feet, tore the foul gag from her mouth, pulled the velvet curtains aside, and grasping the heavily carved alcove's decorative frame for support, peered into the room.

Young Giles was on his feet now, firmly gripped by his mother, her gun pressed tightly to his temple. Just beyond them Gossmar was winding Foote's length of rope around the duke's groom and Quarmayne, the snarled loops draping like pond weed. His Grace of Rawdon sprawled at their feet, motionless. Bratchett lay crumpled just beyond him in a pool of gore.

Louisa's eyes flicked to the fireplace a few feet from the alcove. Forgotten tools leaned there, rusty, tangled with cobwebs, but they would be serviceable enough for what she intended. She dropped to her knees behind the furniture, began crawling toward them, knees pulling her gown tighter and tighter at the neckline, forcing her head down. Just beyond her Lady Fortescue was muttering in disgust as she watched Gossmar creating hopeless tangles in the rope. Louisa pulled up her burdensome skirts, tucked them in her décolletage, and eased forward now unhampered by voluminous draperies of wet silk, shoulder screaming its pain.

"Can't you do anything properly?" Lady Fortescue barked from just beyond the fireplace. "Useless! Useless—all of you! Here, Cousin—hold Giles. Keep the gun trained on him, you fool! *I'll* tie them up."

Louisa paused, quickly reviewed the tools, and glanced out of the corner of her eye to where Lady Fortescue's boots peeked from beneath heavy maroon silk skirts. Then her eyes flicked up. Foote was staring at her in surprise. His eyes widened, then slammed shut. Louisa brought her feet beneath her, now crouching, a process that seemed to take forever in the interests of silence. She clenched her teeth, reached for the poker which stood slightly apart from the other tools, grasped it firmly, and lifted it away from the wall, tearing the cobwebs which linked it to its brethren. With a sob she surged upward, wavering as another attack of dizziness claimed her, skirts still tucked into her décolletage, then spun toward the little group. She brought the poker crashing down on Lady Fortescue's maroon bonnet just as the woman turned to investigate the unexpected noise. The force of the blow crushed the bonnet, poker connecting soundly with skull.

The fury in the woman's eyes flared, then was extinguished as they rolled upward. With a sigh Lady Fortescue slipped to the floor, skirts ballooning.

Louisa glanced around the room. Rawdon was coming to his knees, shaking his head as if to clear it. Foote and Quarmayne were scrabbling at the rope in an effort to untangle it. Gossmar stood, the tiny pistol dangling from his pudgy hand, eyes popping, mouth open, beside a goggling Giles.

"Give me that!" Louisa said calmly, pointing to the pistol, poker drawn back.

Gossmar handed it over wordlessly, seeming almost relieved that someone else was taking responsibility for it. She took the delicate, ivory-and-silver-handled thing, dropped the poker, examined the weapon briefly, jammed it against what looked to be a heavily stuffed sofa under tattered holland covers, pulled the trigger. There was a click, but nothing more.

"Miss Beckenham," Foote cautioned, "best give me that. Could be it——"

In disgust Louisa hurled the pistol across the room. It struck a table. There was a loud report. Louisa screamed and sank to the floor as Rawdon clutched his upper right arm, cursing.

"—misfired," Foote concluded. "Them little ones often does."

Sixteen

By the time the others arrived, Rawdon's wound had been properly cleaned and bandaged, Harriet Fortescue and her confederates bound, gagged, and distributed between the two alcoves where a pair of troopers now stood guard. Had Harry been there, he would have perhaps noted that one bore a strong resemblance to a strapping flower seller who had, of late, taken to hawking her wares in the vicinity of Grosvenor Square, while the other—except for his clean-shaven face and uniform—was the very spit of a certain jarvey who fancied marigolds in the whip socket of his hackney.

Louisa's abused and aching shoulder had been provided the relief of a warm compress and a sling fashioned from Lady Fortescue's Norwich shawl, her wrists and ankles tended, her sodden gray silk evening gown replaced by an ancient and dusty alcove curtain draped toga-style and girdled by drapery cords. Jasper Foote was, if nothing else, infinitely resourceful and infinitely efficient. He had even contrived a small fire in the baronial-sized grate, and sent Giles on a reconnoitering expedition to the cellars, thus garnering two ancient and highly-welcome bottles of excellent French brandy whose passage through the hands of any Customs official was highly problematic.

A pair of threadbare sofas, divested of their covers, now flanked the small fire. Ventriss, Gracechurch, Fenton, Heath, Winthrop, and Malfont reposed on them in all the glory of their travel dirt—six slightly frustrated, but entirely satisfied warriors. Their mounts might never recover. Their garments were definitely past praying for. They might have arrived too late to do anyone any tangible good. But, the Fortescue was done for.

Giles, after the first flurries of questions and explanations, had joined Foote on the front terrace to share a tumbler of brandy and take a few tentative pulls at his first cheroot. If there was one thing the boy didn't want, it was to be in the same room where his mother lay trussed like a fowl ready for the spit, no matter what she'd done, and even if she was more or less out of sight. He *knew* she was there, and that was enough . . . He was thankful Foote had sent him foraging for wood, water, clean linen (none had been found, and the duke's shoulder had been bandaged with several cravats and the remains of one of Miss Beckenham's petticoats), and whatever could be found in the way of food and drink, so he didn't have to witness the process. To be forced to watch his mother treated so would have been more than he could bear. As for Cousin Gossmar, the sight of the elderly cleric lying bound on the filthy floor, unprotesting even as terror dewed his brow, brought to mind too many childhood images of the parish church just beyond the Lodge, its altar decorated for Christmas, Gossmar sonorously proclaiming the birth of Christ and the redemption of Man.

"What'll be done with them?" he asked into the soft summer air after a long and slightly uneasy silence.

Foote leaned against the stone parapet, staring at the small woods-crowned hill that rose just beyond the gates as he puffed thoughtfully on his cheroot, the smoke curling upward in the still air to lose itself in the scents of wild flowers and dry grass. Above them stars wheeled through a dark sky from which the clouds had flown. The moon was now no more than a smudge of pale light on the horizon, its journey done. Below them, hidden in the tangled grasses, crickets sang—the eternal melody of a peaceful summer night.

"No way to know for certain," Foote responded reluctantly after brief contemplation of the problem. "Not something for the courts—that was decided long ago. Got 'em dead to rights this time, an' they know it, but when all's said an' done, the proof still ain't there—not proof as'd stand up in a court o' law. That there footman's dead, y'see. My fault, an' without him to admit what he done, a clever barrister'd get 'em off in a blink. Word of a vicar, 'mong others, 'gainst one slip of a girl—an' her only real complaint that they was tryin' to marry her off to a cove she didn't fancy? Happens every day, besides which, her brother'd prob'ly take their part." Foote sighed, shook his head. "Transportation's my guess, given rank's privileges—Australia, most like—which'll be no easy berth for the likes o' them. His Grace's been arguing for the nubbing cheat—or to be left alone with the lot of 'em in a locked room with no weapons but his bare hands," he added wryly.

"They wouldn't—"

"No, no—they wouldn't."

"She's m'mother, you know, when all's said and done," Giles apologized. "I didn't think I'd care, but a part of me does. They won't despise me for that, will they?"

"Not likely. T'opposite, rather."

"You think so?" Giles asked, voice uncertain. "What'll they do with me, d'you think? Will they transport me, too? And my younger sisters?"

"Shouldn't think so—not if other arrangements can be made. More likely give *you* a medal."

"I don't want a medal for this!"

" 'Course not. That's why you might get one, life being

what it is, but real quiet-like, as there ain't to be anything official done about this mess."

"What I'd really like——" Giles bit his lip, scowling into the night. "That'd be impossible, though, after all that's happened."

"A pair o' colors? There's been talk . . ."

"Don't toy with me," the boy returned, voice thick. "I know better than that."

"No—my word on it. The lot of 'em's been argufying over it, one time an' another—who was to purchase your colors, an' who was to provide for your mounts an' allowance, if it turned out you was as straight as you seemed to be. Even Lady Cheltenham wants t'help, 'cording to His Grace." Foote threw a comforting arm over the boy's shoulders. "I know they was harsh with you, lad, but you see, they was afraid your mother'd kill the major, maybe even his sister, afore they caught her good and proper, an' put an end to it all. It was a terrible gamble they took to get her, and if it hadn't been for you, they'd've lost it. The major'd've ended up dead on the high road, just like his sister said your mother threatened, and *she*'d've ended up in the Serpentine, an' your mother'd've pocketed all the money she could get her hands on, an' then your father'd've gambled it all away, an' the whole thing would've started over again with some other unlucky fool. Said it yourself—she's a determined woman, an' it don't pay to cross her. If she'd been a man, she could've equaled Wellington hisself for strategy, and with two on 'em, Boney'd've been long done for. Oh, no, lad—they know what they owe you, right enough, and they're fair men. They pay their debts, which ain't perhaps what you're lookin' for, but it's what you can count on."

It was little enough to give the lad after all he'd been through, but it was all the comfort there was. With a sigh, Foote crushed his cheroot, dropped it on the terrace. The duke had won something out of this if he played his cards right, but he was the only one.

"Come on, Master Fortescue," he said, "we'd best be gettin' ourselves within doors, find out what they've decided on. Carriages should be arriving soon."

In a far corner of the room Louisa sat on a hard, narrow window ledge, her back turned determinedly to Rawdon, the soft murmur of voices from the group by the fireplace washing over them like the self-absorbed susurration of a placid stream. They'd been like that, she silently sitting, Rawdon standing behind her making sporadic attempts to open some sort of discussion, for so long she had been able to see a change in the pattern of stars hanging over the far hill.

She'd asked him to leave her be. He had refused.

She'd tried to retreat to the group gathered in front of the fire, claiming she was chilled to the bone. He'd offered her his coat.

She'd pleaded exhaustion. He'd told her to lie down on one of the many dilapidated sofas, with his coat as quilt and his lap for pillow.

No matter where she turned he was there, blocking her way, stubborn, persistent, infuriating, permitting no retreat, however well intentioned. She was not being cruel—only sensible. This discussion he demanded would do nothing but cause them both pain. For her? To her heart. And for him? To his pride, for that was all that was involved—how well he'd proved that at Almack's! It was so unnecessary! And so inevitable . . .

"It was you at Vauxhall, wasn't it?" she demanded, yielding at last, determined to get it over with so she could find some measure of peace.

"I made a regular mare's nest of that, didn't I," he admitted ruefully.

"What in the name of God did you think you were doing?" she demanded.

"Ventriss warned me they were planning to abduct you. I intended to get there first, but in the event—"

"In the event, you did . . . Ventriss, my faithful groom!" she sighed bitterly.

"He was, you know—very faithful. And, unless I've been misled, an excellent groom into the bargain."

"He was. I—Commendatore will miss him." She toyed nervously with the rusty fabric serving her as gown, twisting and pleating it between her fingers, shredding the frayed borders. The moon had set now, though the sky had not yet begun to lighten. The stars were points of fire, almost painful in their brilliance. "Harry's safe," she said finally, the hint of a plea for reassurance in her voice.

"Yes, he's safe enough—for the moment," Rawdon agreed.

"You were connected with all this, weren't you—not just at the end because of me, but all through it. I don't see why. It was army business. Why would a high and mighty duke, wealthy as he can stare, want to involve himself in such a dangerous and tawdry enterprise when he had all of London in which to play his games! What was it—a lark? A whim? Boredom?"

"You've heard of the Coruña retreat?" He gave it the Spanish pronunciation.

"Corunna? Of course! My brother was there. I spent weeks in an agony of suspense until I learned he had survived."

"*My* brother wasn't so fortunate."

"Oh . . . I—I didn't know you had a brother, though come to think of it, Aunt Daphne did say something of the sort once to which I paid little attention." She bit her lip, ashamed, embarrassed by her earlier biting words. "I'm sorry."

"It's all right—it's been a long time now, but thank

you." He paused, scowling, uncertain how much to tell her, how much to leave out, as he adjusted his arm in its makeshift sling. The cursed thing ached like the very devil, destroying what little coherence his thoughts retained. "Christo was their first gull, you see, or one of them. When the dust settled, and I caught wind of the will and where and when it had been drawn, I began to ask questions. I didn't like the answers. I've been after them ever since."

"But when you tried to snatch me from Vauxhall—why, you almost had them because of Harry and me, and then—"

"Something mattered more to me than catching my brother's murderers," he said gently. "It still does."

"Oh . . . All the disguises, and the lies about your identity—?"

"I was hard on Bratchett's heels. His Grace, James Edward Fitzmorris Debenham, Duke of Rawdon, wouldn't've stood a chance of unmasking him. Jamie Morrison did. You do understand the coil I was in?"

"But, Almack's—"

"Was a tactical error," he admitted ruefully. "I wasn't thinking clearly. I had to make an occasional appearance as myself, you see, and I couldn't bear there to be lies between us any longer. I thought it would be the perfect time and place to tell you the truth, enlist your cooperation, with you in my arms and no chance of escaping. I was never more wrong." Would she never be done with her inquisition!? He was beyond exhaustion, nerves raw and jangling, and suffering a letdown at the end of it all that he had never anticipated. He truly no longer cared what was done with his brother's murderers. The catharsis—if catharsis there had been—had lain in the chase, the struggle, the matching of wits, the having of a reason to rise from his bed each morning when living itself seemed to require too much effort. "When I got home that night, I tore up our special license and drank myself into a stupor. It was all my fault, and I knew it, and I couldn't face a world in which you despised me.''

Silence stretched between them, uneasy, colored by all the events of the spring—the misunderstandings, the unexpected joys, the sudden terrors, the despair. She was painfully conscious of the men gathered by the fire, of their pretense that she and Rawdon were not there, or that they themselves were both invisible and inaudible. It wasn't the case, of course. She could hear them well enough, though their words were indecipherable at this distance, their presence at once barrier and unwanted protection. Out of the corner of her eye she saw Giles and Foote join them, the boy standing a little apart as if he did not truly belong in their company. What would happen to *him*, now? He had so adored Harry . . .

"I'm sorry about your arm," she said tightly, body rigid, eyes unseeing, wishing Rawdon would go away now all the explanations had been given, wishing he would stay, not knowing *what* she wished.

"I'll forgive you," he said, "on certain conditions."

She could hear the laughter in his voice, hated and loved it at the same time. "What conditions?"

"I'll tell you in fifty years or so."

"No . . ."

"No? You don't want to be forgiven, then." His tone was light, now, teasing, as if her apology for wounding him, however indirectly and in whatever manner, personally or physically, had been all he waited for. "Your apology was unmeant?"

"You're twisting my words," she protested, infuriated by his sudden assurance.

"You've got to marry me, you know, after all this," he said softly, tried to turn her toward him. She wrenched away, winced. "You've been thoroughly compromised."

"Hardly! Lady Fortescue's been here the entire time."

"But no one will know that—only that you disappeared from Vauxhall, and—"

"You're unscrupulous!"

"Besides, there's the problem of a certain interesting announcement in this morning's journals."

"How did you ever find out about that!" she demanded, whirling to face him. "How *could* you—*What announcement?*"

"Why, that you and I were wed yesterday," he smiled. Then, more seriously, "I'd no idea this would all resolve so suddenly. It had been going on for years, you know—a piece here, a piece there, with much futile effort between. It's damnably difficult to prove a man who appears to have died in battle didn't . . . I wanted you out of danger. If you were married, and the fact were known, you'd be safe from the Fortescue beldame. I instructed my solicitor to send the announcement, anticipating that you'd see sense by the time we reached Rawdonmere."

Louisa stared at him, burst into laughter. "Oh, dear God!" she giggled hysterically. "Compromised? You don't know the half of it! I'll never be able to face anyone again! Exile? Permanent! Send me off with the Fortescues. No, Australia may not even be far enough. The moon— that's it! Send me to the moon!"

"My dear girl—"

"I'm not your 'dear' anything!" she spat. "Damn you all! I won't even be able to return to Marleybourne, and I had thought at least *that* possibility would be left me once Harry comes to his senses."

Rawdon sighed. His arm throbbed as if all the soldiers of hell had maneuvered on it, his head wasn't much better after double treatment by the defunct Bratchett, and after two nights without sleep he was tired past caring. He whipped the cover from a tiny love seat in front of the narrow window, sneezed at the dust he had raised, and sank down thankfully.

"If we are to quarrel—which it appears we are—and you are to wax first cryptic and then incoherent, and I by turns irate and cajoling, I suggest we do so in relative comfort," he said, patting the seat beside him as he looked up at her imploringly. "Come join me. That ledge has to be hard, and it's certainly narrow. This is much better. It's not the thing, to just sit willy-nilly in a lady's presence without her permission, but I hope you'll forgive me. If I try to stay on my feet much longer, I can assure you I'll end on my knees—but it won't be for the purpose of begging your hand."

"You won't, ah, *do* anything?"

"Do?" He gestured at his arm. They made quite a pair. At least he'd had the foresight to sit so his good arm was toward the open space beside him, and as it was her left in a sling, possibilities remained. "What in the name of Heaven *could* I do, encumbered like this?"

Louisa regarded him doubtfully for a moment, then perched primly on the edge of the seat as far from him as she could get. Primness was devilishly difficult to achieve without a pair of hands to fold in her lap. A single hand, lying there all by itself with nothing to do and nothing to hold, appeared so distressingly *vulnerable*, almost as if it were inviting improper advances. She made up for the solecism with an uncompromisingly straight back and an arrogantly tilted chin, hoping they would convey what she intended.

Rawdon chuckled, taking her free hand firmly in his. "This," he said, "belongs to me, I believe—by your own request, if I may be so ungentlemanly as to remind you, as well as according to the *Gazette*, and several other journals of equal repute and authority. I never gave it back to you, you know, and now I'm claiming it. Are you going to persist in sitting on air, or are you going to show a trace of that practicality for which I honor you?"

"I am fine as I am."

"A prevarication, if ever I heard one, but have it your own way for the moment if you must!" He eased his arm from the sling, transferred her hand to his right one, grasped her chin, and turned her face toward him. She stared back at him defiantly. "Now—I, for one, am past the point where I am willing to have patience with conundrums. You'd best explain yourself. Why must you be sent to the moon?"

"You've all been very busy on my behalf," she said bitterly, then burst once more into peals of laughter as tears streamed down her face.

Rawdon watched her for a moment, bedeviled by unaccustomed sensations of helplessness and inadequacy, gave it up and pulled her into his arms, holding her gently and ignoring the fire in his arm. She collapsed against him, at once sobbing and laughing.

"Shh," he whispered, hand stroking her damp hair, "Shh, it's all right. Whatever it is, I'll never let it hurt you. I'll take care of it, love, don't worry."

"Two!" she gasped. *"Two!"*

"Two whats?"

"Husbands!"

His arms tightened, and then he tilted her head where it rested against his shoulder, kissing her brow, her wet eyes, her nose, her chin—anything he could reach but her lips, not quite daring them yet. "No—no, my darling," he said softly. *"One* husband—me. The other doesn't count, even if they made you sign something. I've destroyed the license. It's as if none of it ever happened."

She hiccoughed, raised her head. "You don't understand," she snuffled.

"No, I don't." He retrieved a handkerchief from his pocket, handed it to her. "Blow your nose, and then explain it to me."

"Two announcements," she quavered, and mopped her face, blew her nose, looked doubtfully at the handker-

chief, then tucked it under the drapery cord sash. "I'm not usually such a watering pot," she apologized.

"I know. You'd match Zeno for Stoicism," he said comfortingly. "Now, what's this about two announcements?"

"Lady Fortescue sent one, too, only *hers* says I'm married to Norval Quarmayne, and *it* will be in this morning's papers right along with yours!"

Rawdon stared at her incredulously for a moment, burst into laughter. "Why, you little minx!" he chortled. "An official bigamist? That well and truly tears it! Whatever will the ton say? But," he grinned, "as one of 'em's a duke, I think you'd be wise to keep him, and throw the other back. A duke's pretty highly placed. He might be able to pull the thing off, given time. Oh, the high sticklers may cut you for a while, but they're dull in any case, and even *they*, in time—*Don't hit my arm!*" he yelped. Then more calmly, "You'll have to marry me, now—even you can see that. It's your only way out of the brambles. We'll stay at Rawdonmere for a bit—you *don't* want to see your brother just yet—and when things calm down, we'll return to town for the rest of the season if you want. After all, the ton may be difficult, but they're not impossible."

Louisa stared up at him, tears springing once more to her eyes. "Harry will need me," she said uncertainly.

"Your beloved Harry needs to grow up," Rawdon said firmly, "and the only way you can help him is to stay away and let him get on with the process."

"I suppose you're right . . ."

"I have a nasty habit that way," he admitted, smiling tenderly at her, and kissed her gently on the lips. He'd won, though she hadn't admitted it yet, and he hadn't been entirely sure he would. Women could be both unpredictable and contrary. Strangely, there was no feeling of triumph—only a sense of immense relief and thankfulness.

"Now, madam, I will admit to a certain degree of pain in my arm, as well as an even greater degree of exhaustion throughout my entire body, combined with a miscellany of aches which are rather debilitating, and not the least conducive to dalliance. In short, I have a great longing for a bed—my own bed, preferably, though I will accept any reasonable substitute with one proviso—that you are there beside me, so that once I'm recovered sufficiently I may take immediate and pleasurable advantage of the fact. Therefore, since I'm rather a conventional man when all is told, I suggest we have them untie the whuffling vicar and put him to good use."

"Here? Like *this?"* She stared in dismay at the filthy drapery turned toga, hand rising to her bedraggled hair, her tear-stained, dirt-streaked face. "But—"

"For better or for worse," he said lightly, "which, in your case, means garments of unusual cut and provenance, and in both sickness and health, which for us both means with unsound arms, and until death us do part, which means forever."

"But, I haven't said I'd—"

"I've a special license right here just begging to be used," he said, patting his pocket, *"and* a ring, and every intention of employing both without further delay. I *am* said to be slightly mad, you know, which means it's best to humor me," he grinned. "Besides, given all that's happened, you can see I can't take you to Rawdonmere until we're wed. Foote would never countenance it!" Then his face grew serious. "I love you, you know—more than I ever would have thought it possible to love anyone. I told you that at Muriel Stoking's masquerade, and I've repeated myself every chance I've had since. I fell in love with you when I was untangling you from the cursed mess in your brother's chaise the day you arrived in London, face red with blushes all the while you were desperately trying to pretend you'd fainted, and I was cursing God and the Devil alike because I thought you were already wed. Then your coachman—Robert?—set me right. I love you more than I love life itself," he repeated simply, "and I've never known such despair as when I thought I'd lost you—not even when Christo died. I think you love me. Do you? Because if you do, admit it, and we'll be married tonight. If you don't, I'll see you through all this somehow, and we'll reestablish your credit with some plausible fabrication or other, and then I'll never trouble you again, for there's nothing I want less than to cause you pain."

She stared at him in wonder, speechless for perhaps the first time in her life, then threw herself into his arms, clinging to him as if he were her only hope of life. The peace she found in those strong arms, the warmth, the security, the sense of coming home were beyond anything she had ever dreamed possible, even during the few halcyon days of their betrothal. Rawdon winced at the searing pain in his arm, smiled. The pain was worth it.

"I've been very silly, haven't I," she whispered into his shoulder.

"Very," he agreed, "but I'll forgive you, as you've come to your senses."

"My damnable pride . . . I *do* love you, you know. I have all along."

"I know," he murmured. "If you hadn't, you'd never have been so angry. That was the one thing that gave me hope." Then he turned his head, glancing over his shoulder. "Gracechurch, Fenton," he called to the group by the fireplace, "untie the vicar. I've a pressing need of him."

It was a week before they allowed Harry Beckenham to see Gwendolyn Fortescue, and then permission was grudgingly granted only at Percy Fenton's repeated insistence following a complaint from Carlton House.

The Horse Guards were not entirely in charity with Lord Henry Beckenham, now truly as well as officially sold out, nor with his insistence that a gross miscarriage of justice was being perpetrated on at least one innocent member of the Fortescue entourage. Indeed, tempers were wearing thin as he pounded desks and hurled impossible demands at the heads of those few senior officers in possession of the story, ignoring rank and civility, and throwing their damning evidence back in their faces as if it did not exist.

Harry was, by the end of four days, both desperate and irrational, close to becoming a danger to himself as well as to others. Indeed, he had attempted to call out his former friends and comrades, individually and collectively, for refusing to assist him in procuring Gwendolyn's exoneration and release. No relationship, however close, was proof against his scathing tongue and bitter demands. Face haggard, scar pulsing, stump reopened, raw and bleeding under its bandages, he stormed government offices, badgering anyone he could bring to bay, forsaking sleep and food, even battering at the doors of Carlton House in a futile attempt to enlist the Prince Regent's aid. It was this last attempt that provided Fenton with the needed leverage. Permission was granted for a private interview with the girl. Papers were drawn, orders issued.

In the interim, Dickie Fotheringham and his mother had gratefully accepted Lady Daphne's invitation to join her in her town home, quitting Cribb's establishment with profuse thanks, and—on Fotheringham's part—a promise to return as soon as he was able. Tom the Toff had found permanent—if somewhat irregular—employment with certain members of the Horse Guards, his talents admired and his shortcomings overlooked. Major Ventriss departed for home on a well-earned leave, hair properly trimmed, mustaches gone, and uniform thankfully once more upon his back until the next time, the blandishments of Lady Daphne's cook one of the few humorous memories of what could only be termed an infernal coil. Winthrop and Malfont, awaiting orders, were preparing to return to the Peninsula and making the most of their last days in England. The Season had not yet drawn to a close, and the feverish rounds of gaiety suited their tempers just then, permitting a welcome forgetfulness. The others—Fenton, Gracechurch, and Heath—would be in London slightly longer, tying up the scattered loose ends of an unusual and, ultimately, highly successful clandestine operation.

The simultaneous announcements of Louisa's two marriages in the *Gazette* caused a considerable stir when they first appeared. Morning calls, dinner parties, routs, balls, had only one topic of conversation—*was* the girl wed, and if so, *to whom?* Bets were laid at White's and Brook's, with Quarmayne the odds-on favorite given Rawdon's reputation and Louisa's spinster status. Interest faded slightly two days later when a retraction of one announcement was printed beside confirmation of the other, the two enclosed in a box and labeled CORRECTION. For a miracle, no titillating speculations about the announcements and the facts behind them were printed in the tattle section. Perhaps money had changed hands, and perhaps the unusual omission was merely a case of prudent self-interest. His Grace of Rawdon was well known for his temper when provoked.

That night, a schoolroom miss dressed in her older sister's finery invaded a rout at Lady Sefton's, clambered onto a chair and, teetering well above the heads of the throng, declared at the top of her lungs, knife clutched in her hand, that she was with child by her brother's tutor and would kill herself then and there if she wasn't permitted to marry him. Louisa and Rawdon were instantly forgotten.

The disposition of the Fortescues, Ephraim Gossmar, Norval Quarmayne, and their solicitor had been decided: Australia would claim them for her own. They were already aboard the penal transport that would carry them there, the one concession to their former positions two minuscule cabins—one for the four men, and one for the two women. Dexter Fortescue had renounced his title in favor of his son, declaring he had no more use for it, and so young Giles was now Lord Giles.

The two younger girls were given the choice of accompanying Gwendolyn and their parents, or remaining in England as wards of their brother, the Crown to pay their expenses temporarily as recompense for services (unspecified) rendered until he could regularize his finances. Rawdon's solicitor, in the official capacity of trustee and temporary guardian, would oversee their well-being until Giles reached his majority.

Lady Daphne had spent long hours convincing the two girls to accept the wardship, and resign themselves to life within the confines of an exclusive Bath seminary until it was time to make their come-outs—which she promised to sponsor. Australia was neither romantic nor civilized, she told them, no matter how invigorating or healthful the climate. Confused by the sudden changes in their lives, uncertain as to what had truly occurred and why their parents and older sister were deserting them—supposedly for the sake of their mother, whose health, they were told, required the dryness of the antipodes—they had clung tearfully to their older brother, then resignedly permitted themselves to be packed off to school. Lady Daphne held some hope for them. Vain, silly, pretentious, and overly impressed with the glory of the Fortescue name they might be, but that had been their mother's doing. Her own daughters had attended Miss Peckminton's Seminary, and Lady Daphne was well acquainted with Amanda Peckminton. If anyone could knock the silliness out of Sophronia and Belinda Fortescue, and instill in its stead some grace, some common sense, and a modicum of decorum along with a little much-needed humility, she was the one to do it.

For Giles, now a baron and in possession of what was left of the Fortescue estates—primarily the Lodge along with the entailed land, and the house in town—life for the past week had been a confused whirl of conferences with first Rawdon's and then Harry's solicitors. On their advice, he had put both properties up to let, signed papers to the effect that all revenues, with the exception of a penuriously modest allowance for himself and a slightly more generous provision for his younger sisters, should be devoted to clearing his parents' debts, and left the entire mess in their capable hands. The debts had been called in and tallied, and while a few might be still lurking here and there, the total was essentially known. The burden was large, but it would be discharged in time.

Gracechurch, Fenton, Heath, and the others, even Rawdon on a flying trip to town, and Harry Beckenham—the only time he condescended to sit down with them—had met with Giles on the fifth day to offer him his cornetcy. The boy declined, refusing to explain, proffering one lame excuse after another, until Harry had called him an ungrateful fool and a traitor to his family and class with no sense of honor or responsibility and stormed from the room. Giles had watched him leave, expression determinedly unreadable, then turned to the others.

"I accept, of course, and most gratefully," he had said calmly, masking the profound hurt Harry's words had caused, "but you can see how *he* is. I don't want to leave him to himself just now. It's bad, and it's going to be worse once he's seen Gwennie, 'cause I know what she's likely to say to him, and it ain't nice. And, when she and m'parents sail, it'll be even worse for a time. I don't know—six months? A year? Whatever it takes, and then I'd be honored to accept. Until he's all right, I just can't see my way free to do what I want—not with what *they've* done to him . . . I'm the head of the family now, and seeing to him's my responsibility. He still don't believe she's what she is, you see. He loves her, or at least he thinks he does. She's going to kill that. I'm just afraid she'll kill what's left of him as well."

He stood slowly, an old man of eighteen, looked at each of them in turn. "It's been an honor to call you my friends, even if you haven't called me friend," he said. "You couldn't. I understand that. But . . . try to forgive them if you can, because *I* can't, and they need someone's forgiveness. I'll—" His head came up proudly. "Don't you worry: I'll be waiting for Harry when he comes off the ship from seeing her, and I won't leave him to himself—I promise."

Now Henry Beckenham, sixth viscount Marleybourne, former major in His Majesty's Army, wounded at Salamanca, invalided home missing an arm and with his face forever scarred, stood at the base of the rough wooden gangplank leading aboard the *Dancing Mermaid*. His eyes traveled the vessel from stem to stern. She wasn't much—a graceless merchant hulk under charter to the Navy, designed for superior hold capacity rather than speed and comfort, her barely raked masts stubby, her beam broad, and her proportions clumsy. An afternoon mist was rising from the river, curling in filmy tendrils around her improvised bulwarks, catching in the shrouds, so that she seemed to hang suspended in the air, a ghost-ship who might vanish if one's eyes left her for only a moment.

She moved slowly with the oily rolling of the Thames,

rising and falling at the dock, hawsers creaking, planks groaning.

Ships were such damned noisy things, even the best of them, talking to themselves like addled old women. How Gwendolyn, with her delicate constitution and refined sensibilities, was bearing the sounds, the stench, was beyond Harry's imagining. She must be half-mad herself by now, he thought furiously, confined in such a way in such a place, and all so unjustly—the helpless victim of the mindless fools at Whitehall and the Horse Guards.

A soldier peered at him over the gunwale, hawked, spat, the gobbet landing precisely between Harry's boots.

"Be ye one"—he consulted a list—"one Henry Beck-enham?" he shouted.

Harry nodded, placed his hand uncertainly on the gangplank railing. The dock was strangely deserted, and until the man had poked his head over her side, the ship had appeared more derelict than functioning craft. The hairs crawled on the back of Harry's neck, issuing their standard warning of things not quite as they should be.

"Well, be ye commin' aboard, or bain't ye?" the man demanded. "I ain't got all day! Instructions are, ye got half a hour, countin' from when ye sets foot on that there gangplank, an' a hand's just as good as a foot by my reckoning—'specially when there's only one on 'em."

Harry grimaced, forced himself to place one foot in front of the other, gained the ship's side, clambered into her waist, bracing himself against the deck's slight movement.

"Docooments?" The man held out a grimy paw.

Silently Harry reached in his pocket, retrieved a sheaf of papers, handed them over. The man examined them laboriously one by one, referring to his list, shuffling them, cross-checking them, sucking on his hollow cheeks and thrusting his furred tongue between browned stubs of teeth, until Harry thought he would go mad.

"Hurry it up, will you!" he growled.

The man cocked his head, studying the tall ex-officer. "Ye ain't got no official status here, *my lord*," he said slowly. "If'n I say these here docooments ain't in order, ye gets no farther, unnerstand? An', I ain't so sure but what somethin's missing."

Harry clenched his teeth, reached back in his pocket, felt for his heavy purse, slipped out a guinea, extended it. "Is this perchance the document you're missing?"

"Here, now! Ain't no call fer—"

"Is it?"

"Might be," the soldier admitted after a moment's careful consideration. His hand flashed. The gold coin vanished. "All right—I'll be takin' ye to her. Arrangements've been made. Won't be no one else in there with ye, but I'll be standin' guard right outside along the others, so no untoward moves, ye unnerstand?"

Harry nodded, not trusting himself to speak. That this dregs of the army, unworthy even to tend a sutler's mules, should have the guarding of Gwendolyn, have the right to issue her commands, hold her very life in his filthy mitts . . .

They traversed the ship's waist, plunged down a dark companionway smelling of tar and cordage and rotten food and human filth and sweat and stagnant water and mildew—stenches so deeply impregnated in the timbers that not all the fresh breezes of all the oceans of the earth could have swept them away. Gimballed lanterns swung slowly from crossbeams at irregular intervals, keeping rhythm with the gentle tidal swell, their fitful golden light heightening the sense of nightmare. Everywhere was silence except for the ceaseless talking of the ship to herself and the occasional soft chuckle of a wavelet against her side. Nowhere was there a hint of habitation by man or beast.

They followed one low passage, then another, Harry

stumbling helplessly behind the soldier as he steadied himself with his single hand. Then they turned into still another passageway, lower and narrower yet, so that Harry had to bend over.

"Here ye be," the soldier said, gesturing at a heavily barred plank door guarded by two thickset men in ordinary clothes whom Harry could have sworn he recognized from the night at Cribb's—one by his crooked nose, the other by an ear so blossomed by bludgeonings that it had lost all semblance of a human orifice. Both sported evil-looking knives and efficient pistols in their belts. "This be the one. Ye're to let him in. Them's the orders, crazy or not."

The men turned wordlessly, lifted the heavy bars, twisted an iron key in the well-oiled lock, eased the door open. The cubby was dark, unventilated, lit only by a small lamp with the wick turned low, the porthole covered by thick boards nailed securely in place. There was a figure in the darkness, a graceful silhouette against the far bulkhead. Harry took a hesitant step forward, then another.

"Well, get on in wi' ye!" the soldier snapped. "Told ye—I ain't got all day."

Harry pressed his lips together, took a deep breath, and stepped all the way inside. "Gwendolyn?" he whispered uncertainly.

"Yes, it's me." The voice was as beautiful, as mellifluous, as perfect as ever—but cold, so *cold!* "What ever are you doing here, Lord Beckenham? What do you want?"

"I came to see you." Harry held out his hand. "I *had* to see you."

"Why?"

"Why? Because I love you!" he exploded. "Because I can't bear what they're doing to you! Because——"

"You should have thought of that before," Gwendolyn Fortescue said, came slowly into the light, not quite looking at him. Her cloud of glorious russet hair was perfectly arranged, her dress of sprigged jonquil muslin, with its ruchings of deeper yellow and fluttering ribbons and knots of palest green floss, in the highest stare of fashion, the shawl draped daintily over her arms of the finest silk. "Shouldn't you have? This is all your dreadful sister's fault, you know," she pouted. "What you want with any of us after what she's caused to happen I shall never understand."

"My dearest darling—"

"Don't call me that!" she shuddered. "I am not your darling. I'm not *anyone's* darling. Mama promised I should never have to be, not if I did as she told me."

"We were betrothed," he said helplessly, confused. "As far as I am concerned, we still are. Let me help you," he pleaded.

"Why ever should you want to help me—as if there were any way you could!"

"I'm prepared to marry you here and now," he persisted, holding out his hand, taking another hesitant step forward, fighting for her, fighting for himself, fighting for their future together and the hope of heaven it offered him, "take you home with me if they'll permit it, or sail with you if that's the only way."

"*Marry you?*" Her silvery laugh filled the tiny cubicle as she turned slightly away, fingers caught nervously in the deep fringes of her shawl. "I should think not! A cripple? Scarred? With a coarse, *brown* face? Heavens above— what do you think I am? I have some standards, after all! *I,*" she declared, tossing her head, now looking directly at him over her shoulder, "am a Diamond. I can have the best. What would I want with *you?* Not that you aren't very nice in your own way, I suppose," she conceded graciously.

She smiled sweetly, turned, and gestured to one of a pair of stools flanking a rough deal table bolted to the cubby's floor. "Oh, dear—I've been remiss. I should at least have made you comfortable before we began speaking, though it's impossible for me to offer you refreshment beyond the water in that bucket. Would you care for some? No? Well, it's not very nice water, so there's no harm done. In fact, it's rather nasty, if you must know.

"Do be seated, my lord, and I shall be also. I find it most disconcerting to balance on this unsteady deck. You appear to find it equally so." She sank gracefully onto one of the stools, arranged her skirts, and gestured impatiently toward the other. "Well, do be seated," she snapped. "I have invited you to be, after all! It's perfectly proper. Mama told me I might ask you to be seated, so long as we kept the table between us, as I do so detest standing in this place. Do you like my dress? Papa says it lends me the appearance of a ray of sunshine, which we all need in these dingy surroundings.

"They've permitted us to keep all our clothes, you know. Mama says she intends to establish a series of subscription dances in the manner of Almack's as soon as we arrive, so I shall even have a use for my ball gowns. Is that not wonderful? Mama is *so* resourceful! She says we're sure to enter into the very highest levels of the Antipodal ton instantly, though Papa isn't so sure. Do you know how the ton organizes itself in the Antipodes?"

Harry stumbled forward, collapsed on the stool, eyes never leaving her face.

"What are you looking at me like that for?" she demanded peevishly. "Did you *really* believe I loved you, or would ever have truly married you? How foolish! I have never loved anyone—not even Mama, though I respect her judgment infinitely. Love is a quite improper emotion, belonging to the lower orders. A lady should have nothing to do with it."

"You're doing this to spare me," Harry implored

hoarsely. "You don't mean it. You're trying to make parting easier for us both. Oh, my poor, brave angel!"

"Why should I try to make it easier? It's easy enough," she returned indifferently. "You will stay in England. I will depart for Australia. In a matter of days uncounted miles of ocean will separate us. I don't have to do anything. *You* don't have to do anything. It's being done for us."

"But it's so unnecessary, so unfair! You weren't involved in your mother's plots. An angel like you? You *couldn't* have been!"

"Not involved?" she laughed. "Why, my lord, however could I not have been? Naturally I knew what she was doing, and I approved entirely. She was sparing me the lowering necessity of marriage, you see. I was much more valuable to us both as I was."

"You *knew?*" he said incredulously.

"That you were to die? Of course. What possible use would you be to us otherwise? After all, you had to die sometime," she smiled consolingly, "and this way your death could be of some use to someone. That's much better than it's just being meaningless, isn't it?"

Harry stared at her in dawning horror, gripping the edge of the table with his single hand. "Louisa?" he asked, certain now of her answer, voice low and weary.

Gwendolyn Fortescue shrugged. "She was to marry Cousin Norval, and then conveniently die. Childbirth, if Mama could arrange it. An accident, if she couldn't."

"Good God!" he groaned. "And Rawdon's brother? The rest?"

"There were ten all told, I believe, or was it twelve? And then there are you and the young handsome one with the funny name. Freemantle? Farthingale? Something like that. I'm never quite certain if I should count the two of you or not," she said lightly, a pensive finger pressed to her cheek, her attitude all beauty and grace, "as you are still alive. Don't look so shocked. I didn't ask any of them to marry me. *They* asked *me* to marry *them*. It was all their own silly faults. Whom did we harm? They all died thinking me deeply enamored of them, and the memory of my faithful love comforted their last moments. What more could a man want? Certainly, very few get as much," she concluded petulantly. "Besides, Bratchett didn't have to see to *all* of them. Three, I believe, met their ends naturally—if death in battle can be considered a natural end—before it became necessary to encourage their demise."

"But *why?*" he groaned.

Gwendolyn stared at him in startled surprise. "We had to live, after all," she said. "You expected us to starve, or give up our rightful place in the ton? You are indeed a foolish man!"

Harry stumbled down the gangplank moments later, the heavy purse of golden guineas he had intended to give Gwendolyn to ease her way in Australia if all else failed still in his pocket. Giles watched him come, lips compressed, hardly daring to breathe.

"What're you doing here?" the former major snarled when he spotted the newly elevated baron.

"Waiting for you," Giles said. Then, "I'm sorry, Harry. Oh, Lord, I'm so sorry!—but you had to know. I'd've snuck you on board if I had to, bribed everyone from here to Lisbon. Thank God Major Fenton agreed."

Harry closed his eyes, standing there on the rough cobbles while the earth turned beneath his feet, spinning on its axis, traveling around the sun as it always did. Nothing essential had changed, but nothing would ever look the same. "I'm not sure if I should thank you or curse you," he said slowly, voice dead.

Giles seized his arm, exerting a gentle pressure away

from the ship. "Well, while you're figuring it out, what d'you say we head for Marleybourne? From what you an' Miss Beckenham told me about it, I'd like to really see the place, spend some time there," he prattled, desperately trying to fill the leaden silence. "Wasn't there long enough to tell much of anything the last time. Beautiful this time of year, an' peaceful, she said. I could use a little peace. We could stop at Rawdonmere on the way, if you like, offer your sister an' the duke our best wishes if it ain't too soon for paying calls on 'em. Or," he shrugged, "we could swing by White's, have an early supper, an' a few hands of piquet. Or, we can go to Lady Cheltenham's. Door's always open to both of us, she told me. Or, there's always Cribb's, or—"

Harry wrenched away, snarling, then glanced down at Giles's young-old face. Concern and sorrow and anguish and desperation radiated from the boy like heat from a bonfire.

"Give me a moment alone," Harry said more evenly.

"I don't have a moment to give you."

"Damn you—"

Harry turned his back, went to lean against a stack of barrels awaiting loading, eyes screwed shut, breaths slow and shallow as he clenched and unclenched his single fist. He knew what he was, now. She had shown him. He was no more than a relict of the Peninsula—a damaged, pathetic excuse for a man, unworthy to look at any woman with warmth, undeserving to have any give him her regard, an unpleasant reminder of the less glorious aspects of war. His missing arm, his scarred face defined him. For if, in her desperate plight, Gwendolyn could not force herself to turn to him, what woman ever would?

Harry sighed, opened his eyes, and stared around him. "Not Rawdonmere," he said softly as Giles hesitantly joined him. "Couldn't face my sister yet. Not my aunt's—same problem. My God—what a blind fool I've been!

Bad enough I almost cost myself my life. I almost cost Louisa hers as well . . ."

Slowly he turned, eyes roving the ship, her masts lost in the thickening mist rising from the river, as if to memorize her. Then his gaze fell to a pair of boarded portholes just above the waterline.

"You tried to tell me," he said softly.

"Yes, I did."

"But, I wouldn't listen. I don't think I could . . . Marleybourne," he said curtly after a moment. "We'll go to Marleybourne. You're right—you'll like it there. Lots to do."

Surreptitiously he slipped his hand into his inside waistcoat pocket over his heart, pulled out a small gold case with an ornate chased frame, opened it, studied it for a moment, then dropped it into the slowly rolling Thames and watched it sink from sight in sweeping gentle curves.

The two young men turned their backs on the ship, the docks, the river, and began walking toward the waiting hackney, the ghost of a silvery laugh echoing after them.

Two days later the Fortescue Diamond set sail for Australia. By then Giles and Harry were halfway to Marleybourne, slogging determinedly along mired roads, mud-spattered and wet and cold, collars turned up and hat brims pulled low, their horses' hooves slowly eating up the miles in a steady and dispiriting rain. Giles's one hope was that Harry had forgotten to pay attention to the date or time. It was a false hope. Harry was more conscious of that distant dock, that graceless vessel and the woman she bore down the Thames past Woolwich and Margate, through the Dover Straits and into the Channel, than he was of the dripping hedgerows and sodden fields they passed.

A new man was emerging from the one Giles had so admired. The fires were banked, the enthusiasm damped. Only a calm, cool, courteous shell remained, observing the world through faintly cynical, unamused, bitter eyes.

But, there was a detail of which neither Giles nor Harry was aware: a week following her rather unconventional wedding, Louisa Debenham had gazed across the dinner table at her new husband, the slightest frown marring her smooth brow.

"Well, minx?" Rawdon grinned at her. "You've that considering look again. Is it Rawdonmere, England, the entire Earth, or only my own life I should fear for?"

"I feel rather guilty," she admitted, the faintest flush staining her cheeks. "For me, it's all turned out so wonderfully well, and there Harry is, from what you say more impossible and miserable than ever. And then, there's young Giles Fortescue . . ."

"The lad has had it hard recently," Rawdon agreed, "and I suppose I can't complain about your concern over your brother. It's natural enough, though there've been more than a few times in the past weeks when I could've cheerfully wrung his neck!"

"D'you think, just possibly"—she hesitated, toying with the single full-blown red rose at her place, eyes falling from the clear deep gray eyes meeting hers with amused speculation—"that I might perhaps write little Patsy Worth at home? Not everything of course, but hinting the Season hasn't been unbounded bliss, that Harry's diamond played him false, and they're both in need of a friend? Patsy's such a dear little thing, and Harry's so accustomed to her following him about, that—"

"Dear God—what're you attempting to engineer?"

She gazed at him guilelessly, at which he chuckled.

"Does it run in the family," he inquired with a twinkle, "this apparent necessity to put the entire world to rights— for its own good, of course?" And then, at the look of hurt, he reached across the sparkling napery to grasp her hand. "Lady Daphne's plots are expert," he conceded. "If

you're to take her place one day as the family miracle-
maker, I suppose you've need of some practice."

The discussion was continued even after the candles
had been snuffed and only the ruddy glow from the grate
lit the darkness of the ducal bedchamber of the lords of
Rawdonmere. In the end a very *small* hint, Louisa and
Rawdon agreed, would be enough. At Louisa's protest
that she was not the interfering sort and *quite* out of her
element he guffawed, suggesting that to request the hand
of a down-at-the-heels gamester named Jamie Morrison
in marriage had been interfering on the grand scale.

"*Must* you persist in recalling that time," Louisa wailed,
torn between fury and mortification as she whirled in the
bed, burying her head in the pillows. Rawdon handled
both embarrassment and fury quite skillfully, turning her
thoughts to other matters. But, he knew the note would be
sent on the morrow. Life at Rawdonmere would never
again be dull or despairing—not with Louisa at his side—
for which he was immensely grateful.

An alerted Patsy Worth would haunt the rain-soaked
lanes as she watched for a pair of horses, one a deep-
chested bay called Thunderer bearing a one-armed former major in Wellington's Peninsular forces, the other—
called Gorgon, and no prettier than her namesake—the
ginger-haired boy with whom she had danced at her
come-out.

And what Harry would say to *that* the duke had a fair
notion. With a mental note to review all arriving post
before his bride glimpsed it, he gathered her into his arms
and continued those exercises which might, eventually,
hasten the arrival of the next duke.

ZEBRA'S REGENCY ROMANCES
DAZZLE AND DELIGHT

A BEGUILING INTRIGUE   (4441, $3.99)
by Olivia Sumner

Pretty as a picture Justine Riggs cared nothing for propriety. She dressed as a boy, sat on her horse like a jockey, and pondered the stars like a scientist. But when she tried to best the handsome Quenton Fletcher, Marquess of Devon, by proving that she was the better equestrian, he would try to prove Justine's antics were pure folly. The game he had in mind was seduction — never imagining that he might lose his heart in the process!

AN INCONVENIENT ENGAGEMENT   (4442, $3.99)
by Joy Reed

Rebecca Wentworth was furious when she saw her betrothed waltzing with another. So she decides to make him jealous by flirting with the handsomest man at the ball, John Collinwood, Earl of Stanford. The "wicked" nobleman knew exactly what the enticing miss was up to — and he was only too happy to play along. But as Rebecca gazed into his magnificent eyes, her errant fiancé was soon utterly forgotten!

SCANDAL'S LADY   (4472, $3.99)
by Mary Kingsley

Cassandra was shocked to learn that the new Earl of Lynton was her childhood friend, Nicholas St. John. After years at sea and mixed feelings Nicholas had come home to take the family title. And although Cassandra knew her place as a governess, she could not help the thrill that went through her each time he was near. Nicholas was pleased to find that his old friend Cassandra was his new next door neighbor, but after being near her, he wondered if mere friendship would be enough . . .

HIS LORDSHIP'S REWARD   (4473, $3.99)
by Carola Dunn

As the daughter of a seasoned soldier, Fanny Ingram was accustomed to the vagaries of military life and cared not a whit about matters of rank and social standing. So she certainly never foresaw her *tendre* for handsome Viscount Roworth of Kent with whom she was forced to share lodgings, while he carried out his clandestine activities on behalf of the British Army. And though good sense told Roworth to keep his distance, he couldn't stop from taking Fanny in his arms for a kiss that made all hearts equal!